The Devil in Soho

BY

J M SHORNEY

Published by M-Y Books

187 Ware Road
Hertford
SG13 7EQ

m-ybooks.co.uk

DEDICATION

Dedicated to the memory of my lovely husband Michael.

CHAPTER ONE

–

A GIRL NAMED CAITLAN

DUBLIN, NOVEMBER 2011.

I'm aware of a man, drunk, his clothing rough and dishevelled, being propelled out of the bar by a tall heavyset individual. Innumerable expletives pursue the drunkard from the big guy, as he is thrown into the street. The guy, who I imagine must be the landlord, pauses to regard me with no more than a cursory attention.

I judge the man whom he threw into the street to be about 50. His greying hair and beard are as rough as his clothes. He squints his bloodshot eyes into my face as the landlord disappears inside his pub.

"If you're planning to go in there, mister," the drunk gestures in the general direction of the bar, "don't fuckin' stare at the singer's tits whatever you do, or ould Flanagan'll throw you out."

"Wouldn't dream of it," I assure him. "So who is she, the singer?" I ask although I'm certain that I won't gain much conversation from him in his drunken state.

"She sings like a fuckin' angel don't she?" I couldn't help but nod my agreement. "But ould Flanagan's barred me so I'll have to try down the road."

His whisky-soaked breath is enough to make me turn away and, without bothering to observe him stagger off down the street, I involuntarily push open the green painted door.

The place is, I'd guessed correctly, heaving. Most of the punters are crowded around the bar; nevertheless, there are a few vacant seats at green painted tables.

A group of young men, well on their way to being drunk, stagger ungainly to the bar. They cause me, for a weird moment, to believe that I am back home because their accents are unmistakably English. I conjecture mainly South London. I guess this is some kind of stag party.

Approaching the bar and leaning an arm across it, I see her. Not only does she sing like an angel, she also resembles one.

"The night was dark, the bottle empty.
The moon shone down O'Connell Street.
I stood alone and brave men cried.
Fighting for his country bold.
He fought for Ireland."

She's standing on a sort of raised dais at the side of the bar. Some of the punters are dancing to the music on a cleared floor area. The music is rousing, melodic and smacking of something akin to rebellious. Maybe this is a Republican Bar, although Uncle Sheamie assured me that the majority of political 'shenanigans' had evaporated by the nineties, even in Belfast. Still, sometimes, I can't help but wonder.

She isn't overly tall, maybe 5' 3" in her stockinged feet, as she isn't wearing any shoes. A short tartan skirt, worn at least 4" above her knee, compliments a black figure-hugging sweater. Her hair is long, past her shoulders, a dark tawny colour curled up at the ends. Her features are small, almost elfin; her lips are full, sensuous and set as if in a permanent pout.

Dancing in time to the accompaniment of her music, she belts out the numbers to her more than receptive audience.

"Only a tramp was Lazarus, they left him to die like a tramp on the street."

"That's an old Hank Williams song doncha know?" Her accent is pure Irish, with a lilt behind it as she sings.

"What'll it be, mate?" A man's voice growls at my elbow, serving to distract me from my reverie. Reluctantly I steer my gaze from the singer. "A small whisky, thanks."

"Bushmills?"

"Sure."

"She's sure something else ain't she, our Cait? She's my barmaid y'know."

I recognise the man who'd thrown out the drunk. I guess this has to be Flanagan. I ask him if she's the resident singer in the realisation that I really would like to get to know this woman and not allow her to be the one who got away. "Mostly, it was only after she'd been working here a coupla months that I knew she could sing. Talk about hiding your light under a bushel," Flanagan chortles, adding, "ain't seen you in here afore."

Sipping the whisky, I make a face. It is a fraction stronger than I'm used to. Maybe I should have ordered a beer and made it last, because she has drawn me in, distracting me. I have no intention of leaving without an introduction, I reason. Even if she tells me to 'piss off', at least I intend to try.

"I only arrived yesterday."

"You sound as if you've been here all your life."

"Oh the accent, I was born here, but left when I was a kid."

"So where you been then?" Flanagan pauses to rub a big hand across the rather flushed features of, I suspect, a secret drinker. He also appears to be the only one serving.

While he talks, there are innumerable punters lining the bar.

"London," I tell him.

He gestures toward the bunch of lads congregating about the stage, now embarrassingly heckling the singer to "get 'em off, darling," as if she is little better than a stripper.

"That's where those boys come from," volunteers Flanagan. "She'll give 'em short shrift if they heckle her. She does stand-up too."

"Stand-up?"

"Stand-up comedy. Och, sure if she ain't pretty versatile is our Cait."

"A coupla Guinness's, Flanagan," a man addresses the barman impatiently. In turn, Flanagan sports a long-suffering expression on his big bearded countenance when he clocks the newcomer.

In his mid-twenties, I note that his hair is long and straggly; a sort of blond colour that falls around his face and which he keeps swiping back with irritation at intervals. He wouldn't have been bad looking I suppose, if his lean-cut features were not so badly pockmarked with the remains of acne scars, or the fact his hair wasn't quite so overloaded with grease. He's wearing a black leather coat thrown over a pair of loose fitting jeans and a check shirt. His hands are encased in black leather gloves. He pushes in, almost needling me out of the way. I entertain an initial stab of anger, but allow it to subside. The man slaps his money onto the bar and Flanagan goes to fetch his drink.

The drinks paid for, the man grabs them. Moving away, he leaves me oddly relieved somehow because there is something about him, a something I fail to pinpoint. I catch the words, "fuckin' Blackwood," muttered from Flanagan at my elbow. I frown and enquire, "What are you talking about?" "Him, Shaun Blackwood, her fella." He gestures to the stage. "Caitlan deserves better than him, sure she does." As he moves away, Flanagan heaves a sigh before going to serve another punter.

So she has a fella, at least according to Flanagan. It serves to surprise me, however, that someone who looks the way she does, sings so beautifully, could possibly be interested in this refugee from the movie 'The Lost Boys'.

It is almost ten in the evening and pitch-dark outside, apart from an assembly of street lamps located along the quayside. Of course, with the bar being so close to the river, if someone was drunk enough they could easily fall into the Liffey and be swallowed up by the waters. I bring myself up sharply for what I'm contemplating.

I now mentally scrutinise the punk, or whatever it is he purports to be. He has a couple of pals with him. One is skinny, with black greasy clothes while the other sports a plaid shirt that stretches every conceivable inch of his leviathan girth. It also becomes swiftly apparent that I'm not the only one who's favouring the three punks with some attention. In fact, it seems that the majority of the locals are staring them out disdainfully.

Meanwhile, the English boys are pretty well on the way to becoming rat-arsed. Even though they aren't in their own country they still manage to heckle, "fucking Paddies," and Flanagan - this beefy, broad-shouldered guy - is having none of it. He moves from behind the bar uttering more expletives than I have heard one-person string together in a couple of minutes, making it plainly obvious that the big Irishman is his own bouncer. "C'mon, lads, fuckin' break it up before I have to call the law and you wouldn't want to end up in one of our Paddy jails would you?"

The boys turn on Flanagan with a load of abuse and cheek before he catches hold of a couple of them by the scruff of their necks and quickly hauls them out of the door. He brooks no argument, while those present applaud and cheer. While the two remaining English boys passively trail in the wake of their friends, ould Flanagan rubs his hands and spits into his palms before returning to his place behind the bar, nonchalantly.

Caitlan sings again and she informs everyone that it is to be her last number of the evening as Flanagan needs her help behind the bar.

While she sings, I observe in surprise that there are tears in the eyes of the man who, but minutes before, had thrown out four potentially troublemaking English boys without batting an eyelid.

The song is called 'The Fields of Athenry'. One I recollect my mother singing when I was a child.

"By a lonely prison wall
I heard a young girl calling
Michael, they have taken you away
For you stole Trevelyn's corn
So the young might see the morn
Now a prison ship lies waiting in the bay
Low lie the fields of Athenry
Where once we watched the small free birds fly
Our love was on the wing, we had dreams and songs to sing
It's so lonely 'round the fields of Athenry"

I successfully manage to locate a seat at one of the green circular Parisian-style tables. Although my attention is mostly riveted on Caitlan, as is everyone's, I can't avoid flicking innumerable glances in Shaun Blackwood's direction where, I observe, he's now deposited himself onto a seat nearest the stage. The almost adoring looks he favours the barefoot singer will attest to the fact that maybe he does care about her and that maybe his feelings are reciprocated.

"It takes all sorts," I think to myself and wished that maybe I'd shaved instead of convincing myself into growing a beard. It is still in the early stages of 'bum-fluff' and stubble. With my dark hair, it will ultimately develop into a full-blown effort in a matter of days. I have scarcely made an effort any more than Blackwood has, in tight black jeans, check shirt, plus an old battered leather jacket.

The song has ended but I fail, long after she's concluded her act, to erase either her or that song about 'The fields of Athenry' from my mind. The way she dances, performs in her stockinged feet, the microphone in her hand as she bends over in order to reach the crowd. She is obviously a very popular young woman.

Blackwood and his pals are on their feet applauding and cheering with everyone else. Blackwood assists her down from the dais. Jesus, I haven't even spoken to her but I am already growing jealous of the acne-scarred punk because he is able to attract such a beautiful girl.

Then Flanagan switches on his jukebox and the old traditional 'When Irish eyes are smiling' plays into the crowd.

Caitlan is escorted by her punk boyfriend to the bar, his arm encircling her waist. I wonder if Blackwood can swim. The Liffey appears pretty cold at this time of the year. I can particularly taste the anticipation of throwing him in, in order to find out, certain that no one here will miss him. I watch, or maybe torture myself, as he kisses her. Did I imagine it, or is it simply wishful thinking on my part, that Caitlan attempts to extricate herself from his embrace? Blackwood releases her reluctantly.

"I'll help you clear the tables, Flanagan," she offers. Her voice is a little husky, I guess from all her singing.

"When she's famous we can all say she started off in my bar," Flanagan declares proudly.

With such a high esteem he lavishes on her, I wonder if she might be his daughter. The name Caitlan Flanagan sounds a bit of a mouthful, whereas Caitlan McRaney sounds much better.

Naturally, I am merely dreaming. I am only going to be in Dublin for a couple of weeks as I have a landscape gardening business to run back in London. My brother Harry has gone to Milan with his wife, Sue, and her children Antonio and Gina. Sue's ex-husband Gino Sanguiletti, a racing driver, had been killed on an Italian circuit. His grief-stricken parents persuaded Harry and Sue to bring Antonio and Gina, Sanguiletti's children, to live with them in Italy. Having saved up enough money to go, on leaving Harry had requested that, instead of merely being an employee, as his brother I should take on the business. Although his parting shot was that I should run it, I believe he added 'and not into the ground.'

My son Patrick is in England. Of course, London is my home now. Anyway, the beautiful singer is far too out of both my league and my reach, so I resolve to forget her, or I would have done if she wasn't standing right in front of me. Lost in my own retrospection I had not so much as witnessed her approach.

"Hi." Her greeting is friendly, while the scintillating emerald green eyes snap wide. The curling, sensuous lips are conducive to illuminating a perfect alabaster complexion. She carries a tray on which rests a couple of bottles, plus several glasses.

"Hi," is all I can manage. Even that solitary greeting manages to adhere to my throat. What follows then, is in all likelihood, to be located in 'The Twilight Zone'.

"Have you finished with your glass, Sir?" she asks with an accent, which seems to flow from her as gentle as the softest breeze on a summer's day.

"Sure." I pass the glass across the table and swallow when I discover myself staring into the alluring green eyes. "What time do you get off?" It isn't me, honest, it must be my braver, alter ego.

She laughs, displaying a perfect set of even white teeth. Her laughter is silky and a little husky. "Sure now if I had a few euros for every guy who asked me that, y'know something, I'd be a wee rich girl now."

"So what time do you get off?" I repeat, observing her colour, before the beautiful sculptured cheeks transform to ashen as she pauses to glance over her shoulder to where Blackwood is trying to outdo his pals by displaying his proficiency in knocking back a full bottle of Guinness in less than three minutes. "I'm sorry," she says quietly. I can barely hear her, before she returns her attention to me. In addition, I wonder did I imagine the peculiar hint of something in those wide green eyes. Is it a look almost of longing?

She retrieves the glass, about to place it onto the tray when I close my palm over hers, conscious of Flanagan stiffening, grey eyes negotiating surreptitious glances in Blackwood's general direction. He need not have worried however, for Blackwood continues to display more interest in swallowing yet another full glass of Guinness, showing off to his pals.

"Please Sir." Caitlan seems quick to display her embarrassment over my attention. "If you need another drink, Sir…" She pulls her hand away deftly, the efficient barmaid once more. I watch Flanagan breathe a relieved sigh.

She is gone, but not before she throws me a brief furtive glance, one I am quick to exchange. God, she is so lovely. It is also plainly obvious that she is scared of Blackwood and if I'm not much mistaken, so is Flanagan, a man with precious little compunction at throwing out a group of drunken Brit revellers, or the odd paralytic I'd initially encountered.

So what is it with this guy? He refuses to scare me. After all, he is merely some greasy, outmoded punk.

The crowd thins and I ease myself from the table. Moving to the bar, I catch Flanagan's attention as he leans his elbow on the counter towards me.

"Want another?" he asks. "The pubs like this in the 'Big Smoke' then?"

Caitlan is at the till in the process of counting out someone's change.

"Not as a rule. Usually live bands or juke boxes."

"Not proper music, not like my Caitlan then?"

"So, is she your daughter, Mr Flanagan?"

His mouth splits into a wide grin doubtless at my expense. "It's just Flanagan, son. This place used to be called 'Flanagan's', but since they introduced the euro, the big city suits reckoned that 'Flanagan's' sounded too... too," he fishes for the correct words.

"Irish?" I arch a brow.

"That's it, my young friend," he guffaws, "too Irish. All that change in London. The Docklands. I lived in the Big Smoke for a while when my old man took us across the water. However, I had to come back. I know it's an old saying, but it's true all the same. You can take the Irishman out of the country, but you can't take the country out of the Irishman. You wanted to know if Caitlan's my daughter, God no, but I wish she was. If you read them posters outside you'll see her name is Caitlan McKenna." He leans his elbows onto the bar in his familiar pose, before lowering his voice conspiratorially. "Every guy who comes in here, whether they're my age or yours, gets smitten by that wee girlie, you're probably one of a hundred Mr..."

"McRaney. Aidan McRaney."

"Mr McRaney. They try to get off with her, but he..." He gestures at Blackwood; the latter is engaged in earnest conversation with her.

Flanagan continues, "He, Blackwood, is a nasty piece o' work. It's himself that thinks she's his possession. I've seen him pull a knife on anyone who as much as looks as if he might get off with her. You're a good looking man, Mr McRaney. If you want to stay that way I'd give that wee girlie a wide berth, so I would."

While Flanagan talks, his back is turned from them. He is seemingly oblivious of Caitlan deep in conversation with Blackwood, the latter suddenly grips her left wrist forcibly. No one appears to notice, or if they have, they prefer to turn the proverbial 'blind eye', but I'm aware of her pretty face tightening as she attempts to wrestle her arm free of his grasp. When he finally releases her, he pushes her away before signalling to his companions, as if she is no longer of any consequence. He moves away. Caitlan rubs at her wrist, an infliction of pain crossing her face.

To reach the exit, Blackwood and his pals have to pass right beside me. It would be so easy to trip him up with my boot. Nevertheless, I am a stranger here and beginning to enjoy the company of the affable barkeep, Flanagan, and have no desire to cause him any trouble.

The hour is late. I decide to return to my aunt and uncle, aware that the former is a light sleeper and that Uncle Sheamie isn't in the best of health. I'd caught Aunt Clodagh in tears after the less than

8

optimistic news when I'd taken them to see the consultant at St Patrick's. I had been about to enter the kitchen when I saw her by the sink. She was washing up and wiping tears from her eyes interminably.

Aunt Clodagh, a no-nonsense lady who had moved to London temporarily when I was about 11, to help bring us kids up after our ma died. In addition, my dad, Aunt Clodagh's brother, had taken to the drink big-time.

I hated seeing her so upset. The moment I appeared, however, she hastily blinked back her tears and was the familiar bustling lady again, as if she were capable of turning off her emotions like a tap I was a guest in her home. As she wouldn't accept any money from me, I opted to do a few jobs around the house.

"You've got enough to pay for, Aidan, with your ex-wife and all that." Whenever she referred to Judy my ex, the contempt in both her speech and in the tightness of her lips was ever present. Although she adores my son, Aunt Clodagh had once intimated that Judy had trapped me into marriage. Notwithstanding, Auntie never once mentioned the fact that I'd gone to prison for eight years. I killed a man, in my capacity as mob boss Frankie Lamond's minder. The guy who had shot Frankie, leaving him a cripple, had murdered Leanne. She was the woman with whom I was in love.

The beer has lasted for the duration of Caitlan's presence in The Liffey, when I realise she has vacated the bar. Reasoning there is nothing to hang around for, the majority of punters have left anyway once they realise that the singing is over. Flanagan shakes his head, regretfully, bemoaning that he'd probably lose much of his trade if Caitlan decides to leave.

"'Course she's got her own life. It's a pity she's tied up with that evil wee bastard."

"Evil?" I echo. "That's rather a strong word isn't it?" However, Flanagan had moved away without a reply, as if he'd said too much and the last I hear of the friendly landlord is him calling, "time, ladies and gents."

The Quayside is marginally lit in parts, although certain areas remain dim and shadow enshrouded. A three quarter moon ascends the indigo sky and manages to illuminate my surroundings somewhat.

I roll and light a much-needed cigarette, my hand cupping the Calibri, as a wind has sprung up from the river. I imagine I hear a voice that has nothing remotely to do with the wind. A female voice, imperceptibly faint at first, but growing distinctly urgent with cries of "let me go, please, please let me go!"

A few passing stragglers begin to quicken their pace. They have obviously heard the sound, but have no intention of getting involved. It is not my concern either. I need to return to my aunt and uncle, having no desire to wake Aunt Clodagh by coming in late and abusing their hospitality. That is, until I see the woman who is crying, pleading to escape the man's clutches is *her*, Caitlan.

I'm conscious of the dark, partially lit alleyways, the closed-in urban screen of dirty red-bricked walls.

The girl attempts to struggle free from her captor. The man holding her, her hands thrust behind her as if manacled, pushes her belligerently over the bonnet of the car. It's Shaun Blackwood. She's crying, pleading, "please, it wasn't my fault, Shaun. Please, please let go of me. I really am sorry. I didn't mean to..." she begs and the upraised hand that is about to crash across her lovely face is poised but intercepted before he can bring it down.

"What the fuck!" Blackwood hisses, surprised, because I grab both his hands, pinning them behind him, push him face down onto the bonnet of the vehicle that's parked nearby. The girl screams, runs a trembling hand toward her mouth, but I'm not about to let up. I guess it won't be too long before someone calls the Gardaí, but I intend to deal with Blackwood before that happens.

"Who the hell..." he starts, but his words are muffled due to the fact he is eating metal, while I propel his hands so far behind him, I could snap his arm if I'd wanted to.

"Your fuckin' nemesis, pal," I spit.

The instant he releases the girl I grab him. She's just standing there, her entire body trembling.

"Is that the way you treat your women, you bastard?"

"Who the hell are you?" He attempts to twist his body around to face me. This close, in the yellow fluorescence of the street lamps, his face is even greasier; the pockmarks resemble livid craters in his unprepossessing features. My free hand continues to push his head onto the car.

"He... he might have a knife," she half-whispers. She really has no need to inform me of that fact because, before he manages to locate it, I scramble around in the pockets in his coat, my fingers closing over the handle of the knife as Blackwood attempts to lash out with a boot in a vain endeavour to connect with my balls. Now the knife is in my hand. It's a switchblade. I spring the weapon and the ugly punk finds himself staring at the silvery halo that bounces off his blade, reflected in the moonlight. His eyes widen to an impenetrable black, filled with fear. When I lay the blade across his throat, I hear Caitlan yelp, the sound reminiscent of a wounded animal. I pay her scant attention because a sense of anger has already overtaken me.

"Okay, you bastard, you don't even touch her. You let her go and you try following us you know what I can do." I make my voice deliberately chilled and lowered, so that it is only Blackwood who hears it. The anger abates somewhat. Only the ostensibly clinical anticipation remains.

His Adam's apple undulates, he swallows noisily, rasps, "I don't fuckin' know who you are, but didn't I see you at the bar in The Liffey?" He makes a futile attempt to struggle free from the restraint I maintain on his arm and to twist his body away from me, but the arm is pinioned so far back, he is now bent over the car in an uncomfortably contorted position. "You're fuckin' hurting me, you bastard!"

I hear Caitlan gasp and I observe, from my peripheral, that she has both hands covering her face, so that she doesn't have to look.

At this stage I have no idea whether her fear is for him or me. Some women are tolerant of abusive men and dare anyone to interfere. I also have no idea whether either of Blackwood's two cohorts might be lurking somewhere in order to ambush me.

I have pushed their leader onto the bonnet of a car and held his own blade to his throat. The more he attempts to talk, the more I press the blade across the exposed area of his neck.

"Sure that was me and you've got my attention, punk boy, or whatever the fuck you're trying to be. Now I want you to piss off, understand me?"

Blackwood sucks in a breath harshly, his gaze lowering uneasily to the switchblade I continue to hold against his throat.

"You don't know the fuck who you're dealing with, fuckin' pretty-boy." His words convey an obvious threat. I've heard enough and I crash my free hand viciously across his face, pummelling him harder onto the bonnet.

Raising his head slightly, he levers a mouthful of saliva in my direction but I scarcely notice as I hurl another crack against his jaw. It's enough to send him spinning away from the car and crashing to the ground at my feet. I tower above him, all 6' 2" of me, slam a boot down onto his chest and keep it there.

"You fuckin' bastard!" he rasps angrily. "You won't get away with this…" His acne scars flush an angry crimson and it's not difficult to observe there is an unmistakable hatred in his eyes. "Like I said, you don't know the fuck who you're dealing with, Mister." Sprawled on the ground, he presses a gloved palm against a split and bleeding lip.

"Yeah, save it for someone who fuckin' cares," I retort. Resting a boot on his chest, I remove it eventually and pulling Blackwood to his feet, I grab him by the scruff of his neck. He is in pain, half gone; his eyes are glazed, cold, unremitting.

Careful to maintain a lowered voice, I hiss at him, "next time, you fuckin' bastard, I'll have a gun. I've killed before. They're right, it does get fuckin' easier, pal," before I push him out of the way as if he really is a lifeless body, into the muddied puddles of the alley.

I notice for the first time, I guess it has not registered before, Caitlan has donned a blue mackintosh-style coat over the sweater and skirt, and that she now wears a pair of high black suede boots.

Blackwood struggles slowly, warily to his feet in case I might hit him again. He almost overbalances when my hand comes up to stroke my face, teasing him.

In the process of wiping blood from his mouth with a sweep of his hand, he retorts, "you really will be sorry you did that, you bastard. And you…" his face screws up ugly with so much anger prevalent inside him and he points a leather-encased digit at Caitlan, "and you, darlin', you'll be fuckin' sorry too. If it's 'pretty-boy' you want, but he won't be so fuckin' good looking when we've finished with him."

Her face remains buried in her hands. She weeps quietly, disconsolately. Momentarily, I pay her a cursory attention because I worry that Blackwood intends to return with his pals then, plans to jump me when my back is turned. As Frankie Lamond instructed, 'you don't turn your back on anyone, Aidan. You never know when they might pull a shooter.' Sound advice, Frankie.

He limps away, a frightened brow beaten animal, yelping in pain, blistered lips curling into a venomous snarl, elevating a couple of digits in my direction. I mutter at him to, "piss off, punk."

It is a while before I turn my attention back to her. She's slipped behind the wheel of a dark green Peugeot, the same one I'd pummelled Shaun Blackwood's head onto. She sits behind the wheel unmoving when I half expect her to drive away and hope to God that she doesn't. I guess I can't blame her if she does decide to drive away and leave me standing there.

Seizing my opportunity I crack open the car door and slip into the seat. She jumps instinctively, regards me wide-eyed and fearful, a different girl from the confident barefoot singer with the voice of an angel who had captivated her audience tonight. Now she appears so incredibly small, fragile and remarkably younger than I had at first thought, maybe no more than 18.

"You okay?" I ask gently. She continues to tremble. I touch her arm lightly. She emits a frightened gasp before pulling away as if I am contaminated. When she utters something under her breath, she is shaking so much I fail to catch the words. "I'm sorry." I long to place an arm about her shoulders, but she so resembles a frightened rabbit, I am scared she will leap out of the car and go running into the night.

"Thank you for what you did." She turns to face me finally. She appears so inordinately white, ghostly in the reflection of moonlight. Maybe she is a ghost, a pathetic wee wraith, one of those phantom hitchhiker types. You know, the sort you pick up in your car on some lonely road only to discover that they've disappeared. Maybe if I touch her she might disappear also.

"I'm sorry if my violence scared you," I offered, if that is why she seems so afraid. "So is this your car? Caitlan isn't it?"

She nods.

"Maybe we should get out of here in case your boyfriend comes back," I counsel. "I take it he's your boyfriend."

She shivers suddenly. "Yes. Shaun…Shaun Blackwood." She hesitates on his name. "Thank you again but I'll be fine now Mr…"

"It's Aidan. Aidan McRaney."

"Caitlan McKenna." She sighs. "You shouldn't have done that, Mr McRaney. He… he's bad news."

"Then why do you go out with him?"

Her mouth tightens whilst she attempts to turn the key in the Peugeot's ignition. Her hand shakes so badly she drops the keys a couple of times and curses beneath her breath. "Please…" her words trail. Burying her face in her hands, she sobs uncontrollably. "Please, you… you'd better go. If he comes back and finds you with me."

"Sweetheart, Caitlan, I'm not going anywhere. I know I'm not on your insurance and all that malarkey, but darlin' I'm going to drive, so where do you live?" I ask authoritatively.

Raising her head, shining tear-filled green eyes snap wide as if she is afraid of me again. "Fenian Street."

"Fenian Street? So where's that?"

The green eyes regard me incredulously. "The other side of Temple Bar. You live in Dublin?"

"No, darlin' I don't."

"But you sound as if you do."

13

"Sure, I was born here. I lived in O'Connell Street 'til I was almost 10. Then my parents uprooted us to live in London. That's where I've been ever since. So you going to let me drive?"

She allows me to touch a palm to her face and flinches because the beginning of a nasty bruise is already discolouring her cheek.

"And if I do, how do I know I can trust you?" she says anxiously. A frightened rabbit again.

"You don't, sweetheart, but I wouldn't harm a hair on your beautiful head. Look I'm staying with my aunt and uncle in Marrowbone Lane for a while. No strings, I mean it. You're welcome to come back with me. You can tell me about Blackwood, or not if you prefer." I add when I observe her shiver again.

She allows me to take the Peugeot's steering, composes herself beside me and I swing the vehicle out into the street. She says, "Mollie'll worry if I don't come home."

I say stupidly, "who's that, your cat?" Mollie seemed the appropriate name for a cat.

"No." she smiles a little unevenly. "No. Mollie's my sister."

"Oh, sorry." I laugh. "Only we had a cat called Mollie when I was a kid."

"I share a flat with her in Fenian Street. I saw you in The Liffey tonight. You and about a dozen other punters were staring me out at the bar."

"Well, you were the centre of attention. You don't have to come back with me. I mean I'm not kidnapping you or anything."

"I didn't say you were but I hardly know you. I've never known anyone take on Shaun Blackwood before. 'Course you don't live round here or you would know about him."

"So what's there to know that I don't already? That he's a vicious bastard who enjoys beating up defenceless girls."

"Shaun Blackwood's also a drug dealer."

I attempt to suppress a niggling warning signal. "A drug dealer huh? So he's your boyfriend then? And I'm going to say, what's a lovely girl like you, who could have anyone, doing with an ogre like him?"

"I told him I didn't want to see him anymore. He gets jealous because the male punters chat me up. He thinks I'm his possession. So where did you learn to fight like that? Are you in the army or something?"

"God no!" I laugh, unwilling to confide in her that working for the mob has taught me a great deal, that is how to handle punks like Blackwood.

"Just a wee bit streetwise that's all. So what would have happened if I hadn't turned up?"

"I would have gone back to his place as I usually do. We would have had sex." She colours, averts her eyes.

"It's okay, sweetheart." I touch her knee, surprised when she does not flinch. It would be so easy to slide a hand beneath her coat, inch my way upward. I resist with an effort, suggest, "so we could go and clean up that pretty face at my aunt's place, or you can tell me how to get to Fenian Street."

"It's okay." Her smile illumines the beautiful emerald orbs. "I'll call Mollie. Tell her I won't be home tonight."

CHAPTER TWO

–

SHARING CONFIDENCES

She continues to shiver and bundles her coat around her as if for protection. Her face remains ashen so that the bruise inflicted by Blackwood stands out in marked contrast. He has obviously upset her badly. She is still the frightened rabbit, or a kitten, small and delicate, this child/woman. Her mascara has run, affording her the proverbial 'panda eyes' and I wonder, when she washes off her make-up, what will it reveal? How old she really is? I guess that thugs like Blackwood entertain precious little compunction at having sex with an underage girl. She had to have been 18 however, or she wouldn't have been allowed to work in the pub. I long to enquire her age but the way she looks and acts, she might think I had an ulterior motive for asking.

She hasn't called her sister hitherto. On the journey to Marrowbone Lane we lapse into silence. It remains for me to remind her about the call and she promises to call her when we arrive.

"And you're happy to come with me? I'm not a mad sex maniac y'know. Well, not all the time." I inject a note of light-heartedness in order to hopefully, put her at her ease. While I concentrate on the drive through the streets of night time Dublin, I continue to feel her eyes locked my way.

"I meet a lot of folks in the bar when I sing. A lot of men have asked me out. I know, because they run it by Flanagan first as if asking his approval. Because they live around here and they know Shaun, no one has dared to ask me outright and if they'd seen what happened tonight, they would have hurried by."

"Jesus, you could have been raped or something. How could anyone let that happen?"

"I'm saying that you were very brave, that's all."

"Sure I'm brave, darlin'. Blackwood's just a thug. I'm sure any guy would have taken him on when they saw him abusing you."

"Och, no they wouldn't, believe me. Sorry, I've been so wound up, you told me your name and I've completely forgotten it."

"It's Aidan. Here we are…" I pull the Peugeot into the front drive.

"Thank you, Aidan, and I really don't know a thing about you, except that all I need to know is you took Shaun on tonight. You're either very brave or very foolish."

"Why foolish? You said he was a drug dealer. Is that supposed to scare me?"

"Sure it's not. Let's not talk about Shaun anymore. Let's talk about you."

Killing the engine, I lean an arm across the back of her seat. I have secrets far too numerous to confide in this ostensibly scared wee wraith of a girl. "What do you want to know?"

"What do you do in London for instance?"

"Look, your make up's smudged, maybe we could get your face cleaned up." I trace a finger the length of her upper cheek. Her bone structure is artistically high, asymmetrically sculptured. In spite of the panda eyes and the bruise, the pallor of her complexion, she is undeniably beautiful, reminding me of those old sepia biopics of Mary Pickford that I had seen somewhere. She could so easily have fitted into that time. I can imagine her with bobbed hair, furs and a fringed Charleston dress. Or maybe the sixties. Her hair is long and thick, curling past her shoulders. She would have looked good in a mini skirt and high suede boots. Very Mary Quant.

"What's wrong?" Her green eyes narrow. "Why are you staring at me? It's the blotched mascara isn't it?"

God, it is growing increasingly difficult to resist fitting my lips to those beautiful, sensuous rosebuds, or slipping an arm about her shoulders and pulling her into my body. The hardness prevalent in my jeans is an uncontrollable animal pacing its cage.

Instead, cracking open the Peugeot's door, I suggest we go inside. "You can make the call…"

She already has the phone in her hand. Closing a palm over it, she whispers, "I thought you said you didn't want to wake your aunt and uncle up."

"I don't."

"Then I'd better make the call before we go in. You don't know my sister. Hi, Moll…"

Leaning an arm on the car door, I can only listen to the one sided conversation.

"I'm fine now honest. I… I met someone." Raising her eyes to my face, she smiles delicately. "No it isn't Shaun. Sure I had some trouble but Aidan… Aidan, the guy I met tonight. He's staying with his aunt and uncle." Caitlan heaves a prolonged sigh. "Yes he's nice and he... no, he doesn't seem that sort and the only reason I'm calling you is 'cos I know how you worry about me. No, for God's sake, Moll, I'm almost 20 years old. I'm not a child. Jesus." She snorts indignantly as she closes her phone. "Sisters!"

So, she is 19. Ten years my junior. A wee bit younger than the women I am used to. I'd dated women my own age and Verdi, who was almost 40, 20 years older than Caitlan.

"Tell me about them," I tut. Ushering her ahead of me we enter the house.

"You have a sister?" she asks.

"Sure. Two, I mean one." I amend quickly. Predictably, she pauses to regard me oddly.

"Don't you know how many sisters you have?"

"Sure I do. But she died."

"Oh I'm sorry. How?"

I am saved from a reply when, her bag slung across her shoulder, her attention diverts elsewhere. She rakes her gaze around the first room we enter, which happens to be the kitchen. "This is nice. A wee bit olde worlde but nice all the same, and cosy. Is your aunt very old?"

I shrug, "in her early seventies I think but Aunt Clodagh isn't the kind of woman you think of as old," I say defensively.

Again, she seems more interested in the room than in my defence of my aunt's age. The kitchen units are all fashioned in dark oak with marble effect worktops. There is also a large oak table spread with a blue checked cloth. Aunt Clodagh and kitchens are a match made in heaven. This is her domain as our kitchen had been in Shooters Hill when she lived with us.

Aunt Clodagh and Uncle Sheamie must have long since gone to bed. After all, it is almost midnight and I dismiss, or at least attempt to dismiss Shaun Blackwood from my mind.

"You like a drink or something?" I ask, inviting her to take a seat at the table. She asks if I have herbal tea, preferably Chamomile.

"Herbal tea?" I laugh. "I don't think Aunt Clodagh's budget stretches to herbal tea. It's just tea or coffee."

"A weak tea then please, I can't drink coffee, it makes me a bit jittery."

"Jittery?" I busy myself putting the kettle on to boil, searching amongst Aunt Clodagh's array of jars and spices for tea and coffee. "What do you mean, as in nervous?"

"You must think I'm such a scatterbrained wee thing. I'm not always jittery. I went to London once you know, to Oxford Street with Mollie to do some Christmas shopping."

"That was nice."

"Sure that was fine but I got jittery on the underground and Mollie had to take me home, well, back to the hotel where we were staying. Do you go on the underground much?"

"Sometimes, but I'm not often down Oxford Street. Shopping's not really my scene. Besides, I prefer to drive everywhere."

"In London!" she exclaims in surprise.

"I live near Blackheath, Shooters Hill, that's in South London. I don't take any notice of driving in London. Maybe I've been there too long. Anyway, from what I've seen, the Dublin traffic can be just as busy." The kettle boils and I fix her a weak tea, simply by showing the teabag to the hot water. That's all it is, virtually hot water with a trace of brown liquid. I ask her if it's okay. I'm surprised when she says, "it's lovely, Aidan, thanks. So you here on holiday then?"

Joining her at the table, I set a black, sugarless coffee in front of me. I nod my response.

"So how long are you here for?"

"A couple of weeks, Uncle Sheamie isn't too well and I take him to St Patrick's for consultations. They don't drive, so it saves them taxi fares. So what about you? Aunts and uncles? Mum and Dad?"

I am astonished when her face turns even more ashen. She swallows, shakes her head. She shrugs. "Sure. A few aunts and uncles I don't see much of. My ma…" she pauses to swallow uncomfortably again.

"She died and da walked out on us a while ago. So there's really only Mollie and me. Her and Niall will be getting wed soon."

"Who's Niall? That her fiancé?"

"Yes. She'll probably move out of the flat. Flanagan says I can live in the flat above The Liffey if I want to. He has the other one but I can't imagine not living with Mollie. Sure I know she nags at me something dreadful at times but she does have my best interests at heart."

"Anyway, let's get you cleaned up," I suggest, about to ease from my seat when she touches my arm.

"So who do you have besides your aunt and uncle? You're a wee bit older than me, but not by much I'm thinking."

"I'm 29. The big 3-0 next June."

"Really? You look younger. I thought you were about 25 or 26. So what do you do in London? You didn't tell me when I asked before. Can I guess?"

"Sure," I laugh dropping back into my seat. "You'll never guess."

She taps her mouth thoughtfully as she considers. "You're an actor?"

"God no! Where did that come from?"

"I don't know. Maybe you look like one of those Shakespearian types. Or a poet? A male model then?"

"I'm flattered. But you're way off."

"Then you're a photographer, a solicitor or maybe a singer or an artist. Something like that. Maybe it's the hair."

"Now you're clutching at straws. Try landscape gardener."

"Never! I'd never guessed that. In London?"

"Believe it or not, people do have gardens in London. Anyway, we go to other places outside London, like Dartford in Kent, or Surrey."

At the mention of Surrey, I wonder if I should confide that I have an ex-wife and son, but decide against it at this early stage in what I hope will become a blossoming relationship. "But the artist bit. You're partially right in that assumption. When I was in…"

I catch her staring at me pointedly. She clings onto my every word, every inflection, as if I am about to dive into the deep end and confess that I have sold some paintings while in prison. She obviously picks up on my hesitation and prompts, "yes, go on. You were saying."

"When I was in the Tate Modern, that's an art gallery in London…" I've never been to the Tate Modern in my life. Nevertheless, that is close, McRaney. I expel a breath. "I… I was inspired by the paintings there."

"We have quite a few galleries in Dublin. I love art too. You'll have to let me show you the city. I expect it's changed a wee bit in 20 years. I love it here," she enthuses dreamily. "Sure I haven't lived anywhere else, but I couldn't imagine living anywhere else but in Ireland." That piece of news is hardly conducive to heightening my spirits. Everything in my life, particularly my son, are all tied up in London. Ireland had once been my home. Now I can't imagine living here again.

"I'd love you to show me around, as long as Blackwood don't…"

A slender finger presses against my lips, the touch soft on my flesh. I wonder again if she is a wraith, a ghost, a beautiful phantom.

"Don't let's spoil it. I want to forget him. So tell me about your family. Your ma and da, do they live in London too?"

"My mam died. Dad lives in London. I have a sister, Bridget, she's 34. Two brothers, I'm the middle one. Harry's the eldest, he's 41. And there's my kid brother Ru, Ruairi, he's 21."

"So we've both lost our mothers."

"Mine died in childbirth. Then my 18 year old sister died."

"Was she ill?"

I nod painfully with the lie, unable as I am to confide that my sister was raped and murdered and that Verdi, my girlfriend, and I had taken revenge on the man responsible.

"Och, if it isn't so painful when someone dies? It's best not to talk about it and then you can almost make believe it never happened."

It seems a strange thing to say. Then I've begun to realise that she is a strange elfin child. "You're a funny wee thing, you know that?"

She giggles. "That's what Flanagan says. He's such a sweet man. He's been like a da to me. His wife died a while ago and sometimes I find him weeping up in his room over her picture and I cry with him. I can't help it, even if I don't know the person and I never met his wife, I still weep for them. Now you know how stupid and pathetic I am."

"Not at all, it shows you care." My heart goes out to her. I realise that I never want her to leave. Anyway, I'm not ready to leave *her*. When I return to London - and I know I will have to eventually - would an interminable stretch of water always be there to separate us?

Reaching for her hands across the table, I'm pleased, and ultimately surprised, when she fails to pull away. "You're neither stupid or pathetic but a gentle, caring person Caitlan. I'd like to see you again and don't tell me that Shaun Blackwood wouldn't like it," I stress, observing her face whiten once more, "because I can handle him. I don't care whether he's a drug dealer or a gun-runner. I'm made of sterner stuff than that but if you're not interested, then tell me now because I won't pursue it further."

"Now you sound like a poet. I'd love to see you again. Can I tell you something?"

"Sure, fire away and if you say you don't like guys with beards, I'll shave it off immediately. I've only just started to grow it anyway."

"No, I think the beard suits you. Beards suit men with dark colouring like yours. I was going to say when I saw you in the bar at The Liffey, although I was busy singing, I saw you and I thought you were very good looking. I wanted to say more when I took your glass away but I was scared of antagonising Shaun. Besides, I lost my nerve and was scared that you'd think I was some stupid wee girl for making the first move."

"I felt the same way about you the minute I saw you."

"You did!" she enthuses, eyes shimmering. "But what I also wanted to say was, unless your aunt's got a spare bedroom, now you've brought me back here, where would you like me to sleep?"

*

Caitlan really has no idea how her question of where she is going to sleep has excited me. I am all too intrinsically aware of where she should sleep or maybe she does. If we were back at my Shooters Hill flat, the question of sleeping quarters would not have arisen. If she's willing to sleep with me - of course no pressure at this stage, I can be patient - this is my aunt and uncle's house and I am merely a guest. "You can have my bed," I offer. It isn't what I really want to say but if Aunt Clodagh decides, as she has since I've been here, to enter my room with a wake up cup of coffee and discovers me in bed with a girl, she may not approve. Not that she'll come right out and say so of course. She isn't a prudish sort of woman.

"If that's what you want," she shrugs and I can hear the disappointment in her voice. It isn't what I want. Not at all. "So where will you sleep?"

"I'll take the couch."

"If you're sure. That's very gentlemanly of you, Aidan. If it was Shaun he would have pulled me into his bed by now."

Unwilling to hear any more about that man I say, "I'm not Shaun. I thought you said you didn't want to discuss him?"

She allows me to grab her hand, escorting her up the stairs. "My aunt has three bedrooms but uses the other as a junk room." I smile at her. "She doesn't like to get rid of stuff."

Caitlan giggles again. When she isn't shaking she seems to have acquired a penchant for the giggles. A palm clasps her mouth, the other clutches mine, she attempts to stifle her laughter as we mount the stairs. It is odd and a feeling I should shelve if this lovely girl and I are to have any kind of relationship. I hope we will; but right now my hand in hers is more in the way of a fatherly gesture than that of a potential boyfriend. At 29 I am beginning to feel inordinately old all of a sudden, something I've never felt before. The eleven-year age gap between Verdi and I had scarcely concerned me, even though she was almost 40. With Caitlan, somehow...

Halfway up the stairs she almost overbalances in her boots. I'm compelled to slip an arm around her waist as she staggers against me and whispers, "Shush. What if your aunt and uncle hear us? Will they go mad?"

"No, why should they?"

We reach the bedroom and opening the door, we enter together. I close the door behind us. The room is quite small. Although she's moved a lot of her things out, it's obvious the bedroom is very much Aunt Clodagh orientated. She does all her own decorating; wallpaper instead of paint, the innumerable pink and red roses being the first thing your eyes alight on upon waking, plus the holy pictures of course. "Jesus you're Catholic too!" Caitlan exclaims. Her voice is barely above a whisper as if she's just entered a church.

"Afraid so. And Mollie, she don't have the holy pictures?"

"Mollie won't have religious stuff in her flat."

"I'll get rid of it if it bothers you. I don't really do religion myself but my aunt takes hers seriously and still goes to mass and stuff." So does my sister, I reflect. Rumour has it, courtesy of my kid brother and my ex-wife, my sister is having an affair with her priest, Father James Mulligan.

"It's okay," she shrugs and allows her eyes to travel the room thoughtfully. "It's pretty and so feminine. Your aunt has good taste. A wee bit old fashioned but there's nothing wrong with that," she giggles again. "Did I say feminine, well apart from your shorts and shirts thrown over the chair…"

"I'll apologise for that too. I'm not the tidiest of men."

"Men can't be tidy. That's what Mollie says anyway. It's not in their nature to be tidy. So stop apologising," she teases.

Suddenly she is in my arms. Covering my lips with hers, we kiss, unmindful that Aunt Clodagh and Uncle Sheamie are in the next room. My hand lowers to her small behind and pressing it tightly, pulls her against me. I feel her fingers inch behind the belt of my jeans.

She murmurs, "Oh Aidan, I wanted you from the first moment I saw you. I wanted to know what it would be like, a man like you wanting to make love to me."

I have little time to dwell on whatever that might mean because while we kiss I realise we've moved closer to the bed, hear the springs creak with the pressure of our bodies collapsing onto it. Impatient hands loosen my belt; this giggly childlike woman is a nymphomaniac suddenly, unexpectedly. I am the one holding back, unwilling to rush her. Now it's all up to me. As my hands move all over her, sliding beneath the short tartan skirt, feeling the silk of her panties, I relish the inevitability of having sex. There is so much I can teach her or maybe she knows it already. Yet not here, not here in my aunts home, even if I am hard, as proud as a fuckin' stallion. Her hands close around my erection, hear her murmur my name with a sort of pride and impressiveness. I locate that membranous well; play with her clitoris and ease her legs apart, about to enter her. Her breath is hot, be-laboured, waiting and expectant in readiness to receive me. I want her so much and miraculously she wants me, until Aunt Clodagh's kindly but oddly disapproving face rises to my mind's eye all at once, with the recollection that she's a light sleeper.

I hate myself. The loveliest girl I've seen in a long while, the woman I've wanted from the first moment I walked into The Liffey Bar. About to slip my length into her, suddenly I hold back. This isn't what I want. She lies beneath me, her sweater pulled up, her skirt raised high reveals green silk panties, matching filmy lace bra. She's nubile, boyish. Dark hair spread across the contrasting white of the pillow, a solitary curl dangles scintillatingly across the bra. Here I am idiotically swinging my legs over the edge of the bed. Cool fingers trail the length of my back. My shirt remains open but I don't remove it.

"What's wrong Aidan? Don't you fancy me enough to make love to me?" Disappointment edges her words. She offers it to me on a plate when I believe I will have to wait for her.

"Oh God no!" I twist around to face her.

"You mean you don't?" She quickly eases herself up in the bed, her beautiful face registering shock. "I thought you did, the way you looked at me or was I misreading the signs? I mean, when a man looks at a woman the way you looked at me tonight, I really believed you wanted me."

"You know I want you, Caitlan," I say. The sound of my voice is scarcely my own. "You're beautiful."

Her mouth tightens. She breathes raggedly. Swinging her legs over the end of the bed she pulls down her sweater and skirt, reaches for the boots she has unzipped, peeled off the moment we entered the bedroom. "I can hear a 'but' in the tone of your voice, Aidan. Sure, I know what the problem is."

"There's no problem," I reach for her, but she pulls away instinctively.

"It's because of Shaun isn't it?"

"Bejaysus I'm not scared of Shaun Blackwood, darlin'. Didn't I prove that tonight? And I've still got his fuckin' knife in my jacket."

"No I didn't mean that." She faces me squarely; the beautiful green eyes snap wide, an inflection I've come to associate with her. "It's because I told you he had sex with me. You can't bring yourself to touch me. You saw the way he looked. Pockmarked, greasy and you probably think he might have something…"

"Jesus, Caitlan." I leap off the bed, move around to her side and drop my weight beside her. She allows me to slip my arm around her waist. What she suggests has not occurred to me hitherto. "That's not it at all." Slipping a forefinger beneath her chin, my thumb plays with her lip, which she hasn't ceased biting since I pulled out of her. Tears sparkle her eyes. I say gently, "I just don't like that bastard touching you but that's not the reason why I pulled out. I'm a guest in my aunt and uncle's house. I want you, God knows I do, but if you really want me too we can wait."

The tears abandon her eyes. She smiles through them. "You're scared your aunt and uncle will hear us having sex? Oh, and it's not because I've been with Shaun?"

"No, sure it's not and I mean it, but if you're serious about us having a relationship, then I want to know that Shaun Blackwood's out of the picture. I need you to sever your ties with him."

Admonishing myself for not giving in to my ardent sexual drive for once, I reluctantly return downstairs, leaving a girl in my bed while I take the couch.

'What the hell's wrong with you, McRaney? A beautiful girl offers it to you unreservedly, without inhibition, half naked and you prefer to sleep on a couch – alone.'

I hope I've managed to reassure her that my abstinence is not because Blackwood has been having it with her but because of my aunt and uncle possibly hearing the creak of bedsprings. The bed is of the wooden variety, quite old, the mattress worn. Anyone making love on it can be, in all likelihood, heard throughout the house. Then of course, there is the rather pious picture of Jesus, a golden halo surrounding him, his eyes kindly, smiling, as if either to give us his blessing or to say abstinence is good for the soul and a holy accomplishment. Aunt Clodagh has even placed rosary beads over the picture.

Caitlan is obviously disappointed. It further surprises me when I initially intended not to rush her. I also hope I've convinced her to sever her ties with Blackwood.

I lie on the couch and pull the blanket I found in the airing cupboard over my near nakedness. Thoughts of killing Blackwood and throwing him into The Liffey grow in dominance. I had killed Stephen Fitzwalter and helped Verdi bury the body of Fitzwalter's homosexual partner, Nicholas. Also, with Verdi's help, I succeeded in throwing the treacherous woman I believed myself to be in love with, Joanna Sheldon, into Ray Lamond's crematorium in his Maze Hill grounds. Plus the guy in the Copper Kettle restaurant in Soho in 2003. None of which Caitlan has any knowledge of and no way in the world is she ever going to find out. She believes that I am solely a landscape gardener back in London and if she ever chances to meet my family, I'll make certain they allow nothing to slip about my being in prison for killing a man. Somehow, it is imperative she is contained in the dark. She is gentle and so very young, hardly a woman of the world as the others were. If only I can erase the stupid notion, I entertain, of being more of a father figure to her than a lover. Haven't I stupidly proved that?

She is scared of Blackwood, that much is certain but does she care about him? Tomorrow night when she goes to the bar I plan to escort her, remain for the duration, and then leave with her. After all, I'm used to minding jobs and this particular one will be a pleasure.

All manner of unresolved thoughts scramble around in my brain, until sleep finally arrives and I drift off. I then blink into wakefulness with no idea of the time and throw a hand across my eyes when the curtains are drawn back allowing the lowdown November sunshine to intrude into the room.

"Och, Aidan, you gave me such a turn seeing you there, so you did," Aunt Clodagh exclaims, a hand clasping her heart region. This morning she wears a dark blue knitted dress, over which she's tucked a small floral pinny. Despite being in her early seventies, she has a slim figure, accentuated by her height. Like all of the McRaney's, she's really quite tall.

"Sorry, Auntie." I ease myself from the couch and realise apart from my shorts, I am naked. "I didn't hear you come down." I was hoping to have dressed before she did.

"It was just a wee bit odd to find you in here."

"There's a girl in my bed." There is no point in lying because Aunt Clodagh is regarding me with her brows in the speculatively upraised position.

"A girl? What girl?"

"I met her last night." I refrain from mentioning the fact we'd had a spot of bother with Blackwood. Aunt Clodagh has lived in Dublin all her life; it makes me wonder if she might know him. Nevertheless,

I refuse to question her. "I hope you don't mind. I know I'm only a guest. I should have asked."

"A good looking boy like you, it's only natural you should find a girlie soon enough."

"You don't mind? Anyway, what other reason did you think I was on the couch? I didn't wet the bed if that's what you were thinking," I tease her.

"Aidan." She plumps cushions in all the chairs in her less than spacious lounge. A wooden coffee table, plus a 32-inch TV and two chairs occupies every conceivable inch of the room.

"Do you remember when I first came to London to look after you wains? You were a very frightened wee boy after your poor ma died and you used to wet the bed."

At this juncture I can't help but colour with embarrassment. Aunt Clodagh has the perfect knack of causing it. The embarrassment increases when Caitlan appears and greets us with an effervescent, "good morning."

Neither one of us have heard her enter the room. It's plainly obvious that she must have caught the gist of that conversation because she attempts to conceal a smile behind her hand.

"Good morning, dear. So Aidan gave up his bed?" There's no mistaking the subtle reprimand in her voice. She rakes Caitlan over questioningly, ingesting her appearance.

Caitlan's dressed in the black sweater, tartan skirt, high black suede boots. Obviously, she has no other clothes here.

"That's because he's a gentleman," Caitlan says and smiles at me proudly, while I am subjected to the endurance of two women's appraisal, as if I am a prize bull at a market or they are aware I am practically naked beneath this blanket.

"Sure he's a gentleman," Aunt Clodagh agrees. "My favourite nephew. Of all Dermot's children, Dermot, Aidan's father, is my brother; I would have taken Aidan on and brought him up as me own, 'cos me and Sheamie couldn't have any children." She shakes her head as if to clear it of the memory. Coming to, she's the brisk hausfrau once again. "So do you have a name, child?" she asks.

I haven't imagined it, but I am certain that I saw Caitlan stiffen when Auntie calls her 'child'.

"It's Caitlan," she says quietly.

"Caitlan. That's a pretty name. So would you like a drink? Tea or coffee?" Auntie asks.

"Caitlan likes herbal tea but I couldn't find any last night," I tell her and wonder if Caitlan is mad at me for not having sex with her. I'm beginning to feel guilty as well as a complete 'wuss' because I was scared my aunt and uncle might hear us.

"Oh no, I don't have herbal tea, dear."

"A weak, normal tea will do then, Mrs…" Caitlan fishes for her name.

"It's Mrs Connolly but you can call me Auntie if you like."

I wonder if my aunt heard us last night when we came in. If she did, she's given no sign. "So how's Uncle Sheamie this morning?" I ask.

She shakes her head negatively. "He's very tired so he is and has been since that consultation with the doctor at St Patrick's."

I nod sympathetically. "When does he need to go again? You know I'll take him."

"Thanks. You're a good boy, Aidan. I shall miss you when you go back to England." Tears appear in Auntie's eyes. If I wasn't half-naked, I would have sprung up from the couch to comfort her.

"I'm sorry your husband's not well, Mrs Connolly." Caitlan offers her sympathy. At a look from my aunt, she corrects herself hastily. "Auntie."

"Anyway, I'll get your breakfasts. Aidan has coffee." She clucks exasperatedly. "He drinks too much of that stuff and smokes. Do you smoke dear?"

Caitlan shakes her head. "I have to preserve my vocal chords."

Aunt Clodagh's gaze encompasses us both. I explain that Caitlan is a singer in The Liffey Bar.

"A singer! Wow!" Her 70-year-old eyes illumine in surprise. "So what sort of things do you sing, Caitlan? That pop music I suppose?"

"No. She sings the stuff you like to listen to, Auntie, while you're doing the washing up."

It is Aunt Clodagh's turn to blush and she points to herself in pretend disbelief. "You've heard me sing?"

"Sometimes," I smile, my heart going out to her.

"Country music?" Aunt Clodagh wants to know.

"Sure. Irish country music, Auntie," Caitlan says.

"Och, that's my favourite. Now I'll go and fix your breakfasts and you can tell me all about it." She exits the room, but with her departure there is an unmistakeable trill to her voice when she launches into 'Galway Bay', as soon as she's out of earshot.

Caitlan drops onto the couch next to me and closing her lips over mine, we kiss.

"You're not pissed off with me about last night are you, sweetheart?" I slide an arm around her waist, pull her against me. "You know about us not having…"

"Sex." She presses a finger to my lips. "I didn't lie to your auntie when I said you were a gentleman, respecting your aunt and uncle and me."

"So how much of that conversation did you hear when you came in?"

"Oh, you mean the bit about you being a frightened wee boy who used to wet the bed?"

"I thought you might have done." I make a face.

"After you took on Shaun last night, I can't imagine you as a frightened wee boy. You were my knight in shining armour."

"I wouldn't go as far as to say that, darlin'. Look, do you mind passing me my jeans so I can get dressed before my aunt comes back."

"Sure." She retrieves the Levis from the floor, passes them. "So you want me to turn my back?"

"It's a bit late for that ain't it? I mean after last night."

"How did you manage anyway?"

Pulling on my jeans, I regard her obtusely. "Sorry, manage what?"

"You know." She shrugs, colours. "You were as hard as a stallion. I mean, did you have to work yourself off?"

"Not really. That picture of Jesus above the bed is better than any contraceptive."

She giggles again. Then, as if she remembers something, her pretty face transforms to ashen once more. "You said you still had Shaun's knife. Where is it?"

I'd left my jacket over the chair in the kitchen. "Jesus, it's in there!" I gesture in that general direction.

"What if your aunt finds it? She might wonder what you're doing with a switchblade knife in your jacket."

She appears so incredibly young in her anxiety.

"I'll get rid of it, okay? Anyway, I might need it."

"Why should you need a knife?" Her eyes widen questioningly. "You're not like him. You're nice but you really did know how to handle yourself last night. Most men would have been scared. Weren't you scared?"

"Of that bastard? Jesus no." I have begun to savour the taste of her obvious hero-worship. "I'd do it again if I had to. And listen…"

planting my hands firmly onto her shoulders, she's unable to avoid staring into my gaze. "If you want me to, I'll pick you up tonight, take you to The Liffey, stay there until you finish. Then I'll take you home."

"You don't have to, but I'd like that."

"That's settled then."

Aunt Clodagh shouts from the kitchen that breakfast is ready. I am surprised that she's done us a full English and I catch Caitlan regarding the beans, bacon, sausage and two eggs on her plate a fraction uneasily.

"By the time I leave here, Auntie, I'll be as fat as a pig," I tease her.

"Och now, that'll be the day." Auntie scolds good-humouredly. "You're as skinny as a rake, so y'are, isn't he, Caitlan?"

She smiles, but refrains from tendering a response.

Uncle Sheamie appears, taking his place at the head of the table. He looks tired, older than his 72 years. His hair's whiter than when I had seen him last. It is still thick and now resembles a snowy thatch. Naturally, he requires an introduction, which I duly fulfil.

"Hullo my dear. I thought I heard you two come in last night, Aidan," he remarks, a twinkle in his aged gaze. Aunt Clodagh colours to the roots of her still dark hair.

"Hush now, Sheamus Connolly, don't tease," she admonishes him, a twinkle in her eyes.

*

Aunt Clodagh mentions something about changing her bedding, washing to do. She continues her habitual bustling about the house while Uncle Sheamie prefers instead to retire to the lounge with his morning papers, his spectacles perched on the end of his nose. Caitlan elects to do the washing up while I adjourn upstairs to shower. Returning downstairs, I observe Caitlan sitting at the big oak table in the kitchen. I can't help noticing it is in close proximity to where I've left my jacket draped over the chair. I promise to get rid of the knife and that she isn't to touch it. In reality, I have no intention, at least for a while, of losing the knife. I see myself not merely as Caitlan's potential boyfriend but also her minder, that the switchblade might come in useful. I hope that I won't have need of it, but it's simply comforting to know it's there.

Uncle Sheamie asks if I wouldn't mind helping him lift a sack of potatoes Clodagh has ordered, as the van is here.

Needless to say, I won't allow my uncle to lift the sack. When the driver pulls up and unloads the potatoes from his van, I seize my opportunity, despite my aunt's protests that I wasn't to pay for anything. I pay for the spuds before hefting the sack into her kitchen where Aunt Clodagh is in the process of loading her washing machine.

Caitlan is noticeably absent. When I ask where she is, Aunt Clodagh shakes her head. "She went off in some kind of huff, son."

"Huff? What huff? What do you mean?"

Aunt Clodagh gestures toward the window.

"Isn't that her car parked next to yours, Aidan? It looks as if she's got into it and is going to drive away."

"Not without saying goodbye she isn't."

From what I've learned about Caitlan McKenna in the few hours since I have known her, I realise she is prone to mood swings. Giggly one moment. Sexy. A scared rabbit caught in the headlights the next.

I fling myself out of the house in time to observe her fire the Peugeot's ignition. She's about to back out of the drive, when I position myself in front of the car in order to intercept her, before moving around to the driving side. Leaning an arm on her wound down window, I demand to know what she thinks she's doing.

"Have I upset you or something?" You were leaving without saying goodbye. Is it something to do with that knife?"

She brakes the car. Her mouth is tight, factious. Green eyes narrow when she regards me again. "No not exactly. I thought you were different, that's all."

"What's that supposed to mean?"

"You're just like the other men I've been with. Shaun often lied to me, in a different way but he lied."

"What am I supposed to have lied to you about?"

For the first time I feel oddly uneasy. Has Aunt Clodagh told her that I'd been to prison and why? If she has, then judging by Caitlan's reaction, I have lost her irretrievably.

"That you're married!"

"What!" I almost laugh and cry with relief simultaneously. "I'm not married."

"I found your wallet. There was a picture of you with a little boy. He can't be your brother because you said he was 21. So he's obviously your son. He looks so much like you."

Jesus was that all? "Yeah I have a son. Patrick, he's nine but I'm not married. I was but I'm divorced. We... we couldn't get along. I have fortnightly access but I'm definitely not married, sweetheart."

Cracking open the Peugeot's door I slide into the seat put my arm around her shoulder. "So were you checking up on me?"

"No. I was looking for the knife."

"And?"

"Like I said, I found your wallet so I looked inside. I'm sorry but I couldn't help it. I saw your driving licence and stuff. Then I saw the photo of you and the little boy. I didn't mean to jump to conclusions but, as I said, men I thought I could trust have lied to me in the past."

"You were upset. Then I do mean something to you?"

She slowly traces my cheek with her fingers. "I think you're beginning to, Aidan."

"Look when I go back to London why don't you come with me? You told me your sister's getting married soon and you'll be on your own."

She swallows. "You... you mean leave Ireland? But this is my home. London is... is... so..."

"Scary? Sure, we can always avoid Oxford Street and the underground."

She bites her lower lip with her teeth anxiously, as if I've just asked her to fly to the moon. "Now you're making fun of me."

"I'm sorry, I didn't mean to."

She seems a child when she wants to be, scared of leaving the comforts of her home. Last night she came to me as a woman. Now, as she is about to drive away, I am angry with myself for not giving into my natural male urges and taken what she offered. I don't want her to leave, while I have no desire to leave Dublin and Caitlan behind. Maybe this is simply a transient holiday romance, that we'll forget one another once we're separated. Alternatively, I am unwilling for that to happen.

"It's just that I don't want to say goodbye to you when I leave, it would be so final."

"We've only known each other for a few hours but I'm beginning to feel the same," she admits. "So why don't you stay in Dublin? We... we could get a flat together or something."

"Sweetheart I'm sorry. As much as I'd like to, I can't live here. Ireland isn't my home anymore and I have my son in England."

I'm aware how selfish I sound, but during my sojourn in prison, if it wasn't for Bridget's intervention fighting tooth and nail against Judy and her domineering mother, I would have been lucky to have seen Patrick at all. As it was, Mrs Lisle, Judy's mother, instructed her daughter and her grandson to sever all ties with the McRaney's. To abandon him now would be playing right into those treacherous women's hands and my sister's hard work would count for nothing

Her mouth tightens again. She pushes herself back into the driving seat so that I have little choice than to lower my arm from around her shoulders.

"I also have a business to run. I'm not that good at it but my brother Harry's sodded off to Italy and left me to run it. Apart from your sister, you said yourself you have no one."

Firing the ignition, her face turns pale, she snaps, "you don't understand do you, Aidan?"

"You're right about that darlin'. Sure, I can understand why you don't want to leave Dublin. You have your singing and you're probably worried what ould Flanagan'll do without you."

"It's not just that but I have to go now. Mollie will be worried."

"I'll see you tonight?" I practically hold my breath in fear her response will be a negative one.

"Sure." She smiles. "You'll pick me up you said."

"I promised to, didn't I? Seven o'clock was it?"

"You know where Fenian Street is?"

"No but my aunt will give me directions I'm sure."

She allows me to kiss her.

"Sure I want to understand, sweetheart," I say. "And I don't want to lose you when I return to London."

*

I check my jacket after Caitlan leaves. She hasn't taken the blade. So unobserved, I slip it out and into the leather coat I plan to wear this evening. I'm in the process of shaving, debating whether or not to keep the beard. Maybe I will. She seems to like it. I'm negotiating the razor around my face when a rather tentative rap sounds on the door and Aunt Clodagh calls, "are you decent?"

Informing her that I am, I unlock the door and usher her into the bathroom.

"Something wrong, Auntie?" I'm only wearing my jeans. My torso is bare and I'm conscious of her presence. It appears however, that Auntie doesn't seem to notice.

"No not really. I suppose you're going to see that wee girlie tonight?" she maintains a deliberately lowered voice.

I afford her my full attention. "Is that a problem? You sound as if you don't like her."

"Oh but I do and I can tell she's got you smitten, so she has. She's a sweet girl."

It's obvious that Aunt Clodagh is itching to say something and doesn't know how to. "That's good then." I pause from my shave to place a hand on her shoulder. "C'mon Auntie, spit it out. You and I have no secrets between us. We never did and I don't plan on having any now. You know a lot about me and I know you won't tell Caitlan."

"If you're planning on having any kind of relationship with that girl, then you shouldn't have secrets, Aidan."

"Sure I know that but sometimes if too many secrets are revealed, I could lose her. She seems like a scared rabbit at times. If I'd told her I'd been to jail and why, she could run a mile. I might never see her again. See what happened earlier. She went off in a huff."

"What was that all about?"

"I think she's trying to find out stuff about me." I refrain from mentioning the switchblade I'd confiscated from Blackwood. "When she saw the picture of me with Patrick she assumed I was married. So she knows I have a son and an ex-wife back in England. Anyway, Auntie, I don't think that's the issue here, the reason why you couldn't wait to discuss this when I came downstairs. You'll have to excuse my half-dressed state."

"Och, it's nothing I haven't seen before, boy." She waves a hand about her dismissively. "I mostly brought you up, remember. Sometimes I thought of you as my own. I know what you did and why you went to jail. I always reckoned it was 'cos you was uprooted from your Dublin school, then your poor ma dying and that brother of mine drinking so much, the threat of you wee wains being taken into care. But it's all in the past and you've become a fine young man from the scared wee boy who used to come home after being bullied by those English boys."

"Sure, I know all about that but you've obviously got something you want to say. I have to pick Caitlan up at seven to take her to The Liffey"

"The reason why I wanted to talk to you here is 'cos I didn't want your uncle to overhear. It'll only lead to a frightful row and I don't want to antagonise him the way he is. Och now, you'll think I'm being silly."

I have never seen her quite so tongue-tied before. Whatever it is she intends to say, she is obviously finding it difficult.

"Dear Aunt Clodagh," I slip an arm around her shoulders, "you're a wonderful woman and I love you dearly, I always have. If it hadn't been for you and Brid I'd never have got through my growing up years and it's Aidan your nephew you're talking to. So what is it I'll think you're being silly about?"

"That wee girlie?"

"Caitlan?"

"She's got a secret too. A big one."

"Is that what she told you?"

"No, she told me nothing but I… I read her aura."

"You did what!" Despite her perturbed and serious expression, I attempt to stifle the rising tide of laughter. "What aura?" I manage to calm myself with an effort.

"Och, I didn't go out of my way to do it. It just happened. It does sometimes. If I try I can't do it, it has to come out of the blue so to speak. And hers is strong."

"And?"

"And it was sort of dark, as if she's had a lot of sadness in her life. Something happened to her a wee while ago. I don't know what it was but it had to do with death. Now I've said it. Sheamie doesn't believe of course."

"And neither do I, Auntie. I thought you were going to say something serious, that she'd told you something about herself." I resume my shave; concentrate on the mirror and not on my aunt.

Persistently she adds, "I know you don't believe, Aidan. Well, believe this then. I know that just after your poor sister Laurena died, you saw your mother's apparition in Bridget's house."

I froze, aware it is the truth. Swiping a towel around my face with a thinly disguised nonchalance, I attempt to brush it aside.

"My silly 'churchy' sister been talking to you again? Sure, I thought I saw something but I was either dreaming or it was Brid standing there. She and Mum had the same hair colour and practically the same style. Besides, after Laurie's death I'd cried a lot and hadn't slept."

She rests a hand lightly on my arm. "Bridget didn't tell me, Aidan."

"Then how?"

Aunt Clodagh taps her nose enigmatically. "I know these things, same as I know you're psychic, boy."

"No wonder Uncle Sheamie don't approve. Like I said, I love you dearly but I don't believe in all that nonsense, okay? I was sleep deprived when Laurie died, I was bound to hallucinate."

Plus, I was also coming down on Verdi's joints.

*

Garbed in tight black jeans, black shirt, over which I'd thrown the black leather coat, I sit behind the wheel of the hired Audi outside

Caitlan's block in Fenian Street. I'd texted, informing her that I'm waiting, having no desire to be interrogated by her big sister. Alas, too late, her returning text reads, 'can you come up? Mollie wants to meet u.'

Jesus. Vet me more like. Sighing, I am almost prompted to text back 'we might be late. It's nearly 6.30 already.'

Albeit reluctantly, I exit the vehicle and enter her block. On announcing my presence I am instructed to, 'come on up, Aidan,' by Caitlan.

The door opens immediately on a woman who is definitely not my girlfriend. I have no idea what to expect.

A white fluffy towel drapes her head, turban style. Wearing a matching towelling robe, she pauses to rake me over practically to the point of embarrassment.

"You'd better come in." Her eyes are of the self-same emerald green as Caitlan's, equally as snapping but without the familiar alluring endearment, or maybe I am simply being biased. She also appears to be a lot older. Her features are a little coarse, while a rather large nose serves to dominate an overly flushed face. Her full lips would have been as sensuous as Caitlan's if she didn't appear quite so shrewish. In marked contrast to her sister, Mollie is on the plump side. Her robe pulled so closely about her; the tie continues to work loose each time she moves.

Clutching a cigarette between thumb and forefinger, she says, "Cait's still getting ready."

She's just texted me. I assume it's because she is ready to leave. It is obviously a ploy for her sister's interrogation.

"I thought she was ready." I vocalise my thoughts.

She ushers me into the room after closing the door. The place is smaller than I expect, after my own spacious flat in Shooters Hill. There is room enough for a 28-inch TV, a beige settee and matching chair, plus a low coffee table, one that is liberally piled high with various women's magazines. A dark unit occupies most of one wall, cluttered with books, ornaments and a telephone.

The shrewish mouth opens, exposing a tongue slicking around screaming red lipstick, I can only imagine as salacious.

"So you're my sister's new fella?" She makes it sound like an accusation, while she's engrossed in sizing me up as a buyer might, wishing to purchase a horse in a market.

"I hope to be," I reply noncommittally. I want to be 'her new fella'. Yet somehow, in her sister's presence, I have no idea why, I've no desire to leave myself unguarded.

Mollie's expression is one of suspicion, as if she's capable of interpreting my thoughts and has knowledge of my past. Alternatively, how can she?

"Well now, you are or you aren't." She speaks tersely, which instinctively gets my back up. Her tone is caustic, denoting her to be the kind of woman who'd been around the block a little.

My mouth tightens in response. "I hope to be but we've only just met. It's still early days."

"'Course," she shrugs, pulls on her cigarette. "Drink?"

Slipping a hand into the pocket of my coat, I regard her with feigned obtuseness. Again, the red lipstick mouth parts, the tongue appears licking the lips. Eyes widen, less narrow, while thinly pencilled brows arch with, I consider, an amused speculation.

"You asking if I do, or if I want one?" I deal her a sardonic smile. We confront each other, this woman and I.

She invites me to a seat. "If you want one."

Dropping my weight into the armchair, I explain that I'm driving, adding, "so is Caitlan going to be long?"

She shrugs again. "If my sister started getting ready at five, sure now, she might be ready by seven, especially if she's on a date... so I thought Cait said you was English from London. You sound more like a Dubliner to me."

"I'm a Dubliner from London," I quip. "I've lived in London a long time."

"You haven't lost your accent then."

"No, I was 10 when I... Anyway, where's Caitlan hiding? Or has this been your plan all along, darlin'?"

The crimson flush dissipates. "Plan?"

"Apart from the blinding light flashed into my face, I would say you wanted to interrogate me."

"Now that's far from my thoughts, darlin'," she mocks, crushing her cigarette into the tray vindictively. "So, Cait told me you took on Shaun Blackwood last night, Jesus, nobody takes him on, not if they want to keep their head on their shoulders and their knees where God intended."

"I was just looking out for your sister, that's all."

"Hi, Aidan, sorry to keep you waiting." Caitlan appears from an adjacent room and grabs my arm as I'm already halfway out of my seat. She speaks quickly and animatedly, obviously before her sister can add more.

"Pity." Mollie shakes her turbaned head. "Just as me and Aidan were getting acquainted. You look after her, darlin' or you'll have me to answer to. She's precious," Mollie addresses me. About to ignite another cigarette, she jabs the unlit smoke into thin air.

Cuddling Caitlan and kissing the top of her head, I tell Mollie, "that's my intention, to look after her. She's precious to me too. Nice to meet you, Mollie." I can't help my sarcasm.

The wink she deals me, in accompaniment with her salacious smile, isn't difficult to interpret. So, Mollie McKenna might be engaged as the large diamond sparkler on her ring finger testifies, but I'm aware that she isn't averse to savouring the attentions of her sister's boyfriend.

*

"So what do you think of Mollie then?" Caitlan is eager to know. Predictably, she would ask. What can I say? That she fancies me? That much is obvious. I expected a gentler kind of woman, maybe a woman rather like my sister Bridget, adorned with far more scruples than most of her gender or perhaps it's because I'm beginning to miss my own dear sister. We are so close, Brid and I. The longer I remain here, the more I miss her. I realise I haven't contacted her since the first night I arrived in Dublin.

We are en route to The Liffey Bar. I smoke profusely while I notice that Caitlan has wound down her window. Her sister smokes in that small flat without any complaint. "She's okay," I shrug. "So, are you and she very close?"

"Sure we are. Go on, I can tell by your expression she wasn't exactly what you expected."

"Alright, since you asked, no she wasn't. I thought she would be more like you."

"Mollie's so much more self-assured than I am. I'm just a stupid scatterbrain at times."

"So what does she do for a living?"

"Who? Mollie? She's a teacher. Primary School. I guess that surprises you."

"A little. And you, have you always been a singer?"

"What! And working at The Liffey you mean? God no, I wanted to be a children's nanny."

"So what happened?"

"Things I don't want to talk about, Aidan. If I don't talk about them…"

"They didn't happen right?"

She cuddles closer to me. "That's right. The past is the past isn't it… and Shaun Blackwood's in the past like all the other horrible things in my life. I feel now that I've met you, things can change for me and what you asked me I've given a lot of thought to."

"What did I ask you?" I feign nonchalance because I half hope that what she is about to say is exactly what I want to hear.

"We could have a trial period of course."

"A trial period for what?"

"For me to come to London with you when you go."

"You really mean that? I mean you don't know me that well and you're prepared to leave your home, your country to be with me." Don't spoil it now, McRaney.

"What's there to know? I just want to be with you that's all, as long as we can return to Dublin often."

That might cost a wee bit but caught up in her enthusiasm, I refuse to dampen her spirits.

"I'll probably be homesick and I'll miss Mollie and Flanagan and what will he do without me? I've never thought about leaving Ireland before but you have your son in London. I know you have to return. Mollie thinks I'm being foolish when I told her what I decided but if you go I'll miss you more than anyone."

"That's great, sweetheart. I'm not being selfish am I, asking you to uproot yourself when I'm not prepared to do the same? But, as you said, we could have a trial period and we'll come to Dublin often."

"It will be like that story by Dickens."

"'Oliver Twist'?'" I tease, although I know exactly to what she refers. "You mean 'A Tale of Two Cities'?"

"That's the one. Instead of Paris and London it'll be Dublin and London."

"You sure you want to come back with me?"

Her pretty face is swiftly crestfallen. "You did mean it didn't you, Aidan? You weren't just saying it?"

"God no, 'course I wasn't. I'd love you to come to London. I have my own flat, well Ruairi my kid brother stays sometimes when Brid nags at him but he's okay. You'll like him."

But not too much I hope. Ru has a way about him. He is 21 but sometimes he behaves like a 12 year old, all wide eyes and little boy lost. I was nothing like Ru at his age. When I was 21, I faced an eight-year prison sentence.

"When are you thinking of leaving anyway?" she asks.

"My, we're in a hurry. I said I'd stay for a couple of weeks. I promised to take Uncle Sheamie for a couple more hospital appointments. He has to have a scan next week. We're the closest my aunt and uncle have to a family, even if we all live in London. I said I'd do a few jobs around the house, fixing stuff and anything that Uncle Sheamie can't do any more."

"You're so sweet, so normal, so…"

"Ordinary?"

"Sure but it's a nice ordinary."

If only she knew the truth. I really want her to believe I am ordinary – always. "Anyway, are you going to sing that lovely song for me tonight?" I ask in an endeavour to change the subject.

"Which song?"

"The one about Athenry."

"'The Fields of Athenry'. Sure, I will. Just for you, Aidan."

I swing the Audi into the rear car park of the bar and cracking open the door, I alight before she does. Taking her into my arms when she steps out of the car, I move in to kiss her lips.

*

My excitement mounts when I think of Caitlan returning with me to England, showing her off. I'm certain that Bridget and Ruairi can't fail to be as enamoured of her as I am. There is Judy of course but she and I are divorced. She has no hold on me anymore. Harry is in Italy, Milan. So he is in no position to deride me over everything, as he invariably does, as does my dad. Well, I am convinced that Dad will approve of Caitlan. She is an Irish colleen after all. In fact, I dwell on little else than Caitlan and I being together in London, when I sidle up to the bar and order a Coke, aware of Flanagan, already half pissed by half past seven. He's sporting a large white bandage wrapped about his left wrist. I am concerned enough to enquire the reason for it.

Leaning the elbow of the self-same check shirt that I'm certain he wore the previous night, he says in an almost conspiratorial tone, "bastard glass. I was washing the wee bastard when it decides to break, don't it? The water must have been too hot or somethin'." He holds up his injured hand. "So, what's your beverage tonight, Aidan? Remembered your name, so I did."

"Just a Coke please, Mr Flanagan."

"It's just Flanagan."

"You must have a Christian name."

"Och no, it's Flanagan." He frowns. "A Coke? What do you mean? Coca Cola?"

"That's the one Flanagan, with ice."

"Most of my punters usually order whiskey and Coke or rum and Coke."

"Just Coke please, Flanagan."

"Bejaysus, boy, if they was all like you I'd have to close the fuckin' bar."

I smile and pay for the drink, aware of Caitlan taking the stage with her backing band, launching into my favourite, 'The Fields of Athenry'.

Sunday evening. The bar isn't as crowded as it was the previous night. When I ask Flanagan the reason, he throws back his big bearded features and lowering his face close to mine, so close I manage to catch a whiff of his whiskey soaked breath, "church," he says. "Fuckin' church, boy. You and Caitlan ain't at church then? Or do you bat for the other side?"

Misunderstanding his meaning, I frown because the expression, 'batting for the other side' usually means you are gay.

"Sorry?"

"The Proddys. You have been away a long time ain't you, boy?"

"Oh you mean Protestants?"

"Shush. You want to get thrown out. This is a staunchly Catholic bar."

"Sorry, no, I don't bat for the other side, as you call it. I'm Catholic too. Lapsed."

"Me too, I only go to the kind of church where the prayer books have fuckin' handles," he guffaws.

"So what denomination is Caitlan then?"

"Demon…?" He struggles with the word.

"Is she Catholic or does she 'bat' for the other side?"

"Och, she's Catholic right enough but I don't think she goes to mass and stuff, not since…" He clears his throat noisily as if something has stuck there. "Anyway…" he leans even closer, so that I almost gag on his whiskey laden breath. I like the guy, so I attempt not to show it. "Heard Shaun Blackwood got his comeuppance last night." His voice has sunk to such a conspiratorial level, I am compelled to strain my ears in order to catch what he says. I attempt not to stiffen and drain the Coke quickly.

"Did he?" I pretend nonchalance at the news.

"Jesus, what happened?"

Flanagan draws closer, while Caitlan launches into song, 'The Flight of the Earls'.

"I can hear the bells of Dublin. In this lonely waiting room…"

He says, "I heard he got done over by someone. No more than the wee bastard deserves. Blackwood's a nasty piece o' work."

"So why are you telling me, Flanagan? I don't even know the guy."

"So we're over here in Queensland and in parts of New South Wales."

Although I am barely conscious of the action, my hand closes over the switchblade in my coat. Caitlan isn't aware of its presence. I promised her that I'd toss it away safely into a bin. I have no other weapon to hand, not that I should have need of one. Nevertheless, gangland had taught me a lot. Even here in Dublin, when I believed I had left it behind, it continues to rear its ugly head like some maleficent cobra.

"Nothin', no reason son." Flanagan raises his voice an octave. Straightening to his full height, he wants to know if I require another Coke.

"Please Flanagan, och c'mon man, lay your fuckin' cards on the table. You're thinking I did Blackwood over aren't you? I might have only met you last night you ould bastard but I can still read you like a book."

He regards me with a worried frown. "I ain't saying nothin', boy but whether you did for Blackwood or not, all I'm saying is she…" He pauses to gesture towards the raised dais where Caitlan has now kicked off her shoes. "She's his, Blackwood's. Take care."

Tonight she's wearing tight faded jeans, an orange short-sleeved jumper, her hair is in a ponytail. She more resembles a 16-year-old schoolgirl than someone almost 20, belting out the number and dancing on the stage.

"Take these chains from my heart," while the punters clap and dance right alongside her.

It's my turn to lean across the counter, observe Flanagan pull a Guinness from his pump. "I always take care, Flanagan and I can take care of myself. Anyway, Caitlan's mine now. Oh, and when you're ready, maybe I'll have a whiskey. Just the one 'cos I'm driving."

"Sure." His grey bearded features break into the semblance of a grin. "You can't just drink that fuckin' shit all evening and I reckon you really can take care of yourself. You may look like a pretty boy with your hair but I reckon you ain't all you seem."

*

Caitlan's concluded her set for the evening. She vacates the dais to assist Flanagan behind the bar. I wonder what the big guy will do when she leaves to live with me across the water. Seeing me at the bar, she is in my arms. We kiss and from my peripheral, I'm conscious of Flanagan's uneasiness. It causes something indefinable to shoot through me. His hand. Was it really a broken glass as he claims or something more sinister?

Savouring the whiskey, I make it last. Could have done with another now I've got the taste. Ould Flanagan's whiskey is pure Irish; Bushmills and the best. Alternatively, I need to keep a clear head if I intend to drive us back to wherever Caitlan wants to go. She moves away but my arm is wrapped around her waist because I'm reluctant for her to leave. Finally, I allow her to go.

As accomplished a barmaid as she is a singer, she laughs and jokes with the punters. They all seem to know her; they address her familiarly as 'Cait'. She knows them too, calling them by their names. A blond guy waits to be served. I judge him to be in his early twenties. Evidently they are acquainted, I hear her address him as 'Johnny'. He is tall, slimly built. His hair is long, very blond like a thatch, it sweeps to the collar of the blue denim shirt he is wearing with tight blue jeans. The shirt is slim fitting enough to accentuate his athletic frame, hard muscles, with the fresh face of a farm boy. She is obviously enjoying the attention he lavishes on her. She pulls a pint for him, passes it across the counter. As she does so, he smiles and touches her fingers with his own. Colouring with embarrassment, no doubt, because I'm watching them, she deftly pulls her hand away. I'm scarcely aware of it but instinctively my hand closes over the knife. I have no idea that I'm capable of such jealousy when I see him with her. I'd been jealous of Blackwood to a degree, but he's ugly, greasy. This guy is young, good looking and obviously knows Caitlan remarkably well. Rather than give in to my jealousy and pull the knife, aware that if I did I'd be no better than Blackwood, I'd also risk being thrown out by Flanagan and arrested by the Gardai for possession of a weapon. I opt to go outside for a much needed smoke.

All the while, all I can think of is her with him, the blond farm boy. Maybe I shouldn't have left them, I reflect, rolling the cigarette. Planting the smoke between my lips, a hand cupped across the lighter, I consider it's probably all perfectly innocent, Caitlan and the farm boy.

Jealousy is a new found sensation for me. I'd never been jealous of Verdi, of the other man she took as a prostitute. I had only entertained relief when Jude had Andrew Lumsden. Maybe it's because for the first time I'm beginning to feel uncomfortably old. I'll be 30 in June. She has yet to reach 20. The farm boy doesn't appear much older. How much longer will it be before I'm searching my hair for grey, half way to middle age? 'Stop torturing yourself, McRaney. Even when you're 40, she's yet to reach 30.'

CHAPTER THREE

-

THE QUAYSIDE HOTEL

"Does Flanagan have a place out the back?" I ask her, my hands planted firmly on her shoulders. Against my 6' 2" height, she appears insignificantly small. Huge green eyes manage to eclipse every other feature and are narrowed suddenly, wary. "Sure, he has a kitchen and sitting room. Why?"

"Look, why don't you stay here?" I suggest, plumping her into the nearest chair.

Flanagan looks across at Caitlan before turning his attention to me somewhat reproachfully, as if I am bullying her. With all the stuff that has happened to me since coming out of prison, I can't help but be on my guard. Or maybe it's just me and I'm simply growing paranoid.

"Are you sure you're alright, Aidan?" Caitlan asks. "You are behaving strangely. It's nothing to do with me talking to Johnny is it?"

"Johnny?" I echo. I've practically forgotten about him and the jealousy which had driven me outside.

"No, of course not," I say, a little too sharply, for her pretty face whitens and she starts the familiar lip tugging process again. "I'm sorry, sweetheart, I didn't mean to snap."

"Something's happened, I know it has."

"Just stay here okay. I won't be long. Then we'll go."

"Good, because I have a surprise for you," she enthuses, brightening as she reaches up to kiss my lips.

"A surprise!" With the way I'm feeling, the last thing I desire is a surprise. First, I need to talk to the landlord. I follow him to the back room where he's disappeared with a tray full of glasses. Barely have the double doors closed behind him when I discover myself in his kitchen. It is olde worlde, pleasantly furnished and a veritable bachelor abode.

Almost dropping the tray when he sees me, his eyes widen in disbelief, he hisses, "what the fuck!"

I have no idea what his reaction will be. He is pissed, that much is obvious. Maybe he'll be angry or he'll hit me. Either way I need some answers. Certain I'm not barking up the wrong tree, I am prepared to take my chance.

"What do you want, boy? Bejaysus, you gave me a fuckin' start so you did. I never heard you come in. Them glasses cost me a pretty penny and I almost dropped 'em." He carefully lays the tray onto a table.

"I'm sorry for barging in like this, but I need to talk, Flanagan."

"What about?" Funny, but he doesn't sound as pissed as I first thought, which somehow fills me with a tremendous relief. It means that I can have a comparatively decent conversation with him.

He squints up at me, eyes half closed quizzically. "Who are you really? You talk like a Dubliner. I didn't see you around here 'til the other night and I know all my regulars. So, is that accent for real, or are you really a Brit from the Big Smoke?"

"No, Flanagan," I sigh. "Yeah, I'm from the Big Smoke, as you call it but I'm as Irish as you are. I told you I'm here on holiday, staying with my aunt and uncle, Sheamie and Clodagh Connolly. You can check if you like. Anyway, I'm the one asking the questions. So how did you really come by that hand injury?"

His face tightens, he flushes and not merely from the drink. "So what, you a doctor now? I told you, boy, I was washing up and..."

"And Shaun Blackwood didn't come round here by any chance?" I interrupt, allowing my words to trail because, judging by the transformation of crimson to ashen, I've struck a raw nerve. Flanagan plumps his weight into the nearest chair wearily, running a big hand across his perspiring countenance. "Yes, yes, it was Blackwood. He was all cut about the face and fuckin' angry with the guy who did him over. And you're a fuckin' astute bastard ain't you, boy?"

"So what the fuck's going on, Flanagan?"

"I did cut me hand on a glass when I was washing up. I ain't lying boy, honest. Except if I tell you this, you promise you won't tell her."

"You mean Caitlan?"

He nods feebly. "Last night I was just closing up when Blackwood practically bursts in here."

Plunging a hand into my coat pocket, I ask him what Blackwood wanted.

"'Cos you done him over, he was curious to know who you was. He'd seen you talking to me in here. 'Cos you know how to handle yourself and you wasn't scared of him, he thought you might have been sent from London. That you was a cop or something." He pauses. "Got a fag, boy? It's okay; you can smoke if you want."

Handing him one of my hand rolled cigarettes and lighting another for myself, I smile inwardly to think Blackwood imagined I was a cop. That had to have been the funniest thing I'd heard in ages. "So why did he think that? I mean, he must be guilty about something?"

"The drugs probably. There's a lot of dealing both sides of the river, boy. Rumour has it the Gards don't want to make too many waves, so they got the Brits to look into it. You know, Special Branch and that. Only, you ain't heard it from me."

"Sure, Flanagan. And I'm not a cop, just a guy who can take care of himself. So, about your hand. You were washing up…" I prompt.

"That's when he sees his opportunity like and he breaks one of my glasses on purpose, makes me wash it up. I was so fuckin' nervous that I couldn't help but cut myself."

Flanagan pauses, covers his eyes with his hand momentarily. His shoulders are shaking and I imagine he's about to break down. I touch a placating hand to his shoulder. "You're not as hammered as you make out are you, Flanagan?"

He raises his head and regards me wistfully. I thought, if I'm going to miss anyone I guess Flanagan will be high on my list. "Sure, if it ain't all part of the act. Don't tell 'em will you? Ould Flanagan's the people's friend."

"Sure. So what about Caitlan?" I gesture in the general direction of the bar where I left her.

"Blackwood reckoned she's his," Flanagan says.

"No one belongs to anyone else and I'm going to make sure that bastard don't touch her," I add.

"Look Aidan." I'm astonished to observe there really are tears in Flanagan's grey eyes. "When you return to the Big Smoke take that wee girlie with you, I can tell you and she are made for one another. Okay?"

"Actually, now you've put it into words, that's what I plan to do. But why do you say it?"

"Simply because Blackwood uses and abuses her, she's been through enough."

"What's that supposed to mean?"

"You'll have to ask her yourself."

*

Why did Flanagan say he uses and abuses her? Short of forcing him to talk at knifepoint, which is something I have no intention of doing as he is far too likeable to get heavy with. He suggested that I ask her myself.

We are alone in my hire car. I enquire where she wants to go. Back to Mollie or to my aunt's place?

"Neither," she giggles and linking her arm through mine as we drive through the night-time streets, the lights of South Dublin winking either side of us, she declares, "the Quayside Hotel."

"The Quayside Hotel!" I echo in surprise. Flanagan's words return to me all at once. 'Blackwood uses and abuses her.' What for? A prostitute?

"Because I can be alone with you, no aunts and uncles, no snooping sisters and no Holy pictures, hopefully. I couldn't pretend I wasn't disappointed when you pulled out. I really wanted you to make love to me."

"But a hotel at this time of night?"

"Sure, at this time of night. I thought you'd be pleased, Aidan, I just want to be alone with you. Besides, I've already booked us a room."

"You've done what!" I almost crash the Audi into a bollard I fail to see at the side of the road.

"Careful." She steadies my hand on the steering wheel. "I know I should have told you about the room, but I wanted it to be a surprise. Now you sound angry."

Maybe I am paranoid, but coming on the wake of Flanagan's words concerning Blackwood using and abusing her, am I reading more into it than I really should? I wonder at the real reason why a woman suggests bringing a man to a hotel. Naturally, I want sex with her, but I don't want to think that she might view me as merely another prospective client.

If I accuse her, I might lose her if she is innocent and she simply does want to be alone with me.

"I'm sorry, sweetheart, I am pleased. So where is this Quayside Hotel?"

"Och, it's not far. It's near Temple Bar." Clasping a slender, braceleted hand over mine on the gear stick, she enthuses, "I hope you didn't mind, but I booked us in as Mr and Mrs McRaney. Only I couldn't spell your surname."

*

"Mr and Mrs McRaney," I read the name on the register that the bespectacled young clerk passes across to me over his counter.

"That's not how…" I begin, but shrug dismissively, before signing my name in the book.

The clerk appears little older than 18 with his horn rims worn over nervously blinking blue eyes. So I sign 'Mr A McRaney' beneath Caitlan's approving gaze. The hotel room is rather basically furnished and contains two single wooden beds which Caitlan tuts over exasperatedly and urges me to place together, which means moving out the interconnecting bedside cabinet.

"Fancy giving us separate beds."

"Fancy," I murmur my agreement.

There is a white slimline telephone beside the bed which I see is connected to room service. A small refrigerator in the corner of the room is revealed as a drinks bar when I look inside.

I have to admit I haven't stayed in too many hotel rooms, except for the one in Marbella when Frankie, Leanne and I had gone to Spain for a couple of weeks. I'd half expected the sojourn to Spain to have been a proper holiday, but I should have known people like Frankie Lamond rarely have holidays. I was compelled to accompany him on some of his rather nefarious deals with the 'Spics', while poor Leanne was left to her own devices. I'd contemplated on occasions giving Frankie the slip and returning to the hotel to join Leanne for a spot of illicit loving.

"So, Caitlan, do you come to hotels often with guys?" I have to ask it in spite of my reluctance to do so.

She's busy inspecting the drinks bar. As if she hasn't heard me, she says, "shall we call room service? Strawberries and champagne in bed?" There's a glint in her eye.

"Strawberries and champagne?"

She pouts, I guess, at my less than enthusiastic response. Then, flinging herself into my arms, she wraps hers around my chest and gazes up at me. I hear her excited breathing; her body is hot against me. I want her so much, then why do I entertain these stupid doubts? Maybe if I hadn't had that talk with Flanagan.

"The best looking guy I've seen in ages and he doesn't show any enthusiasm when I mention strawberries and champers in bed."

"Anyway, who's paying for all this, darlin'? Strawberries and champagne. Hotel rooms, en suite bathroom. I'm just a humble landscape gardener. I don't get paid that much."

"It's my shout. Don't let's spoil it by discussing boring stuff like money. If you don't talk about it…"

"I know, it doesn't exist." I tap her nose affectionately. "We won't get far without it. So, you didn't answer my question."

"Aidan." She tuts and shakes her head with exasperation again. "Why all these stupid questions anyway? Sure, sometimes I come to hotel rooms."

"So Flanagan must pay you well."

"He pays me well enough for my singing and I come to hotel rooms to be alone, to get away from Mollie sometimes. She can be an awful nag. I don't ask you all these questions Aidan, and I know there are two sides to you but I don't want to know what they are. So come on, relax. I can tell you're wound up about something. Why don't we have a shower? That'll help to relax you, then we can…"

"Why don't we shower together?" I suggest.

I don't want to question her, maybe afterward. Right now, this close to her, I feel her small breasts pert and undulating beneath her sweater. She reaches a hand behind the waistband of my jeans and gazes up at me as she does so, green eyes glinting with arousal, a half smile flirting with her lips, pleased that I'm ready to give in. I'm not holding back, I want her now and my senses play a rhapsody when her cool fingers close around my rapidly ascending erection. All the questions and anxieties evaporate when I am with her. She laughs on recollection of the clerk's face when he enquired if we had any luggage. "Who needs luggage?" she says.

I start to undo the buttons of my shirt, but sweeping my hand aside, she tells me that she wants to undress me. Her movements are slow, meticulous as she opens the buttons and eases the shirt aside, exposing my bare torso. Lowering her mouth to the dark forest of chest hairs, she manoeuvres her lips gradually, licking my flesh with her tongue, raising her eyes to my face. She's unzipping my jeans, easing them over my hips to reveal my shorts, the hardness pulsing against them. I pull her hair away from her face; allow the tendrils to spill through my fingers before I hold the hair back, twisting it tightly around my hand. The action is rough, almost aggressive. She yelps. Aware how much I'm hurting her, I look into her face, witness the tears in her eyes before my mouth descends to hers and I push my fingers into the flesh of her small behind, slamming her into my body. Dominant. Hard. Ruthless when I want sex and I want this woman. She brought me here, eradicated my inhibitions. Parting her lips with my tongue, I caress her mouth before sliding my tongue around it, searching her teeth, feeling the warmth of her saliva as she attempts to swallow. Still kissing her, I peel open the zipper of her jeans, they slide from almost non-existent hips, go unnoticed on the floor. Closing her eyes, she speaks my name breathlessly when I pull my tongue from her cheek. I want her to kiss my organ and she does, my head spins because that beautiful mouth is so hot, burning and moist.

Momentarily I entertain the sharp pinch of her teeth, as she grins up at me. From now on, I'm the only man to take her, not Blackwood, not the skinny farm boy. This is the woman I want enough to ask her to marry me, even if we have only known one another for less than 48 hours.

Naked, apart from a filmy white lace bra and panties, she stands before me when I pull her up and she continues to play with me, her fingers burn like fire when she cups my balls. We move closer to the bed but without releasing one another, I collapse into the satin haven of white pillows beneath my head, pull her unceremoniously on top of me.

When her fingers move to my lips, begin to caress her way around my beard while she lays on top of me, she tells me. "You can be almost animalistic can't you, Aidan?"

"Isn't that what you want? Don't you like it that way? Only it's the way I am with a woman. I don't mean to hurt you."

"It's okay." She places a finger on my lips, silencing me. "I knew what kind of man you were when I first saw you. I want you to dominate me."

"Jesus, Caitlan, I don't want to dominate you, but I can if you like it that way. Anyway, why did you suggest strawberries? It's November. Is that what you've had in hotel rooms before?"

She stops moving to regard me quizzically. "I might have done. Does it matter? You want to know if I've brought men to hotel rooms."

"No, no I don't. I don't want to know about other men. I'm the guy you're with now. Like you said, if you don't talk about it, it never happened, a good maxim." I grin.

The green eyes snap wide, the pupils enlarge, illumine with a greenish incandescence.

"You're learning." She laughs.

"So why don't we take a shower? Is that why you stopped? Because I'm too dominant? I can be anything you want, darlin'."

"I don't usually like to be dominated, but with you it could be exciting."

I've never thought about dominating a woman before. The very idea sends a wild, ecstatic excitement coursing through me, as I relish the idea of bending her to my will sexually.

She clutches my hand and I follow her into the bathroom and run the shower. She giggles, an excited child, but no less a woman as the water slithers its descent like a sensual waterfall cascading across her full-ripened breasts. I cup my hands about the delicate pert aureoles. She ploughs her fingers through my hair, almost lost in the tangle of black curls. "I love your hair," she murmurs.

Her own hair is wet, streaming below her shoulders, spilling down her back. Our faces are awash with water, the squelch of our bodies slam against one another noisily. Our hands, wet and slippery traverse every inch of each other, our mouths locking in kisses ad infinitum.

When I push her unceremoniously against the shower wall, she emits a small giggle, I guess with the unexpected coldness on her back. Pinioning her arms behind her, she squirms, but I refuse to release her. She is slammed against the wall with the intensity of my strength. She appears even smaller in contrast to my height towering above her. Spying a white towelling robe that is draped over a hook on the door, I slide out the belt, clasping it between thumb and forefinger as I step back into the shower.

"What are you going to do, Aidan?" she eyes the belt narrowly, warily.

Grasping her hands, I fasten them behind her with the belt. "You wanted dominance, remember. I'm just giving you what you want. You're my prisoner now, baby and there's nothing you can do about it." This is the man that I can be. No longer the ordinary, gentlemanly landscape gardener, who gives up his sexual desires for fear his aunt and uncle will hear him fucking a girl.

"So less talking, more fucking, hey." My words are raspy, belligerent. I've probably lost her by being this dominant. Nevertheless I'm too far gone to care when she takes the full force of my penis as it invades that fantastic, hedonistic wall of paradise, like a raging torpedo, a warhead unleashed.

I imagine I hear the discordant trill of a cell phone somewhere in the regions of the bedroom. Let it ring. This woman is mine. I want to hurt her as much as she wants my organ inside her.

With no chance of fitting a condom, not with the water, maybe for the first time in my life, I don't care that I might make her pregnant. I want to give her a child in order to substantiate this wonderful union we have between us.

We shower quickly, collapsing against one another I reluctantly release her hands, which she rubs. I long to enquire if I've hurt her but I restrain myself because, I have to admit I savoured the dominance. I'd never been this way, not even with Verdi. It's a new experience for me, an exciting addendum to sex. We dry each other; kiss again, my arms wrapped about her, aware that if my son wasn't in England, I would remain in Dublin with her.

Rubbing the large white towel with 'The Quayside Hotel' emblazoned on it in blue lettering over every inch of her, she whispers, "I love you, Aidan," so softly that the words are barely audible, merely the gentlest breath in my face.

Gathering her into my arms I swirl her around. She and I perform an idiotic waltz of sorts on the soaking wet floor. "I love you too, baby," I say and push a hand through her wet hair.

"Do you think we should clean up the floor or something? They'll wonder what we've been doing."

"If they have to wonder that, then they must be pretty naïve."

Giggling again, she throws her arms around me. "I enjoyed having sex with you; I knew I wouldn't be disappointed. You're a very sexy man. And I do love you; I wasn't just saying that in the heat of the moment."

"And I meant it when I said I love you. You can fall in love with someone in a matter of minutes or you can try to love a person for years, but can't. So why don't we go back to bed. We may as well stay the night. You have to call Mollie?"

"I've a good mind to let her stew."

"She might be worried. You'd better call her, tell her you're with me. Or would that worry her even more?"

"Sure if she doesn't worry about me with any man, as long as it's not Shaun Blackwood."

"Do you think you've seen the last of him?"

"Please, Aidan, don't let's talk about him." She shivers involuntarily, a frightened wee wraith in my arms.

"Don't worry about Blackwood or anyone else. I'm here now and no one's gonna touch you while I'm around."

Clutching my hand, she pulls me back onto the bed. "Do you know what I'd like to do?"

"Again?"

"No, well yes, but what I was going to say was, who was that singer in the seventies who stayed in a hotel room with his wife? I think she was Japanese, Yoko or something."

"You mean John Lennon and Yoko Ono! I'd love to do that." We are on the bed. My arm is around her waist. I pull her close, she snuggles against me. Laying back on the pillow, she invites me to play with her unfettered breasts, uplifted and beautiful in the subtle incandescence of twin bedside lamps.

"I still have that damn business to run back in London and don't say if I don't talk about it, it don't exist. My big brother might have something to say about it if I don't return. Of course my secretary manages the business quite well when Harry and me aren't there."

"You have a secretary?"

"Sure," I tap her nose playfully.

"Is she pretty? I can imagine her sitting on your desk with her legs crossed and…"

"Stop it!" I laugh. "She's about 40 odd and wears those no-nonsense tweeds and brogues and looks closer to 50 than 40. Plus she's too plump to sit on anyone's desk. You're a funny wee thing, you know that!"

"So you keep telling me. See, I'm jealous of anyone you meet. There must be lots of pretty girls in London."

"Lots," I tease. "But none of them are as pretty as you and even with all the girls in London I had to come to Ireland to find someone. That must tell you something."

The mobile ringing in my coat pocket startles both of us.

"Jesus," she pats her heart region breathlessly. "That scared me. You'd better answer it, it might be your auntie."

I reach for the leather coat I'd draped over a chair, fumble in the pocket for my phone and curse when I see who is calling.

"Who is it, Aidan?"

I make a face and run a hand over my beard absently. "It's Judy, my ex."

I drop back onto the bed as Caitlan slips her arms around my waist and I slap her hand playfully when her fingers begin to trail in the direction of another developing erection, only for it to sink into obscurity instinctively as Judy begins, "Oh, Aidan, I've been trying to reach you for ages. I couldn't get a signal. Are you still in Dublin?" She is partially yelling, her voice hysterical and punctuated by sobbing.

"Jude, calm down. Whatever is it? And yes, I'm still in Dublin. What's wrong?"

"It's… it's Patrick, he… he's in hospital."

"He's what?" I leap off the bed, my heart hammering against my chest. "What's happened to him?"

"He has suspected meningitis Aidan, and he's asking for his Daddy. Can… can you come. He's in the Royal Surrey."

"Sure, sure, Jude, you know I'll come. I'll catch the first available flight."

I conclude the call to Jude and Caitlan regards me with a concerned expression.

"What's happened, Aidan? You have to go back to London don't you?"

"I'm afraid so, sweetheart. My son's in hospital with suspected meningitis." I believe Caitlan has never had the occasion to witness me bustling about quite so much, or making so many phone calls. She dresses quickly and throws on a coat, while I struggle into my own clothes before attempting to locate the earliest possible flight to Heathrow. Apparently there are two Aer Lingus flights from Dublin, "at 6.20, sir," I am duly informed and wonder how anyone can possibly make an Irish accent sound so impassively BBC. I ask her what time that particular flight gets into London.

"The Aer Lingus 152 flight's estimated time of arrival at Heathrow is approximately ten minutes past eight in the morning. This flight will leave at Terminal 2 Dublin. You will need to be there for departure at least 90 minutes before take-off."

Concluding the call and making a face at the phone, I tell Caitlan, "apparently I have to wait 'til morning."

"I'm sorry, Aidan." The timbre of her voice is small. My heart goes out to her.

"Come here. It's me who's sorry. You've probably gathered by now my son means a lot to me. And if he has got meningitis…" My words trail because I really don't want to go down that road.

Joining me on the bed she puts her arm around my waist; the action is more companionable than sexual. It's as if the wonderful, exciting moment of sexual attainment we had just shared might never have been. "I've never had a child so I don't know…"

I am already calling London and my sister. When I'm in this state of anxiety and sheer blind panic there's only one woman I can turn to and that is Bridget. Although only five years my senior, sometimes I perceive her as a small substitute for my beloved mother. She and Brid were so much alike.

"For fuck's sake, Brid, pick up. Where the hell can she be at this time of night? I bet she's asked that Maura from church to mind the kids." I'm speaking my thoughts aloud and mostly to myself as if Caitlan isn't present.

"The mobile you have called is switched off."

"I need her to pick me up the other end," I tell Caitlan absentmindedly. "I wonder if she knows about Patrick. And if she does, why didn't she tell me?"

"What are you going to do now? You'll have to pack and what about your aunt and uncle?"

I'm forced to admit that Aunt Clodagh and Uncle Sheamie are the last people I have thought of and what I had promised whilst I was there. "What about you?" I ask her.

"What about me?"

"I asked you to come to London with me."

"Perhaps later. You go and make sure your son's okay. I don't want to intrude."

"You could never intrude."

"I'll stay. I can't just up and leave now."

"You mean your sister and Flanagan? I'm sure they'll understand."

"No, it's for the best."

"But you'll come to London? I'll give you my mobile number, the address of my flat in Shooters Hill."

"I don't even know where that is."

"Aunt Clodagh will tell you. Anyway, I really need to call my sister."

"Sure." She lapses into a subdued silence. I plant a conciliatory kiss on her cheek.

I try Brid's landline. Finally, a familiar voice I recognise as my brother, Ruairi's, greets me with a tentative, "hullo?"

"Ru." God, I have never wanted to hear my brother's voice quite so much.

"Aid!" he echoes, surprised. "You home?"

"Not yet. I'm still in Dublin but I'm catching a flight back in the morning, 6am. It gets in at…" I think quickly, "7.45." If I tell him the correct time, he'll probably be late.

"But you've only been there a short time. You okay, Aid? You sound agitated about something. Uncle Sheamie hasn't died has he?"

"No, he hasn't died. It's Patrick, Jude's just called me. Patrick's been admitted to hospital with meningitis, or at least it's suspected meningitis."

There is a momentary pause the other end.

"Ru, you haven't hung up on me have you?"

"Who's that, your brother?" Caitlan asks.

I nod perfunctorily and hiss into the phone, "You still there, Ru?"

"Yeah, course. I thought you said Patrick has suspected meningitis."

"I did. Did you or Brid know? Anyway where's Brid?"

"No, we didn't know. Then you know your ex, she doesn't share stuff with us. And Brid's gone to some church thing in Dartford with James." He adopts a pseudo-posh accent when he refers to the priest. God knows why. Father Mulligan is as Irish as I am.

"I assume you mean James Mulligan?"

"Who else and who gets lumbered with babysitting nearly every night? Don't get me wrong, Sammy's a good kid but…"

"But you'll pick me up in the morning?" I interrupt.

"'Course I will. Do you want Brid to call the hospital when she gets back?"

"No, don't worry her. When you pick me up, we'll go straight there. He's in the Royal Surrey."

"Sure, Bruv. Where will you be?"

"What do you mean, where will I be?"

"What terminal? I've never had to pick anyone up from the airport before."

"The terminal where the fuckin' Dublin flight lands, I don't know. Just be there, Ru, okay?"

"Sure, Aid. What time?"

Rolling my eyes, I tut, "7.45am. Comprendi?"

Concluding the call to my brother, I haul on my coat, holding out my arms. She throws herself into them and we hug for a while. I say dryly, "we'd better go back to my aunt and uncle's. We can't stay here, we have things to do. I'm sorry, after we'd planned a night of loving."

"Why is it I'm scared I won't see you again?"

"Hey, don't say that. What we have is far more than some stupid holiday romance."

Uplifting her chin with a forefinger, I promise to call her as soon as I know how my son is. She nods flatly. I'm conscious of the tears in her eyes and I wipe them away. "You really are a sensitive girl aren't you?" The scared 'rabbit caught in the headlights' again.

When I remind her about the money she has paid for the hotel room, she merely shrugs. "It's not the money that's important. It's knowing, even if I don't see you again, that I have this wonderful memory of you."

*

When we return to Aunt Clodagh and Uncle Sheamie's, it is late, almost one in the morning. I will have to leave about a quarter to four if I intend to catch the Dublin flight. It scarcely affords us much time to sleep and I won't hear of Caitlan leaving my side with the precious little time we have left. I am reluctant to return to London, but I really need to know how my son is.

Entering the house quietly, I inform Caitlan that perhaps I should leave a note for my aunt, as I don't wish to disturb her and promise to call her when I arrive in London. "I don't hold with notes." Half scaring us to death, Aunt Clodagh appears in the doorway of the kitchen where we are.

She is clad in a thick white candlewick robe; the robe is tied discretely with a matching belt. The frilled neckline of her nightie is just visible above the robe. Twin rollers are coiled in the front of her hair.

"Aunt Clodagh, sorry to have woken you," I apologise. "I have to go back to London. I'm so sorry I can't do those jobs for you."

"Och, stop apologising boy, why do you think I got up? And you didn't wake me. I wasn't asleep. Something's wrong back in London ain't it?"

"How did you know?"

"Och, let's say it was a premonition, son."

"Aidan's ex-wife called. His son is in hospital," Caitlan offers.

"Again, I'm sorry auntie, but I do have to leave soon and I need to pack."

"What's wrong with the poor wee mite?"

Aunt Clodagh places a hand on her heart region anxiously and tugs at her lower lip.

"I thought you were psychic," I tease lightly. "Patrick may have meningitis."

"Dear God in Heaven!" The hand with which my aunt clutches my arm begins to tremble a little. "Poor wain. Poor Aidan. 'Course you must go, my boy."

"Shall I start your packing, Aidan?" Caitlan is halfway up the stairs.

"Sure sweetheart, I'll be up in a minute."

"I did all your washing, son." Aunt Clodagh lowers her voice conspiratorially, as if she doesn't wish Caitlan to know how much she enjoys fussing over me. "All your shirts, tee shirts and jeans."

"You didn't have to skivvy for me, auntie."

"I did it because I love you like me own, I told you that. And if you ever get custody of that boy and you come back for her..." she gestures up the stairs towards Caitlan, who has already disappeared into my bedroom, "you can stay with us – always. I shall miss you, so

I will. I hope Patrick will be alright. I'll pray for him. So what time you gotta leave?"

"Just after four apparently. There's a flight leaving at 6.20 in the morning, it gets into Heathrow at 8.10. Ru's going to pick me up."

I head upstairs. Caitlan has already opened my suitcase and is piling in my clothes. "Oh Aidan, I've just remembered," she exclaims suddenly.

"What!" I regard her with a frown.

"The knife you confiscated from Blackwood, is it still in your jacket?"

"I'd forgotten about that."

"I'll take it. You try getting through the airport with that you'll get arrested by the Gards faster than you can breathe. After all the troubles, we have a tighter security than most."

Closing a hand over the switchblade, I hand it to her, handle first. Taking the weapon, she slips the knife into the pocket of her coat.

"You'll get rid of it, Caitlan?"

"Sure I will!"

"You promise?"

"Yes, Daddy."

I stiffen. "Don't call me that."

She pouts. "Sorry, I was just teasing, you're nothing like my da anyway. He's old and wizened even though he's only in his early fifties, because he drinks a lot. You're very good looking and sexy with your hair and the beard suits you. You should keep it."

Running a hand over my erstwhile facial hair, I ask if the beard makes me look too old.

"God no, you don't even look 29. Remember, when I first saw you, I thought you were 25 or 26."

As it transpires, or is it teleported, Aunt Clodagh appears in the room, declaring, "I've made some sandwiches, Aidan, for the journey."

"There'll probably be something to eat on the plane, auntie."

"Och now, their food's far too expensive. Sheamie had a meat sandwich that didn't agree with him on the flight to London."

Despite the overwhelming anxiety permeating my insides over my son, when Caitlan giggles behind my aunt's retreating back, I can't avoid a smile. Her giggling, instead of finding it irritating as with some women, is oddly infectious. Perhaps it's because this lovely girl can do precious little wrong in my eyes, while her occasional childlike ways are conducive to making me love her all the more.

I didn't have to ask Aunt Clodagh's permission for Caitlan to stay, especially when the latter suggests that she doesn't have to work during the day, plus she'd take my uncle for his hospital appointments. There was the question of the car I'd hired and had hardly used. Caitlan promises to return the car and see if she can get a reimbursement. I instruct her to give any monies to my aunt. In turn, Aunt Clodagh informs Caitlan that she'll be welcome at her home any time. It is plainly obvious that Caitlan has won over my aunt and uncle as she has me. I'm also glad she has somewhere else to go. I'm concerned that she'll fall into Blackwood's clutches again.

We lie together on the single bed, my arm around her. We refrain from making love, however. It is merely comforting just to lie together. When the hour rolls around to 4 o'clock, she is the first up, waking me from a dreamless sleep. Aunt Clodagh is also up, kissing and hugging me, with tears in her eyes, promising she'll try to come to London for Christmas, if Sheamie is up to it of course.

My first Christmas with my family in eight years. Naturally, neither Aunt Clodagh nor Uncle Sheamie have referred to my being in prison to Caitlan. The former counselled me that I should find the right time to confide in Caitlan that I'd been inside and why, if I'm planning to have a serious relationship with her. The trouble is, I'm too scared of losing her if I confess that I shot a guy while I was a minder to a London hard-man. She isn't Verdi, who knew everything about me and failed to care anyway.

Caitlan drives me to the airport. I check in. That's when we part. It is imperative I see my son. It's growing increasingly harder to leave her with a stretch of water between us. She is crying when she leaves me. I promise to call her and make her promise to come to London. After all, there are several hourly flights from Dublin. She tells me that she will.

*

Away from Caitlan, on the flight, my thoughts revert to my son and what the implications of meningitis mean. Deafness. Blindness. Brain damage, if it's serious. The worst-case scenario: he could die. No, I must stop torturing myself.

By the time I arrive at Heathrow, anxiety has got the better of me. With Caitlan I hadn't had too much time to dwell on the fact my beloved son could either die or suffer brain damage. Now I am this close, all manner of terrible reflections issue to haunt me.

Checking out, I resolve to go in search for Ruairi. It is a while before I find him in the car park and only when he toots the horn.

Behind the wheels of my black Cabriolet, he is intent on stuffing his face with a burger in a bun, one of those cholesterol-ridden monstrosities that loosely pass for food, tomato ketchup and salad dressing oozing out of the side.

Cracking open the door, I admonish him about getting bits of salad, already dropping from his burger onto the Cabriolet's floor, while I deposit my case into the back and slide into the seat beside him.

"Morning, pleased to see you too. I was hungry. You said quarter to eight. That bird on the tannoy said the next flight from Dublin wasn't 'til ten past."

"I know what you're like."

"Sorry about Patrick but Brid and me didn't know anything about it. Hey, Aid, I hardly recognised you with the beard. Or were you too busy to shave?"

"Both," I mutter. "Just drive, hey, Ru?"

Stuffing the partially eaten burger into his mouth, he backs the Cabriolet out of the car park.

"Watch it!" I realise I am growing irritable, mainly because I'm upset at leaving Caitlan and overly anxious about my son. I'm pleased to see my kid brother, but he does have some annoying little habits at times. "Mind the other car and stop spilling that stuff. Couldn't you have brought your own car? Do you want me to drive?"

He glares at me. "I know you're upset, but give me some credit. And my motor has sort of..."

"Sort of what?" I pick up on his hesitancy.

"Sort of been repossessed, 'cos I couldn't keep up the payments."

"Sorry, Ru, I didn't mean to sound so..."

"Nagging." He swings the Cabriolet expertly out from the car park and into the street. "I know you're upset about Patrick, I wonder why Judy didn't tell Brid."

"That's my ex-wife for you. Anyway, I could use a smoke." In the process of rolling a cigarette, planting it between my lips, I ask him why he couldn't keep up the payments on his car.

"I thought you were paying with your university grant, or rather Brid was."

"Brid don't approve 'cos I've decided to take a gap year and she's stopped subsidising me."

"Good for her. So what's this 'gap year' business about?"

"You serious? A gap year is time out from uni for a while."

"To do what?"

He shrugs nonchalantly. "A lot of people who take gap years take holidays, y'know, back packing and stuff."

"And you? You sure it's not an excuse to bum around? Only if it is, you can come and work for me."

"As a landscape gardener?"

"Why not?"

"So how was Dublin?" He changes the subject quickly.

"It was still standing when I left, if that's what you mean."

He grins. "So you met a bird then?"

I regard him in surprise. "How did you know?"

"Brid told me. She found out when she rang Aunt Clodagh to see how Uncle Sheamie was after his hospital appointment. Auntie said Aidan's met a nice girl."

It is my turn to change a subject that's grown painful since leaving her. When opening the glove compartment, several CD's plus sweet wrappers and cigarette packets spill onto the floor. "Jesus, Ru, how long have you been driving my car?"

"Since you left, why? What you looking for?"

I manage to stuff some of the junk back before slamming the door of the compartment. "I left a pair of shades in here."

"This them?" he hands me the sunglasses.

I mutter, "thanks," and put them on.

CHAPTER FOUR

–

MUNCHAUSEN BY PROXY

Despite polishing off Aunt Clodagh's cheese sandwiches on the flight, by the time Ruairi and I arrived at the Royal Surrey hospital a little before 9am, I am practically starving. Maybe later, I need to see my son first.

I guess I look a mess. I haven't shaved or bothered to comb my hair. Ru doesn't appear any less dishevelled. He got up late, he says, rushed into his clothes which consist of jeans and a sweater over which he's thrown a black wool coat.

Neither one of us convey our thoughts, nevertheless I am certain he is probably transported to the night when our sister Laurena died. Not this particular hospital but to me a hospital wherever it is, is still a hospital. The Royal Surrey, with its long antiseptic-smelling corridors, the plethora of metallic lights set high into the white plastered ceiling is no different.

We are directed to paediatrics, located down several clinically white corridors until we find the ward we're looking for.

An extremely young nurse, starched apron encompassing a light blue uniform requests our names.

"I'm Aidan McRaney and this is my brother Ruairi. We're here to see Patrick McRaney, he's my son," I volunteer, a fraction breathlessly because my heart is hammering much too fast in my anxiety. I guess the next move she makes will be to consult her computer. She doesn't, instead she smiles pleasantly, enthuses "Oh, you're Patrick's father. He's a lovely boy isn't he?"

"Sure, I know that. But how is he?" I demand impatiently.

"I'll get Dr Malone to come and see you."

Ru and I exchange uneasy glances. When a nurse, no matter how pleasant her smile, appears awkward and suggests contacting a doctor to talk to you, in my mind that means it's serious. It has to be for Jude to have called me back from holiday. "He… he isn't…" I can't bring myself to conclude my sentence. I feel Ru's hand on my shoulder. When I regard my brother, it isn't difficult to deduce that he too is remembering the night our 18-year-old sister died.

"He isn't what Mr McRaney?" she asks, a small frown puckering her brow. When I fail to respond, she informs me once again that she'll fetch Dr Malone, adding that Patrick's mother is with her son and has been all night.

"Then why can't I see him if his mother's there?" I demand and entertain the familiar aggression surfacing.

She's gone and Ru whispers in my ear, "Blimey, I could give that one."

"Jesus, Ru not here," I hiss. I'm aware for the first time of the nurses and patients milling about in the corridor, as they begin their day. Cleaners too are mopping floors, garbed in pale blue scrubs. Flicking the clock a cursory glance denotes it is now a few minutes after nine and I wonder, with a pang, what Caitlan might be doing, guessing she would have returned to her sister's.

The nurse reappears, this time she's accompanied by a slimly built doctor. He's wearing dark blue scrubs and looks to be around his early to mid-thirties. Sporting a sandy beard and short crinkly hair, he greets us with an enthusiastic smile, "Mr McRaney?" His glance transfers from Ru to myself. We both respond and Ru says, "he's Patrick's Dad," gesturing to me.

"Dr Edward Malone," he introduces himself. I wonder, does this guy ever stop smiling? I guess that is a good sign. "So you've just arrived from Dublin?" he asks, as if my son's health might be of secondary importance. I also detect a familiar Irish accent. "How is the ould place? I've been away for five years and I'm still homesick. Sure if I wasn't quite envious when your wife said…"

"Never mind all that, Doc," I cut him off tersely.

He scarcely appears to notice while the smile remains firmly in place. "How is my son?" Taking both me and I guess, Ru also by surprise he declares, "Patrick's fine. Would you like to see him?"

"Sorry?" I frown, disbelievingly, "I thought Patrick had suspected meningitis. What do you mean he's fine?"

It is Dr Malone's turn to frown. "Not you too," he says strangely.

Have I stumbled into what I term a 'Twilight Zone' moment? You rush into hospital, half-expecting God knows what. My son to be wired up to all kinds of apparatus and an 'I'm sorry we did all we could but…' "I'm sorry." Maybe I'm still half-asleep from the journey, although you can hardly consider it as 'jet lag' from Dublin to Heathrow. "What's that supposed to mean?" Dr Malone holds his smile. Jesus, is it fixed there like the fucking Joker?

"I'll explain later. I'm sure you'd like to see your son."

"Well then, can I?" I didn't mean to sound quite so impatient but I feel the guy is stalling for some unaccountable reason.

"Sure."

"So, what is wrong with him? My ex-wife…"

"Your ex-wife?"

"Yeah my ex, what's she been saying?"

"Maybe I misheard, but Mrs McRaney said she was your wife. You're divorced?"

"More than four years. I received a phone call while I was in Dublin from my ex." I stress the 'ex' and blush on recollection of what Caitlan and I were doing when the call came. "She was hysterical and she said that Patrick had been admitted to this hospital with suspected meningitis."

"Not even close Mr McRaney. He has a bad head cold for which I prescribed 'Karvol' and some children's paracetamol, as he's only nine. There was a slight rash on his chest, but examining him revealed the rash to be the result of too much washing powder or something similar used on his clothes. Your wife, I'm sorry, ex-wife was hysterical when she brought Patrick in. She did the right thing of course. You can't be too careful, especially with children. Look." He touches my arm lightly. "You go and see your son Mr McRaney. Then I'd like to talk to you in my office."

Initially, the relief is tremendous. Ru has tears in his eyes, the sentimental wee bastard. We hug momentarily.

The relief turns into a sense of anger, a feeling I manage to shelve. However, when Dr Malone escorts me into the room where Patrick is, I request Ru to fetch us both coffees. He acquiesces.

The ward contains two beds facing each other. Patrick is sitting on the floor playing with a younger boy with straight blond hair falling into his eyes. The boy holds his left arm raised because it's enveloped in a huge white cast, while his free hand races a small car across the floor, the two children making accompanying sounds.

Judy sits on the bed watching the boys vigilantly as if expecting something untoward to happen.

"Hi," is all I can manage. My throat is dry, while I'm overwhelmed at seeing my son again.

"Daddy! Daddy!" Patrick leaps to his feet immediately when he sees me and he flings himself into my arms.

"You okay, Patrick?" I hold him at arm's-length critically.

"I'm fine." He sounds a trifle blocked up with the cold, but otherwise he appears both fit and healthy.

"Oh, Aidan!" Judy is in my arms and sliding a hand around my waist. Her hair is shoulder length and curly. She's wearing a short black skirt with a white linen jacket and outrageously high heels. She gives the appearance more as if she's ready for a night out than an anxious mother whose son might have meningitis. Her eyes are a fraction red rimmed, as if she's been rubbing them, although her face is quite heavily made up with the addition of red lipstick.

"Oh, Aidan I was so worried." She clings to me possessively. "But now you're here it'll be okay."

My mouth tightens, while I attempt not to display the anger that is threatening to surface. Naturally, I am overjoyed to see my son. He clutches my hand, pulling me towards the bed where the other boy is playing and urging, "Look Patrick that's your car," chortling triumphantly because the vehicle is now on its side.

"That's Michael, he's hurt his arm."

"So I see." I ease Judy's clinging arms from my waist. "So Jude, what made you think Patrick had meningitis, just because he had a cold?"

"And a rash," Patrick interjects, lifting his sweater. If there was a rash, it has practically vanished now. A small purplish area above his navel is all that remains. "So when did you bring him in?" I ask.

"Last night. I tried calling you but you weren't answering your phone or I couldn't receive a signal or something, I don't know." She tousles her hair purposefully.

If only she knew why I wasn't answering my phone. "But you got me eventually and I caught the first available flight." Again, I attempt to prevent the anger that is beginning to well up inside me from materialising. "Not in front of Patrick," I think to myself, aware how much it upsets him when Jude and I argue. I am angry. I can't help it, because I had to leave HER and Jude has used our son to force my return. "So, can Patrick come home?"

"It's up to Dr Malone."

"He talks like you, Daddy." Patrick continues to clutch my hand. I sit on the bed because he wants me to meet Michael. So I talk with them for a while.

"Your son can go." Dr Malone stands in the doorway. "I've never seen a healthier youngster." He grins. "I think the rest of your fan club have arrived, Patrick."

We regard him nonplussed, failing to comprehend his meaning.

"A rather irate flame haired Irish woman demands to know how her nephew is."

I look at Judy and am in time to witness the colour drain from her made up features, at the mention of my sister.

"Aunt Brid!" Patrick rushes from the room, almost knocking Dr Malone over.

"He's a live wire," he observes, still smiling.

Definitely not a child with meningitis.

Brid appears as surprised as Ru and I were when Dr Malone announces that Patrick is fine and free to leave.

"Are you the doctor in charge?" she asks in an authoritative tone. She's wearing her uniform. Bridget is a ward sister at Blackheath General. A beige jacket is thrown over the uniform but fails to conceal it.

Dr Malone tells her that he is Patrick's paediatrician, when Brid is aware of me and she flings herself into my arms. We hug, my sister and I, as if I've been away for months instead of a few days. I hold my sister, as I never wanted to hold Judy, whom I see is holding back from any demonstrativeness.

Pulling apart from me, my sister surveys me critically and plays with my beard. "What's all this, Bruv? I hardly recognised you and you've got thinner."

"Jesus Sis, I've only been away for a couple of days."

"I know." Her voice softens. She strokes my face as if we are the only two people in the room. Embarrassment doesn't cut it.

"So, there's nothing wrong with Patrick? You told Ru he had suspected meningitis. Anyway, I'm glad to see he's okay now, although I half expected him to be…"

"In Intensive Care," I finish for her. She regards Judy with raised brows. "At least he's alright, that's the main thing. So how are you feeling, Patrick?" Brid asks. Neither she nor Judy exchange pleasantries, or even acknowledge one another considering the two women were friends and worked at the same hospital.

"I'm fine now, Aunt Brid," he replies. "Just a bit of a cold I think."

"That's good then, so it is. Oh Aidan…" she presses my hand tightly, "it's so good to have my brother back."

"Thanks Sis," Ru mutters from behind me. Sipping his coffee, he hands me the one he's been clutching for the past 10 minutes.

"Now we've established your son hasn't got meningitis or anything else, I'd like a word, Mr McRaney," Dr Malone reminds me, his smile fading. Now I think it's serious.

"Do you want me to come as well?" Judy wants to know.

"Why didn't you tell me, Jude?" Brid's tone fairly bristles with accusation.

Judy colours, tugs at her bottom lip now she is forced to face Brid directly. Like me, my sister has a temper. "Because I didn't want to worry you?" she says lamely.

"Well you worried me, Jude." I have to say it. "I was a bloody nervous wreck, you can't imagine, on the flight back." Several pairs of eyes search my face in the event, I guess, of my erstwhile anger asserting itself. I, for my part, realise how much I need both a smoke and a drink and I don't mean coffee.

"You're his father." Trust Judy to come up with that one, as if that fact excuses everything. Coming on the wake of Ru informing me that Brid had called Aunt Clodagh in order to enquire how Uncle Sheamie was, I wonder had Judy called Brid and had the latter mentioned that I had met someone in Dublin? Is that the reason why my ex had invented the preposterous lie that my son was ill in an endeavour to force me back, knowing that nothing else would ensure my hasty return more than my son… and why is she so 'dolled up'? If I'd just brought my child in with suspected meningitis, I'd hardly bother to either comb my hair quite so meticulously or apply fresh make up.

Judy surveys Dr Malone with suspicion. "Whatever you wish to discuss with Aidan, if it's about our son, you can tell me," she says haughtily.

Dr Malone appears a trifle edgy. As if thinking quickly, he says, "You might find it all a wee bit boring, Mrs McRaney. I want to talk to your ahem… ex-husband about Ireland, seeing as how he's just come back."

"What little bit I saw of it," I mutter. "After all, I had to leave in a hurry didn't I?"

"Patrick's your son, Aidan. Surely no holiday means more to you than your son," Judy snorts indignantly.

I hiss, "Bitch," involuntarily. I hadn't meant to utter the expletive in front of Dr Malone but Judy seems to always bring out the worst in me.

"I suppose you'll be going back to Ruairi's?" she retorts.

"No, Jude I'm coming back to Esher with you," I say, watching her face pale. She tugs at her lip agitatedly again. What does she think I'm going to do, kill her?

"That…that's good then, I'll wait for you outside, Aidan. Patrick's pleased to have his Daddy back."

Dr Malone ushers me into his rather small, basically furnished office. The chair before his desk confronts another opposite. A tall, overgrown rubber plant takes up the remaining space. "You didn't really want to talk about Ireland did you, Doc?" I ask, dealing him a wry smile.

Before tendering a response, he drops into the chair pulled up at the desk, on which rests the photo of an attractive red haired woman with a charming smile and a profusion of curls that tumble about her face.

"My fiancée," he heaves a protracted sigh, "another reason why I'm homesick, Mr McRaney."

"It's Aidan."

"Edward. But I prefer to be called Teddy."

"So, Teddy," I stress the name heavily. "Then you do really want to discuss Dublin?"

"Amongst other things and I didn't lie, I really do miss the old place."

"Then why did you leave?" I ask the obvious.

"Because I like working with children."

"There are still quite a few children in Dublin, probably more than anywhere when the Catholics don't believe in birth control."

He grins. "You have a great sense of humour, Aidan."

"You've seen my family."

"You're lucky to have them all over here."

"Sure, but I reckon if I moved, say to Australia, they'd probably follow me. So you like working with children then?"

"Now that makes me sound more like a paedophile than a paediatrician. I worked in a couple of hospitals in Dublin until this one was built and I was offered the job here, more money, less hours. But no, that isn't exactly what I want to discuss."

"I didn't think it was, Doc, Teddy. It's about what happened with my son?"

The smile fades in accompaniment with the wistfulness in his voice when he speaks of his beloved Dublin. "Last night your ex-wife brought your son in. She said she was a nurse."

"She is. She works at the Pilkington Clinic in Godalming. But she used to work at the hospital in Blackheath where my sister works."

"Oh, the Pilkington. I know it. We send patients there on occasions. The Pilkington is supposed to be one of the best plastics clinics in southern England, possibly in the country. Your ex is a very privileged lady to have a job there, which makes it seem rather strange that she should behave the way she did."

"Sorry?" I frown, as something oddly reptilian begins to uncoil itself in the pit of my stomach.

Previously I had cause to wonder if this cheerful Irish doctor ever stopped smiling. Now, this youthful face with its wispy sandy beard suddenly appears in deadly earnest.

"I could tell immediately that your son didn't have anything more life threatening than a bad head cold. We gave him tests of course. They all came back negative. As I said, the rash was due to excessive use of a chemical on the sweater he was wearing. In fact after the tests I discharged him last night."

"You did what!" I'm out of my chair, scarcely realising that I've done so, before plunging my weight into it again. "Then... then why was he still here?" I swallow. My head spins. My heart hammers angrily. Now I really am ready for a showdown with that woman.

"Because your ex-wife created such a fuss. She was a nurse, she said, and if I didn't do more tests and keep him in for observation; she intended to sue the hospital."

"Jesus!" I run a hand through my hair abstractedly. "Man how could she?"

"Have you ever heard of Munchausen by Proxy, Aidan?"

"Vaguely, I think my sister Brid mentioned it once. Isn't it something to do with a mother making a child sick in order to gain medical attention or attention for herself?"

"You've practically nailed it. It's a form of maltreatment of a child by the mother - it is also called 'Factitious Disorder by Proxy.' It's psychological of course, in which the mother, as you said, makes the child ill to gain attention for herself. Nurses have been known to do it too, for example Beverley Allitt in the early nineties. I've been a paediatrician for almost 10 years, both here and in Ireland and for the first time I was compelled to consult another colleague over a patient at the mother's instigation because she wanted a second opinion. She was extremely insistent that Patrick be kept in last night. She had even brought in his pyjamas because she was convinced it was meningitis. Because both my colleague and I suspected Munchausen's, I'm afraid we had to give Patrick a brain scan, an MRI. It proved negative of course, but it is a well-known fact that Munchausen's parents have banged their children's heads against a wall or shaken them in order to inflict injury. Luckily we found nothing."

I feel all colour abandon my face. "Jesus, what was she thinking?"

"Your son is a healthy boy. I'd like to see him stay that way."

CHAPTER FIVE

-

RECRIMINATIONS

Exiting the hospital I realise instinctively that Judy is conspicuous by her absence. Maybe she decided to return home without me, knowing how I feel and she is feeling guilty because of what she'd put our son through.

Brid is stamping her feet in her boots, wrapping her gloved hands about herself because of the cold. Ru's smoking a cigarette. When I appear, he lights another for me. My faithful brother and sister looking so concerned.

"So what did that doctor say, Aidan?" Brid asks. "We knew something was wrong didn't we, Ru? I mean, surely Judy would have told us if Patrick was ill."

I suggest we head for the car park. At this precise moment I am more interested to know where my ex-wife has gone, taking my son. I briefly explained to Ru and Brid what Dr Malone had related.

"So there was nothing wrong with Patrick after all?" Ru pulls on his cigarette and shakes his head. "I always knew it."

"Knew what, Ru?" I ask him.

"That bird's got a screw loose." He presses a forefinger against his right temple. "But I've never heard of that, what did you call it Munchausen's?"

"'Munchausen by Proxy'," Brid says knowledgably. "I learned about it as part of my training. It's a wee bit extreme isn't it, even for Judy?"

"So you going to have it out with her?" Ru asks eagerly.

"Well if you don't, Aidan, I shall. Poor Patrick having to undergo an MRI scan. That must have scared the poor child out of his wits. 'Course it's all to do with you, Aidan?" Brid joins.

"It wasn't Aid's fault, Sis. He wasn't even here."

"Thanks, Ru. When you called Aunt Clodagh to ask her how Uncle Sheamie was, Sis, did my name crop up at all?" I want to know.

"Sure, I asked her how you were. Aunt Clodagh said you had taken Uncle Sheamie to St Patrick's for his scan. Why?" A frown puckers my sister's brow.

"He means did anyone mention Aid had met a bird in Dublin?" Ru interjects.

"Aunt Clodagh mentioned something. I didn't really take a lot of notice." She flicks a grin at me. "You're always meeting birds."

"Did you mention anything to Judy?" I ask. We cross the grass verge, heading in the direction of the hospital car park.

Brid explains that she'd mentioned something before she snaps her fingers suddenly. "I remember now. Judy reckoned she was put out because you hadn't called her. You'd called Patrick on his mobile. I think she'd been drinking. Only for God's sake, don't say I told you so, Aidan, it'll only cause trouble. But she was spoiling for an argument. I've known Judy for a long time, I can always tell when she's being argumentative because she said, 'that's typical of your brother, he don't fuckin' care about me or Patrick'."

"The bitch! How could she?" I fail to avoid the anger already spilling out of me.

"So, I sort of said…" Brid hesitates and tugs her lower lip somewhat shamefacedly.

"You said what, Sis?" I prompt.

"Well I was angry and you and Judy are divorced. It's not as if I'm gossiping and you and her were still together."

"What Brid's trying to say, Aid, is that she sort of let it slip that Aunt Clodagh had told her that you had met a girl," Ru says.

"I'm sorry, but I was angry, I don't know what it was, you know how placid I am…"

Both Ru and I have to smile at our sister in disbelief.

"Well I am," she retorts defensively. "It's just that Judy seems to bring out the worst in me. She didn't used to, but the way she acted when you were in prison sort of severed any real friendly ties that Judy and I once had. She's always digging at me, so she is. Now, since Mark's left me, she really enjoys picking."

We arrive at the car park to find Judy at the wheel of a dark green Astra. She's obviously waiting for me.

Brid says, "Anyway, I have to go to work. As long as Patrick's okay, that's all that matters." Sliding an arm around my waist, she hugs me closely.

"Oh, Ru, don't forget whose car you're driving," I remind my brother as he is about to slide behind the Cabriolet's steering.

"I know it's yours man. So you're not coming back to London? Only your case is in the back."

I instruct him to take the case back to my flat. Bridget and Ruairi have parked a discreet distance from Judy. When she sees me, she gets out of her car and stands beside it, shielding her eyes against the sun's glare with her palm. I am aware of her observing us but she refrains from approaching.

"And clean out the dash before you bring it back."

"Okay, okay." He throws up his hands in mock submission. "I'll clear it out!"

Slipping the wallet from inside my coat, I hand Ru some money and ask him if he can pick me up in a while, adding, "Go to the shops or something."

"When do you want picking up?"

He kills his cigarette and dons sunglasses. "Only I won't come anywhere near her," Ru gestures in Judy's direction, "at least not without a stab vest."

"Ruairi!" admonishes Brid. Placing her hands around his neck lightly, she pretends to squeeze it.

"Get off." He laughs. "See what I gotta put up with, that's why I've been staying at your flat. That's if you don't mind."

"I suppose that's in as much mess as my car," I tut.

"No it isn't, I cleaned it up yesterday," Brid volunteers. "Now I really must go and Aidan, don't do anything you might regret." She lowers her tone, a hand partly covering her mouth in case Judy might be in earshot.

"Like murdering her you mean?" Ru quips.

"I mean anything that might prejudice your case for custody of Patrick, that's all."

Alone with my brother, I request that he pick me up outside a pub called 'The Galleon' on the outskirts of Esher. It is also a restaurant so I decide that we'd have lunch there. Ru promises he will since he's driving my car. "Don't worry, I'll take care of your precious motor."

While she waits for me, Judy is about to slide behind the wheel of the Astra. At my approach, she says sarcastically, "sometimes I wonder about you and Bridget. You two are always hugging each other."

I glare at her reproachfully. Her eyes are shadow ringed, lack lustre. Ultimately, my gaze drops to the back seat. My son is curled up asleep, his black curls awry and the familiar forelock spilling across his forehead. "Oh just get into the fuckin' car, Jude," I hiss.

Obligingly without a word, she slides into the passenger seat when I tell her that I'm going to drive. My thoughts return to Caitlan

McKenna and the reason why I had to leave her, on the fantastic time we shared, on what was interrupted in the Quayside Hotel room. It was all conducive to building up further resentment toward my ex-wife. Donning shades and lighting a cigarette, I wind my window down. While I smoke I observe her open her mouth as if to speak, but it is tight and set and she appears inordinately put out. If she is about to reprimand me about the cigarettes, I guess she's changed her mind.

The journey isn't far and is made in comparative silence. When we arrive at her house, I am the first to alight and, cracking open the car door, move to pick up my son. He is already awake. "Oh, Daddy, are you staying?" he asks. His eyes are bleary but wide and expectant for my response. "Sure, for a wee while."

Sliding gracefully from the passenger side, Judy allows me the sight of the short black skirt, the fact it has ruched up to display sheer black stockinged legs spilling into high, equally black stiletto heeled shoes.

The bitch is teasing me. Instead of it turning me on as it normally does, it is conducive to make me entertain further anger toward her for what she'd put our son through. In spite of my well of anger, she still knows how to make me fuckin' hard, a sensation I really don't need right now.

I park the Astra at the bottom of the drive. Dark red paving meanders from the road to the house. A small wooden gate encloses a perfectly tended lawn, a high fence separating her house from her neighbours.

A woman calls out to Judy as we walk to the door. The woman appears to be about Judy's age, is slim, attractive. Her blonde shoulder length hair is worn in a sixties-style bob. She wears jeans with a blue sweater. Waving at Judy and Patrick, she greets them both by name. In turn, Judy calls back, "Hi, Joanie."

Joanie calls "hi" to me when she sees me. I merely smile and say nothing but I am conscious of Joanie continuing to stare at me until I enter the house. "So who's that?" I ask Judy, piling my shades into my hair.

"That's Joanie, my next door neighbour. We're in the same position, so to speak. Joanie's divorced. She has a small boy too, Nathan. The nights we've cried on each other's shoulders. The funny thing is, her ex-husband's Scottish and mine's Irish and Nathan's the same age as Patrick, they go to the same school. Oh, and don't even think about it, Aidan."

"I wasn't fuckin' thinking anything, at least not about your neighbour."

"Mummy, can I have a bath?" Patrick is a small voice, plus a small figure framed in the doorway.

"Can't it wait 'til later?" she retorts irritably.

"Don't talk to him like that," I round on her. "What's wrong with him taking a bath?"

"Because he likes me to run it for him, that's why."

"Jesus, Jude, I'll do it."

"You staying then?"

"For a couple of hours."

"That's it, when you get bored, you run off." She stands, her back arched against the draining board in her spacious kitchen.

She has no idea how often she's come close to my physically striking her, or maybe she does. Alternatively, I am aware to do so in front of my son would undoubtedly prejudice my intended custody case.

Upstairs I run Patrick's bath, lay out his fresh clothes and attempt to allow my anger to subside. He asks me to soap his back, place his toys in the bath. I want to know if he is okay after what had happened last night.

"I had to go under this big machine and I was scared. That nice doctor said it was to make sure I didn't have any brain damage. Mummy was acting funny. I knew she'd been drinking. She does that when you're not here."

"I'm sorry but I'm not always going to be here. Would you like to come and live with Daddy?" He begins splashing around with a small yellow duck, letting the duck bob up and down on the water, as if he were stalling for an answer.

"In your flat?"

I attempt not to stiffen at the thinly disguised disdain in his voice, when he refers to my flat. I guess my small apartment in Shooters Hill scarcely matches this ostentatious house.

"Maybe I'll get a house soon." Although I really have no idea how I can possibly afford one in London. Then I say, God knows why, "suppose... suppose." I falter.

"Suppose, what?" Huge brown eyes search my face. His tone is almost stilted, pregnant, waiting on my response.

"Suppose we moved to Ireland?" I half-close my eyes in fear the idea might be rejected.

"But what about Mummy, would she come to live with us in Ireland?"

"Mm-er... no, Patrick." I clear my throat, my hesitation painful. It is akin to manoeuvring my way through a difficult maze and wondering if I will ever discover an exit and not say all the wrong things. "You see, you know when I went to Dublin?"

He nods, bites his lower lip uneasily. I guess he wonders where all this is heading. "I met someone. She's a wee bit younger than me and we started a relationship. I asked her to come to London with me but when I left in a hurry, she wasn't ready to leave Dublin. But I still want her to come and live with me."

"No! No! Daddy, there's no one else. I don't want to live with you if it's not with my mummy."

His reaction surprises me and he begins to splash about in the bath until my shirt is soaked and I am compelled to lift him out. Allowing me to wrap a towel around him he stands there, a little boy lost, shivering, his chest heaving in half sobs. "These women you have, Mummy says they're only loosies."

"Loosies?" I frown. "What are you talking about Patrick?" I dry him off. There is water over the floor of Judy's expensively tiled bathroom.

"There isn't really anyone else is there?" He grows calmer. "No more loosies."

Momentarily I fail to understand what 'loosies' means. Losers. Floosies. I guess it has to be the latter.

"You live with some woman and I'll never come and live with you. You're winding me up. There is no one is there, not really?"

I think of Caitlan. How much my heart aches for her with the need and longing of the beautiful childwoman I'd left in Dublin.

A white towel, with a big red duck emblazoned on it, is draped about him, his unruly black curls so like my own, are wet and awry. His sweet, angelic features, those eyes so brown, so trusting, my eyes, this small replica. The little boy whom Bridget had vouchsafed me photos of his growing up years whilst I was in prison. The small boy who had kept me sane and prompted me to study hard until I was finally released. He stares at me imploringly, half reproachfully because I've dared to bring another woman into the equation.

"There's no one else is there, Daddy?" It is almost as if he were hypnotising me, daring me to refute him.

And I am compelled to shake my head negatively. It's so difficult to deny the woman I realise that I really love as I believed I'd never love another woman since Leanne. "No, no, there's no one. I, I was just winding you up."

Flinging himself into my arms, he hugs me tightly.

Reciprocating, I can only stare at the surrounding bathroom wall with the utmost regret. This is my life and I realise that I can't have both another woman and my son. "Now you go and get yourself dressed," I counsel him. "I want to talk to your mother."

"You and Mummy won't argue will you?"

This time I didn't promise that, and I shake my head uncertainly.

I find Judy busy preparing a salad for lunch. Her back is turned and I enter the room quietly. She's tucked a small apron about her black skirt and is in the process of slicing tomatoes on a wooden board. I catch her around the waist; the action forces her to drop the knife. It clatters onto the board noisily. She gasps in alarm, her eyes enlarging in her surprise, but not in anger. "Oh, Aidan, I didn't hear you come in. Are you staying for lunch?"

I wonder how she can remain so calm. I've pushed her arm so far back behind her, I could snap it if I wanted to.

"What the fuck have you been teaching our son?"

"Oh, Aidan, you're so…"

I interrupt, "I asked you a fuckin' question, Jude. What are you doing to our son, that fiasco of last night for instance? Patrick said you'd been drinking. What's happened to you?"

"What!" This time a ferocious light appears in her eyes. "Don't turn the fuckin' tables on me, Aidan McRaney, you're fuckin' torturing me, you bastard."

I recoil as if she's physically slapped me. "I haven't touched you."

"I don't mean physically. The way you are, the way you look. I think about you all day, all fuckin' night. I can't help it if I want you, you bastard. You fuck me then you leave me fuckin' wanting more than you're prepared to give."

"So, is that the reason why you put our son through so much? A fuckin' MRI scan, Jude. He told me he was scared. Dr Malone reckons you might have something called 'Munchausen by Proxy'. Do you know what that is?"

"Yes, I know what it is. And you, you bastard," she hisses. Her eyes continue to blaze with a strange, almost malevolent illumination, something I've never had occasion to witness before. "'Cos you are a bastard." Her free hand comes up, is about to crash across my face. I see it coming. Before she is able to throw the punch, I intercept it and force her bodily against the wall, both hands thrust behind her.

"Don't you dare fuck me, you bastard. Like I said, you're torturing me."

"You bitch! You don't take it out on our son. Dr Malone says he discharged Patrick last night."

"Yeah that's it, you Paddy's always stick together."

"What's that supposed to mean?"

"I saw how pally you were with that Dr Malone, just because you both come from Dublin."

"That's not fair, Jude. How dare you turn this back on me? You need help, psychiatric help, do you know that?"

I release her abruptly. She turns back to the sink. "You really don't understand do you?" Sobs begin to wrack her body.

"Then tell me, Jude." I force her to face me. "Sure now, I don't fuckin' understand. All I know is that nobody in their right mind takes their child into hospital, insisting that because he has a bad head cold and a slight rash on his chest, that he has meningitis. Sure, you did the right thing having him checked out but you're a nurse, you should have known. If a doctor discharges your son, then you accept that."

"Isn't all this accusation because I called you back from Dublin?"

"You know it is. I promised to help my aunt and uncle. Sheamie's not well. And there were tears in my aunt's eyes when I had to leave in such a hurry."

"Is that the real reason, your aunt and uncle? I can see how angry you are. So who is she, Aidan? That's the real reason why you're so angry isn't it? There was a woman. There always is with you."

"Okay, sure, if that's what you want to hear." All the pent up anger spills out of me now. I push her from me, really let it rip, realise I can't help it. Anger comes far too readily to me and there I am, vehemently throwing up my arms, my eyes blazing so fiercely that she is compelled to shrink away from me.

"Yeah there was a woman, Jude. She's 20 years old. She's beautiful. And I'm in love with her," I spit at her un-mercilessly, uncaring how much I hurt her. "I don't know what you said to Patrick but you've poisoned his mind against me finding someone else. We're divorced Jude, nearly five years. You have your life and I have mine."

"I suppose she's Irish too?"

"Yeah, she's Irish. Her name's Caitlan. I'm not going to lie to you, if that's what you want. It's not as if I'm a straying husband. I'm a single man, Jude. You have no fuckin' hold on me. So don't try coming on to me with your short skirts and high heels. It's all for nothing."

I'm aware how cruel it sounds but she's pushed me too far. I've had enough. She starts to cry and I wish that I didn't feel quite so sorry for her.

"I don't like it when you argue." His face ashen, his thumb in his mouth, Patrick stands there, huge tears slithering down his cheeks.

"Patrick, I'm so sorry." I rush to comfort him. Shrugging out of my arms, he flings himself from the room with, "why can't you love Mummy anymore? I don't want you to have anyone else, Daddy."

CHAPTER SIX

-

A NEW VENTURE

I'd never eaten at 'The Galleon' pub and restaurant before. It was my first port of call before returning to Shooter's Hill since I'd been a visitor to Judy's, which was in order to take Patrick out on the few accessible dates I was allocated. I'd even met Verdi at the pub once.

There is another drinking area in the restaurant. Ru whispers to me, "Blimey, this is a bit posh ain't it?" when we first enter, particularly considering the way we are dressed. Catching sight of my reflection in a long wall mirror facing the seating, I wish I hadn't. My hair is long, with unruly dark curls that appear not to have seen a comb in days with the addition of the dark beard and shadow-ringed eyes. In my old check shirt, tee shirt, black jeans and the leather coat thrown over the lot, it makes me wonder if we should have come here after all.

Ru doesn't appear much different. His own features are unshaven; unruly dark hair he's allowed to grow recently, in faded jeans and rumpled shirt. He mutters to me that because I got him out of bed so early, he hadn't had time to do more than brush his teeth. I'd left Dublin a little after 6am. Did he expect me to feel any better?

When I ask him what day it is, predictably, he mocks, "Jesus, man, you been in a time warp or something? It's Monday, I think."

It is obvious we have hit the lunchtime rush, a little after 1pm. The suited and booted are omnipresent here, poring over files and laptops on the tables. I guess this is where the majority of office workers come to enjoy their midday meal.

Our entrance has not gone unnoticed by the smartly dressed punters, toying with their food, discussing the day's events. I can tell that Ru is made uncomfortable by his surroundings. He has one eye on the clientele, the other in the mirror. Personally, I figure that my money is as good as anyone's is.

We are guided by a skinny, pimply-faced youth to our respective table. "The waitress will bring you a menu," he says awkwardly when my brother is set on maintaining a derisive grin for his benefit.

Several punters crowd the bar area, while three young women, bedecked in dark red skirts and blouses with an embroidered motif of an old sailing ship decorating the breast pockets, act as waitresses. One of the girls, tall, pretty and blonde, although overly made up for my tastes, approaches our table to deposit a red covered menu.

"Thanks, darlin'." Ru's eyes never once move from her face, making her blush to the roots of her blonde hair.

She duly informs us that she'll come back for our order when we're ready.

Ru continues to stare at her so predominantly; the poor girl is left with little choice than to avert her own gaze with embarrassment. To break the spell, I kick him lightly on the shin.

"What did you do that for?"

"Stop staring, it's rude."

"I only stare when I like what I see. Anyway, let's look at this menu. Then I got some stuff to tell you. So how did it go with the witch of Esher?"

"What do you mean you gotta tell me some stuff? It went badly if you must know." In the process of scanning the offerings in the red book, I explain briefly what had occurred between Judy, I, and Patrick. How he'd reacted when I told him I'd met a girl in Dublin.

"So, is it serious, Aid, you and this bird? Only I know you and birds. I mean, there's a stretch of water between you. You might meet someone over here and forget your Irish bird, especially if she's willing to..."

"For God's sake, Ru, do you know how shallow that makes me sound? Sure, it's serious. Since leaving her, I've felt really low, you know what I mean, depressed. I asked her to come back with me. Then Jude phoned and Caitlan said she didn't want to intrude because we didn't know how ill Patrick was then. You should see her, Ru, she's beautiful. She's a singer in The Liffey Bar. It's a pity I didn't stop long enough to take a photo of her. When Jude called, do you know where I was?"

Ru pauses to consider, then leans across the table. "Giving it to her, I bet."

"Jesus, do you have to be so crude? But I was in this hotel."

"Hotel, I thought you were staying with Aunt Clodagh? So what were you doing in a hotel, Bruv?"

"For someone who seems to know his way around women, you're pretty naïve. I wasn't actually staying at the hotel, well, I was going to spend the night if Jude hadn't phoned. Caitlan booked us into this hotel and we..." I sank my voice to a conspiratorial level, "did it in the shower."

"Blimey, you fuckin' lucky bastard. And you still feel the same about her?"

"Sure I do. Anyway, you said you had something to tell me," I remind him.

Ru is about to respond when the waitress returns to our table. His mouth closes automatically, his eyes never once leaving her face.

"Are you ready to order yet?" Blue eyes encompass Ru and I expectantly.

"It's not on the menu, darlin'." He leans closer to her. The girl shifts uncomfortably. "Steak and chips please, sweetheart, with peas," I say. "And drinks."

She jots our orders on her notepad, careful to maintain her gaze lowered from Ru's.

"You driving?" I ask him. "Or do you want me to?"

Ru shrugs. "It's okay. I'm enjoying driving that motor while I got the chance. Anyway, you probably need it more than I do."

I look at him. "What?"

"The drinks, Bruv," Ru grins. "What do you think I meant?"

"Nothing." I grin back and order a double Chivas Regal on the rocks.

"A double Coke on the rocks for me, darlin'," Ru says. She smiles at that.

"What's your name, sweetheart?" he asks her.

"Jesus, Ru," I hiss at him.

"It's Sandra," she replies quietly. "Your meals shouldn't be too long." Ignoring Ru she turns on her heel, about to leave when he calls after her, "and your phone number, Sandra."

"Now you sound desperate. Jesus, I can't take you anywhere. She's obviously not interested."

He runs a palm over his scrubby, beatnik beard ruminatively. "Maybe I should have shaved. Though I reckon some birds like all that scruffy bearded shit."

"You hope they do."

"So, she didn't mind your beard, this Caitlan sort?"

"She's never seen me clean shaven has she? Anyway, talk to me, Ruairi. You had something to discuss. It sounds serious."

The girl returns to our table with the drinks. Before moving away, she pauses to scribble something on her notepad. Tearing the paper off, she passes it across the table toward Ru. "What you asked for, Sir." She flicks him a demure smile.

She'd written her phone number on the paper. Ru can't stop grinning. "Still got it, even if I do look like shit," he says, stuffing the paper into his shirt pocket.

"So, you going to call her?" I sip the whisky, feeling it warm my insides.

"What do you think? 'Course, I'll keep her waiting for a while. You know, not to be too eager. Yeah, sorry, I suppose I'd better tell you."

"Tell me, Ru, does it involve me, whatever it is?"

"Oh yes Bruv. You see, Harry's selling the business."

"He's what!" I almost choke on the whisky. "Selling the business? What do you mean? I haven't heard that before."

"He was going to ring you, but he didn't want to spoil your holiday."

"So where does that leave me? I'm supposed to be running it while he's away."

"He thought he'd be doing you a favour. He knows how much you didn't want to do it."

"Sure, but that's not the issue. It'll leave me without a job. I don't suppose he thought of that."

"Well, yes, he did as a matter of fact."

I scramble around abstractedly in my coat pocket for cigarettes. "Shit, I forgot, we can't smoke in pubs now, can we?"

"'Fraid not, Bruv. I could do with one too."

"So, you were saying about Harry. If he's sold the business, then he must have a buyer."

"Well it sort of fell into his lap. He didn't intend to sell the business, not originally. He enjoys living out there, y'know in Milan."

"Sure he does," I mutter, "and fuck the rest of us."

"Apparently, out of the blue this guy contacts this solicitor. Sue has a family solicitor. This solicitor guy tells Harry that someone is interested in buying his landscape gardening business. Harry was hesitant at first, but then this solicitor on behalf of this guy, I can't remember what Harry said his name was, Horlem or Howlem or something, Brid knows. She was the one Harry called. Anyway, this Howlem guy offers Harry £350,000 to £400,000 for the business."

"Fuck me. You sure it's on the level? I know I'm naturally suspicious and I don't think Harry would fall for a con trick."

"'Course, Harry jumps at it don't he? It means he can buy a villa out there and," he enthuses, "he's thinking of us. He's asked us, once the deal has gone through, to go out and live there."

"Live in Italy? Jesus." I realise I've drained the whisky in one swallow and need another.

"Yeah, in Milan. That's why I've booked this gap year. I ain't one to look a gift horse in the mouth, Bruv and neither should you."

"And to think I've just got out of going to South America." I'd spoken my thoughts aloud, for I incur a perturbed frown from my brother.

"South America? You were going to South America, why?"

I wave a hand dismissively. "No reason. So, Harry's agreed to go ahead with this deal?" I change the subject quickly.

"Yeah, why not? And I said I'd go out there. We can soak up the sun, man. Get out of this country."

"Sure, if it doesn't sound tempting but I have my son to consider. At the moment, as I told you, Patrick isn't best pleased with me. If I could get full custody maybe I'll think about it, but I'm not leaving my son in Judy's clutches. She might have him hospitalised for some other fake illness. So it's definitely no con trick then? I mean it does sound a wee bit too good to be true."

"No con trick. The guy's kosher. Harry's selling the business. And like I said, he wants his brothers to join him out there."

"And Brid? We have a sister too, in case you'd forgotten, and Dad. We can't leave him, he still thinks he's in Dublin. At least the people speak English. In a foreign city he's only going to get even more confused."

"Harry asked Brid, but she reckons those hot countries won't suit her skin and her colouring."

"And Dad?"

Ru has to admit that he hasn't thought about our father, the fact he might be in the throes of early onset dementia and tugs his bottom lip indecisively.

"You can go out to Milan and bum around in your sandals and shorts, Ru. I might go there for a holiday, but I'm not leaving my son or my sister and my dad."

"While you look for work, and can't find any 'cos you're an ex con?"

Sandra appears with our steak and chips, settling the plates carefully onto the table.

"Can I have another double scotch please, sweetheart?" I smile at her sweetly. She nods and blushes.

"Blimey, Aid, you plan on getting hammered?"

"Sure, that's the general idea after what you've just told me." Before starting on my steak and chips, something draws my attention toward the bar. Amidst all the chatter of conversation and the mêlée of customers filing in, I'm aware of a powerfully built guy wearing a loud plaid jacket nursing a beer, his ample behind overflowing the small stool, regarding Ru and I with an ill-concealed disapproval. Ru doesn't appear to notice. He's already tucking into his food in earnest.

The restaurant and bar are already decorated for Christmas, with an assortment of fairy lights and various other yuletide paraphernalia. Lights sparkle brightly in the large bay windows and a tall fir tree is decorated and lit by the bar. Very Esher, very suburban Surrey. A far cry from The Liffey Bar in South Dublin, with 'ould' Flanagan in his check shirt and greasy trousers, his big bearded face looming over his customers. All conducive to making me realise how much I suddenly miss the guy, his bar and above all, his beautiful singer. I'm homesick for a place I hardly know any more, but it has hit me all at once. If I move to anywhere, it's more likely to be Ireland rather than Italy.

Two double scotches later and I'm beginning to feel slightly pissed. I've only managed half of my meal. I've polished off the steak, leaving most of the chips which the human dustbin of a kid brother wants to know if he can finish. I am athletically built and wiry but Ru is a veritable beanpole on legs. God only knows where he puts it all.

Sandra has left the bill so I inform Ru that I'll pay it. He reckons that the money I had given him had consisted mostly of euros. With them, he had paid a visit to the car wash in order to clean up the Cabriolet.

Hauling on my coat, I head to the bar and leave Ru to finish his food. Counting out the money I take care to ascertain there are no euros amongst it. I chat to Sandra who is curious to discover my brother's name. As usual, I have to spell it and explain that it's an Irish name. As I move away, the burly guy at the bar suddenly mutters, "fuckin' Micks," when I pass him. I judge him to be older than I had first thought, at least in his early fifties. He is bullish and ugly with a big, red neck that overrides his shirt collar.

He's sweating profusely, his features as crimson as his neck. His eyes are small and half buried in that mountainous hulk of flesh and balding scalp.

I halt in my tracks, the old red mist surfacing, the scotches fuelling my bravado, not that I need any. I'd taken on Shaun Blackwood who'd been toting a switchblade. Was fat and ugly any different?

Swirling around on him, I hiss, "What did you say?" My voice is deliberately chill and I stare him down.

"You heard," he murmurs, but somewhat less self-assured. "You want to do something about it, pal?"

"We, we don't want any trouble in here, sir. I'll, I'll have to call the manager." The pimply faced youth appears on the point of collapse.

"Let's go." Ru grasps my arm. His voice rings with both concern and unease.

Shrugging him off, I really have no idea what has possessed me, but there I am flailing my arms about angrily and moving threateningly in 'ugly's' direction. The crimson having transformed to an unhealthy ashen, the big guy appears inordinately scared and shrinks away as if I have actually struck him. As big as he is, as wiry as I am, I would have enjoyed kicking seven kinds of shit out of the bastard, Ru knows it. It is only when he whispers, "you don't want to, you know…" anxiously at my elbow that I relent.

Shrugging resignedly, I follow my brother, but my anger remains a living, breathing entity, reminiscent of a caged animal, requiring a much-needed release inside me.

*

Ru is behind the wheel of my Cabriolet smoking profusely, saying nothing momentarily, not even to admonish me. I apologise to him as soon as I join him, suggest that maybe it was the scotches that had fuelled my aggression.

"Apology accepted Bruv, but you know what I meant when I said you didn't want to end up, you know where. I couldn't say you'd been inside, not in front of them, but you got form, you could have got sent down again if you'd hit that guy. Not that the bastard didn't deserve it, probably. I couldn't bear it if you went inside again. I was still at school when you went to prison, but it's not just me, it's all of us. We all fell apart when you went inside. I started playing truant from school and stuff. Now I like to think that you and me have drawn closer."

"Sure we have, Ru. Again, I'm sorry."

"So what did he say to make you so upset, anyway? I noticed him looking down his nose at you at the bar, but I didn't catch what he said. Was it about your hair, your clothes or something?"

Rolling a cigarette and planting it between my lips, it is a while before I deign to respond.

"Aid?"

"My nationality. 'Fuckin' Micks', was what he actually said."

"Jesus, you don't have to be so sensitive about that."

"Well I am. I can't help it. Maybe I've been sensitive about it since I was fuckin' 10 years old."

"Man, that's a long time to be carrying a chip on your shoulder. Harry had to suffer a lot of crap from the squaddies when he joined the British Army. In the eighties, people were scared of the IRA. So he was 17, 18, but he managed to rise above it."

"And I'm nearly 30 but I can't help it. You don't get it in Ireland."

"Well you wouldn't would you?" he grins wryly. "They're all fuckin' Micks out there. They probably say, 'fuckin' Brits'."

"Like I said, maybe it was the whiskies talking."

"Maybe," he agrees.

I, however, remain totally unconvinced by that assumption.

*

We arrive at my flat to discover a man in my garden. Slimly built, he isn't much taller than about 5' 6". He's wearing a light blue, short-sleeved shirt, which seems incongruous in this weather when Ru and I are wearing coats. The man appears to be dressed for summer.

Ru mutters, "Jesus," beneath his breath when he clocks him.

"What's wrong?" I alight from the Cabriolet simultaneously as he does.

"Your new neighbour," declares Ru, grinning all over his face. "Or maybe he's always been there, only you haven't seen him before. You know what the 'fuckin' Brits' are like. We keep ourselves to ourselves."

His hair is short, a sort of crinkly dark blond that is plastered flat to his head as if he's just showered. His forehead is high. His features small and birdlike, attested to by a rather hooked nose. He is bustling about in the garden, calling something that sounds like "Moo, Moo."

"He's looking for his pussy," Ru attempts to explain between stifling his laughter behind his hand.

"Then why is he making cow noises?"

"Its name is Mouflan, apparently."

At sight of the man, my brother's erstwhile good humour is swiftly restored. "Mind you, Bruv," Ru adds, tongue in cheek, "that's the only pussy he's ever likely to be looking for."

"You mean he's…"

"As a fuckin'…"

The gardens are neatly tended by the GLC and are comparatively small, while the grass is hardly long enough to conceal a mouse, let alone a cat.

"You looking for your puss... I mean cat, David?" Ru asks derisively.

David halts in his search the instant we appear, to inform Ru in affronted tones that he is, when his gaze settles on me, only for it to linger almost to the point of embarrassment. I return his eye contact until he is compelled to avert his gaze.

"Your cat might have strayed," I suggest. "You won't find him in the grass." I entertain the feeling that his search for a cat in that neat lawn is merely a pretence.

"It's a she. I'm sorry, we haven't met before. I'm David. David Lennard. I've just moved into the ground floor flat. I had to leave a lovely house in Putney you know. But when relationships break down, you have to live where you can." He shakes his head regretfully.

I merely nod sympathetically. He's obviously awaiting an introduction. "I live upstairs, David," I tell him noncommittally.

"Aren't those flats so warm? It must be even worse upstairs." His tone is unmistakably feministic. He extends a hand loosely, one I purposely ignore.

He adds, "you hardly need to wear much clothes do you?"

"Yeah, we often walk about starkers, don't we Aid?" Ru teases.

A flush of colour appears on Lennard's pale countenance immediately.

"I wouldn't go that far," I say wryly, and to Ru, "why don't you go and make us some coffee, Bruv? Actually, David, I'm a wee bit pissed, so I think I'll go and grab a coffee."

Ru disappears indoors leaving me alone with David. His open neck shirt reveals a large Star of David medallion denoting him to be a Jew.

"Too much lunchtime carousing?" he observes with a smile. "I didn't catch your name."

"That's because I didn't give it. It's Aidan McRaney."

"How do you spell that? H-A-Y-D-O-N?"

"No. A-I-D-A-N."

"You're Irish too. There's a pretty red haired lady who comes here sometimes, are you two an item? She doesn't stay long. And she usually has a chubby little girl with her."

"That's my sister Bridget and my niece Sammy."

"Oh dear." He clamps a hand across his mouth suddenly. "I thought she might have been your girlfriend. Her hair is so red and you're so dark."

"That's from my mother's side of the family, I'm more like my father."

I'm aware the guy is fishing and it's imperative that he knows that I am definitely straight.

"Like I said, I gotta go and get that coffee. I hope you find your cat soon, David."

I refrain from saying 'pussy'. Turning on my heel, I head for the door when he calls out, "are you seeing anyone at the moment, Aidan?"

I stiffen momentarily before I swirl around on him quickly, the familiar aggression welling up inside me and I bunch a fist inside the pocket of my coat.

"No, David, let's get this clear and you won't need to ask it again, I'm not…"

"Gay. I'm sorry, I was just teasing." He smiles to reveal less than white teeth as if they haven't seen a brush in a while.

"But you are a very attractive man. Of course, I knew I wouldn't be that lucky."

I allow the anger to subside at the element of sadness in his eyes.

"Yeah, sure I'm seeing someone. Are you always this forward?"

"Life is too short to be backward, Aidan."

I'm unwilling to remain any longer, particularly at the way this conversation seems to be going. Again, I tell him that I hope he finds his cat.

"Yes, I have two. Blue Persians. Mouflan and Blue. I bet she's pretty."

Jesus, doesn't this guy ever give up? When I favour him with a less than understanding frown, he adds, "your girlfriend."

"Yeah, she's very pretty."

"So where did you meet her?"

"In Dublin, so what's it to you?"

"Nothing. Just making conversation." He turns away with the parting shot. "I'd like to meet her."

This time I choose to ignore him, guessing the guy must be lonely. Upstairs, Ru's fixed us both black coffees, plus rolled me a cigarette.

"Jesus, Bruv, I was about to go downstairs and rescue you. He never stops fuckin' chatting does he?"

Hauling off my coat, a cigarette anchored to my lips, I tell him that David Lennard has only made a pass at me.

"Jesus, Aid."

"You mean he's never made a pass at you?"

"Yeah, once or twice but I told him to go fuck himself. Do you know what he calls me or so Brid told me?"

"Rude?"

"Probably, but no… One morning, when she mentioned something about turfing me out of bed 'cos it was her laundry day or something, it was when you were away, he asked her, 'where's 'young Lochinvar' this morning?' Meaning me!"

"He probably fancies you as well. We walk about the flat starkers remember."

"Yeah, I bet he was imagining that and wanking himself off." His voice trails when he sees I'm in the process of examining a cream vellum envelope that is addressed to me.

"What is it?"

"I don't know. A letter, it looks official."

Slitting the envelope I discover the letter inside bears the heading: MAXWELL SORENSON SOLICITORS

My heart performs a double somersault. I mutter, "What the fuck?" beneath my breath. I check the postmark. "It came the day after I left."

"What is it? You ain't half gone a funny colour. Bad news?"

"I don't know, but it's from a guy called Maxwell Sorenson. He's a solicitor with offices in Wardour Street, Soho apparently."

I read aloud:

"Dear Mr McRaney,

If you could possibly make an appointment on this number, I have something of interest to impart. It concerns the estate of Mr Raymond Lamond. If you will contact me as soon as possible.

It's signed by a 'Mrs L Haynes' Maxwell Sorenson's secretary."

"Jesus, Aid, something of interest, hey. Ray Lamond isn't dead is he? I thought he was banged up."

"He is, but 'the estate of Mr Raymond Lamond' sounds as if he's dead. Or maybe if he had died, wouldn't it have read 'the estate of the late Mr Lamond'?"

"I dunno Bruv, but there's only one way to find out. Why don't you ring that number?"

CHAPTER SEVEN

-

MAXWELL SORENSON

In the wake of making the appointment with Maxwell Sorenson, the secretary isn't giving anything away. I ask her what the solicitor wished to see me about. She merely responds stiffly, "Mr Sorenson will tell you when you come, Mr McRaney."

I manage to secure the appointment for 10.30 the following morning, after explaining that I'd been on holiday for a few days.

Ruairi is excitedly speculating what Maxwell Sorenson might want to see me about. Both of us are all too intrinsically aware that Morey Sorenson, the latter being his brother or his father, had been the lawyer Frankie Lamond had hired. Consequently, I was let off with an eight stretch instead of a possible 15 or 20 for killing the guy who'd shot him and Leanne in the Soho restaurant in 2003.

Once again like the proverbial bad stench, gangland was, in all probability, rearing its ugly head. Whatever his relationship to Morey, Sorenson ultimately worked for the Lamond brothers who were indisputably the latter day Kray twins. I'd learned recently that Frankie had died in an Eastbourne nursing home from the bullet that had lodged in his spine. Ray is banged up for tax evasion and possession of both firearms and a crematorium in the grounds of his ostentatious Maze Hill residence.

After making the call, I can't help but reflect on Caitlan and Patrick and wish that I hadn't. I voice my thoughts to Ru.

"Look, there's no harm in going to find out what this Sorenson guy wants is there?"

"If it's money it could be stolen, and you were the one who was scared of me going back to prison."

"Like I said, there's no harm in finding out. I'm curious if you're not. Maybe he's left you the key to one of them safe deposit boxes or something."

I pace the floor like an expectant father while he makes a futile attempt to watch 'EastEnders' on TV. Smoking profusely, I deride him, "safe deposit boxes. Jesus Ru, where did that come from?"

"You know. Isn't that where crooks stash their ill-gotten gains? Or maybe he's left you one of his shooters or something. Maybe he wants you to pull a blag."

"I don't believe you sometimes. Maybe you watch too many crime shows." I grimace inwardly at the way my brother's mind works sometimes, with his wild imaginings. "I might be a lot of things, Ru, but I don't pull blags. Maybe Ray's got wind of the fact I wanted to try for child custody and he's hired his solicitor to help me."

Ru looks doubtful. "Not without wanting something in return, Bruv."

"You don't know Ray Lamond, Ru." I sit down finally; observe the frown that knits my brother's brow.

"What ain't you telling me?" he asks suspiciously. "Is it about that money Ray Lamond gave you? You mentioned something about South America. He wanted you to go there didn't he?"

I regard him in surprise. "Jesus Ru, how did you know that?" I wonder what else he knows.

"Harry told me. Well, Brid. You know what Brid's like. She gave him the third degree. Did he know why Aidan had suddenly come into so much money? It was while you were in Ireland. 'Course she ranted and raved. Harry told her that you'd told him the money was for you to go to Rio or somewhere, because someone wanted you dead and you preferred to go to Ireland instead. Jesus man, I would go to Rio like a shot. I'm a sun worshipper. You can't get much of that in the Emerald Isle."

*

Missing her so unbearably, I call Caitlan later in the day, before I know that she has to leave for work at the bar.

"Caitlan McKenna's phone, her sister Mollie speaking." She sounds almost robotic and rather off-putting. Because it isn't Caitlan herself I'm almost tempted to conclude the call, but I need to know how she is. Ru watches me curiously.

"Hi, Mollie," I clear my throat a couple of times. "This is Aidan."

"Aidan who?"

"Aidan McRaney" I sigh. I wonder if she's genuinely forgotten or is she feigning ignorance? A momentary pause, maybe she's rung off. "Caitlan's boyfriend."

"Oh, the one who pissed off back to England and abandoned her when he thought things might get serious."

"I didn't abandon her, Mollie. I had to fly back to London because my son was ill. Can I speak to her?"

"So, how is your son now?" She sounds as if she doesn't believe a word I say.

"He's a lot better thanks."

"So it wasn't meningitis then?"

"No, Mollie, it wasn't meningitis. So, can I speak to her?" I hear the impatience in my voice.

"No you can't. She's lying down with one of her migraines. She seems to be getting a lot of them since you left."

"I'm sorry. I'm not getting migraines but I am…"

"Men don't get fuckin' migraines. They just get pissed and you sound pissed. Is that why you had the nerve to call?"

My sigh is one of exasperation. I try to be amicable but Caitlan's sister really is getting my back up. It's almost as if she's got some kind of grudge against men. I pity her poor fiancée. "I'm not pissed, okay, and I'm sorry Caitlan isn't feeling well. Will you tell her that I called, please? That I'm missing her and I haven't abandoned her. I love her." I chose to ignore Ru muttering, "Jesus, man."

"Well, she's enamoured of you too. I must agree though, she's better off with you than she is with Shaun Blackwood. Seems he's disappeared. The trouble is you have a bolthole."

"What's that supposed to mean?"

"Your bolthole, it's called London. She's well enamoured of you, but if you break her heart my Niall's a big fella. He'll come over there and break your fuckin' legs, so he will."

I think to myself that I'd like to see him try and realise that Mollie has already concluded the call while I am left still staring at the phone. "And I thought Jude was a bitch."

"What! She ain't dumped you has she? God, I hope not, you're fuckin' angry now. I'll never be able to control you if she has." Ru looks worried suddenly.

"You make me sound like some head case, Ru."

"Well, you are sometimes. You scared me this afternoon. I really thought you was going to land one on that guy at the bar. So has she dumped you?"

"Hopefully not," I muse uneasily. "That was her sister."

"Blimey. That didn't sound like it went well."

"Mollie, her sister, believes I abandoned Caitlan when I came home because Patrick was ill. Caitlan was lying down with a migraine and couldn't come to the phone. And what's that look for, Ruairi?"

"It sounds as if your precious Caitlan whispered to this Mollie sort, 'tell him I've got a migraine 'cos I don't want to speak to him.'"

"That's where you're wrong, Bruv. Mollie reckons Caitlan was 'enamoured' of me."

"Enamoured?" Ru laughs. "How old is this Mollie bird?"

"It's difficult to judge. I'd say she was about the same age as me, but the way she talks she could be 50."

*

"So you're selling the business then, Harry?" Nursing a double Chivas Regal on the rocks, I talk to my brother on the landline. This time I plan to get well and truly hammered.

"Sure I am, Aidan. You don't sound none too pleased. I thought I was doing you a favour."

"By putting me out of a job?"

"I'm sorry if you feel like that. Didn't Bridget and Ru tell you that I've got enough? Yes the money's come through, £375,000, into my bank. You and Ru can come and stay here a while. I don't hold any hard feelings about what happened between you and Gina. Sure, I was angry at first. Anyway, Gina's hoping to get into a university here in Milan. You should see the girls out here, Aid, well they all look like Gina. Beautiful olive skins, long black hair. If only I was 15 years younger and unmarried. I know Ru's sold on the idea."

"And it's not a con?"

"Trust you to think of that. I'll admit I thought it was at first. It came out of the blue, the offer from this fella, George Howlam. He owns several landscape gardening businesses in London and the South East of England."

"And he wanted to buy you out?"

"That's about the size of it, Bruv. So how was the 'ould' country?"

"It was fine, but getting back to Italy, what about Brid? And Dad? You can't just abandon him."

"He can come as well."

"Oh, sure he can, Harry. He thinks he's in O'Connell Street even though he lives in Billet Road, what the fuck's he going to do in Milan and what about Patrick? I'm definitely not going to leave him behind."

"Look, I'll give you, Ru, Brid and Dad some of the money and Dad'll be okay. Didn't Ru tell you? Dad has a woman to come and look after him, a Mrs Jenkins, apparently. She's a neighbour, a widow."

"No he didn't." How long have I been away for Christ's sake? "All I hope, for your sake Harry, is that it's not a con." I am tempted to confide in him about the letter I'd received from the solicitor.

Conscious of the Sorenson's being the Lamond brother's lawyer's, I refrain.

*

I park the Cabriolet in the main car park, the nearest one to Sorenson's suite of offices and check the address on the letter. Ascending a lengthy flight of stairs, I'm duly informed by a tired looking male receptionist after announcing my presence, to take a seat while he called Mrs Haynes, Sorenson's secretary.

The waiting room is spacious. A dark blue corner suite occupies the entire length of one wall. There is the inevitable water machine, plus a stone fireplace and a small marble table on which rests innumerable magazines that consist mainly of 'Country Life' and 'The Lady', neither of which I am interested enough to pick up. I am alone in the room and fidgeting with my tie, when a middle-aged woman appears. Wearing a blue pleated skirt and white blouse, her hair is short and neatly permed. A pleasant smile radiates her mature features to a more youthful iridescence. Extending a palm, the woman introduces herself as Laura Haynes.

"Mr McRaney?"

"Sure," I respond and wonder why I am suddenly feeling so nervous.

"Mr Sorenson will see you now."

"Is Maxwell Sorenson any relation to Morey Sorenson?" I dare.

"Yes, Mr Morton Sorenson is Maxwell's father, but he's retired now," she explains as I follow her down the long white corridor. Beneath my boots a deep pile, green patterned carpet springs to attention as we near a brown wooden door that is marked simply, 'Private'. Laura Haynes raps tentatively and we are invited to enter.

The office is surprisingly ostentatious. A couple of rubber plants stand sentinel-like behind the desk of a slimly built man I judge to be somewhere in his mid-forties. He's wearing an expensive looking grey linen suit with a dark patterned tie. His hair is dark and closely cropped, while a pair of thick tortoiseshell horn-rims straddle the bridge of a long Jewish nose.

Piles of papers in a wire tray plus a telephone are the only items on his desk. Rising from behind it at my entrance, he introduces himself as Maxwell Sorenson and instructs his secretary to fetch us some coffees. "Or would you prefer tea, Mr McRaney?" I want to tell him that I'd prefer a whiskey. Nevertheless, smiling politely I say that coffee will be fine.

"Do sit down." He motions me into the chair facing him at his desk.

This room is also quite spacious, containing a couple of filing cabinets. The same dark green carpet is here as in the corridor.

"I'm sure you're wondering what all this is about." Sorenson slides out a grey file from the remainder in his tray.

"Can I ask if this has anything to do with my gaining full custody of my son?"

Sorenson's perplexed frown makes me realise instinctively that my assumption is radically incorrect.

"I'm sorry, Mr McRaney but I'm afraid it isn't. Look, I'll be up front with you. I visited Mr Lamond in prison recently. In an endeavour to clear up some of his affairs and by affairs, I mean those that consist of a nightclub called 'The Black Garter', plus his Maze Hill residence, he has been forced to sell in order to pay off some of his taxes. It is the nightclub I'm concerned with here. You see, Mr Lamond has nominated you to mind it for him, the club as it were. While he's inside, he wants you to manage The Black Garter club. According to the authorities, I believe that Mr Lamond is going to be in prison for quite some time."

CHAPTER EIGHT
-
A PRISON VISIT

It is becoming increasingly difficult to come to terms with the fact that Ray Lamond has requested me to run The Black Garter while he is inside.

Maxwell Sorenson's secretary has brought in a tray containing the coffees plus some wafer thin chocolates on a plate. She must have guessed somehow that he has explained about the club, for she flicks a hurried glance to her boss then to me, sitting there frozen in disbelief. Finally, I find my voice to exclaim, "you've gotta be fuckin' kidding! Run that den of iniquity?" in horrified tones. "I'm sorry about the swearing but this has come as something of a shock."

Slipping the horn-rims from his nose, Sorenson rubs the bridge before replacing the spectacles and interlacing his lean, brown fingers. Supporting them on his desk, he says, "I'm sorry you feel that way, Mr McRaney."

"That place holds a lot of bad memories for me."

"I know what happened in 2003 and I sympathise, but you must know that Mr Lamond is grateful to you for looking after his brother's interests so well. He also feared that you might refuse the offer."

"Then why did he ask me?"

"Because he is aware of all the obstacles that have been put in your path recently."

"What obstacles?"

"Didn't someone try to kill you? The relatives of the man you shot dead in 2003?"

I hadn't expected him to rake that up. I also wonder how much Ray Lamond knows. I trusted Verdi enough not to grass to the police, aware that if she did, I would drag her down with me.

"It seems that Fitzwalter has disappeared, to South America, apparently," I say.

"That's alright then. So, other than the reason you gave me, what other reason is there for your refusal? All you have to do is oversee things. You'd be the owner, the guy who did the hiring and firing. Do you have any other concerns, Mr McRaney?"

I'm on my feet suddenly. "I'm sorry you've been put to any trouble Mr Sorenson, but you can tell Ray Lamond I don't want anything to do with that place."

"Then you'd better tell him yourself."

Sorenson's face is grave and tight, I guess he hasn't taken too kindly to my refusal. He tosses a typewritten paper down onto the desk in front of me.

"What's that?" I regard the paper dubiously.

"It's a prison visiting order. Mr Lamond wants you to go and see him to discuss the club and what he wishes you to do."

"A prison visiting order!" I echo and plump my weight in to the seat again. "Prison, I can't go inside a prison again. You wouldn't either if you'd spent eight years in the joint. I'm sorry, but you can tell Ray nothing doing. Can't he get some other wee bastard to run his wretched club? I'm sorry he's in the situation he is, but he's picked the wrong guy."

"I'm sorry you feel that way." He shakes his head regretfully.

"So, is the club closed down now? Not that I'm interested you understand."

"No, the staff are still there. As long as you're satisfied, then the original staff can remain. Like I said, all you have to do is run the place. You called it 'a den of iniquity'. Mr Lamond knows where your feelings lie."

I sip the filtered coffee absently, whilst my mind works overtime. "Gangland will never let me go will it? Just when I'm trying to build a new life for myself."

"Which brings me to the point Mr Lamond intended to make. You see, as I was about to say, he knows how you feel about gangland and he wants the club turned around legitimately."

"Jesus!" I practically choke on the coffee. "Legitimately, there's nothing legit about that dive. Personally, no offence to Ray, but they should raze it to the ground."

"Really? You do have strong feelings."

"Anyway, suppose I decided to run the joint, not that I intend to of course, what's in it for me? I can't run the place on shirt buttons y'know."

"You wouldn't have to. Mr Lamond has money tucked away in several Swiss banks that the law can't touch. Whatever you may think of Mr Lamond, he is a businessman. You won't have to worry about money. There was something else you mentioned when you first come here."

"What was that?"

"You were under the impression when you first arrived that this was some kind of child custody case."

"Sure. So what are you saying?"

"I'm saying, Mr McRaney, that a child custody case can take weeks, even months of social worker's supervision. You'd get a social worker assigned to you and if you know anything about social workers, they're a relentless bunch, digging out everything about you, digging up things even you didn't know you knew. Get my drift?"

"Sure, if I haven't had dealings with social workers," I muse thoughtfully. Well, not me exactly. When our mother died, Dad and Aunt Clodagh looked after us. I was about 11, 12; Ruairi was three, Laurena a baby. We were threatened with being taken into care, while Dad roared at them from an upstairs window, 'you ain't fuckin' taking my kids,' invariably in a drunken state. Sorenson was saying, "then there would be a court case. It wouldn't be in a large courtroom, not the kind you were in when you were sentenced, but the case would still come to court. Do you have a partner? Are you cohabiting?"

"Only with my kid brother," I grin.

"I mean, is there a special someone in the picture?"

"Sure, I'm hoping there will be soon, she's living in Dublin at the moment. Why?"

"Because if you have a partner, then you and your partner will have to legally adopt your son."

"Adopt my own son?"

"Yes, I'm afraid it's the law. Then there's your ex, Judith McRaney..."

"Man, you have been busy."

Steepling a bridge of interlaced fingers, once more he pauses to regard me pointedly. "It pays me to know as much as I can about you. Your ex-wife would probably contest the case. Plus, as I said, child custody cases can go on forever and sometimes things get messy and who would suffer at the end of it? Your son, Mr McRaney, that's who. The Americans call it 'a tug of love'. Would you want that?"

"God no! Then what are you saying?"

"No courtroom. No social workers, no months of drawn out anguish for your child. A 50/50 access option, if that's what you prefer. You can't deprive a mother of her child any more than you can deprive a father, and the only way you could hope to obtain full custody would be if your ex-wife was found by law to be an unfit mother."

"She drinks. And she almost had Patrick hospitalised." I relate the incident, which had brought about my hurried return from Ireland.

"A good case but not a strong enough one to prevent her from gaining that fifty per cent."

"I'd be happy with that. Which means what?"

"Four days a week, nights staying with you in one week, three nights with your ex. Then vice versa the following week."

"And if I don't run Lamond's club?"

He smiles enigmatically. "You get the picture, Mr McRaney, Aidan."

My expression hardens and I entertain the familiar well of aggression. "This speaks of bribery and blackmail to me, Mr Sorenson. Maxwell," I stress his name sarcastically. "Why does Lamond need me to run that club so much?"

"Because he trusts no one else."

"Someone must be running it now."

"Yes... a Mr...." he pauses to leaf through the pile of papers in his tray, before locating the one he wants, "Mr Ronald Engels."

"Ronnie Engels!" I echo in surprise.

"You know Mr Engels?"

"Not personally. I met him once but I do know Engels is a pimp, amongst other things, probably. And if I manage the club, no prostitution, no drug dealings. All above board or nothing doing, understand?"

"You sound as if you're considering it."

"Okay." I expel a ragged breath, almost of resignation. "And Engels?"

"I told you, you do the hiring and firing. It seems that Engels is sitting tight at the moment. It's up to you to see he... ahem... leaves."

Oh, I was way ahead of him. Whichever direction it took, it all invariably led back to gangland and what I believed I had left behind nearly 10 years before.

"I'm sure you can handle Mr Engels, discreetly of course."

"And the child custody thing, what do I have to do for that?"

"See Mr Lamond. Then once you've decided, maybe a trial period, see how you get on. A few simple questions and we'll get the child custody case underway. As I said, you will have access to your son for the main part of the week and if you do find something amiss with your ex-wife, that she's failing in her duties as a mother for instance, then we'll review the case for full custody."

"I can see why you're a gangland lawyer. You know I'd do anything to gain custody of my son."

"That's good," he smiles again. "But I prefer to be called a criminal lawyer."

"Whatever," I shrug.

"Anyway, Mr Lamond will furnish you with more information."

I see that the prison order is for the day after tomorrow. The place is HMP Lexford, which I observe is located out Colchester way. "It's a semi open prison," Sorenson informs me.

"Semi open! For Ray Lamond?"

"Oh Mr Lamond knows he can't escape. Besides, he has too much to lose. The prison is newly opened for people with similar convictions. If you need a map…"

"I'll find it," I snap.

"You probably don't need me to tell you but you will have to remove all your jewellery. Your rings," his gaze descends to my hands, "a necklace if you have one."

"I wear a crucifix."

"That too I'm afraid. So you will see Mr Lamond?"

"Sure. I guess I don't have a choice do I?"

"Good man." Sorenson pats my shoulder in a friendly gesture. "You know it all makes sense, Mr McRaney."

As far as I am concerned, there is nothing about this that remotely makes any sense.

*

"Ru, you little shit, pick up your phone."

Returning to the Cabriolet, just sitting there in contemplation, I'd never wanted to hear the familiar sound of my brother's voice quite so much. I'd texted him, but that failed to meet with any response. Finally, he deigns to enquire, "Aid, you okay? How did it go with that solicitor? Was it anything to do with you getting custody of Patrick?"

"Sure, part of it. But it comes at a price."

"What do you mean? You gotta pay for it?"

"Not exactly, where are you?"

"At the pub."

"It sounds noisy." I can barely hear him. Leaning against the Cabriolet's headrest, all I can do is chain smoke.

"I've met some mates from Uni. We're out Camden way. Why don't you come and join us?"

"With 20 year olds? I'm not driving out there. Besides, I'm not in the mood."

"You sound terrible. What's happened?"

"I'd tell you but there's too much noise. I'll wait 'til you get back to the flat."

"It's okay, I'll go outside. The way you sound, if it wasn't good news, you know I'll be there to pick up the pieces, man."

"You sound pissed."

"I'm not pissed, Jesus, Aid," he retorts defensively. "Look, hang on a minute."

A short while later I hear my brother's voice again. "What's happened? So it was something to do with…"

"Shut the fuck up Ru and listen." I hadn't intended to snap but all I can do is dwell on the impending visit to Ray Lamond, while I wonder if I can ever step inside a prison again.

"I'm sorry." He remains affronted, I guess after the way I spoke to him. "Whatever it was it's obviously left you in a bad mood."

"I'm sorry, Ru, I didn't mean to snap." I relate the majority of what had transpired with Maxwell Sorenson, the fact that he wanted me to manage The Black Garter club in Ray Lamond's absence, concluding with, "What the hell do I know about running a fuckin' nightclub, for God's sake? If I run the club, he'll consider the custody case."

"That sounds like blackmail. But on the plus side…"

"There's a plus side?" I echo incredulously.

"I think it's a brilliant idea. I only hope you'll ask me to help."

I make a face. "I'm glad you think it's so fuckin' brilliant. What do you know about running a nightclub any more than I do? I suppose I could sell it. Sorenson didn't mention anything about that."

"That's called 'pulling the rug from beneath his feet', Bruv."

"So Ray Lamond hasn't done the same to me before?"

"What I meant was, I've done a spot of deejaying before, and I've helped behind a bar when it's busy, this one in Camden actually."

"Oh, that's helpful. There's more to managing a nightclub than a wee spot of deejaying and bar work. There's other stuff too."

"So you've got to see Ray Lamond in prison to discuss it?"

"It would seem so, or I could just call it all a fuckin' day and not bother."

"Come on, don't be a defeatist, I think it's a great idea and a challenge. I know you can't resist a challenge - we'll run it together. How hard can it be? I've taken that gap year from uni. That's if you want my help."

"You know I do, Ru."

Somehow, my brother and I have begun to draw closer and I realise that I am beginning to rely on him and value his opinions. He was 13 when I went inside. A moody schoolboy. We often argued when I was sometimes left with him and Laurena to babysit. Ru would 'go off on one' when I refused to allow him to watch television after 10 o'clock when Brid said he should be in bed if it was a school night. Of course, I preferred to be out with my mates than watching my brother and sister. Then I'd gone to prison and hadn't seen Ruairi again until two years off my release when he came with Brid to visit. I couldn't believe how much Ru had changed from that spotty 13 year old into a fine young man of 19.

*

My brother scarcely needed any persuasion to drive me to HMP Lexford, mainly because he enjoys driving my car, for which I'd put him on my insurance. Secondly, because I know he is concerned about me. He may be eight years my junior, but he's suddenly developed a sort of 'mother hen' persona towards me. Today his young face, with the 'bum fluff' beard he's attempting to grow, regards me with concern because he is all too aware how difficult it is for me to enter a prison again. If it hadn't been for someone's promise to grant me a fifty per cent access to my son, I wouldn't have considered taking on that iniquitous den, letting it close down or be razed to the ground, I didn't care.

Ru appears rather bemused by my apparent 'striptease' when I remove my rings, my watch, the crucifix that Brid had bought me as a 'coming out' present. Divesting myself of my coat, I invariably wear a tee shirt beneath my shirt. I leave the shirt unbuttoned, although it is cold outside. It has begun to snow, a few scattered flakes beating against the Cabriolet's windscreen.

"You'll freeze without a coat." Ru shivers in indication.

I tell him it's one less thing to check. "You've been to see me in prison. You know what they do. You can look after my stuff 'til I return."

"You sure you don't want me to come?"

"Without a visiting order you won't get inside the door."

"I could always pass myself off as you."

I stare at him and smile at his suggestion. "Thanks Ru, but you wouldn't be able to deal with Lamond. He's a crafty wee bastard. He has to be handled a certain way. I'm the only one who knows what makes him tick."

"I'm not scared of him, if that's what you mean."

"I know." I breathe harshly. "Let's fuckin' get this over with."

Cracking open the car door, I step out as a blast of cold air slices through me, making me realise how much I miss my coat. I regard my brother enviously as he sits in the warm motor. He's brought a carrier bag with him. Hitherto I have no idea what it contains, until I ask him what he is going to do while he waits.

"Read some comics, Aid. Don't worry about me, I'll be fine." Reclining his long legs onto the dash, he settles down to read.

"I won't," I mutter. Reading his comics, he reminds me of the 13-year-old schoolboy once more.

*

Her Majesty's Prison Lexford more resembles an old rambling country manor house than a jail. A couple of uniformed guards restraining huge Alsatian dogs stand sentinel-like outside as I approach the red bricked building that now appears less like a stately manor than a forbidding castellated prison.

As requested, I show my visiting pass and I'm instructed to enter the vast stone-flagged area. There are other visitors there, both male and female. I can't help but feel apprehensive, as if, once they close those huge iron studded doors behind me, I'll be trapped inside for another eight years.

Predictably, the checks are thorough. When you're an inmate, you don't realise how much a visitor's personal belongings are open to inspection. Two more guards, with accompanying dogs, are inside. The dogs are straining at their leashes as if in readiness to attack, but are obviously there to survey a person for drugs. Then comes the hair inspection and I close my eyes tightly when I feel rough male hands roam through my hair, searching for what, nits? I recollect those nit inspections when I was a kid.

"Jesus, mate, you've got a lot of fuckin' hair for a man," a disgruntled middle-aged guard mutters sourly.

I am apprehensive enough and none too pleased myself, so I refrain from a reply. Judging by those cold-eyed guards, they are chosen both for their inherent ugliness and their dour expressions.

A young woman, standing next to me, shudders involuntarily when a guard begins searching through her hair before the hand descends to her body in the tee shirt and jeans she is wearing. I long to admonish him about what he is doing, the way his big mitts hover over her slender form quite so lasciviously. "Please…" she starts to protest.

There are two women present, the pretty blonde next to me plus a much older woman with straight bobbed hair, who keeps blinking nervously when the rough male hands run over her.

I manage to whisper to the blonde to ask if she's okay.

She turns my way and I am aware of the tears standing in her eyes. Her hair is quite long and pulled back by one of those comb grips, which she is compelled to remove. In her nervousness, she lets the comb fall to the floor. Quicker than she is, I retrieve it for her. She deals me a small grateful smile from perfect white teeth and mouths her thanks.

"You can go through," the guard hisses, half pushing me forward, serving to incur the familiar anger inside me. It would be so easy to retaliate over the way visitors are treated. Maybe the dogs are telepathic because one of them begins to growl low down in his throat. The dog bares its teeth, as if it is about to spring, guessing what I am about to do.

I hiss back, "down, Fido," before the guard calls him off and flashes me a warning look. Moving away, I'm conscious of the pretty blonde approaching the desk ahead of me. Without a word, I pass the visiting order to another guard behind it. His dark eyes favour me with speculative glances, I guess, when he sees who I am visiting. After all, Ray Lamond is an ex mob boss.

I have no idea what to expect from Lamond. Vindictiveness, pleasure at seeing me? I'm about to discover when I'm escorted by another guard to an adjacent room. I half expect to join the other visitors as my family had done when they visited me.

"Through there." The guard holds open another iron door.

It's a solitary room. Does this indicate that Lamond hasn't been behaving himself? Why would he be put in 'solitary' if he hasn't been? However, I doubt if he would be allowed to receive visitors.

The door closes behind me. The self-same iron framework incurs a return of all the bad memories, memories that continue to haunt me. 'Lights out!' The screaming and swearing in the dead of night. Dennis Mitchell my cellmate, "hey you, got a fag, McRaney, you old paddy bastard."

Mitchell growling, well it seemed that's all he ever did. "They have to put me in a cell with a fuckin' moody Mick."

I'd say nothing, just keep my head down and attempt to keep my temper in check, not rise to the familiar taunts parodying my name, 'hey, Ada,' and such like, the way the bullies had done in school.

Eventually Mitchell and I became reasonably good friends, particularly after I'd opened up to him the reason why I was there. In his eyes and most of the other jailbirds, to shoot someone was enough to warrant a pedestal.

And there he is, the infamous mobster Raymond Lamond, decked out in a blue regulation jacket and trousers, a fluorescent orange band criss-crossing his chest. His greying hair is cut unaccustomedly short as to be practically shaven. Now he resembles the convict that he is rather than the suave businessman, smoking his elegant Havanas in his ostentatious Maze Hill residence.

Standing sentinel-like, his back adjacent to the wall is another guard even uglier than the last; a broad shouldered frame filling out his uniform almost to bursting, a cap partially screening his eyes. It makes me wonder if the guards I have so far encountered are either clones or robots fashioned from cold metal into forbidding sentinel machines.

"Blimey, McRaney, you got more prison pallor than I have," Lamond declares and drops his weight into the chair facing mine. A wooden table separates us, that is all, and open prison or not, Ray Lamond sports handcuffs fastening his wrists in front of him.

"Ray, it's good to see you," I try to enthuse, only for it to drop flatly. "What's all this about, 'The Black Garter' club? You want me to run it while you're…" I flick the guard a glance from beneath an elevated brow, "while you're away."

"You don't have to stand on ceremony here, Aidan. That's Barry the screw, ain't it, Barry?" He addresses the guard as if he were an imbecile. Barry fails to acknowledge him, however. "So you've spoken to Maxie then?"

"If you mean Sorenson, that's why I'm here. And you gotta know, I don't fuckin' play along to blackmail, Lamond." Leaning an elbow on the table, I'm conscious of the guard moving closer.

"Don't worry, Barry." Lamond raises his hands as if he is the one in command. Knowing Lamond as well as I do, my assumption is probably correct. "Me and McRaney go way back. You don't wanna worry about him."

"Blackmail?" He points a digit to himself, while an injured air negotiates his expression. His black hair has really become quite grey, his face narrower.

"Getting me to run your club with the promise of fifty per cent access to my kid."

"Old Maxie'll do it for you an' all. He's Morey's son you know. 'Course I was too deep in the shit for me to get let off with a lighter sentence, but he got me a single room, plus I don't have to sit with the riff-raff listening in when I meet a visitor."

"A snob to the last, hey Ray, so what about this club?"

"You sound interested, Aidan."

"I didn't say I was interested. I don't know the first thing about running a nightclub. Besides, according to Max Sorenson, Ronnie Engels is a sitting tenant, so to speak."

To my surprise and consternation, I guess the guard Barry is too, for he moves forward again, Lamond fashions a gun firing motion with two finger resting against his right temple.

"It's okay, Barry, just messing," Lamond grins. One I fail to share, while something akin to icy tentacles dance a rhapsody the length of my spinal column and I narrow my eyes deliberately.

"I hope you mean sack him, Ray."

"If you like," Lamond shrugs but holds a smile, which serves to indicate a more sinister interpretation.

"You know I don't do that kind of thing anymore. So if I do decided to run this club of yours, it's strictly legit, understand. No drugs, no prostitution or protection. You know I don't like dealing in that stuff."

"Of course. You run it your way, as long as I've got a club to return to when I do eventually get out. Get that kid brother to help you. The one who's all arms and legs. What's his name? Rory?"

"You make him sound like an octopus. And it's Ruairi."

"Whatever, same funny, paddy name."

"Actually he's agreed to."

"What about the other one, the 'ex squaddie'?"

"Harry? Harry's in Italy with his family. That was odd too."

"What was?" Do I detect a rise of colour flowering Lamond's otherwise ashen pallor?

"Some guy offering Harry nearly 400 thousand to buy his landscape gardening business, that wasn't down to you was it, Ray? You knew I'd be left without a job and who would employ an ex con these days? Especially one who'd been inside for murder."

"Moi?" Lamond makes a face, adopts an injured air again. "You've got a naturally suspicious mind, Aidan McRaney."

"Do you blame me?"

"So what have you decided? Only if you haven't, there's nothing to say is there? But, if you decide to manage my little club for the duration, then we have things to discuss. It's up to you my young Irish friend."

CHAPTER NINE

–

THE BLACK GARTER CLUB

Lamond observes me with diligence as he awaits my response, one I'm not certain I want to give. Still I suppose I could do worse and I enquire, "why me? Why do you want me to run your club when I've never run a club in my life before? You must have other pals to do it for you, Ray."

Lamond's expression is serious and he shakes his head regretfully. "I guess you heard about poor Frankie," as if to change the subject.

"Sure, Ray and I'm sorry. I'm surprised that he's lived this long with a bullet in his spine," I sympathise and mean it.

Albeit he was a treacherous wee bastard to some, Frankie Lamond had been a good employer as well as a friend.

"There aren't many people I trust in the world, Aidan." His tone is strongly poignant. I half expect to witness tears in his eyes but the grey orbs display little sign. "But I trust you."

"To fuck it up y'mean?"

"No, to turn the club around."

"What's that supposed to mean?"

"Since I was about your age, when you were first banged up, what were you 20, 21?"

I nod briefly. He adds, "I'll be 52 in February. Since I was 21, I've been banged up three times. Whenever anyone mentions the names, Francis and Raymond Lamond, they automatically lumber us with the Kray twins. Mobsters, and because we owned The Black Garter, that gaff became known as the joint where mobsters hang out."

"Sure, if it's not like you to get maudlin' Ray, and if people associate your name with the Krays, it's because you've brought it on yourself. That joint was mob run and you know it."

"'Course I do and I'm not denying it, Aidan. When the 'suits' started sniffing around, I knew my days were numbered, and the reason why you're the only person who can turn that club around is because you want to stay legit. You have your family, that precious son of yours. When people go there they'll know there are no criminal elements. You run it as you think fit. Some of the staff are still there, I expect Maxie told you that."

"Sure, including Engels. So, do I keep the staff on?"

"Only if you're happy with 'em. If not, don't be afraid to fire 'em. I'll leave Engels to you, but make sure he knows who's boss."

"Och, don't worry Ray, I don't like Engels much. I'll make sure he knows who's boss all right. Apart from the staff, what other stuff do I need to know?"

"You could always run it as I did…"

My eyes narrow speculatively. "I thought we were going legit, Ray."

"That hurts, boy," he grins, but it's good humoured, I think. "What I meant was most of the trade comes from the games, you know, the casinos. I've got a good croupier working on that, his name's John Gorman but everyone calls him Jacky. He's a bit on the belligerent side, but he knows the casinos. You can rely on him. You could have theme nights, that always draws in the punters."

"Theme nights?" I echo derisively. "You mean people dressing up in 'Star Trek' uniforms? Something like that?"

Throwing back his greying head, his laughter is a strident guffaw. Even the clone-like Barry has to force a half-hearted smile.

"Well that could be interesting."

"I told you, I don't have a clue about running your damned club."

"What I meant was, well if you're going to come out with remarks like that, you could have a comedy night. You know, stand up. Hire some acts. Two, three times a week there's a DJ, Pauly Lucas, the punters like him. Then there's karaoke nights."

I make a face at the thought of karaoke. "I've been there, so I have. If, and I stress 'if' I decide to run this club of yours, karaoke and cabaret are out."

"You can't pull the plug on cabaret, Aidan. Some of the best acts on the circuit do cabaret. How else are you going to attract the punters? Bingo? Another night you could have a magic act. That always brings 'em in."

"Where do I get them from? See I told you…"

"Aidan my friend…" Lamond allows a restrained hand to touch mine, only for it to be withdrawn at Barry's approach. "Okay, Barry, easy. I ain't passing him nothing, honest." He shakes his head. "Nervous you see. Maxie got a list of some good acts, plus you can get the keys from him. All you need to do is make sure the place runs smoothly. Put some signs out, you know the kind of thing. No rough elements. Suits. No jeans. Ties. There's already some muscle on the door. Make sure the punters have identification, no underage drinkers. I'll get a pal of mine to fix you up with one of them search machines. You know, if anyone is carrying any kind of weapon, even a hair clip'll show up on the machine. All you gotta do is make people know who's the boss. If you wanna hire some lovelies…"

"Lovelies?"

"Birds. You and that kid brother of yours can do that. Dancers. Waitresses," he enthuses, while his eyes glint lasciviously. "Only the pretty ones of course. I can see you're getting excited already. You pick the birds you want. Promise a bit extra in their wages if they'll perform just for you and I ain't just talking fuckin' dancing, boy," he winks knowledgeably. "You're a fuckin' attractive geezer, you can get any bird or anything you want. If I wasn't as straight as a bleedin' die I might fancy you myself."

I was on my feet, guessing this is my cue to leave. "I think we've concluded this conversation, Ray," I say tersely.

"Getting embarrassed, Aidan? But you know what I mean. So you'll consider it?"

"Sure, maybe for a trial period. And if it don't work out…" I allow my words to trail.

"If it don't work out then I'll be the one who'll be sorry," he says ominously.

*

Returning to Ruairi sitting in my Cabriolet I discover my brother smoking profusely with the window wound down. He is still engrossed in his comics. His gaze shoots up when I appear, sneakered feet dropping from the dash, his cigarette tossed from the window.

I slip into the seat, fasten my belt and dwell on how Lamond has changed from the cigar smoking, cocksure man with his crinkly, dark hair to a much older guy than one approaching 52. Prison does that to someone, I'm aware if I'd received a longer sentence I'd probably have ended up looking closer to 40 than 30.

"So how did it go with Reggie?" Ru interrupts my reverie.

"Who?" I regard him obtusely, failing to comprehend his meaning hitherto.

"Reggie Kray," he grins and twisting the key into the ignition, swings the Cabriolet out into the street.

"Don't fuckin' call him that." I realise that the place has left me irritable, angry too, mainly because I really don't want to run that bastard nightclub. Plus, I am missing Caitlan so much it hurts, almost as a physical pain. She hasn't called me after I'd spoken to her sister and guess that the ostensibly vindictive Mollie hasn't deigned to vouchsafe the message. Maybe Caitlan has dumped me. After all, out of sight, out of mind. It isn't the same for me, however, I still want her so much. I feel a jealous pang as I recollect the young blond farm boy she'd chatted to in The Liffey Bar.

"You okay, Aid? I'm sorry. I didn't know you was so pally with his nibs," Ru says.

"Sorry, Ru, it was just that place getting to me, that's all."

"So what did he say? About the club, I mean. Have you agreed to run it for him?"

"A trial period, okay?" I glance at my watch. "We could go and check out the place. It's only twelve."

"Won't it be closed?"

I shrug. "It doesn't matter if it is. So much the better. All I have to do is collect the keys from Sorenson apparently."

"Sure. We'll make a go of it somehow, and you know I'll be with you a hundred per cent. You've made the right decision."

"I hope so." I muse retrospectively, without my brother's faith, however.

Predictably, Max Sorenson is pleased that I have agreed to manage The Black Garter if only a trial basis. Personally, I have my doubts about the place, but Ray wants me to turn it around and I promise I will. I intend to make the club mainly a legitimately, pleasant place people can come to without anyone passing drugs around. There will be no protection rackets, no prostitution. As far as I'm concerned those days are over. I need to keep my nose clean more than anyone because my ultimate goal is gaining custody of my son. If the club works out it could result in a lucrative income for both myself and Patrick. Sorenson promised to get the custody case underway as soon as possible, which serves to make me feel a little better about this business. Nevertheless, it fails to lessen my hurt and jealousy over what Caitlan might be doing or who she is seeing in Dublin, aware that it will be impossible to return there for a while. I promise to give her a call later.

The Black Garter club is located in Soho's Wardour Street, quite near Sorenson's office. Ru's parked the Cabriolet in the car park at the back of the club. The keys jangling in my hand, I step out and kill a cigarette beneath my boot. "Let's do this, Bruv," I tell him. "At least we can…"

"Case the joint," he quips.

"I was going to say look over the place."

Nonetheless, I can't avoid a smile at his analogy. All this seems little different to my brother than opening his presents on Christmas Day. I am the one with all the doubts.

Catching up to me he says, excitement prevailing, "bejaysus, I've never owned a nightclub before." Ru's accent is ultimately South London. Occasionally, a trace of Irish creeps in when he gets excited. Perhaps my erstwhile doubts stem from the fact I remember that upstairs room where Leanne and I had once made love. I recollect even after nearly 10 years how much I had loved and miss her and what that bastard Brian Fitzwalter had done to her lovely face.

From the outside, the place doesn't look like much. A white boarded façade is interspersed with dark brick, innumerable windows, plus the familiarly archaic neon's with the black, stiletto heeled shoe that flash interminably when the neon's are switched on. I hate that sign. It will be the first to go. That shoe. The very name 'The Black Garter' attests to sleazy and sluttish elements. Maybe I am a snob, but any club I manage will be wholesome and pure. Certainly there is precious little to recommend The Black Garter as resembling anything remotely wholesome and pure, or the addition of the muscularly built guy, folds of a red bull neck overlapping from his bald scalp and flapping over his collar, who greets us at the door.

"Fuckin' hell, Aid!" Ru exclaims, a small voice from behind me.

From what I'd learned, during my days as Frankie Lamond's minder, muscle only appears imposing to the untrained eye. Beyond that is merely a soft belly badly running to fat and capable of being winded if you know the correct place to strike. Not that I hope it will come to that of course.

"Club's closed, mate." The bouncer gestures his balding scalp to the sign on the door. "Don't open 'til 7.30."

"Fuck off," I mutter and attempt to push past him. Predictably, he moves in to bar my way.

"Maybe we should come back later." Ru suggests uneasily. Obviously, the 'muscle' bothers him. "I happen to like the way I look."

"Shut it, Ru just leave it to me," I counsel purposely for the muscle's benefit.

He moves nearer to the club entrance and folds his arms across his leviathan girth. He reminds me of a sumo wrestler, even his small pinched up black eyes are reminiscent of a Japanese. Anyway, at 6' 2" I tower above the sumo. Slipping the keys from my pocket, I dangle them in front of him.

The black eyes narrow with suspicion.

"What's your name?" I ask him.

"What's it to do with you?"

"Your name?" I bring my face up close to his, giving him the opportunity to lash out. I am waiting for it, every nerve fibre strained.

"Mike Corman. What's yours, Paddy?"

"Well it ain't fuckin' Paddy for a start. It's Aidan McRaney. Just remember that, Mike," I stress his name, "'cos I'm going to be your boss."

The black eyes open, at least marginally, his expression fills with disbelief. "Fuck off, Mc… whatever it is or I'm gonna call the manager."

"Jesus, you really aren't getting this are you?" My sigh is heavy. I can hear Ru's breathing issuing harshly from behind me. "I am the fuckin' manager."

The vicious blow I deliver hard against that fleshy stomach with my right elbow causes him to emit an involuntary 'ouch' of pain and his hand flies instinctively to the injured area.

"Jesus, Aid!" I hear Ru exclaim.

Another blow sends Corman reeling violently back against the club entrance. Doubled up now, he continues to clutch at his stomach, muttering, "you fuckin' bastard, you nearly fuckin' crippled me."

"Now you get the picture, fat boy," I taunt him. "And I didn't cripple you. But if you'd like me to…" I square up to him, while he attempts to anticipate my next move. He searches my expression as if in an attempt to read my thoughts, but the presence of my shades prevents him. Initially a sense of wild exhilaration courses through me with the old aggressions surfacing. Maybe I shouldn't have done so in front of my brother but tensions have to be released. Momentarily I stare into his young face with his wispy, beatnik beard, dark curls standing out in marked contrast against the ebb of colour on his cheeks. The little boy lost once more, before a wry grin spreads across his face.

"I'm sorry, Ru." I shake my arm, which has now begun to ache a fraction where I'd struck Corman. "You shouldn't have seen that."

We leave Corman nursing his 'wounds' and enter the club to discover that the door marked 'Private' is unlocked. I ask Ru if he is pissed off with me for what I'd done to Corman.

"I was at first. It scared me you know. I knew you could be violent but…" he allows his words to trail.

"Again, I'm sorry." I really am apologetic in front of my brother. His young face, so cherubic, is one I've often mistaken to be innocent and afraid when it came to the rough stuff. I voice my thoughts.

"No, I'm not scared of the rough stuff. I've been in a couple of fights. I ain't scared. There's only one thing I'm scared of."

"What's that?"

"My brother going back to prison again, 'cos if you did I'd fuckin' do something to go to prison with you."

"You stupid bastard." My admonition is friendly. "I want you to stay out of trouble, you know that. It'd break Brid's heart if we both end up inside. Anyway, I'm not going to jail. It's guys like Corman that have to be dealt with before we can turn this place around. So come on, let's see what other goodies or baddies we'll find through that door, Bruv." I grin.

"Sure." He taps my shoulder affectionately. "You know we have to stick together, Aid and I'm going to make sure we do. Well, except when we're with a bird of course and when we take a pee."

"C'mon you stupid wee bastard," I laugh and ruffle his hair.

I hope the place might be deserted, so that we can have a proper look around undisturbed. I might have guessed we wouldn't be that lucky.

Four scantily clad girls are practising a somewhat dubious form of sensual dancing, their slender bodies gyrating in time to some upbeat pop music, against a silver pole on the stage. The proceedings are observed diligently by a short, heavy set man, whose greased back black hair displays a high promontory of a forehead and one that is liberally awash with perspiration. His features are as heavy set as his bulk, all conducive to rendering him an ugly sort of man. Fleshy lips manoeuvre to the semblance of a salacious grin. Leaning an elbow onto the bar counter, he watches the girls from this position.

A young man, in his early twenties I judge, garbed in a white starched jacket and black trousers, wipes glasses on a towel.

The girls continue with their routine and my gaze is drawn to a tall, shapely redhead, mainly because of what she is wearing. It's a similar emerald green bikini as I've seen on Caitlan. Long legs spill into matching green 3" high stilettos. I note how the long titian hair, whether natural or emanating from a bottle, it scarcely matters, compliments the satin bikini. She clocks my glance and smiles my way. One I reciprocate lopsidedly. His mouth open, Ru merely stands there, then piles his shades in his hair.

"What do you want? You a rep, mate?"

The big guy, sweat permeating the underarms of his burgundy shirt, growls at Ru and I. Not again, I think to myself.

"No, I'm not a rep. And you, are you Jacky Gorman by any chance?" I ask. "If not, can you tell me where to find him?"

He regards me with suspicion. "I'm Jacky Gorman, so you ain't selling nothing?"

I shake my head negatively.

"Then what do you want, only the club's closed."

"It's just that you're under new management now." Ru strives to show his authority, while still managing to resemble the university student he actually is.

"Under new management, what's that supposed to mean? Mr Lamond owns this place or at least he did before…"

"He went inside," I finish for him. "Sure, I know. He's asked me to run the place while he's otherwise detained."

Gorman squints gimlet orbs into my face.

"Ain't I seen you before?"

"Then you've got me at a disadvantage."

"I know." He snaps his fingers suddenly. "A photo in Mr Lamond's office, well at least I think it's you, only you look more like him." He gestures his head at Ru.

The photograph, of course. There is a photo of me in Lamond's office. The picture was taken with Frankie Lamond when I was his minder nine years before.

"Fuck me!" Gorman exclaims, "Adrian McRaney."

"Close. Actually it's Aidan."

"So, Ray Lamond's asked you to take over the club?" he echoes incredulously.

"That's right. I'm your new boss, Jacky. So is Ronnie Engels around? Only I heard he was running the place." I glance around the room, my gaze, as if magnetically drawn, coming to rest on the girls again. When Gorman suggests they take a break, they move to the bar.

"Ronnie don't come in 'til two. So why did Mr L ask you to run the show?"

"Because he wants new blood and he wants me to turn this place around."

"Turn it around? What the fuck's that supposed to mean?"

"Change the décor." I wave a hand about me in indication. "Get rid of that fuckin' sign outside for a start. Change the staff too if they displease me."

The girls are all quite pretty of course, a mix of both blondes and brunettes. She is the only redhead and the tallest, at least 5' 10" in her stockinged feet. She appears even taller, leggier in the heels.

She is the last to vacate the pole as she gyrates up and down, hot flesh against cold metal, as if she is making love to it.

"Mr Lamond mention me?" Gorman distracts me from my reverie and I steer my gaze reluctantly from the beautiful redhead, back to the ugly man. I lean on the bar and order a double Chivas on the rocks.

"The club isn't open yet, mister," the young barman states a fraction nervously.

"A double scotch for the man," Gorman cuts in, broking no argument.

Gorman's foetid breath hits me with a kind of salmon sweetness.

"One for me, just a small one." Gorman fashions a half measure with two fingers.

"And this is?" he queries with a frown in my brothers direction.

"My brother Ruairi," I introduce him.

"You want a drink, Rory?"

"It's Ruairi," Ru grins, "but my friends call me Ru. You can call me Mr McRaney, Mr Gorman."

Gorman's laughter at Ru's sally reveals a veritable collection of gravestone like molars, one of which is fashioned in gold. Coming on it unexpectedly, the gold tooth intermingling with the rest appears strangely incongruous. I'm uncertain whether his apparent solicitousness stems from his desire to keep his job or from a genuine respect. I suspect the former.

"He's a card ain't he?" Gorman guffaws.

"So you both planning on taking over the running of this old club? Look, you gotta know, Mr McRaney, I didn't know anything about it. As far as I know neither does Ronnie. It came as something of a shock at first, but I know Ronnie ain't gonna like it."

Nursing the whisky, I observe Gorman speculatively above the rim of my glass. "I know Engels. I can deal with him."

"What about me? I run the gaming tables mainly."

"So Ray told me. As long as you run them honestly."

He blanches. Eyes slitting narrowly, hawkishly.

"'Course they're honest. You won't find nothing amiss about my tables."

"So, what were you doing with those lovelies then, Jacky? Getting off on it?" I grin at him wryly.

The girls have moved to the bar.

I'm aware I only have to throw the word 'boss' into the mix and I reason that I could have anyone of them simply by snapping my fingers.

A petite blonde sidles up to Ru, introduces herself as Lisa. His arm slips about her waist instinctively. My own arm has now found its way around the waist of the redhead and I ask her name.

"It's Suzanne," she purrs sexily.

Guiltily I think of Caitlan and how much I love her. She still hasn't called me and there is that blond boy in The Liffey Bar in Dublin.

Suzanne is gorgeous and willowy, with the longest legs I have ever seen. My palms feel a fraction chill against the heat of her bare flesh. The scotch has already slid down my insides, conducive to warming me and finding her lips, I close my mouth over them. She offers no protestations, as my hand tightens around her waist and I pull her body against mine, the action is almost a belligerent one but she pays it but a scant attention. When she throws her arms around me, I whisper that there is a room upstairs, if she is interested of course.

"I was interested the minute you entered the room, baby," she smiles coyly, "you're Irish."

"Does it matter?"

"God no. I love Irish accents."

"Look, boys." Gorman realises he has lost at least two of the girls attentions. "We should talk about this."

"There's nothing to talk about, Jacky," I say offhandedly. "I'll wait 'til Engels arrives. You just go about your business and I'll go about mine." I wink at him meaningfully before my mouth descends to Suzanne's once more.

I have no idea why I had suggested the room upstairs. Maybe it's because she is hot and begging for it and I fancy the beautiful dancer so predominantly. Or perhaps I simply realise how much I need sex right then and maybe I am on the rebound because I've convinced myself that Caitlan has dumped me. In fact, I received the distinct impression, after I had spoken to her sister that Mollie has somehow managed to talk Caitlan out of a long distance romance. I haven't moved to Australia for Christ sake. There were practically hourly flights from Dublin to Heathrow. Maybe Mollie had suggested to her sister that I might have used my son as an excuse to return to London once I had had my wicked way with her. She as good as emphasised that fact over the phone.

*

The room upstairs above The Black Garter club has changed somewhat. I guess after 10 years, the décor has to. I'm pleased this is so or else those poignantly embittered memories would return to haunt me. The bed has gone. It was my bed. I'd stayed here the nights I hadn't bothered to return to my wife and baby son. Leanne came to me when Frankie was drunk, which was often. Next to the bedroom is a small lounge. That has now been converted into one room. Two sumptuous black leather corner seats encapsulate the length of a wall. Adjacent to the lounge is a small kitchenette. The original yellow wall cupboards have now been replaced by oak. I remember there is also a small bathroom, where Suzanne dives the minute we arrive, while I wander about the room and attempt to forget the past.

"There's a divan." Suzanne appears in the doorway. Her hair is freshly combed and spills in a tangle of waves to her bare shoulders. She's also thrown on a pale blue negligee.

"There is?" I guess I sound less than enthusiastic because she sidles up to me and slips my hand in hers.

"You haven't changed your mind have you, only you seem to have grown quiet? It's this room isn't it?"

"What about the room?" I regard her with a frown.

"Nothing," she shrugs. "Forget I said anything. You still want me don't you?"

"You know I do." Sod to the memories. They might never have happened. She is here with me now and I want to make love to her.

She helps me to pull out the divan. The leather is cold against her skin or there is something else that makes her shiver. The divan is large, almost the equivalent of a king size bed.

I allow my arm to slink around her waist, pull her to me and fit my lips to hers, crushing them gently at first, then more dominantly. One arm is around my neck, the other frees my erection when she peels down the zipper of my trousers. I tangle her hair with my fingers entwined around the glorious texture. She has beautiful hair, it falls long, almost to her waist. Her eyes are green, like the sea, enlarged by a little too much mascara for my taste but her eyes are the first thing you notice about her face.

Impatiently, she unbuttons my shirt, peeling it away and the palm she's coiled around my penis brings it into full arousal. I can't help but recollect Caitlan and making love in the shower of the Quayside Hotel, how she wanted to be dominated. I long to be the same with Suzanne but maybe she isn't into that kind of thing.

I unfasten the bikini, toss it across the room. She's thrown off the negligee, the panties follow. Her body is slender without an ounce of fat, her height affords her a nubile modelesque beauty.

Both of us are naked and she lowers her body onto mine on the divan, when I am suddenly aware of a perfume. It's exotic aroma assaults my nostrils. The perfume is one I could have sworn is strangely familiar. I'm about to enter her but the perfume has distracted me and I can't help but comment on it. "That perfume you're wearing is a wee bit strong isn't it? I hadn't noticed it before."

"I'm not wearing any perfume."

"Sure it's not me, darlin'. I don't even wear aftershave."

"You don't even shave," she giggles, playing with my beard.

"I do shave. If I didn't I'd look like the old man of the woods with my dark hair. Maybe it's some kind of air freshener."

"It's odd but I can't smell it."

"Maybe your nose is blocked or something."

"No, a lot of people who come to this room mention that perfume. And you can smell it?"

"Sure. Come on sweetheart, I don't care what the hell it is, I've got better things to think of instead of perfume. Only, if it is yours, I'd prefer it if you toned it down a little."

"I told you it isn't…"

My lips crush hers, silencing her. The scent continues to assail me but I guess I'll probably get used to it, because all I can think about is the woman I'm with. She lays beneath me, warm enticing fingers are caressing my balls before the other hand coils like a sensuous snake around my penis as she brings it closer towards her, halfway to paradise. She takes a condom from her bag, fits it on my organ with practiced fingers.

Suzanne propels herself, this dancer's body, supple, graceful as she bends like a willow, in a sort of wheelbarrow fashion before positioning those long legs on each of my shoulders. This enables me to push my erection further into her and I joke something about, "open wide, here it comes."

Oh, this woman sure knows how to please a man. She's the one guiding me, propelling me further, deeper into her, with her legs on my shoulders. I'm coming and coming as I slam into her with an almost animalistic violence.

I look at her, at lowered, mascara eyelids, the slightly open mouth. She murmurs something unintelligible, unless it's because of all the blood pounding inside my head with my efforts that makes me a little hard of hearing. She appears drugged before her eyes open again, the curl of a pure self-satisfied smile dances and flirts around her pink lipsticked mouth. "Oh, God, it's been a long time since I've enjoyed sex so much. I can die happy now," her words end with a prolonged sigh.

For my part, I have to remove a condom from an organ that refuses to grow limp before lying beside her, pretty much exhausted and barely conscious of the trill of a mobile phone demanding attention somewhere in the room. Probably in my coat pocket but Jesus, I'm far too knackered to get up right now.

She lays across me, our bodies touching. Playing with my chest hairs, her fingers manoeuvre toward my crotch again. I kiss her lips, pull her head down to me, tangle her hair with my fingers ploughing through it with the realisation I want to stay like this forever. Our naked bodies fused together. We had sex but I want it again and I know she does also. The phone rings again. I curse, attempt to rouse myself up in the divan, but she pushes me back playfully. "No you don't, Irish boy."

"I have to get up," but my sigh is heavy, filling with reluctance.

"You don't have to answer it if you don't want to. I don't want this to end. And you're still hard."

Her fingers are gently caressing but intrinsically manipulative and conducive to arousing me once more. And bringing her face down forcibly onto mine, my hand still entangled in her hair, I'm uncaring that I might hurt her, I crush my lips to hers so demandingly hard, she is breathless when I release her. She swipes at her mouth, "Jesus, you're a fuckin' great kisser."

"Now I really do have to get up." I half push her from me. Reluctantly she acquiesces, allowing me to slide my legs over the side of the bed, reach for my shirt, until she stalls my hand. "Not yet," her eyes are slitted, her expression dazed, dream like. "You've got a great body, I want to go on looking at it."

"Thanks for the compliment darlin' but I really do have to go."

"So, you really the new boss of the club?"

Sliding an arm around her waist I say, "Sure, it looks like it. Does that make any difference? Do you mean that's why you had sex with me, to gain favour with the boss?"

"God no! What do you take me for? I wanted to get in first, if you'll pardon the pun, before those other bitches had a crack at you. Jesus, after Gorman's ugly face and Ronnie Engels leering at me behind those stupid brown shades he wears, you're the breath of fresh air this place needs. You're gorgeous and if someone was to ask 'do you fuck as good as you look,' then I'd be the first person to agree that you do."

"Then I'll return the compliment. But I really do have to answer that phone," I tell her when it rings again. Before I do, however, I pull her onto my lap and kiss her again.

Checking my phone, I discover four missed calls from Brid, plus a text, "call me ASAP, Aidan. It's important. Sis."

Sliding Levis over my hips I pause to consider why I seem to receive such urgent phone calls when I'm having sex, as if my sister and my ex-wife know exactly when to strike.

Suzanne is rabbiting on about that damned perfume again and why the room's so cold. It's the end of November, darling, the room is bound to be cold, although I'm warm enough. Sex and a double scotch has that effect on a man.

"What the bejaysus you talking about, sweetheart?"

"So, Aidan, you seeing anyone?"

I afford her but a momentary hesitation. "No, why do you ask?"

"Why does a girl ask a good looking guy if he's seeing someone? Firstly, because I don't want to tread on anyone's toes and because I really would like to get to know you better."

"I told you I wasn't. Anyway, what's all this stuff about the room being cold. It is November."

"Just that some of the girls who have come up here who reckon they can smell that exotic perfume say that the room's always cold even with the heating turned up. A murdered woman is supposed to haunt the club. Well this room really."

"Jesus," I laugh. "With the nefarious reputation this joint has, I reckon there were a lot of murders committed here. I know the place dates back to the fifties, if not earlier. Anyway, you don't seem the kind of gal to believe in all that baloney… do you?"

"I thought you Irish believed in spirits and stuff."

"We Irish believe more in the spirits that come out of bottles, darlin', not in the ghosties and things that go bump in the night."

"I don't believe either, but you ask some of the girls. They won't come up here late at night or on their own. Even Jacky Gorman…"

"Don't tell me 'bulldog man's' scared of a few wee spooks?"

"What did you call him?" she giggles, "'bulldog man', well I suppose he does resemble a bulldog. Even he reckons there's something up here. Somebody stayed in this room one night and they heard this woman sobbing."

"Stuff and nonsense. Now I've gotta take this call." I drop onto the bed. Suzanne joins me and slithers a braceleted arm around my waist, lays her head on my shoulder.

"Brid, it's Aidan. What's so important?"

"Where are you?"

"I'll tell you later." I pause to wink at Suzanne.

"Well, wherever you are," she lowers her voice conspiratorially. I enquire why she is whispering.

"I'm at your flat and she's in the next room."

"Who is?" I ask impatiently.

"Your girlfriend, what's her name? Caitlan. She's just arrived from Dublin."

CHAPTER TEN

–

THE ROOM UPSTAIRS

"I have to go," leaping from the divan, my senses are exhilaratingly high, my heart hammering. SHE has come to see me, although the guilt surfaces because I am with another woman.

"What is it? Bad news?" Suzanne asks, concerned.

I dress quickly, haul on my coat and toss her the robe she'd worn earlier.

"No, just the opposite in fact, but I do have to go."

Suzanne is beautiful and sexy. Under different circumstances, I might have wanted her again. Caitlan is so much more. I realise, however, that I shouldn't push Suzanne away too readily. Nevertheless, there is no way I intend to two-time Caitlan. Two-timing invariably results in losing both of them.

"Look, baby," I plant a forefinger beneath her chin, raising her face to mine, so close. I know she wants to kiss me and that I feel the same but I relent, reluctantly, "I'm sorry."

"That sounds ominous. Go on, hit me with the old, 'it's not you, it's me' kind of thing."

"I wasn't going to say that at all. That call just now was from my sister. I wrongly believed my girlfriend had dumped me, because I am seeing someone. My sister rang me to say she's…"

I have no time to finish my explanation because all hell seems to have broken loose. Alarm bells that I mistakenly believe to be sirens, pierce the comparative stillness of the room. Doors bang. Not merely the odd one or two, but it is as if all the doors in the building are slamming shut simultaneously. "The Polis!" I exclaim involuntarily.

Is all this because Engels has returned to discover that I am taking over his club without his express permission? Has Mike Corman, the bouncer, reported me for assault?

The blast of sirens, the doors banging, all serve to remind me of prison, the sounds reminiscent of the aftermath of an escape attempt.

I race to the window, but can't see any police cars in the street. I feel rather than see Suzanne slip her hand into mine.

"Whatever made you think it was the police?"

I half expect the bill to burst in any moment, armed to the teeth, and order me to lie on the floor while a senior officer reads me my rights before bundling my wrists behind me with handcuffs.

"What the fuck's going on?"

"There's probably a fire, that's the fire alarm. When that goes off, all the fire doors shut at once," she explains.

"A fire. Jesus!"

"We're okay behind the fire doors. Really, we should go to the fire point, but as this room's close to the stairs, it's best not to risk it. Anyway..." she flashes a smile from perfect white teeth, "let's look on the bright side, Irish boy."

"There's a bright side?" At least it wasn't the police.

"You really did go pale, Aidan. A sign of guilt?"

"No, just bad memories that's all. So what's the bright side in all this?"

"Well, it is for me. I'm trapped behind a fire door with the best-looking guy I've seen in ages. 'Course I might have known you'd be seeing someone. Guys like you don't come along every day. Usually the punters at the club are either old, ugly or balding. And they disgust me."

"So why do you do it? And thanks for the compliment."

"I do it because it pays the rent and, I must admit, I enjoy it. It's better than some boring old nine to five job."

Hearing the sound of hurried footsteps on the stairs, I rush to open the door on a livid faced Ronnie Engels.

His mouth opens, then closes, disbelief negotiating his expression. "What the fuck! I thought that was you, McRaney." He flicks me a venomous glance before training the same on Suzanne. "And what the hell are you doing with this toe rag?" His mouth clenched, his eyes rendered impenetrable behind brown-lensed spectacles.

"Ronnie, well this is a surprise," my retort is acidic.

His jacket off reveals a white shirt worn with black trousers. Engels is about my age. His crinkly hair is dark, cut even shorter than when I'd seen him last. He sports the impression of a man who is about to burst a gut.

"Don't you fuckin' 'Ronnie' me, McRaney. And you, darlin', get back to work. And McRaney, I might have known you couldn't keep it in your fuckin' pants for long," he blusters. "The last time I saw you, you was helping a pissed Verdi Benson from the club. So you're not seeing her now?"

"I haven't seen Verdi in a while. I heard she'd moved to Kent."

"I don't fuckin' know," Engels growls.

"I thought there was a fire, Ronnie. The doors all slammed shut and the alarms went off," Suzanne interjects.

"Yeah, some fuckin' short sighted maniac decides to light up a fag in my office."

"Why short sighted?" I enquire.

Engels remains angry. I am determined, however, not to rise to his taunts.

"Because he didn't bother to read the no smoking signs all over the fuckin' show," he continues his tirade. "And I told you to get back to work, missy," he hisses at Suzanne, "and leave this fuckin' toe rag alone."

"Okay, okay," she shrugs. Before she leaves, she smiles my way and I discover myself alone with Ronnie Engels, while I reason that I should be getting back to Caitlan. She's come all the way from Dublin, plus I have cause to wonder what Brid might be saying to her. My sister is a born interrogator. By the time she's finished, I'm sure she will have induced Caitlan to lay bare her life history. What concerns me most, however, is what Brid is telling her about me.

"So, McRaney…" Engels waits a decent interval until Suzanne has gone. I thought of following in her wake but Engels has closed the door. At least his jacket is off. Unless he's concealed anything behind his back, he doesn't appear to be packing heat. "And the bleedin' short sighted maniac I was talking about reckons he's your kid brother."

"Ruairi, Jesus! Is he the one who lit up a smoke?"

"Blimey, how many of you are there? There's the ex-squaddie, built like a wrestler, the pretty sister who died and the other one, the little red headed nurse."

The familiar aggression surfaces again.

"You leave my family out of this."

"Sorry, mate, I didn't mean nothing. It's just that you Micks seem to breed like rabbits. Anyway," he allows himself an unaccustomed grin, or is it more in the way of a grimace? "Your kid brother's got a bit wet. 'Cos when the alarms went off and the doors slammed, the sprinklers came on. 'Course you'll have to pay for the cleaning bills. Oh, I almost forgot, you're taking over the club, ain't you? So Jacky tells me. So you can pay for your own cleaning bills," he chuckles.

"So, you been to see Ray Lamond?"

"Sure I have. If you must know Lamond was the one who asked me to visit him in prison, where he told me he wanted me to run this joint. I also saw Max Sorenson, Lamond's solicitor."

"You oughta know Maxie's more crooked than his old man was."

"It was his old man who got me let off with that eight stretch instead of a possible 20 for pumping that Fitzwalter guy. So I guess you're looking for some kind of fight over this, Engels." My sigh is heavy. His expression alters, unreadable behind the incongruous brown shades. He sinks his weight into the divan. I haven't had a chance to clear away since Suzanne and I...

"You have been screwing her, McRaney!" he exclaims and slaps a hand vehemently onto the unit. "I was fuckin' right. Fuckin' knew it."

"Sure," I edge uncomfortably, guilt surfacing again because of Caitlan's impromptu arrival. "But I'd appreciate it if you kept it to yourself."

"Blimey, I envy you, I always have."

"Why should you envy me?"

"'Cos you got it all."

"What's that supposed to mean?"

"Looks, hair. You work out?"

"No, I don't have time for that fuckin' crap."

"Well the club has a gym and I work out. I reckon though, if I worked out for a month of fuckin' Sundays, I'd never look like you."

I couldn't resist a smile. "I didn't know you cared, Engels, you making a pass?"

"Fuck off, McRaney. So, anyway, back to your earlier question. I'm not looking for any kind of fight. Against you, I'd be mad. Look at what you did to my boy."

"Sorry?"

"Mike Corman. I had to persuade him not to make a case of it."

"That was noble of you, Ronnie," I say sarcastically.

"Look, McRaney, you and me have both done time. We know the score as it were."

"Is this going to take long? I've got a girl on the boil back at my flat. This wee girl has come all the way from Dublin and she's with my sister right now. By the time she's told Caitlan, my girlfriend, stuff about me... well, she'll be on the next flight back. So is there a point to all this huh?"

"Fuckin' hell, McRaney. There ain't many geezers the lovely Suzanne will look twice at, let along get near. Then you got this Mick bird at home. I don't wanna get in the way of your Paddy conjugals. You must have kissed that fuckin' Blarney Stone."

"Funny that, 'cos I've never seen it. Like I said, I didn't want to take over this place, only Sorenson's promised me if I give it a trial period, he'd take a custody case for my son."

"I'm guessing Lamond told you to sack me, right?"

"Something like that," I mutter. Although Lamond had indicated, with that pretend gun firing motion, he'd prefer something more permanent.

"So what do we do? Fight a duel?" I quip.

"No need for heroics, McRaney. You get the correct paperwork, I doubt if Sorenson will hesitate to guarantee that. See, I got my eye on a little club out Essex way. You're welcome to The Black Garter."

I can scarcely believe that Ronnie Engels should relinquish The Black Garter quite so readily. "Why? No arguments, no fight?"

"Not at all, I'm sick of this gaff, sick of Lamond and trying to prevent this club from sinking into the mire as it were."

"What's that supposed to mean?" I am beginning to get an uneasy feeling about this. I expected Engels to bluster, to argue, maybe even throw a punch. Yet he appears almost delighted at the prospect of someone else taking over the place.

"In a coupla months I'll be 33 and I've already got a fuckin' ulcer, you ain't much younger than me."

"I'll be 30 in June. So where is all this leading? And I'm sorry you've got an ulcer."

"I thought when Lamond got banged up that things would be okay. I mean, they have been 'cos me and Jacky have made sure of it. He's a good ole boy is Jacky. He might look like a bulldog chewing a wasp, but he'll stand by you. Jacky reckons you want to turn this club around. Which way?"

"Jesus, what do you mean which way, to make it respectable, what else? And I know you were a pimp because Verdi told me you were."

"Not anymore. The prostitution, the drug rackets, the protection, was all down to Ray Lamond. I don't expect you to believe that, I can tell by your doubting expression, but it's true. Why do you think Ray's in that place?"

"Because he was busted for firearms possession, tax evasion and housing a crematorium in his grounds."

"What I was going to say was, he's in that place because I put him there."

I stare at him in disbelief, while my heart thumps unwittingly. "I thought you and he were good buddies."

He shakes his head. "I know it sounds hard to believe but I was pushed into a corner. Now, no one knows this."

"Then why are you telling me?"

"Because I figured you should know about some of the pitfalls in running this club, about the 'suits'."

"The 'suits'?" I echo, but I already know don't I? Because Verdi had referred to them sniffing around Lamond's gaff before he was arrested.

"You mean the polis?" I feign ignorance.

"No. The filth won't touch Lamond. There's something else. I don't want you going into this 'blind' so to speak. I don't expect you to believe this, McRaney, but I got a daughter. Rebecca. She's six. Something like your ex. My missus divorced me because of the stuff at the club and me working for Lamond, but I get access to Becky. Not much but it has to suffice."

"I can understand that. I have a nine year old son I'm fighting my ex for more access to."

"That's fuckin' women for you," he tuts morosely.

"Sure, but you've lost me. What has all this got to do with your daughter?"

"I'm getting to it. See, the 'suits', I mean I don't know their head guy. Those two were merely hirelings, straight out of the bleedin' X-Files they looked. They didn't give me any names. Just suits. Dark glasses, slicked-back hair. I mean, they could have been fuckin' robots for all I know. They said if I delivered Lamond to them, they'd have him arrested and his concerns closed down. I know me and Lamond didn't always see eye to eye but there was no way I was going to hand him over to anybody. Besides, Lamond's too well protected to do something like that. They said I was to get him pissed, lower his resolve. When I argued against it, they snatched Becky."

"Jesus." I shiver involuntarily, a cold feeling clutching my insides. "So what did you do?"

"I got Lamond drunk at his place. Put the central heating up a bit. He was sweating. So I suggested we went out for some air. The 'suits' had been busy digging up the dirt on him so the bill could burst in and arrest Lamond."

"I thought you said the bill wouldn't touch him."

"The bill let the 'suits' pave the way, so to speak."

"And your daughter?"

"My ex had been all for calling the police but the 'suits' warned me that if she did, we wouldn't see Becky any more. Anyway, she was delivered back to my ex safe and sound. She didn't remember a thing about it or her kidnappers. She said she was asleep all the time. I think they may have kept her drugged but if I hadn't delivered Lamond, it doesn't bear thinking about what might have happened to her. I do know something about these 'suits'. Whoever they are, they're fuckin' manipulative."

I attempt not to allow Ronnie Engels' narrative concern me unduly. Nevertheless, I did worry about Patrick. How safe is he? Maybe I'll call Judy later, recollecting I was seeing him this weekend for a whole two days. Then I thought about Caitlan. A latent excitement was managing to override Engels' story plus the thought of my girlfriend meeting my son. With a fifty per cent access, maybe we can become a proper family, certain that my son, despite his bathroom tantrums, will love her as much as I do.

Engels was mouthing something about, "'Course you've heard about the boys from Brazil, haven't you, McRaney? Or more like the Dominican Republic. That's where the real dealers are."

"Dealers?" I echo obtusely. "Isn't 'the boys from Brazil' a movie or something?" I inject a note of humour into my voice, but one I scarcely feel.

"It's important you don't let them into the club. So do you think you and Shaggy can make a go of this place?"

"Shaggy?" I laugh.

"Sorry, but your kid brother reminds me of Shaggy from 'Scooby Doo'."

When a couple of loud raps sound on the door we both jump, startled simultaneously and regard one another with raised brows. At least the fiasco of the fire alarms seems to have died down. Engels is about to rise, but I get there first and open the door on a rather dishevelled kid brother. His hair is wet, hanging like rat-tails to his shoulders. His tee shirt and jeans appear to be soaked and he rubs a hand down the legs of the latter.

"Can we go now, Aid?" he sounds a trifle vexed.

Engels smiles. I can't blame him, even if it's at my brother's expense.

"It's not fuckin' funny," Ru directs his resentment to Engels.

"Well, you shouldn't have lit up a fuckin' fag should you?" he admonishes.

"The minute the alarms sounded the fire doors bang up and the sprinklers come on."

"Where were you?" I ask Ru.

It is Engels who responds, however. "He was in my office, just mooching around I suppose. Guess it's yours now."

"So you were up here all the time?" Ru accuses.

"I'm sorry." I would have liked to have learned more of what Engels intended to impart. Whatever it was, it sounded far too ominous to repeat in front of my brother. I knew about the boys from Brazil of course, big time drug dealers whom Frankie Lamond and possibly his brother Ray, bought drugs from for exorbitant amounts of money. I wasn't a minder anymore. Once the paperwork was completed, which I promised to attend to tomorrow, the club would be mine.

"Come on, Shaggy," I tease my brother and ruffle his wet locks affectionately. "Let's get you home and out of those wet clothes," which he responds to with a frown and a nonplussed, "You what?"

"No hard feelings, McRaney?" Engels extends a hand.

I shake the proffered hand eventually. "Sure. I guess not."

And to Ru, "now you read the signs next time, hey. Sorry it took so long, but me and your big brother were just doing a bit of male bonding."

*

Swinging the Cabriolet into the street, I inform Ru that Caitlan is at my flat and that I'd received a call from Brid.

"Blimey!" His brows shoot up, astonished. "You mean I get to meet the gorgeous Caitlan? She's turned up at your flat?"

"Apparently." I roll a much-needed smoke and flare my lighter.

"So who was that bird you was with? You and she just disappeared and that was the last time I saw you."

"What bird?" I stiffen. The last thing I need is to be reminded that I'd fucked Suzanne in the room above the club, when I have another woman waiting for me at home.

"Then you must have a short memory, Bruv, 'cos the last I saw of you, you had your arm around her and you was snoggin' her face off. And in case you need your memory refreshed, she was a tall redhead with a model figure and legs all the way up to her…"

"There was no bird. You must have imagined it, Ru. So don't keep talking about it, okay?"

"I know," Ru grins. "You don't want Caitlan to find out you got your leg over with another bird. I take it that's what happened and don't tell me she was just showing you around, 'cos I know you too well, you can't resist a pretty…"

"For fuck's sake, Ru!" I have heard enough, mainly because he is right and I can't resist a beautiful woman who happens to offer it on a plate, as it were. Nevertheless, I decide it's wisest to lie. "There was no other bird, okay. She blew me out anyway. And I didn't get my leg over."

"Okay, okay, I won't say any more."

"Then fuckin' don't. So what's this about you nearly setting fire to the place? What happened?"

"Well, I was with this bird, then Gormless calls her over."

"Gormless?"

"Yeah, that ugly guy Jacky Gorman. She says she won't be long. I tell her I'll wait in that office. I sort of got bored waiting around and I forgot about the no smoking signs, so I lit up a fag didn't I? Anyway, who was that guy you were talking to? You and he looked pretty pally. And what did he mean by 'no hard feelings'?"

"I love you dearly, Ru, but sometimes there are things I can't even tell you, okay?"

"I know you have a past, and the people you mixed with but I don't like secrets. And I'm not some wet behind the ears kid, you know."

"Then stop behaving like one."

"Fuck, man, what's that supposed to mean? Just 'cos I forgot about them no smoking signs. I need you to trust me. So I joke about and that, but I do know what's gone on in your past, man."

"And what's that, Ru?"

"About when you carried a gun and stuff, it won't be like that again will it?"

"What do you mean?"

"That club's got a reputation, always did have."

"Not anymore, Bruv. We'll make it respectable - no more guns or drugs. When I've signed those papers tomorrow, the first thing I'll do is get the decorators in, change that joint completely. Do you know what I'm going to do?"

He shakes his head.

"Caitlan's a singer. You should have heard her sing in The Liffey Bar. Even old Flanagan had a tear in his eye. I'm going to change the place, make it more like The Liffey."

"You serious? That was in Ireland. I mean here in Soho? You're going to turn it into a Paddy club?"

"Why not? It can be done. Please, Ru, have a wee bit of faith in your brother…" I allow my words to trail when the mobile rings in my coat and I ask Ru to check it.

"It's probably Brid wondering where I've got to."

"No, Bruv, it ain't. And I'm not speaking to her."

"Her?"

"Yeah, it's fuckin' Judy ain't it?"

"You there, Aidan?" I hear her voice, it's raised, angry.

"Just tell her I'm driving. I'll call her later."

"Me! Talk to the witch of Esher?"

"Jesus, Ru, she'll hear you."

Ru makes a face. "Judy, he's driving. He'll talk to you later." He is compelled to hold the phone away from him.

"Well, he'd better, 'cos it's important. Don't forget to tell him that, Ruairi."

"Love you too, Jude," mutters Ru under his breath before he concludes the call. "She's well upset, Aid, I think she's been drinking."

CHAPTER ELEVEN

-

A VISITOR FROM IRELAND

"Jude, calm down," I urge. "What is it? What's wrong?"

"Oh don't sound so bloody calm about it, Aidan. You've only gone for fifty per cent custody of Patrick, haven't you?"

"Sure I have." I refuse to deny the fact. Also I'm as surprised by the outcome as she obviously is. So Sorenson was true to his word.

"Don't play bloody innocent with me, Aidan McRaney. I don't know how you managed to do it; custody orders take weeks, social workers breathing down your neck and you've just been released from prison. I allowed you a fortnightly access to Patrick, but that was all. Now I get home today and there was this letter from some guy named Maxwell Sorenson, and I bet he's some relation to that Sorenson guy who got you let off with a reduced sentence. What games are you playing now, Aidan? Are you mixing with gangsters again? Because if you are…"

"For God's sake, Jude! Shut up and listen."

Her angry tirade is reminiscent of a battering ram pulsating inside my head. Ru is right, I can tell she's been drinking. The tone of her voice is marginally slurred.

"Don't tell me to shut up. This is spite isn't it?"

"Spite for what, Jude? I haven't done anything to you!"

"Because I wouldn't let you fuck me."

"Jesus." I run a hand through my hair with exasperation. "That's got nothing to do with it. Anyway, I thought it was the other way round."

"What do you mean?"

"You wanted to fuck me, remember. It's me who said nothing doing."

"You bastard. Trust you to think of that. Who is this Maxwell Sorenson?"

"If you read his letter, then you'll know he's a solicitor."

"I'll tell you something, McRaney. You've got to know I'm not that naïve little girl you can boss around anymore. Or brag to your pals that I'm easy and fuck when it suited you. You know I loved you, you bastard…"

Jesus, she really must be drunk to rake all that up. "I'm sorry for the way I treated you back then. And you've gotta know I'm not that kid anymore…"

"I know what women are like around you, with your looks, all that long curly hair and that fuckin' accent."

"Jesus, where the fuck's all this going, Jude?" I attempt to conceal a smile at her complimentary appraisal of my attributes.

"You've promised some hoods something haven't you? That bloody Lamond guy. I bet he's got something to do with this. You haven't agreed to mind him have you?"

"No, Jude. Lamond's inside."

"Well something's going on. We'll talk this weekend. Fifty per cent access," she muses. "That means you'll have to drive down to Esher to take him to school because I'm not uprooting him. In 18 months, he'll be going to secondary school and I've already selected the best school in Surrey. Then there's your flat…"

I catch myself stiffening with surfacing anger. "What about my flat?" I snap. "What's wrong with it?"

"It's not what Patrick's used to. Shit…"

"What's wrong now?"

"I'm running out of juice, but you're not off the hook, Aidan. I'll talk to you at the weekend."

"I'll look forward to it," I mutter sarcastically, but her line has gone dead.

I hadn't expected Sorenson to come up with the 'goods' quite so soon, especially as I haven't yet signed any paperwork relative to ownership of the club. Not signing anything indicates that maybe I can still back out. I've already gained a reasonable access to my son. Who was I kidding? If I back out now, Sorenson would ultimately discover some means of reneging on the access, of that I am certain.

Alternatively, I am now beginning to actually look forward to it, despite Ronnie Engels' less than positive outlook of my ownership of the club.

Ru has already gone ahead and let himself into my flat, while I consider that every conversation I have with Jude invariably results in us both arguing, and the reason why I preferred to talk with her beforehand and not allow Caitlan to hear anything of our conversation.

I put all these unwelcome thoughts on hold instinctively when I see her. Brid is being her customary, gossiping self. She usually manages to dominate any conversation. My four-year-old niece

Samantha sits on the settee next to Caitlan, who is reading a story to her.

As no one is aware of my entrance, I am able to indulge a moment in which to savour her beauty and hope that nothing untoward will occur to spoil the relationship I am desirous of continuing with her.

Ru is being Ru of course. Half-dressed, he's only wearing his jeans. A momentary jealousy flows through me because his body is on display. Albeit it is scarcely a muscular physique, nevertheless it is still a male body and I am compelled to admonish him, "put some bloody clothes on, Ru, for God's sake!"

"I was looking for a tee shirt," he mutters. Three sets of female eyes shoot up at my entrance. It is Sammy who makes the first move. She rushes headlong into my arms, exclaiming "Uncle Aidan!" excitedly.

"Hey, Sammy, how are you sweetheart?" I collect her up into my arms. My niece is a little chubby with her round apple cheeks and curly red-gold hair like my sister.

"Aidan!" Caitlan breathes my name huskily. She is on her feet and I lower Sammy to the ground gently, moving into Caitlan's arms. "Oh, Aidan, I missed you so much. I hope you didn't mind me coming to see you." She appears anxious when she says it.

"God, no darlin', I missed you too." Wrapping my arms around her, oblivious of my family looking on, I crush my lips on Caitlan's, until I hear Brid clearing her throat. I release her reluctantly.

"Where were you, Aidan? I called you nearly an hour ago," Brid says. "Ru said you bought a nightclub. What nightclub?"

"Sorry, Sis, do you mind if we discuss it later?" Jesus, Ru and his big mouth.

"Sure. I suppose so." She sounds disgruntled at my suggestion.

Caitlan says, "you bought a nightclub?" She searches my face. I release her, haul off my coat, tell her that I haven't as much as bought one, rather it sort of landed in my lap.

"So, you caught a flight or did you come on the ferry?" I ask Caitlan, in an endeavour to change the subject, guiding her to the sofa where I join her. The minute I sit down, little Sammy bounces onto my lap, asking me if Caitlan is my girlfriend.

"Out of the mouth of babes," my sister tuts and appears suitably embarrassed.

"Sure, I'd like to think she is," I tell her.

"I caught a flight," Caitlan adds quietly.

She is wearing her familiar black sweater and tartan skirt with a pair of high, black leather boots. Her hair is pulled back into a ponytail.

"I've never done that before, I mean alone. The last time I came to London…" She turns her attention to Brid. Predictably, my sister's own attention is rapt, reminiscent of a small bird waiting on a few scraps from its parent. "I told Aidan about it," she pauses to smile at me. "My sister came with me. I almost fainted on the underground."

"Fainted?" Trust Brid to pounce on the word, her brows knitted into a frown.

"I guess it can get a wee bit stuffy on there." I dive in swiftly in order to spare Caitlan's embarrassment when Brid regards her with undisguised curiosity. "I prefer to drive most of the time. So what did Mollie have to say when you left?"

"Och, we had this awful row. But then I called her when I got to Heathrow."

"So, you came here from Heathrow? Why didn't you ask me to pick you up?"

"I came by cab. Sure now, I know it was stupid of me, but I think I put your number in my phone in the wrong order, but I had also written down your address, so I got here eventually." She presses my hand and I slip an arm around her.

Ru's dark brows appear to be set in the permanently raised position. He listens in complete fascination. I note that he is wearing one of my tee shirts. It's khaki coloured with a picture of an automatic pistol on the front. "Is that my tee shirt, Ru?"

"Yeah, it's pretty hot ain't it?" he enthuses. "Can I keep it?"

"Ugh. Where did you get that awful tee shirt, Aidan?" asks Brid with thinly disguised disdain in her voice.

"I don't know. I've had it a while. I think Harry gave it to me." And to Caitlan, "did Mollie tell you I called a couple of nights ago? She said you were lying down with a migraine."

"Aid thought you'd dumped him," Ru says, until I silence him with a withering glance before the little shit can say more.

"Dumped you!" Caitlan exclaims in disbelief. "God no. Whatever gave you that idea?"

"Your sister actually, she was under the impression I'd abandoned you when I had to fly back to London."

"And your son, how is he now?"

"He's fine thanks, Caitlan," Brid replies. "You know he's got an ex-wife?" she gestures at me.

"I thought you were married at first, didn't I?" she smiles at me delicately, uncertainly, "when I saw the picture of your son in your wallet."

"We're divorced, almost five years. And when I spoke to your sister, she told me if I broke your heart, she'd send Niall to break my legs, I think that was what she actually said."

"Niall's a big guy but he's a gentle soul. He'd never do that. My sister might though. She bosses poor Niall about something dreadful, even more than she does me."

"Jesus, she sounds scary," Ru observes.

"She can be, can't she, Aidan? He's met her," Caitlan responds, "I suppose after what happened she thinks she can be both mother and sister to me."

"After what happened, sweetheart?" I ask, wondering what is to come and I thought I had problems.

"Sure, I guess we shouldn't have secrets from one another should we?" The beautiful emerald eyes encompass us.

In turn, my sister flashes me a scarcely concealed meaningful regard that refutes me to confide the things I've done.

Predictably, Brid agrees, adding, "secrets have ways of coming out eventually."

Choosing to ignore her, I prompt Caitlan to explain, but only if she really wants to, I tell her.

"Our father left us when I was still at school. He'd been seeing another woman."

I observe Brid nod sympathetically.

Caitlan continues. "They moved to Omagh. Ma was heartbroken naturally. I used to hear her crying in the night. I cried too."

Hugging her close I assure her that she doesn't have to relate any more if she doesn't wish to. Nevertheless, I feel as if she wants us to know. "Mollie was already living in her flat in Fenian Street but I was still at school. I wanted to be a children's nanny, would you believe?" She cuddles Sammy to her when my niece decides to snuggle in-between us. Occupying the facing chair, Brid's gaze never once leaves Caitlan, as if she is determined to ferret out her innermost thoughts on behalf of her beloved brother.

"I was 16. My ma picked me up from school as usual. I could tell she'd been drinking, I could smell it on her breath but I didn't want to say anything. I wish I had. Then she took another route home, one we didn't often use because it took us right into the Dublin traffic. Then she started driving on the wrong side of the road and much too fast. I told her to slow down, well I was sort of screaming at her I suppose. When she crashed the car I think she wanted to kill herself."

"Jesus!" Ru mutters, his face paling.

"Sweetheart," I mouth sympathetically and kiss the top of her head.

"But to try and take you with her, that's hardly fair," Brid says.

"I really don't know but we hit this car head on. Ma was pronounced dead on arrival at the hospital and… and…" she pauses to swallow uncomfortably, "so was I."

"You what!" I guess we all exclaim in unison.

"It's okay, I'm not a ghost." Her gentle laughter returns us to the present. "But I was told that I'd 'died' for more than five minutes. I was in hospital for almost nine months. The migraines started after the accident. I suffered, amongst other things, a fractured skull and bruising on the brain. That's why I get a wee bit jittery and that chamomile tea helps to calm me down. Now, if you want me to catch the next flight back to Dublin… I haven't unpacked my case."

It seems a while before any of us recover from Caitlan's confession, even Ru is speechless for once. It was left to me to remind her that I will prevent her from leaving, even if I have to tie her to the chair.

"She might enjoy that," Ru quips.

"Ruairi, language!" Brid admonishes her brother. "So, Caitlan, how long ago did this happen? You said you were 16." Her gaze falls directly, meaningfully on me. The look is easily interpreted as 'maybe this girl is too young for you, brother'.

She considers. "About three years ago. 2008."

"You're 19?" persists Brid.

"Sure, if that's not a sad story, darlin'," I swiftly interject, before Brid can say more.

"Yes it is a sad story, Caitlan," little Sammy agrees and cuddles up closer to her.

They have only known one another for a short time, my niece and my girlfriend, but they have already drawn close. I am certain that Patrick will feel the same about Caitlan as his cousin does. "My auntie died too. She was only 18," Sammy adds, surprising us all.

"I know. Your Uncle Aidan told me," Caitlan says.

"Anyway," I change the subject, having no desire to discuss my sister Laurena's death. It is much too painful for all of us. "We'll have to keep a plentiful supply of chamomile tea in won't we? It's not something I normally buy."

"Urgh, sounds disgusting," Ru says. "Sorry, Caitlan, isn't it made from flowers or something?"

"It's a sort of herb, Ruairi," she laughs. "But chamomiles are essentially flowers I suppose."

"Caitlan brought some chamomile tea with her didn't you, Caitlan? From Dublin, in her bag," Brid says, as if she is speaking to a child.

My lips purse with a thinly disguised acrimony at my sister. I smile and hug my girlfriend closer. "That's good, darlin'. Saves me buying some for a wee while. So, have any of you tasted chamomile tea?"

"Once," Brid admits. "I'm sorry, but I prefer the original. Peppermint's good for indigestion, apparently. We even serve it in the hospital. So boys, we've skirted around this long enough, with the benefits of chamomile tea. Tell me about this nightclub, Aidan. I hope it's not that awful 'Black Garter' dive in Soho is it?" She shoots us both speculative glances. For his part, Ru appears a fraction sheepish. So I guess it's up to me.

"It's okay, Ru, you don't have to look so worried, man. And yeah, it's The Black Garter!"

"I bloody knew it!" Brid exclaims. "I'm sorry, Caitlan, I don't usually swear but sometimes my brothers infuriate me. That place should have been razed to the ground years ago."

"Well Ru nearly managed to set fire to it," I quip.

"What happened?" Caitlan asks curiously.

I explain about Ru lighting a cigarette and setting off the fire alarms, the fire doors banging shut and the sprinklers coming on.

"So that's why you were wet." Brid's mouth is set. "So how come you got lumbered with that place? I hope you didn't enter into it lightly and you should have burned the place down, so you should. Bejaysus, Aidan, that place of all places," she adds with a snort.

"It's cool, Brid, calm down," I attempt to placate her, "I can handle it alright. The place was going for a song, okay, since the owner's been away." How easy it is to lie rather than tell the truth. That a mob boss had requested I ran his club while he is inside, in exchange for a fifty per cent access to my son. Nevertheless, Brid retorts, "in jail more like," scornfully. "Oh, Aidan!"

I refuse to glance at Caitlan and wish that Brid would give her mouth a rest once in a while.

"Anyway, Aid's gonna turn it around from what it was," Ru says.

"What's that supposed to mean?" Brid demands. "The only way you can turn that place around is like I said, raze it to the ground. So you've bought a nightclub, Aidan. That's a new low, even for you, Bruv. What do you know about running a nightclub anyway?"

"Last time I saw you, you were a landscape gardener, Aidan," Caitlan points out.

"Sure, but my brother Harry went and sold the business didn't he?" I tell her.

"So how you going to turn it around, move it to somewhere upmarket?" Brid says sarcastically.

"No. Aid reckons he's going to turn it into an Irish bar," Ru says.

Rising abruptly from her seat, Brid tuts, rolls her eyes and predictably shakes her head in particular Bridget modus operandi.

"What do you mean an Irish bar? Jesus, Aidan, it'll only attract the wrong crowd."

"The Irish, hopefully," I grin.

"We're not in Ireland. The only people you'll get in your club, if you're trying to cater for the Irish, are navvies, big muscle-bound building workers, especially weekends, whose only interest will be in getting drunk. I'm sorry to put a damper on things, boys, but you sure about this? And Ru, I suppose you're going to help him?"

"I was planning to. What's wrong with that? Jesus, Sis, you never give us any encouragement," Ru retorts.

"And Ru, so you've decided to go AWOL from uni for a year and who is it who pays some of your tuition fees? 'Tis meself, that's who it is."

Brid's accent is so overly pronounced when she is angry that I half expect her to lapse into Gaelic. She addresses Caitlan, whose small frame appears to shrink into my big leather sofa.

"Brid, Sis," I sigh impatiently, "haven't you got tea to make at home? Any shifts to do at the hospital?"

"No, I've finished for the day. I'm sorry, I really don't mean to be a grouch and I'm sure if you work hard, you'll manage to turn the club around. So, Aidan, how much did you pay for it?"

"I... I rented it for a song," I say hesitantly, "does it matter?"

"Och, what must you think of me, Caitlan?" Brid says. It was just a shock that's all. Sure, if I shouldn't be used to my brothers giving me surprises."

There is, however, the semblance of an affectionate smile curling her lips when she regards me. "I suppose I shouldn't try to be a mother to them, but I do care about all my brothers. We lost Mum. We lost Laurie our kid sister. My brother Harry's gone to live in Italy. I've only got these two rogues now. And as I said, I love them dearly but sometimes I could bash their stubborn heads together." Brid places a hand against my cheek, pecks a kiss on Caitlan's. We move to the door preparing to see my sister out when Brid turns to Caitlan. "It's lovely to meet you, Caitlan. Like I said, if you want to come to mass with me next Sunday…"

"Brid, for God's sake!" I exclaim but am forced to apologise for my blasphemous misuse of His name in front of my sister.

Brid says, "I was going to say that our priest Father Mulligan is a lovely man."

"'Course he is," Ru giggles oddly school-girlishly.

"What's the matter with you, Ruairi?" Brid invariably calls him by his full name when she is annoyed with him. "Ignore him, Caitlan, that boy will never grow up. So it'll soon be Christmas. Are you going to stay in London with my brother? Or I suppose you'll be returning to Dublin?"

Caitlan regards me hopefully when she says, "I don't know, it's up to Aidan."

"What about Mollie?" I ask.

"Och, she'll have Niall," she shrugs, making me wonder if the 'awful row' with her sister she'd spoken of has actually been resolved.

"I'd love you to stay, sweetheart," I say.

"Then I'll stay."

"Before then, you must come and have a meal with me, both of you," Brid says, "and you," she turns her attention to Ru, "you can come back with me, give your brother and his girlfriend some peace and I've got a practice with Maura at the church tonight so you can babysit Sammy. And don't give her that pizza like you did last time. It made her sick, Ru."

"Uncle Aidan," Sammy is a small figure barely reaching to my knees, "are you and Caitlan going to get married?"

We all stare at her in astonishment.

"Out of the mouth of babes." Brid clutches her daughter's hand tightly. "Now don't be so nosey you. We'll go before she says anymore."

Lowering my tall 6' 2" height to my niece's level, I have no idea what it is that prompts me to ask her if she really needs an answer to that question.

"No she doesn't," Brid says quickly.

Ignoring my sister, I say quietly, "the answer to that is yes, Sammy. Yes, I'll marry her if she'll have me."

Colouring to the roots of her dark hair, Caitlan mutters, "I have to use the bathroom."

CHAPTER TWELVE

-

MOLLIE'S CONCERNS

I suppose my impromptu response to my niece Samantha's question, were Caitlan and I going to be married, has come as something of a surprise. Even Brid is at a loss for words for once.

Out of earshot of anyone else, Ru whispers to me, "try before you buy, Bruv. Oh, I forgot, you already have." For which he receives a playful push from yours truly.

Brid calls "bye" to Caitlan and to me, "we'll leave you alone now. Sure if she might need a stiff drink after that. I think your wee girlie's in shock, so she is. Are you sure? I mean about getting married again, Aidan?"

"I've never been more certain of anything in my life, Sis."

"She's a sweet girl and an Irish Catholic too."

According to my sister, what other qualifications did she possibly need?

After everyone had left, I wonder with a sense of unease, if I might have been too hasty and upset Caitlan because of it. I hear her bustling around, first in the bathroom, then my bedroom. I observe her from the doorway in the process of unpacking her suitcase. She obviously hasn't heard my approach and I slip an arm around her waist and nuzzle her neck.

"At last we're alone. I thought they'd never leave."

She practically jumps out of her skin at my approach. "Oh, Aidan, you gave me the fright of my life."

"You knew it was me. I'm sorry about what I said about us getting married. If it wasn't much too presumptuous of me. Did I upset you, baby?"

She twists herself around in my arms and I'm astonished to witness tears standing in her eyes.

"Am I that bad to be married to? You've been crying." I trace a finger the length of her cheek in order to brush away the wetness.

"I'd love to be married to you. That's if you meant it and you didn't say it just to shock your sister. I could tell you were getting impatient with her."

"Sure I meant it sweetheart, and it wasn't to shock my sister, but I was getting impatient because I wanted you all to myself. I do love you, you know." How easy it is to say because I have not told a lie. "So what's brought the tears on?"

"Because I love you so much Aidan, and when you mentioned marriage I couldn't believe it. I was so overcome that I felt the tears well up and I didn't want your brother and sister to see them and it was all right to come into this room wasn't it? I saw there was a double…"

Pressing my lips to hers is conducive to silencing her flow of words. "I wanted you to sleep with me," I say, releasing her gently. "If you didn't I'd think you were pissed off with me."

"I'd never be that, Aidan. Do you want to?"

"What do you think?" My hand has already manoeuvred its way beneath her skirt, my palm is hot against the coolness of her thigh. Unzipping her skirt, she drops it to the floor, yanks off the sweater. She has already removed her boots. She begins to undress me. Our clothes tossed aside, both of us naked.

Caitlan lies beneath me on the bed while I straddle her. I'm erect as I've been practically from the outset when I'd first seen her again sitting on my sofa. Our hands rove one another. Her long fingernails claw my back. When I ease myself up in the bed and lay beneath her, she slides herself on top of me, her body overflowing with passion in my arms. Her long hair falling across my face, she lowers her head down, closes her mouth around my organ. I want her to stop momentarily because she is getting me there much too quickly.

"I'd do anything to please you, you know that," she murmurs.

"You please me just being with me, sweetheart."

She straddles me now, while I slam my hardness into her. Sometimes she is the ostensible childwoman. Nevertheless, when we make love, she is indisputably a woman. Again, I refuse to concern myself that I might make her pregnant. I simply want her and would give her a child unquestionably.

The sex act is over. Both she and I are spent, exhausted. She lies beside me, her head resting against my chest.

Realising how much I need a smoke, I raise myself up in the bed and reach for the tobacco and papers I keep in my bedside drawer. Her eyes are closed. I thought she had fallen asleep. She's obviously felt my movement beside her because she murmurs, "what are you doing, Aidan?"

"Just fancied a cigarette, that's all." I was about to roll one when, sitting up suddenly, she exclaims, "you keep tobacco in your bedroom?" in disbelief.

"Sure. I often fancy a smoke after sex," I say with a smile.

"Does that mean you've brought other women back to your bedroom?"

"God no, 'course I haven't. You're the first."

"Have you ever thought of giving up?"

"What? Sex?"

"No, silly," she laughs. "I meant cigarettes."

"Not until now." I return the tin to the drawer reluctantly.

"I'm sorry. I've only been here a short while and already I'm bossing you about."

She gazes into my face when I lapse back onto the pillows again.

"Maybe I smoke too much, but if I'm going to die of something, it might as well be of something pleasant." I reach for her again.

"Personally, I'd like to snuff it after sex." Her laughter is a fraction high pitched but wholly infectious. Green eyes snapping wide, she asks if I want to make love again. "Only I want to talk."

"Less talking, more fucking. People talk far too much I reckon. If we were all mute, we could just get on with it. Or is that a wee bit male chauvinist?"

"A little," she flings her arms around my neck. "I'm sorry about the cigarettes but I can help you quit if you like."

"Make it a New Year's resolution," I declare, whilst I hope she won't hold me to that.

"How long have you been smoking anyway?"

I shrug. "Since I was about 15 I think."

"14 years."

"So what do you want to talk about? It isn't to discuss me giving up smoking is it? Only whatever it is, let's get it out of the way so we can have more sex."

"Aidan, stop it," she reprimands with a giggle. "I didn't come all this way just to have sex with you."

"If it isn't a good enough reason as any. So what is it, sweetheart? Then I can get on with the two most important pleasures in life."

"Which are?"

"Sex and cigarettes. So, let me guess. You want to discuss my family. By the way, since we're conversing, I've actually been allocated fifty per cent access to my son, which gives me one full week with Patrick. And I'm having him this weekend."

"Och, Aidan, sure if that isn't wonderful news. I'll get to meet him. Your wee niece is gorgeous. I told your sister that I wanted to be a children's nanny. I think we'll get asked to babysit. That'll be good won't it?"

"Sure, grand," I mutter. "Oh don't look like that. I love Sammy dearly and I know she loves me, but you start babysitting for my sister, she'll take advantage."

"She told me about her husband leaving her for that teenage girl. I thought what a rogue he must be. Bridget's so pretty. She doesn't look in her mid-thirties. I noticed she bosses your brother Ruairi around quite a lot."

"Ru's anything for a quiet life. Every now and then, he'll retaliate with some quip or other. I think Brid forgets that Ru is almost 22 now and his own person, because between her and Aunt Clodagh, they helped bring us up. What do you think of him? Ruairi?"

"He's really nice. Very good looking like you but getting back to your sister, I can tell she's quite bitter about what happened with her husband. Who wouldn't be? It happened to my ma, so I should know."

"Don't let that bossy act fool you. Me and Ru just let it pass. It's the only way she can get stuff out of her system."

"About her husband?"

"Sure." I explain how embroiled with the church our sister is. Her shift patterns at the hospital, her attempt to keep Ruairi and me on the straight and narrow, scarcely realising that we are both grown men now. I neglect, however, to refer to Brid's ascertaining that Patrick should know me as his father on my release from prison. While we are having this amicable conversation, I long to confide in her that I'd been banged up for eight years for killing a man. Alternatively, I am far too scared of losing her if I do.

"I reckon your sister is right about one thing."

"What's that, baby?"

"This nightclub you said you'd come into."

"What about it?"

"Obviously the magic of The Liffey Bar has got into your system."

"What's that supposed to mean?"

"Och, now, you can't turn a nightclub into a bar like The Liffey. I mean, The Liffey was just that and old Flanagan still managed to maintain it as a pub no matter what the big wigs thought, 'cos it used to be called just 'Flanagan's' back in the day."

"He told me that."

"It's still essentially a pub. In Ireland, particularly in the south, a lot of the pubs play my kind of music. Sure, it's big business but not in the nightclubs in Dublin or Belfast anyway. Here in London, although I've not been to your clubs, I'm sure the kind of music they play is chart music, stuff people can dance to. Can you dance to my music? A waltz, sure, maybe line dancing. I think Bridget is right. Most of our navvies are over here. They'll enjoy having an Irish club in the heart of London. You have been to a few nightclubs?"

"Sure. And you, is that your scene?"

"There were a couple out Temple Bar way I used to go to. It's all popular music. If I sang 'The Fields of Athenry' or 'The Flight of the Earls' or the DJ played it, he'd get thrown out, so he would. Why don't you let the club stay as it is? You could always change the name, what did you say it was called?"

"'The Black Garter'!"

She starts to laugh. "'The Black Garter'! Jesus and here I was thinking that London was the nightclub capital of the modern world, well next to Hamburg that is. Hamburg used to be big. 'The Black Garter' sums up those big breasted blonde bombshells in England and America of the fifties, all gold lamé and sultry singing."

"You sound as if you know a lot about it."

"Not really. It's just that I've been to quite a few nightclubs around Dublin. And you reckon you've done your share of the nightclub scene, you and your brother."

"Ru has, but not me." At least not since 2003.

"Jesus, Aidan, you've got nightclub written all over you. So where you been hiding that gorgeous light, under a bushel?"

In fucking prison, darling. Needless to add, I refrain from mentioning that fact. Before she delves too far into my private life, I tell her how much I really do need that cigarette. That I'd get dressed and take it outside.

"Then I'll succumb to my own wee addiction," she says.

"What's that? Chamomile tea? When I come back I'll help you unpack."

I drag Levis over my hips, haul on a tee shirt and lift her case back onto the bed having removed it to have sex.

"It's okay, Aidan, I can do it."

"What's this?" I retrieve a copy of 'The Irish Times' from the pile of clothes. "You're in London now, sweetheart."

"It's just that I like to keep abreast of what's happening back home. I bought it at the airport."

"You sure you won't be homesick?"

She regards me a fraction askance. "Why should I?" and practically snatches the paper from my hand. It makes me wonder at the sudden alteration in her tone. Have I touched a raw nerve?

"I'm sorry, baby, I didn't mean to pry. Sure you need to keep in touch with what's happening back home. Anyway, while you're here you can see some of our sights like the Tower, Hampton Court."

"You said, 'our sights'."

"What do you mean?" I ask.

"Haven't you forgotten you're Irish too?"

"God no, I'm proud to be Irish. It's just that I've lived in England for a long time. I know my way around London better than I do Dublin."

"Just teasing, Aidan," she smiles. "I'd like that and I wouldn't be scared on the underground, not while I'm with you. It's just that Mollie used to tell me to pull myself together when I got scared. As for me being homesick, sure if I wasn't more lovesick than homesick. It was missing you after you left that made me so depressed. I was scared that the phone call you had from your ex-wife was because you wanted to dump me. That's what Mollie thought anyway. She forced it out of me that we'd had sex. She said that was all you were after. 'Now he's had his way with you, he's gone to his bolthole'. That you only had to get on a plane to London."

"Sweetheart," I placate gently. Wrapping my arms around her, I kiss her, realise how much I want her again. "I love you. I would have sent for you anyway."

"When I was on the flight I was scared that when I got to your flat, you might have someone else or you wouldn't be pleased to see me."

"I was depressed from missing you too, baby," I tell her. Not so depressed that you couldn't shag that dancer Suzanne, less than a few hours ago, in the upstairs room at The Black Garter. A reflection I dismiss instinctively.

"I'll go and have that smoke," I remind her. "Can you do me a coffee while you're making your tea please?"

"Sure."

"Tomorrow I've got some business to sort out at the club. I might be away for a while."

Caitlan swiftly appears crestfallen. "All day? What will I do without you?"

"Sweetheart," I tilt her chin with a forefinger, "I'll pick Ru up, so he won't be here either. You can have the flat to yourself. There's a couple of supermarkets around here. I'm not really very good at that shopping lark, Brid does it for me sometimes."

"If I'm going to stay here I'm to keep house for Aidan McRaney?"

"Whatever made you say that? I don't expect you to 'keep house' as you put it. All I want you to do is to look pretty. Be there to love me." I kiss her lips. "I suggested the supermarkets so that you can go and buy what you want. I'll give you the rest of my euros. I expect you've got some too."

She admits that she has with a nod and I tell her to get them changed. "You have the money. Buy something nice 'cos I want to show you off."

A frown crosses her face, making me wonder if I've said something amiss.

"You make me sound like a trophy wife or something."

"A what?" I laugh. "A trophy wife?"

"A beautiful woman who high-flying businessmen like to show off at parties."

"Jesus, Caitlan, that's pretty shallow. I meant I want to show you off because I love you and you're beautiful and to show what a lucky guy I am."

"I'm the lucky one. And I'm not as beautiful as you're good looking."

"What a strange thing to say. And you are beautiful." I tap her nose playfully. "But you do need to overcome your insecurity though, darlin'."

"I know I'm insecure. I didn't used to be. It was after the accident and I am in a strange country. You'll have to bear with me."

"Sure, but you talk as if London's the other side of the world. You'll soon get used to London. You know what you said about the accident?"

"Yes."

"You 'died' for more than five minutes?" She nods affirmatively and I dive right in. "They reckon if you 'die', you see a light at the end of the tunnel. Did you see a light or anything?"

Her lovely face transfuses paler than I've seen it. "There… there was nothing and I don't want to talk about it… it was far too painful. Now you're thinking what have I lumbered myself with?" She laughs half-heartedly, hesitant. "Some stupid neurotic wee girl."

"Whatever, darlin', we all have our hang ups. And I'm here now, you've got nothing to worry about." I hug her against me before releasing her gently, reminding her that I'm going to have my smoke.

Caitlan obviously has a few issues. Nevertheless, I am determined to help her through them because I'm scared she might want to return home and I'm pleased that she's chosen to journey to London to see me.

Outside, in the garden, it is getting late. I am preoccupied with what everyone had intimated about the club. How Caitlan's brand of Irish country music would hardly be appropriate in that environment, when a less than masculine voice interrupts my thoughts.

"Hullo, Aidan." I am confronted by David Lennard from the basement flat. As before, the large Persian cat is partially squeezed in his arms.

In a blue wool cardigan, white shirt, grey slacks, his thinning hair brushed back, he adds, "I thought that was you. Girlfriend won't let you smoke in the flat, hey?"

I am almost prompted to retort, what's it to do with you? However much he irritates me, I decide to at least try to be polite to the guy. "Sure, something like that. So David, how are you?" I inject an enforced friendliness into my tone.

"I'm fine, Aidan. I've just learned I'm about to become a father."

My brows arch automatically. I echo, "a father!" in disbelief.

"Oh not me, not physically. I'm not interested in that kind of thing." He pulls a face, as if giving a woman a child is utterly repugnant. "No. Moo's going to have babies. Isn't that the most wonderful news, Aidan?"

"Sure, wonderful," I murmur. "So is that Moo?" I move to stroke the fat Persian but it decides to spit at me the instant I touch its back.

"Sorry. She's a bit moody. You know what ladies are like at that time in their lives?"

"I guess," I shrug.

"So, she settling in alright?"

I stare at him nonplussed.

"Your girlfriend, Caitlan is it?"

"How did you know?"

"I was here when she came. She looked so small and lost carrying that big suitcase. I thought she was a runaway. A child at first, well at least a young teenager. She asked me if Aidan McRaney lived here. So I invited her in until your sister and her daughter arrived. Didn't she mention it?"

"No, she didn't. Perhaps she forgot. And she's settling in fine, thanks." It isn't difficult to deduce the guy is fishing and I have no intention of hooking my catch to his bait.

"I told her she was a lucky lady, didn't I Moo?"

He talks mostly to himself or is it to the cat? It does not hiss at him, however. "To land such a catch."

I growl, "what are you talking about?"

Finishing my cigarette and killing it beneath a boot, I was about to head back inside.

"Nothing," he murmurs evasively. "She's a pretty girl and Irish like you. She was taken up with my cats, wasn't she Moo?"

I halt in my tracks, with the realisation each time he addresses the cat, I half expect the animal to respond.

"Do you like cats, Aidan?" he asks.

I am tempted to say that they were okay but that I couldn't eat a whole one, but guess he'll be quickly offended by such a remark. Instead, I merely shrug and move to my door with Lennard's words ringing after me, "she expressed an interest in purchasing one of my pussies when Moo gives birth."

I thought, 'over my dead body' and am practically bursting a gut when I get inside. Unable to stifle my laughter, I encounter Caitlan in the hallway, a frown on her face. Closing the door, she wants to know what's got into me.

"You didn't tell me you met David from downstairs." I manage to regain a semblance of composure because she looks so serious.

"That he offered you one of his pussies."

"Aidan McRaney, I'm surprised at you."

"What do you mean?"

"Mr Lennard's a sweet man. Sure if he can't help the way he is. He prefers men to women, that's all and he's lonely. I met him and he told me that his partner had given him the cats as a present. And that's all he has left of the man he was in love with."

"Jesus, Caitlan, I'm sorry, I didn't mean to laugh." Her words have the desired effect, for I cease my laughter immediately.

"I know it seems funny. We all have eccentricities, even you."

"I don't have any eccentricities do I?"

"Aye, sure y'do." Her smile is enigmatic and she fails to elaborate.

*

The following morning, in the wake of a couple of phone calls, to which his secretary puts me on hold, I attempt to organise a meet with Maxwell Sorenson. When the secretary palms me off with, "Mr

153

Sorenson is tied up all day with business clients, plus he has a meeting," I counter that he has a meeting with me and that I am one of his business clients. My annoyance with the stupid woman is such that, despite Caitlan's disappointing glances, I smoke indoors. It is my flat after all. Not that I'd take it out on her and she hasn't exactly admonished me about the smoking.

I guess my temper is well in evidence at the secretary's palming me off, although I have no idea why, for which I apologise to Caitlan.

While I'm on the phone, Caitlan slips her arms around my waist and wants to know if a cup of chamomile tea might calm me down, to which I tell her I am desperate but not that desperate.

After I threaten to confront Sorenson in his office or at his meeting, I didn't care, I guess she realises I am not bluffing. She duly informs me that, "Mr Sorenson has agreed to see you, Mr McRaney."

Which makes me wonder why he had refused to see me in the first place. After all, he was the one who'd written to me.

I suppose I should at least make an effort, so I manage to dig a suit out of my wardrobe with Caitlan's help. She decides to take a shower. I want to join her but she's locked the bathroom door, which doesn't help one iota.

We'd spent half the night making love. I can't help it if I want sex all the time, but I guess I should respect her privacy. I'd already taken my shower. Changed into the dark suit, adding a black shirt, I'm in the process of searching for a suitable tie amongst my collection of three, when Caitlan's mobile rings on her side of the bed. I stiffen when I see that the caller is Mollie and I debate whether or not to answer it in the wake of the ear bashing I received from her last time.

Heaving a reluctant sigh I pick up the phone and tentatively enquire, "hullo, Mollie, it's Aidan, is something wrong?"

"Hi, Aidan. Nothing's wrong, at least I hope not. It's just I haven't heard from Caitlan since she called me from Heathrow yesterday. Is she alright?"

"Sure, she's alright. Why wouldn't she be?"

I can't help but be on the defensive every time she enquires over her sister's welfare. "You don't have to keep checking up on her, Mollie. She's with me now."

"She arrived at your place safely then?"

"Sure. She's in the shower at the moment. I'll tell her you called shall I?"

"Don't you go palming me off, Aidan."

"I wasn't. I'm getting ready to go to a business meeting this morning."

"At the landscape gardener's convention I suppose."

I blanch at the element of disdain in her voice. I know I shouldn't allow her to get my back up quite so readily, but I can't help but entertain the feeling that Mollie refuses to trust me with her little sister. "Yeah, something like that," I retort. "I'll tell her you called."

"I want to talk to you." This time her tone is even more strident and commanding.

"What about?" I fail to keep the impatience from my voice.

"Don't you go getting impatient with me, if you care about Caitlan as much as you say you do."

"You know I do. I love her. So what's all this about?"

"You know what I told you if you piss her around."

"You'll send your fiancé to break my legs."

"Aye and anything else that gets in the way. Have you got a GP?"

"Sorry?" I fail to comprehend her meaning momentarily.

"A general practitioner. A doctor."

"Jesus, I know what a general practitioner is. I don't think so." Finding a doctor isn't something I have considered after my release from prison.

"Is she going to be... ahem..." I hear her clear hear throat noisily, "living with you? Or is my sister planning to return to Dublin anytime soon?"

"Mollie, what is this?"

"Just answer the question please, Aidan."

"I'm hoping she'll stay with me. Live with me."

"Then you need to get yourself a GP for Caitlan. She has enough medication from Dr Mulcahy in Dublin. But if she's going to stay with you indefinitely, she must not run out of her pills, do you understand?"

"You mean for her migraines?"

A momentary pause before I hear the expletive "shit!" issue in disgruntled tones.

"Sorry, Aidan, I've run out of juice. I should have topped up my phone before calling from this distance. Migraines. Sure, for her migraines. You will look after her, you promise?"

"With my life, Mollie," I assure her. "Why don't you learn to trust me?" The line has already gone dead.

I hear the bathroom door and Caitlan appears, wearing a white bathrobe. She's drying her hair on a towel.

"Who's that on the phone?" she asks.

"Your sister Mollie. She ran out of juice."

"What did she want?"

"She's got to learn to trust me. She said I should get a GP and for you not to run out of your medication. That you were seeing some doctor in Dublin."

All at once Caitlan's perfectly sculptured features transform to ashen, her green eyes widen.

"For your migraines?"

"Sure, for my migraines."

"Can't you get pills for that over the counter?"

"Probably, but Mollie's right, maybe we should get a GP. Don't you have one?"

I shrug, "No."

"How long have you lived in London? 20 years," she answers her own question, "and you don't have a GP?"

I decide that now is the appropriate time to change the subject, while I promise to locate a GP and make a mental note to discuss the same with Brid.

Reaching for the grey silk tie, I ask her if it goes okay with the suit.

The colour returning to her cheeks, her smile borders on adoration. "You look so gorgeous, I'm jealous that another woman will steal you away from me."

"Jesus, sweetheart, I love you and I don't care about other women. Besides, it works both ways, remember."

"What do you mean?"

"I'm jealous of other guys who look at you. What about the blonde guy in The Liffey? I saw him flirting with you."

"Oh, you mean Johnny Rogan."

"I don't know his name."

"He's my friend Orla's boyfriend but he likes to flirt with other girls when Orla's not around. He thinks he's God's gift. As long as you don't think that."

"Perish the thought, darlin'," I grin wryly, in the process of adjusting my tie in the mirror. "Still…" I tease.

"Stop it! I'd die if you ever looked at another woman, so I would. Do you know I fell in love with you at first sight, Aidan?"

I attempt not to stiffen too quickly at her words because Suzanne, the leggy redhead from The Black Garter suddenly springs to my mind. The fact I had had sex with her the same day Caitlan arrived from Dublin. It was only because I believed that the latter had dumped me. Besides, isn't Suzanne merely a cheap floozie who'll dance for any man who'd toss her a few quid? Caitlan represents everything that is pure and wholesome, something I need in my life. I'd had enough of cheap whores. From what I know of Caitlan, my little Irish Colleen, she wouldn't lower herself to do pole dancing.

CHAPTER THIRTEEN

-

TEMPTATIONS

"What's the whistle for, Aid?" my brother asks, regarding me askance. Despite being 9.30 in the morning, I notice he continues to wear the tee shirt and pyjamas he has slept in.

"It's called making a good impression, Ru. If we're going to be running this club, we need to dress smartly. Jeans and tee shirts are out, right."

Ru makes a face. "Oh yeah, it's okay for you Mister Moneybags, but suits and stuff cost money and you know I hate fuckin' ties and I ain't had my breakfast yet."

"That's why I came early. I know what you're like, but if you're making a brew, I'll have a coffee. Where's Brid? Gone to work?"

"Yeah. She took the kids to school and reminded me that you were coming but not that you were going to be wearing a whistle and looking like a fuckin' gangster." Lifting the lid on the teapot that's resting on the kitchen counter, he grimaces.

"I'll pretend I didn't hear that last bit. I don't look like a gangster. Jesus, Ru, I'm trying to get away from all that."

Ru arches a speculative brow. "If you say so, Bruv. Anyway, you had breakfast?"

"A couple of slices of toast, you know I don't do breakfast."

Ru locates a packet of Crunchy Nut Cornflakes from the cabinet. "Well, you won't mind if I do. Then I'll take a shower, but I ain't wearing a whistle."

"Well, make sure it's smart then."

"Yes, Your fuckin' Highness," he mocks. "So, she kick you out of bed did she?"

"No, I told her I had this business meet with Sorenson this morning and one of the things I'm going to ask for is some readies. After all, it's his and Lamond's idea I run this fuckin' club and I can't do it on shirt buttons, and you're going to have to wear a suit if you're going to run it with me or else they'll think you're just another punter."

"Okay, okay," he mumbles grudgingly, pouring milk onto his Cornflakes. "Anyway, I can see why you got together with that Caitlan sort. She's well sexy ain't she? Very pretty too."

"You keep your eyes off, Ru. The only man who touches her is me, okay?"

"I wouldn't dream of treading on your territory, Bruv, you know that. Anyway, you remember that Sandra from 'The Galleon'?"

"Vaguely. Not that I dare show my face in there again."

"Not after you nearly attacked that guy for calling you a 'Mick'."

"Actually, what he said was 'fuckin' Micks'. I'm still having nightmares, man. So, what about her?"

"I asked her out and she's only accepted. I told her that me and my brother are going to manage this nightclub in Soho. I think that was what really clinched it. Birds are impressed by that sort of thing, ain't they?"

It is almost an hour before Ru is finally ready. Dressed in his best Levi's and denim jacket, we make it out to Soho where Max Sorenson has his suite of offices.

*

Judging by the surprised expression on Sorenson's immaculately shaven features, he had not expected a visit from both my brother and myself. As we are running the club jointly, I express the desire for Ru to add his signature to mine.

"Of course, Mr McRaney." Sorenson appears somewhat nonplussed. His piercing blue-eyed gaze never once strays from my brother, his demeanour effortlessly interpreted, 'he's nothing but a kid'.

At Ru's age, I had been in prison for almost six months, had killed a man and known my way around firearms as adequately as any soldier. I guess Ru, with his lanky frame and wild tousled hair which he makes a vain attempt to control, plus his 'bum-fluff' beard, all attest him to be some kind of Bohemian-style student.

Shifting uncomfortably in his seat, Ru is about to sign the paper Sorenson passes across his desk until I restrain him. My brother frowns and enquires what's wrong.

"Before either my brother or I sign anything and before I consider running that club, you know that it can't be done on shirt buttons," I stress. "In short, we need money. I'll accept a cheque. I'm sure it won't bounce will it, Mr Sorenson? 'Course cash would be preferable."

Interlocking my fingers and leaning my elbows on the desk, I steeple a bridge, conscious of Ru grinning like a Cheshire cat before he says, "how much do you reckon we'll need, Aid?"

"Och, maybe…" I pause to consider, although I am already aware how much I want. I note that Sorenson has paled beneath his tan. An element of alarm registers on his face as if I'd pulled a gun on him with the intention of committing a hold-up.

"Fifty thou should cover it for now, until I've had a chance to work it out." I ignore the 'core, blimey!' from my brother.

"Fifty thousand pounds! Good Heavens! The club practically runs itself," Sorenson blurts.

"Well, it's like a car you've filled up with petrol. When the petrol runs out the car breaks down, follow me? Okay, let's make it seventy-five thousand and I'll consider taking the club."

"I've already acquired a fifty per cent access to your son for you, despite your ex-wife practically blasting my eardrums down the phone."

That sure sounds like Jude, I grin thoughtfully.

"Yeah, thanks for that, man, but I still need the cash."

"You certainly drive a hard bargain, Mr McRaney."

"As I see it, you don't have a choice, Mr Sorenson. I'll run the club if you give me the dough."

"I'll lend you…"

I cock a brow speculatively, interrupting him. He clears his throat noisily, uncomfortably.

"I'll give you the money. Short of pulling a gun on me, Mr McRaney…"

"That won't be necessary, Mr Sorenson," I smile coldly.

∗

It is almost midday when Ru and I arrive at the club having first decided to grab some lunch. I call Caitlan to discover she's in the supermarket. She informs me that she's managed to change our euros and is beginning to find her way around. Naturally, she wants to know when I'll be home. I promise not to be too long, that Ru and I are going to oversee things at the club. Over the phone, she reminds me how much she loves me. I reciprocate and pretend to ignore the wry grin on my brother's face.

"She's sure got the 'hots' for you Bruv," he observes. "It's time you found a nice girl, better than that Verdi Benson."

"I know you didn't like Verdi but I won't have a bad word said about her."

Verdi and I had been through so much. She knows all my secrets as I know hers. What she and I have done I couldn't possibly allow my family to discover.

The club isn't closed, not even at this time of day. A few lunchtime punters are wandering in. We find the dancers with Jacky Gorman doing what he is best at, ogling them. The girls are busily decorating the main bar for Christmas. Despite my love for Caitlan, I can't prevent my senses from reeling when I clock the leggy redhead Suzanne up a ladder. She is about to place a fairy, in a red outfit and wings, atop an 8ft Christmas tree. She's wearing the tightest pair of jeans, she must have poured those long legs into them. The jeans are accompanied by a red mohair cardigan and sparkly top.

She greets, "It's Aidan and Aidan's brother."

I observe Jacky Gorman's approach from my periphery. Ru gives the girls a feeble wave, his eyes practically on stalks, I guess at seeing so many 'lovelies' all in one place.

"Suzanne," I greet her with a smile, which she returns with pursed lips and raised pencilled brows.

"Still ogling the girls, Jacky?" I quip sarcastically, to which response his mouth hardens.

He mutters, "supervising, that's all. Just supervising. So, you get the papers son?"

For a start, I'm not his fuckin' son. I allow it to pass, guess he's just trying to be friendly. "Sure I have," I answer. "Shall we go into my office? That's if you can tear yourself away, Jacky."

He continues to appear affronted, while I reason that perhaps I shouldn't make an enemy of the guy.

Gorman ushers Ru and I from the bar area and down a red carpeted corridor at the end of which is a white painted door marked 'Private. Manager's Office'.

I was soon to discover that manager and owner aren't the same person.

Ray Lamond was the owner of The Black Garter in as much as he purchased the place practically 25 years ago with his brother Francis, when they were both in their mid-twenties. It transpires that Ronnie Engels is actually the manager, I'm deemed the owner. With Engels' imminent departure, it will fall to Jacky Gorman to be installed as manager.

I'm not overly surprised to discover Ronnie Engels seated at his desk behind a green-baize table, in the process of leafing through a pile of papers, while simultaneously scratching his head as if perplexed over the laptop at his elbow.

"Aidan!" As if relieved from his duties, Engels moves from behind the desk to shake my hand. His pleasure evident, he actually smiles.

"Ronnie," I breathe somewhat uncertainly.

"I thought you might have changed your mind," he says.

"About running the club?" I take a moment to scan the room. The office is spacious, as I remember, although the door has changed. A couple of paintings I recognise as Jack Vettriano's grace the wall. A grey marble fireplace with a large dried flower display rests in the hearth. Some decorative tinsel adorns the walls and the fireplace.

Engels invites Ru and I into the chairs pulled up at the desk, while Gorman remains standing. Today the ugly man is wearing a loud houndstooth check jacket that is accompanied by a white shirt and black trousers. Complimenting me on the suit, Engels suggests that I appear to be a nightclub owner already.

"'Course, as I expect you know, the club practically runs itself," he began. "That's if you keep the same staff."

"So what's the turnover? And how many staff are there, Ronnie?" I stress his name heavily.

"The turnover is roughly 50 grand a week, more weekends. Friday and Saturday are our busiest times of course. We are fully staffed. We also have eight cleaners who cover their own respective areas. As you know, Jacky manages the table with our female croupiers. We have various theme nights. Monday, Wednesday and Friday we have our resident DJ, Pauly Lucas. He knows his stuff and he's very popular with the kids."

"Let me stop you there!" I interrupt, raising a hand. "I have a singer."

"You have!" exclaims Engels, regarding Gorman with raised brows. It is the kind of gesture that is conducive to making me uneasy, with the realisation that if Gorman refuses to 'play ball', then he'll be out on his ear. I am the owner now. Lamond has requested that I run the place, which means I have the choice of acts I want.

"So who's this singer, Aidan?" Engels, fashioning a steeple with his fingers, rests his chin thoughtfully.

When I explain who the singer is, he says, "oh, one of your countrymen or rather woman, I should say. How did you find her?"

"In his bed probably," Gorman says sarcastically.

I stiffen involuntarily. Throwing him a withering glance, I observe 'Bulldog Man' swallow hard.

Engels affects an awkward cough behind his hand and shifts in his seat uncomfortably. Engels is well aware of the kind of man I am, how quick I am to react. No one messes with Aidan McRaney.

Ru, who hasn't spoken, merely sports a knowledgeable grin.

"I saw her in Dublin. That's in Ireland, Jacky," I say sarcastically. I watch him blanch but he refrains from a response. Ignoring him I continue, "she sang in a bar near the quayside called The Liffey. She has the purest voice you've ever heard. Anyway, this isn't an interview. I'm the guy running the show now."

"Absolutely!" Engels confirms. "But…" he clears his throat again, "you have to cater to the punters, not the other way round. Then there's a magic act. That's usually Sunday nights and karaoke of course."

"No karaoke," I shake my head emphatically. "I'm not doing karaoke and what magic act? Next you'll be telling me there's a ventriloquist."

"Well actually…" Engels' hesitation is painful suddenly. "It's what the punters expect, Aidan. Look, why don't you see how it pans out. And your singer…"

"Caitlan. What about her?" I demand. I am about to reach for a smoke when Engels mutters, "I wouldn't if I were you," and points to the 'No Smoking' signs.

"Remember what happened to me, Aid," Ru reminds me, speaking for the first time.

"So, what does she sing?" Engels wants to know.

With Gorman's black piercing eyes boring into my back, plus Engels' interrogation, it is as if I'm a prospective employee hoping for a job rather than the new owner of the club. I find myself growing increasingly angry in their company. "She sings Irish country music."

"So what does that entail?" asks Gorman. "Only I don't think country music's big in The Black Garter."

"Then I think it's about time that it was." I listen to the rising well of aggression I attempt to control, but it seems there are too many people pissing me off just lately and I spit, "we've signed the papers. My brother and I now own this joint and if I want to change the acts, then I will and karaoke's way out in the nineties. Ventriloquism in the seventies, before I was fuckin' born, man, so are magic acts and if your DJ doesn't please me, then I'll get someone who does. What kind of stuff does he play?"

I observe Gorman and Engels exchange disconcerted glances. It is Gorman who says, "he's black, Mr McRaney. He plays rap mostly."

"Rap? What the fuck's that?"

"Your kid brother probably knows what that is," Engels says sotto voce. "You had been inside quite a while hadn't you? Look, come back tonight. Sit in on the acts and get this Irish bird to come and try out with the band. Like I said, I got this little club out Essex way. I hope everything works out for you boys."

Engels shakes our hands when we rise to leave. Ruairi and I accept the proffered hand reluctantly, while I'm more concerned with finding a way to eliminate Jacky Gorman from the equation. I entertain the disquieting sensation that Gorman will always be looking over my shoulder, expecting me to put a foot wrong.

In truth, I have to admit I have no real idea how to run this damned club. I promised Lamond and in turn, he has professed to trust no one else. So I vow to make a good attempt to do the job, even if it means I tread on a few toes in the process.

*

Returning to the Cabriolet, Ru and I enjoy a much-needed smoke when he says, "Jesus, Aid, those guys scared the shit out of me."

"What do you mean?" I laugh, feigning ignorance.

"Old Gormless and the geezer in the brown shades. I wouldn't like to encounter those bozos on a dark night down a lonely alley." He shivers in indication.

Cupping gloved hands about my lighter I nonchalantly tell him they are nothing I can't handle.

"I suppose you're used to dealing with those kinds of guys, but I'm not. I could never have gone through what you did at my age."

"You sound as if you're having regrets about this."

"I do want to help you. I enjoy your company and I look up to you. I know I used to be a pain in the butt when I was a kid and you had to babysit me sometimes. No, I'm not having any regrets. What about you? I could tell you were getting angry. I've seen you get angry a lot lately. So what sort of acts did you have in mind? Apart from Caitlan of course."

"Not fuckin' karaoke that's for sure, or ventriloquism and magic shit and if this DJ guy don't work out, you can do it. You said you'd done some DJ work. How hard can it be to play a few CD's?"

Ru is about to reply when a small blonde about his own age, sporting Shirley Temple curls, wearing a plaid dress and white jacket, her arms folded across her small breasts with the cold, touches Ru on the arm tentatively. "Sorry about the other day, Rory."

"It's Ruairi."

"Whatever," she shrugs. "I just want to apologise, that's all. I didn't mean to blow you out but Mr Gorman called me back to work and I was afraid of getting fired if I didn't do as he asked."

"Don't take any notice of him, darlin', I'm the boss now. You answer to me, right," I say.

Ru looks uncomfortable and snapping his fingers exclaims, "it's Angie, right?"

"You remembered!" Her eyes light up. "That's right, it's Angie. So you're the new owner Mr McRaney?" she addresses me as if I'm royalty. I half expect her to curtsy.

"Sure now, Angie, things are going to be a wee bit different around here. So what do you want with my brother?"

"Just to talk to him, that's all." Her smile is sweet. She really is quite pretty. Her features are small, almost elfin. Her eyes a sultry translucent blue.

"Go on, Ru," I urge. "You want me to wait? Only I'd better be getting back to Caitlan." I flick my watch a cursory glance.

"It's okay, Mr McRaney, I won't keep him long". She holds her smile.

"I'll wait then," I tell him. I watch as they head towards a door at the rear of the premises. I guess Angie intends to profess how much she really wants to apologise to my brother for leaving him in the lurch. I am left alone to wonder if I can actually make a go of this club any better than I have the landscape gardening business. Or would someone pull the proverbial rug from beneath me as my brother, Harry, had done.

Whilst I wait, I kill a cigarette, about to light another when a husky female voice purrs at my elbow, "Aidan McRaney, I thought that was you." She'd thrown a trench coat over the sweater and jeans and pulled her auburn hair into bunches that make her appear younger than she probably is. Sure, I'd fancied her earlier but I have Caitlan now and no way am I prepared to two-time her.

"Suzanne, darlin', what do you want?" Albeit there is precious little enthusiasm in my greeting. 'Set up' springs to mind all at once. I hope I am wrong. "I told you I was seeing someone."

"So," she shrugs and devours me with her eyes. "Can't a girl talk to a man without him wanting more? I know you told me you had someone. It's a pity. You got one of those?" She extends a slender braceleted hand for a cigarette.

"It's only a roll up."

"A cigarette's a cigarette whatever you do with it."

I roll the cigarette, plant it between her lips and light it. "So, you want me to smoke it for you as well?"

"Jesus, you're tetchy today. Girlfriend not giving you your just desserts?" she teases. Red lipstick sucks on the cigarette almost sensuously, giving me cause to avert my gaze for obvious reasons. I don't love her the way I love Caitlan but try telling that to the erection over which I have no control.

"Fuck off, Suzanne. I'm not in the mood." Liar, McRaney. "I'm a wee bit worried about running this place, that's all."

"You'll be fine. The girls will help. They'd do anything for you and if your girlfriend runs out of steam, 'cos I know you won't, if that shag you gave me is anything to go by."

I blanch at the intimation behind her words. Bringing my face up close to hers I rasp, "what happened between us never happened. Get my drift, darlin'? And if Caitlan, my girlfriend, comes down here to rehearse, you say nothing, alright?"

"Rehearse? What does she do?"

"She sings. She has a beautiful voice. So did you get your little friend Angie to drag my brother away so that you could come onto me?"

"You're the boss-man now, Irish boy. You can have any girl you want, you know that?"

"There's only one girl I want, thanks. Tell my brother I'll be in the car when he comes out."

"Sure, boss." She kills her cigarette beneath the heel of an outrageously high stiletto. "So, whereabouts in the Emerald Isle do you come from?"

"I'm from Dublin, but I've lived in London for 20 years."

"Really? You haven't lost that gorgeous accent then. Anyway, thanks for the cigarette." Her arm slips against my waist. I should pull away. So why don't I?

"The room upstairs is free, boss," she teases, winking salaciously.

She is the one who moves away, leaving me with both my own thoughts plus a hard on that a fucking stallion would have been proud of.

CHAPTER FOURTEEN

-

NIGHT TERRORS

Caitlan is noticeably absent when we return. Pressing the buzzer to my flat, I speak through the intercom, only to receive no response. Ru suggests she might still be at the shops.

It is a little after three in the afternoon. Letting myself in fails to reveal her presence. Initially I imagine she might be lying down with one of her migraines. Moving through each room, I fail to locate her. It is Ru who discovers the three bags of unpacked shopping on the kitchen counter.

"Maybe she's gone for a walk," he suggests. "You want me to unload the groceries, Aid? Jesus, there's a lot of fruit here. Chamomile tea. Coffee. What's this? Another herbal thingy? Valerian."

"Valerian?" I frown. "Never heard of it."

"She really does like her herbal stuff. You sure she isn't a witch? She's sure cast a spell on you, Bruv."

In the process of rolling a cigarette, I request him to fix me a coffee.

"Jesus, I get to do all the household stuff and I ain't even married."

I pat him on the back good-naturedly. "Good training for when you are then."

"You sound worried. You don't think she's got lost do you? I mean London's a fuckin' big city. She could be halfway to Edmonton by now."

"If she is, Bruv, then she's either caught a bus or a cab. Nobody can walk that fast. Anyway, there's only one way to find out where she is." Dialling her number on my mobile, it's a while before she responds.

"Aidan!" she sounds surprised, "where are you?"

"Where are you, sweetheart? Only I'm upstairs in the flat."

"Oh, sorry," there's an element of panic in her voice. "Sure if I didn't forget about the time. I'm downstairs with David."

"David?" I allow a semblance of jealousy to wash over me until I remember who David is. "You mean David downstairs, the…"

"Sure," she interrupts quickly, "I'm on my way now. See you in a minute."

"Sure, baby." I conclude the call and turn to Ru. "She's downstairs with David Lennard."

"What's she doing with him?"

"I don't know," I shrug. "The other day I came in after talking to him. As usual he was discussing his pussy," I grin wryly, "and I was laughing fit to burst, right. She had a right go at me."

"Since I've got to know your bird, she's definitely a lady with morals. So," he lowers his tone in conspiratorial fashion, "have you told her where you spent the last eight years, Bruv?"

"Fuck no and risk losing her? I can't afford to take that chance."

"I agree with Brid for once. You really shouldn't keep those kinds of secrets from a bird, not if you're serious about her and you obviously are."

"I am serious about her. Very." I drag on my cigarette thoughtfully.

"About marrying her you mean? Only if you intend to get that far in a relationship you should tell her. If she loves you, and I'm certain she does, I'm sure she'll be fine with it. Tell her, Aid."

"Tell me what?" Wearing her plaid skirt, white sweater and high boots, Caitlan stands on the threshold. Neither of us had heard her enter the room.

Before my brother or I can respond, she adds, "you're not angry with me because I spent too much money are you?" All at once she looks worried.

"No my darling," I tell her and hear the immeasurable relief in my voice because she hasn't sought fit to pursue her question. I slip my arm around her, hug her to me and kiss her lips gently, before her mouth possesses mine.

"Jesus, get a room," Ru jokes. "I forgot, you already have."

"Hi, Ruairi," she greets him. "Thanks for putting the groceries away."

"So, Caitlan, what's that Valerian stuff?" he asks. I detect a note of suspicion in his tone as if he imagines she might intend to poison me.

"Valerian is a herbal tea. It helps me to sleep," she explains. "I heard you walking about last night, Aidan. You should try some."

"Sweetheart, for a start I wasn't walking about. I was out like a light and I'm not that desperate to try herbal anything. So, you going to make that coffee, Ru?"

"Yes, Sir," he mutters. "So Caitlan, what did the woolly… I mean David," he corrects himself hastily when Caitlan purses her lips warningly, "have to talk about?"

"I was worried about you," I tell her.

"There was no need to be." Extricating herself from my arms, she moves to the lounge and sinks her weight onto the sofa. "I met David at the supermarket. He drove me back with my shopping. He likes chamomile tea too, so he invited me back for some."

"That figures," I say.

"What's that supposed to mean?" she sounds affronted because I dare to criticise him.

"Nothing sweetheart."

"He really is quite lonely. So was I while you were at that club."

"Does that guy ever work?" I ask.

"He owns a book shop apparently. I forget the name of the street. The shop wasn't busy, so he decided to go to the supermarket. He's promised me a kitten when Moo has her litter."

Killing my cigarette vigorously in the ashtray beneath Caitlan's disapproving gaze I tell her I really don't want an animal in my flat, adding, in hopes of bringing a smile to allay her obvious disappointment, "I've already got my brother and he is housetrained," with a wink in his direction.

"It's okay," but her response is a half-hearted one.

"So what will he do with them? Sell them to a pet shop or something?" I ask.

"Or dr…" Ru begins, before I fix him with a, 'don't you dare mention drown' sort of glance. Shrugging, he carries on fixing the coffee.

Luckily, I believe that Caitlan hasn't heard him. He can be quite tactless sometimes, can my kid brother. Changing the subject, she enquires how we got on at the club. Was I returning there tonight?

"I thought we'd have a quiet night in. You going out, Ru? Or are you going back to Brid's?"

"I'm going out. If I go back to Brid's she'll only want me to babysit again."

"We could babysit, couldn't we, Aidan?" Caitlan enthuses.

Babysitting isn't really what I had in mind. "Maybe some other time," I placate her. Not if I can help it. Sitting next to her on the sofa, my arm around her, I say, "tomorrow, if you want to, you could come to the club to rehearse some of your songs."

"Really!" Her eyes shimmer with an inner excitement. "Do you think they'll like my songs as much as they did in The Liffey?"

She lapses into anxious mode again.

"Sure they will, sweetheart. They'll love you as much as I do," I tell her, choosing to ignore Ruairi's doubtful expression.

Of course they will love her. She is the breath of fresh air that stale old club needs. A club that has changed precious little from the sixties and seventies and one I am determined to introduce to the 21st century.

*

Ru is sensitive enough to realise that I need to have some time alone with my girlfriend. Informing me he has a date with 'that Sandra sort' from 'The Galleon pub', he wants to know if he can borrow my car to drive down to Esher. I agree, with the reminder that he isn't to overload it with cigarette packets and rubbish as he had when I was in Dublin. Promising that he won't litter the Cabriolet, I toss him the keys.

Caitlan suggests lying down on the bed as she hadn't slept much the previous night. She remains convinced that I was walking about. She should know, as I'm the one lying beside her, but she is convinced that when she put her hand to my side of the bed, I wasn't there. Maybe I'd got up to use the loo, I suggest.

Looking in on her later, mainly because I want to make love, I observe that she really has fallen asleep. The tartan skirt is ruched up around her, affording me the invitation of bare flesh. Not wishing to wake her however, I decide to take my mind of a raging hard on and cook something.

She awakes as I finish cooking steak and chips and open a bottle of wine I'd sneaked out purposefully to buy from the nearest off licence. I'm surprised when she regards my culinary efforts with an ill-disguised disapproval.

"What's wrong, sweetheart? I can cook you know." I throw her a smile but it is barely reciprocated, merely a small puckering of her lips is all I receive. Maybe she is still tired. "I've lived on my own for a while and Judy, my ex, never really bothered to cook much."

"Why not?" She pushes her weight into the chair facing me at the kitchen table. With the realisation that I might have vouchsafed too much information about my past, I quickly add, "oh, Jude and I were never that close."

"Then why did you marry her, Aidan?" she asks the inevitable, a hand covering her glass after I half-fill it with wine. "Just a small one.

Wine gives me migraine if I have too much. Anyway, you didn't answer my question."

"Why did I marry Judy Lisle? Because she was expecting my child and I didn't want to lose sight of him. Plus, with her mother and Bridget arguing over where Jude and I should be married, in a Catholic or Protestant church, and with Brid managing to win against such an over-powering woman as Mrs Lisle, I was barely 20, Jude 22, I guess we were both carried along with it all without a say in the matter."

"Did you love her?"

I make a face. "Hey c'mon, baby, don't let's spoil our meal by discussing Judy. As it is she's enough to put you off your food." My laugh is hollow.

"Is she ugly then?"

"What Jude? God no. She's not as pretty as you but she's an attractive woman, more so in command of herself now. Well, most of the time, except when she got hysterical and called me back from Dublin with the pretence our son had meningitis. Now she's a nurse to this top plastic surgeon guy in some exclusive Surrey clinic. Sure, she's turned out to be quite a sophisticated woman from what she was."

Did I imagine it, has the colour instinctively drained from her? She begins to toy with her food while I realise how hungry I really am. I'm a steak guy, recollecting there had been innumerable salad items amongst the groceries Ru was packing away in my kitchen cupboard.

"What's wrong, sweetness? Isn't it to your liking?" I ask, concerned.

"It's fine, so it is. It's just that I'm not very hungry just now."

"You what!" I exclaim, but manage to regain my composure with an effort. I'd enjoyed cooking for her. Now she regards my culinary offerings with something akin to disdain. "You're not on some stupid diet are you? I mean, if you're not all skin and bones now. I hope you're not thinking of Judy. I don't love her. It's you I love, Caitlan McKenna, I'll carve it on a tree if you want. The only time I see her is when I go to pick up my son."

"I'm not sophisticated, Aidan," she says flatly.

"Thank God. I fell in love with you the first time I saw you. Look, don't worry about the steak. Is there something else you'd like me to cook? I'm sure Ru will eat it later."

"But it'll be cold."

"Och, Ru's a human dustbin. If he can eat cold pizza for breakfast, he can eat a cold steak and I'm not really a wine kind of guy either. I prefer a scotch. You want some more?" I hold the bottle towards her. Predictably, she shakes her head.

"I don't drink much. I'm sorry I'm so boring."

Half expecting her to break down, my meal barely finished, I am out of my seat and cradling her in my arms.

"You could never be boring and maybe I'm a wee bit set in my ways. I love you. I need you, sweetheart. Sod the food. We could always live on love. God, you are light aren't you?" I whirl her up into my arms as if she were weightless. She places hers around my neck and I carry her into the bedroom, where we both fall sprawling and laughing onto the bed.

"I've never done that before, carried a woman into my bedroom," I tell her.

"Not even Judy on your wedding night?"

"God no! Remember, Judy was pregnant. I could barely manage to carry one person, let alone two."

I trace a forefinger the length of her cheekbones; they're as chill as alabaster beneath my touch. "You remind me of a fine oil painting, d'you know that? I used to paint. Maybe you could sit for me one day. I've never asked a woman to do that for me before either, but you have such a beautiful bone structure."

"I didn't know you were an artist. You're so full of surprises, Aidan."

And I thought, darling, you don't know the half. At this juncture it would have been so easy to confess I have been in prison and why. Alternatively, I really am so afraid of losing her. As Ru outlined, Caitlan is a lady with high morals. Maybe the notion that her boyfriend has been to jail for murder might send her scuttling post-haste back to Ireland.

It isn't difficult to reason that Caitlan scarcely approves of my predilection for whisky. I'm not exactly an alcoholic but I cannot fail to appreciate a good malt. So I smoke, I drink, enjoy a good steak. Isn't all that a man's privilege? Nevertheless, I'd relinquish them all if there was a chance of losing her.

She refrains from saying anything. After all, I could start an argument about why she refuses to eat my food or drink the rather expensive wine I bought especially for her, mainly because I am under the misguided impression that women prefer wine to any other drink. I love her too much to argue with her.

I'd fallen asleep. Lately I've been sleeping much better. After all, I've been out over six months, plus I've grown accustomed to this old flat. I wasn't dreaming, although I'd been in the throes of a fairly deep sleep, one that is suddenly disturbed by an ear-piercing shriek that almost succeeds in shattering my eardrums. I hear my name screamed loudly and coming to, I rub my eyes, attempt to adjust to the sight of Caitlan sitting bolt upright in the bed and shouting, "Aidan! Aidan! There's someone in the room!"

"What!" I come fully awake now.

"Caitlan, sweetheart, what... what do you mean there's someone in the room?"

Rousing myself in the bed, I slip an arm around her and realise she is shaking uncontrollably. There is something else too. A definite sensation of wetness has begun to seep in the general direction of my bare legs. I'm wearing shorts, nothing else. She is only clad in her panties. I see they are wet and clinging to her back.

"Caitlan, what's happened? Jesus."

Momentarily confused, I run a hand through tousled curls, across my beard and realise my hand is also beginning to shake.

"Oh, Aidan, I'm... I'm so sorry," she starts to cry when she sees the suppurating patch of water I've been lying on.

"It's okay." I leap out of bed and attempt to console her, my arms around her. I feel her body shudder beneath mine. "It was just a nightmare, sweetheart."

Raising huge emerald eyes to mine, I see they are filled with unshed tears. She whimpers, the timid childwoman once more. "I couldn't help it but I really did see someone in the room."

"Stay here!" the command issues far more stridently than I intended, but anger has now begun to surface, in my conviction that Ru has come in drunk and thinks it funny to scare my girlfriend half to death with his stupid jokes. It's time that little bastard was taught a lesson and grew up.

"Where are you going, Aidan?" She's standing there, hugging herself, small and frozen. She'd gathered the quilt around her, the only item of bedding that isn't soaked in urine.

"Wait here," I instruct her, "It's time that fuckin' wee bastard brother of mine fuckin' grew up. I'm sorry about the swearing, darlin' but I've had enough of his antics. As far as I'm concerned he can go and sleep in the park."

"Aidan, it wasn't Ruairi!" she calls after me but I barely hear her because I am already on the landing outside my brother's door. Bursting in, I see he's in bed, alone. So he hasn't brought Sandra back, unless she's hiding in the wardrobe. I practically kick down the door with a bare foot, stubbing my toe in the process, but I'm far too angry to concern myself over a little pain.

"What the fuck, Aid!" Ru exclaims, rousing himself up in bed he rubs eyes, bleary from sleep. "You fuckin' scared the shit out of me, man, bursting in like that."

"Not as much as you fuckin' scared the shit out of my girlfriend," I rasp. "Now fuckin' get up and apologise."

Deep down I know, unless Ru is an accomplished actor, it isn't him who Caitlan has seen. Almost in tears, he reaches for his robe and hauls it on. I do not apologise because I need to blame my brother. If it is one of his practical jokes, then I'll admonish him, but at least I'll be relieved. And if it isn't Ru, then who the hell has Caitlan seen in my flat?

CHAPTER FIFTEEN
-
NIGHTCLUB SINGER

Neither Caitlan nor I slept much after that. Leaving her on the settee, I remain awake nursing a couple of straight whiskies. I realise it is almost 3am and that I seem to be increasingly turning to the bottle.

I put the washing machine on and pile in the wet bedding. Sitting in the kitchen, I'm beginning to feel guilty at the way I treated my brother when I realise how much I love and need him. When I'd accused him of sneaking into our room and scaring Caitlan, he'd vehemently protested his innocence. I noted he'd also been close to tears. Ruairi is quite a sensitive young man, I hadn't known how much hitherto. The realisation makes me long to hug him, explain how sorry I am, but something holds me back, the anger I guess. Or is it the fear that someone had slipped into my flat without my knowledge? Caitlan was convinced she'd seen a man in our room. If I'd waited to hear her explanation, she'd have tearfully informed me that it wasn't Ru. Common sense also indicates that if it had been Ru, I would have come awake immediately and probably caught him in the act. I'd leaped from the bed instinctively. Whoever or whatever she had seen had frightened her enough to make her wet the bed. She'd also insisted that she hadn't seen him before. Perhaps later, as I'm a fairly decent artist, maybe I can sketch one of those photo-fit pictures the way the police do, I promise her.

So the intruder wasn't Ru. That much is obvious. In truth, I didn't actually believe it was. So much has happened to me since my release. I've been stalked. Had fallen foul of people I believed I could trust. Needless to add, I refrain from confiding this to Caitlan. Of course, all this might stem from another source, one I really have no desire to entertain. That Caitlan might be imagining things. I'd attempted to console her that it had been nothing more than a horrific nightmare. Haven't I had enough of those? She'd shaken her head adamantly. It had been far too real, she said. So after a thorough search of the flat, I discover nothing, certainly no sign of an intruder such as a forced window.

I must have dozed at the kitchen table because I hear my name. Wearing his pyjama bottoms with a grey tee shirt, Ru moves into the room. I guess he's still angry with me after I'd burst into his bedroom, accusing him.

"Ru, Jesus…" I come fully awake now and rub my face. My eyes are stiff from lack of sleep and too much scotch. I observe the time is almost five. "I must have dozed off."

"You look like shit," he remarks tersely, "that bottle was almost full when I saw it last." He gestures to the almost empty bottle of Chivas Regal at my elbow. "I'm really sorry, Ru. What can I say?"

"You want some coffee?"

"Sure. Black. Plenty of it. Did you manage to sleep?"

"What do you think?" he mutters barely audibly. Opening the fridge door, he scans inside momentarily, then shrugs and lifts out a carton of milk. "You want the percolator or instant?"

"Do you mind doing the percolator?"

"No, if that's what you want."

We are skirting around one another. He looks tired too. His long hair is tousled and he runs a hand through it distractedly.

"What's a plate of steak and chips doing in here wrapped in cling film?"

"That's from last night. Caitlan wasn't hungry. I'd cooked an' all. You can have it if you want."

Ru makes a face. "No, you're alright. So where is Caitlan? And why's the washing machine on so early? She ain't got you spring cleaning or something has she?"

"Jesus, man, you ask a lotta questions, but at least you're speaking to me. I really am sorry, but Caitlan was convinced there was someone in our room." Fumbling in my jeans, I locate cigarettes and light one. "And the washing machine. She had a wee bit of an accident."

Ru is in the process of searching my kitchen cupboards, opening doors, letting them slam, muttering, "where's the fuckin' cornflakes?" The noise is beginning to exacerbate the beginnings of a headache. "With the accent on 'wee' hey, Bruv?" He flicks a smile. "You mean she wet the bed?"

Dragging on the cigarette, I nod, too uptight to respond momentarily. "She really was scared, man. Honest, you should have seen her."

"But how could anyone have got in? We're on the second floor for fucks sake. He could have used a ladder I suppose and got in through a window. Personally, I think she had a nightmare. I was reading about those things called 'Night Terrors'. Some people believe they've been taken up in UFOs, that aliens have been in their rooms. They've actually been convinced of it."

"Jesus, Ru." I can't help but smile at what he intimates. Making one of those eerie, spooky noises, I quip, "maybe it was a little green man."

He manages to find the cornflakes and pours milk into his bowl.

"'Course you know what I reckon," he lowers his voice conspiratorially before joining me at the table, "maybe she drinks too much of that chamomile tea and that 'Valerie' stuff."

"It's called Valerian, Ruairi," Caitlan appears, fastening her robe. Her long, tawny hair tumbles dishevelled and awry about her shoulders, while her face is whiter than alabaster.

Ru mutters, "shit," beneath his breath guiltily, between mouthfuls of cereal.

"You okay now, sweetheart?" Slipping from my seat, I move to her side, envelop her in my arms and catch her gaze alighting on the almost empty bottle of Chivas on the table, before turning her head away, doubtless at the stench of stale whisky on my breath. Guiltily, I realise that Ru and I have been making fun of her predicament. Her mouth is tight, green eyes widening larger than I've seen them. "I know you don't believe me, either of you."

Ru carries on eating his cereal as if she hasn't spoken.

"I believe you, sweetheart," I placate her. "But it could still have been a nightmare, night terrors or something."

"I'm sorry about what happened. I'm going to take a shower. Then I want to talk to you, Aidan." Her voice is carefully controlled.

"Don't mind me," Ru shrugs. He hasn't even greeted her. "But if you're really convinced someone broke in last night, then we'll have to call the Gendarmes."

"Gendarmes?" she echoes disbelievingly. "You mean the police?"

"I don't think we need to go that far, Ru," I put in quickly as I catch Caitlan regarding me with a frown. My love affair with the constabulary is practically non-existent and if they check and come up with my name, things might come to light which I have no desire to expose.

"Caitlan, darlin'," I touch her shoulder lightly as she prepares to exit the room, "let's talk now, okay?"

"If you want. Then I need to take a shower."

Out of earshot of Ru, I suggest that maybe we could take a shower together.

"Oh, Aidan, I love you so much." She places a hand against my cheek.

"But. I can tell there's a 'but' in that sentence somewhere. Is it because of the scotch?"

"I didn't know you drank."

"Look, baby, it's cool. It was only because I was upset. I'm afraid you'll have to take me as I am and I love you too. Does all this mean you regret coming to London to be with me? That you want to return home?"

She silences my words mid-flow, a finger against my lips. "I don't want to go home. I want to stay here with you. I'm not so selfish as to make you turn your back on all the stuff you have here. I was scared after what I did, that you'd want to send me home. Maybe it was just a nightmare after all." She turns her back and wrapping her arms around herself, as if she is cold, she adds with a shiver, "I don't know. But that man, ugh, he seemed so real."

"Can you describe him?"

"He was oldish with a grey beard. I've never seen him before but I'd know him again. His eyes sort of glinted wildly and he held a hand outstretched toward me. He… he also…" she swallows uncomfortably, "didn't appear solid, as… as if he were a ghost. Oh God, am I going mad?"

"You're not going mad, sweetheart." I cuddle her close, listen to the erratic beating of her heart pumping against my chest. "And my flat isn't haunted." I stifle the impulse to laugh, "because ghosts do not exist, believe me. Anyway, you fancy coming down to the club this morning? No rush. Make yourself look pretty. And as you said, we need a shower."

"Sure, Aidan, I'd love to see your club and you won't send me back to Dublin will you?" Tears stand in her eyes again with her anxiety.

"Not unless you want to go, baby."

Caitlan buries her head in my bare chest, while I cuddle her close.

"I want to be with you always."

I dare to enquire about Mollie.

"Mollie has Niall. She doesn't need me," she says quietly.

*

My intention of introducing Caitlan to The Black Garter club is to enable her to 'try-out' with the resident band. She starts to protest that she isn't ready, particularly after last night. "All you need to do is run through a couple of numbers. No pressure," I assure her, "and I'll be there."

She continues to remain uncertain and holds back a little when we enter the place. The cleaners are there, a mix of both young and mature women. They are busy piling chairs onto tables, mopping floors and dusting. All the kind of things cleaners do.

I introduce myself and Caitlan and enquire from one of them, a young blonde who offers her name as Elaine, who else might be there at that time of day.

Elaine carries on piling chairs onto tables so I decide to help her, for which she mutters a grateful 'thanks'. "Oh the usual," she adds. Whoever that is.

There is a guy on the stage. I figure him to be some kind of stand-up comedian, to whom he's advocated the cleaners as his audience. "A magician friend of mine. You know the sort, knew his job." He pauses briefly to arch his thick beetling brows with the customary inflection all stand-up comedians I had ever seen seem to entertain, as he continues with his story now that he has an attentive audience. I judge him to be around his mid-forties. Wearing a check jacket, grey trousers, his dark hair is crinkly, cut short, his features are polished, immaculately shaven. "This magician pal had this awful nagging wife. She hated what he did. This particular night he got a little drunk. You know what I mean. 3ft 2" in his stockinged feet. A little drunk…"

"Jesus," I whisper exasperatedly to Caitlan.

"Well, he used to work with mice. Most magicians work with rabbits but he had this mouse act, you see." He begins to laugh a fraction hollowly, aware no doubt that he is the only one enjoying the joke, as he nears the inevitable punch line. "Anyway, he forgot he'd stuffed the mouse down his trousers see. When he went home to his wife, his wife said…" He pauses again. Now his attention diverts from the cleaners to Caitlan and myself. Her smile flirts about her mouth indecisively, while I wait impatiently for a punch line I guess will not live up to its intended expectations.

"That's the first time you've had any movement in your trousers for years." He guffaws raucously, while the cleaners merely favour him with disappointed shrugs and continue with their work as if he is no longer of any consequence.

"Well suit yourselves," he mutters grudgingly and shrugs before vacating the stage and I realise he's heading in our direction.

Extending a chubby brown hand, he enthuses, "you must be Mr McRaney? Steve Walton. You might have seen my billboard, I'm on tonight."

His gaze lingering for longer on Caitlan than I consider comfortable, he waits for an introduction. I accept the preferred hand reluctantly.

"Yes I'm Mr McRaney, Mr Walton."

"Oh, call me Steve. I hear you're the boss man now."

"That's right. So what do you do?" I ask, deadpan.

Caitlan giggles, "Aidan."

Walton's mouth tightens, his eyes darken momentarily before his manner begins to relax.

"Oh you," he laughs.

"I'm serious, Steve," I remain unsmiling, even though I'm laughing inside over his swiftly crestfallen demeanour. Behind my shades, I guess my expression is unreadable. I continue to feel the worse for wear, a shower has done precious little to help. "What do you do?"

His humour subsides instantly. The wide grin has lapsed into a sober moue. I'm conscious of Caitlan paling, no doubt at the iciness prevalent in my tone.

"I do stand-up. What else do you think I do?" He's on the defensive, I've obviously got his back up.

"I thought you were here to entertain the cleaners."

A ripple of laughter erupts from the assembly of women.

"Maybe you should do the stand-up, Aidan," Caitlan suggests with a grin.

"So, Steve, never let it be said that Aidan McRaney isn't a fair man. You do your act tonight and if I like it, you can stay but lose the 'mouse' story. It's not funny, man." I deal him a sardonic smile.

I realise how much I am beginning to relish this managerial position that Ray Lamond has entrusted me with. To hire and fire whoever I want to.

As Frankie Lamond's minder, I was forced to endure countless hours of so-called songstresses who belted out numbers such as, 'I Will Survive' and 'I Will Always Love You', plus an innumerable assortment of bad stand-up comedians to last a lifetime. I guess I do know my way around the nightclub scene.

"But I always do Thursday nights, Mr McRaney," he protests, "from 8 'til 9.30. I was just running through my act."

"That long, huh? Jesus." I shake my head. "Anyway, carry on, don't mind me, but I'll be around tonight and you'd better be good Steve, 'cos if you aren't, I'll have to let you go, do you understand?"

I am aware that my appearance of long, black, curly hair which is habitually pulled back into a ponytail, my all black clothes, jeans and shirt, over which is thrown my leather coat, impenetrable dark glasses and the stony expression I adopted for Walton's benefit are all conducive to leaving him uneasy.

Any semblance of his erstwhile humour has evaporated. He practically shrinks away as if I have physically struck him.

"Of course, of course, Mr McRaney," he grovels subserviently.

"So, Steve…"

"Yes?"

"Is Jacky Gorman around?"

"No… no, it's his day off but the girls are here."

"Girls?"

"The dancers. They're out the back," Walton volunteers, before almost curtsying to Caitlan.

At the mention of girls, Suzanne unwittingly springs to mind guiltily, when I recollect what happened in the upstairs room.

Steve Walton moves away, or maybe slinks would be more appropriate.

"I'm sorry you had to see that, baby," I say apologetically. "Sure if I don't get angry much too quickly."

"I've never seen you angry with me."

I pull her close, kiss her forehead. "That's because you calm me down. Who needs an anger management course when they have you?"

I do get angry far too quickly. I don't suffer fools gladly and that guy was a fool.

Steve Walton is soon replaced, at my request, by the resident band. They are a little older than I expected, possibly a good sign. They might know some of the songs in Caitlan's repertoire. The 3-piece band consists of Georgie Moon, Kenny Collins and the youngest guy, I judge to be in his mid to late thirties, Georgie's brother Derek. They call themselves 'The Moon Brothers and Friend'. Not the most awe-inspiring moniker. I ask if they play rock, but Georgie, thin and wiry, with a lead guitar ostensibly a perpetual attachment to his torso, explains they aren't a hard core band, but mainly session players and accompanists. Georgie's brother Derek, or Del, plays piano, while Kenny is on the drums.

Eager to please the new boss, they take to the stage and invite Caitlan to run through the numbers she usually sings. They'll do their best to accompany her. I say, "you'll do more than that," until Caitlan, clutching my arm, counsels me not to get their backs up before they've barely begun. I smile and kiss her in the knowledge that she is right and definitely the calming influence I need in my life. She is also a far cry from the frightened girl who wetted my bed last night.

A little plumper than his brother, Georgie Moon asks Caitlan what songs she sings. She rolls off some of the titles, 'The Fields of Athenry', 'The Flight of the Earls', 'Galway Bay', 'Fairytale of New York!'

"I know 'Galway Bay' and 'Fairytale of New York'. The others sound very Irish."

"What's wrong with that?" I retort. "It's Irish country. That's what she sings and that's what we are. Irish."

"I can tell that, Mr McRaney. There's nothing wrong with Irish." Kenny's tone is conciliatory.

Derek drops his weight onto the stool before his baby grand. Somewhat nervously, Caitlan climbs, with my assistance, onto the stage. I whisper to her that she'll be fine, adding, "I'm here. I love you."

"Love you too," she mouths and smiles.

"Tonight this place will be packed. At least I hope so and you'll knock 'em dead the way you did in The Liffey."

"I feel I can do anything when you're with me, Aidan. I might be your calming influence but you're my confidence booster."

Caitlan begins to sing and when she does, the assembly pauses to listen. The cleaners doing their work. Steve Walton about to exit. The young barman Jamie, washing his glasses. Even a couple of the dancers. I wonder where Suzanne is and hope it is her day off, aware that every time she sees me, after what we'd done, she invariably makes a pass.

Caitlan is doing what she does best. She is my star. I plan to erect a billboard with her beautiful face on it, as there had been outside The Liffey Bar in Dublin.

As it turns out, the Moon brothers and friend are fine musicians and are quick to pick up on her songs as accompanists and I am transported back to the night I first saw her, as she kicked off her shoes, clutched the microphone and leaned toward her audience.

She notices me and I observe there is so much love in her eyes that it causes my heart to leap. I know in that moment that this is the girl I want to spend the rest of my life with.

She launches into a song I haven't heard before and she sings it whilst her eyes never once stray from me.

'I don't want to hear a sad story; I always know how it goes.

So if tonight you'll be my tall dark stranger, I'll be your San Antone rose.'

Her confidence is fully restored when she sings. I drop my weight onto one of the chairs facing the stage.

'If wishes were fast trains to Texas.

How I'd ride and I'd ride…'

Our eyes lock, hers and mine, aware of no one else in the room.

Elaine, the blonde cleaner has taken the chair from the table for me purposefully and I murmur my thanks, ask her if she wouldn't mind fixing me a black coffee, no sugar, plus an orange juice for Caitlan. With a smile, she promises that she will.

Preoccupied watching Caitlan, I am only marginally conscious of her approach, until I hear a familiar, sexy purr at my elbow, "she's got a lovely voice, Aidan, you should be proud," and Suzanne lowers a cup of coffee and an orange juice on the table.

I feel the guilty colour flame my face, murmur, "thanks" and find myself looking her way reluctantly.

She's wearing tight faded jeans with a white silk top. Her red hair is loose and spills halfway down her back. I tense, anxious that she might consider joining me. I observe Caitlan's momentary hesitation in her song, when she clocks Suzanne, whose partially exposing her breasts in the plunging décolletage of her top purposely in my direction as she places the drinks on the table.

"By the way, there's a phone call," she declares.

I purse my lips with the sense this might be yet another ploy to entrap me. "Well, take it, darlin'," I tell her flippantly.

"They want to talk to the boss and Jacky isn't around. He usually deals with that stuff."

"Who is it? If this is another of your games, Suzanne."

"Don't flatter yourself, baby. There really is a phone call. It's about an act Ronnie Engels intended to book before he left."

"What kind of act?" I enquire, while attempting with difficulty to steer my gaze away from the sight of that plunging neckline.

"A singer."

"We don't need another singer. Caitlan is my singer."

"Then you'd better tell him."

"What are you now, Suzanne? My fuckin' secretary?"

She stands her ground, arms folded defiantly. "If you must know, Irish boy, I am your fuckin' secretary and no funny business, okay."

I sigh with resignation because I have to answer the phone, but wait until Caitlan finishes her number. I explain that someone is calling about a booking, that I won't be long. Her pretty face whitens and she appears crestfallen.

"You promise?"

"I promise." I kiss her cheek. "Love you, sweetheart."

"Love you too, Aidan."

I'm aware of Caitlan watching me uneasily as I follow Suzanne from the room. I am equally conscious of the latter wearing that familiar smouldering smile. Out of earshot of Caitlan she murmurs, "wish you'd whisper those sweet nothings to me like that, baby."

"Go on, Suzanne, let's get this fuckin' call over with." I remain wary, however, that she's about to grab me around the waist, inch a hand in the general direction of my zipper.

The phone on the desk is off the hook. She's obviously been attending to some papers in a filing cabinet because she returns to them.

"Hullo." Snatching up the receiver, I greet the caller tentatively. "Can I help? I'm Aidan McRaney, the new owner of The Black Garter. I understand you require a booking."

"Oh, hullo, Mister McRaney. Yeah, Mister E promised me another gig at the club. I'm Bobby Howes."

"Mr E?"

"Mr Engels. Ronnie."

"Sure. So what do you do, Mr Howes?"

"I sing."

"So what kind of stuff do you sing?"

"Oh, a mixture. Classic songs you know. Sometimes country. 'The Green, Green Grass of Home', stuff like that. I also play guitar and I do warm-up if you want."

My attention has already begun to waver. The guy has a boring voice and Suzanne is busy sifting through some papers on my desk, on purpose I know, as she is bent over far too closely in those incredibly tight jeans.

"Warm-up?" I attempt to immerse myself in the guy's conversation and avoid those fucking jeans that aren't helping me to concentrate.

"Yeah, you know. Warm-up the audience with comedy skits, stuff like that."

"Sure, Mr Howes, I'm happy to give you a try but my plan is to bring this club into the 21st century, not send it back to the fifties."

"Blimey, Aidan, you don't mince your words do you, baby?" Suzanne returns the papers to the filing cabinet.

"I'm sorry if I've wasted your time," I hear him swallow. I imagine he might be about to break down, before he mutters, "bloody Micks," beneath his breath.

Anger swells, but I allow it to subside and placate him, "it's cool, Mr Howes. You come in, I'll give you a listen and if I like your audition, I'll give you a spot in my club. Oh, and Mr Howes, don't call me a 'bloody Mick' okay." He has already rung off. "Jesus, some people." I say it to the phone instead of Suzanne.

"You certainly know how to win friends and influence people, don't you, my darling," she mocks.

"Fuck off, Suzanne. Sure if this stuff is harder to deal with than I imagined."

"You mean booking the acts?" She stretches herself lazily, like a cat, against the filing cabinet. For one wild, crazy moment, I can imagine her as 'Cat Woman' enveloped in skin-tight black leather, until I bring myself up sharply for what I am thinking because the woman I love is singing on the stage next door.

"So, you a secretary as well as a pole dancer now? Talk about multi-tasking."

"I do a lot of things, baby. Secretary, dancer, anything. Anyway, I can see why you threw me over. She's beautiful, Aidan, but I'm not jealous. Well I suppose I am a little bit. She's Irish like you. The only trouble is, when you fuck a girl she stays fucked, if you get my drift."

I intend to respond with a quip about there being no answer to that, when I am conscious of Caitlan framed in the doorway, her beautiful face ashen.

CHAPTER SIXTEEN

-

FACE FROM THE PAST

Caitlan's face is as pale as if it were sculptured in alabaster and I fear she is about to faint. As it is, she has a palm thrown limply across her brow. Suzanne and I turn in unison at her appearance and I take my girlfriend into my arms.

"You alright, sweetheart?" I ask with concern.

"I felt a wee bit faint, Aidan. That's why I came to find you. I think I have one of my migraines coming."

Suzanne quickly reaches for a chair, "would you like me to fetch you a glass of water, Caitlan?" she arches a concerned brow in my direction.

Caitlan sinks her weight into the chair and Suzanne slips an arm across the back of it. When Caitlan glances her way, it seems to me like her green eyes are dark with reproach for the dancer, only for the look to disappear as swiftly as it came. She nods, "please?"

"Of course." Suzanne favours me with another anxious glance before she fetches the water.

"You've probably done too much, sweetheart," I tell her. "Maybe I shouldn't have pushed you like this."

She deals me a wan, feeble smile. "Sure, but I enjoy it. I love singing. That's when I'm happiest. When you were out there watching me, I was on cloud nine."

"Let's not talk about it now, huh," I counsel when Suzanne returns with the water. She hands the glass to Caitlan, who begins to sip from it slowly.

"Maybe you ought to take her home, A… boss," Suzanne corrects herself quickly. The smile she directs me above Caitlan's head speaks volumes, but one I choose to ignore. I'd have to be one insensitive imbecile not to realise that Caitlan is obviously jealous. Coming upon Suzanne and I closeted in my office, although the call was genuine, after what the dancer had said about 'a girl staying fucked' is evidence enough to send a volatile woman like Caitlan over the edge.

"That's exactly what I'm about to do." I inject a note of acerbity into my voice for Suzanne's benefit.

She twists her lips, moving from Caitlan's side. "Of course, boss. I'll leave you alone. I can come back later if you want. Only, since Ronnie's left, that filing system is…"

"The filing system is the last thing on my mind," I snap.

Suzanne scarcely deserves the way I spoke to her and I am certain she understands.

With a, "hope you'll be feeling well enough to sing in the club tonight, Caitlan," she exits and closes the door quietly.

"When you're ready we'll leave, sweetheart. You've hardly eaten anything since you arrived. Look, if you want I'll cook you something, not steak. Just tell me what you like."

She nods feebly, clutches my arm and I kiss her.

We vacate the club and she composes herself beside me in the Cabriolet. The streets are busy. It takes practically all of my efforts to concentrate on the traffic during the drive from Soho to Shooters Hill.

Curled up in the seat, her back is turned from me. I touch her shoulder occasionally; enquire if she is okay, only to receive no response.

"I don't think you'll have any trouble pleasing the punters tonight if you're feeling up to it, but maybe if you get some rest now. I'll cook up some of your salad or whatever. Not that you cook salad." I'm rambling, in the main to release some kind of conversation from her. When she refuses to respond I shut up, commence checking out the streets in silence. Suddenly she says, "did you fuck her?"

"What!" My heart begins to hammer both with guilt and the unexpectedness of her question. I am compelled to brake the Cabriolet abruptly or risk colliding the vehicle into the car in front when we reach the traffic lights.

"What… what did you say, sweetheart?" I ask, although I heard her plainly enough.

"That woman at the club, Suzanne. Did you have sex with her? It's a simple enough question, Aidan."

"Jesus, no!" I concentrate on the lights instead of looking her way, glad of the shades so that she can't read the guilt in my eyes.

"Sweetheart, you're the only one I want, you know that? I love you, Caitlan, why should I look at another woman?" Jesus, ten Hail Mary's for that, McRaney.

"I mean after I met you and you had to rush back to London."

"You know why I had to rush back to London. Because that stupid ex-wife of mine reckoned Patrick had meningitis. There was nothing wrong with him. If you need to worry about anyone it's Judy. Not that I've had sex with her, but she can tell all sorts of lies to me and about me."

"It wasn't Suzanne who called you back and you were on some kind of promise was it? What did she mean, 'when you fuck a girl, she stays fucked'?"

"God no, where did that come from? Another thing, I didn't know Suzanne when I went to Dublin and I wasn't seeing anyone. I fell in love with you and knew you were the woman I wanted. Now, let's get through this damn traffic and I'm going to pamper you more than David Lennard pampers those cats of his."

Her smile is weak. "I do want to trust you so much Aidan, but men have hurt me in the past."

"I'm not those men, darlin' and you have to trust me, please…" I allow my words to trail as a momentary panic seizes me because I have fucked Suzanne. I've been in prison. I've done some bad things with Verdi Benson's help. All I hope is that Caitlan, so delicate, so gentle, will never discover it.

*

I let her rest a while and guiding her to the bed, refer to the pills and ask her where they are. The mention of her pills reminds me that I should sign us up with a GP as I promised. She insists on searching through her bag, although I urge her to rest, that I'll look for them. For some reason she is reluctant for me to know anything about them. I suggest she might be able to purchase migraine tablets over the counter.

Shaking her head, she remonstrates that they aren't strong enough. Are her migraines so bad that she has to only have pills on prescription?

She starts to protest again when I discover the small bottle containing white tablets labelled 'Teva-Olanzapine' – 20mg. To be taken once a day. Also printed on the label are her name, Miss Caitlan Bernadette McKenna, which I decide has a beautiful ring to it, plus the name of her doctor, S J Mulcahy, the Merrion Square Clinic, Dublin.

"So what happens if you run out of your pills then?" I ask, dropping onto the bed beside her. "Do you have to go back to Dublin? Only if you do I'll come with you."

"There's no need if you sign me up with a GP here."

"Sure. I'll talk to my sister. She deals with all that medical stuff. Will you be okay tonight?"

"Sure I will. I'll try for your sake, Aidan. I know what it means to you. Will… will…?" Flinging a palm across her eyes, she says, "will that Suzanne be there?"

I attempt not to stiffen. "I suppose so. She's a resident dancer after all."

"Can't… can't…" she swallows.

"Can't I what, sweetheart?"

"Can't you sack her? I mean I saw how you were with that stand-up guy today."

"Sack Suzanne? If she puts a foot wrong, maybe I will. Look, baby, you don't want to worry about her. You're my girlfriend and she knows that. Now, stop being so insecure. There's no need to be."

"I know, but I'm such a pathetic creat…"

The kiss I plant on her lips is conducive to silencing her.

"You're beautiful. You have the voice of an angel and with a name like Caitlan Bernadette McKenna, who can possibly compete with that? When you get up you're going to eat something. Can't have you fainting on me can I? But now, I'll give Brid a call, get her to sort out a doctor for you."

"And for you?"

"I don't need a doctor, sweetness. I'm pretty fit."

"I can testify to that," she smiles.

"I really don't deserve you."

"No, darlin', I don't deserve you, I really don't."

*

I could have called her sister Mollie in Dublin. If I had, she would, in all likelihood, have furnished me with more information concerning Caitlan's medication. Alternatively, I sense that if I ask her too many questions relative to her sister, she and her fiancé Niall will be over here demanding Caitlan return with them to Ireland.

Bridget is a nurse and there is stuff I need to know. So, cloistering myself in the bathroom, locking the door in case Caitlan decides to get up, I contact my sister.

"Aidan, how are you? How's Caitlan?"

"Are you at work?"

"I'm on a break at the moment. There was an RTA on the M25, we had most of the injured come to us, so it's been a wee bit busy here. If you wanted to meet up for a late lunch or something, it'll be nice to talk to you after the morning I've had."

I let her talk for a while. She sounds exhausted, even at that time of day. "Sure, I'd loved to Sis, but I can't leave Caitlan."

"What do you mean? She's not ill is she? You sound worried, Aidan. What's happened?"

"I'm not worried. Look, you've got a doctor haven't you?"

"A doctor?" Now Brid sounds really concerned. "She is ill, or you wouldn't need a doctor. Is there anything I can do?"

"No, Sis. She's lying down with a migraine. You know she told you about the accident?"

"Sure, but you can get migraine relief over the counter. My friend Maura gets migraines near her period. She swears by that Migraleve. If you want me to drop by with some…"

I explain to my sister about Doctor Mulcahy in Dublin, prescribing a drug called Teva-Olan – something or other.

"Teva-Olan? What the hell's that?"

"Search me, Sis. I don't know anything about medical stuff."

"So what did you want?"

"Your doctor. The GP. Is he local?"

"Blackheath. Why? It's Dr Southern. He's a good man when I can get in to see my own doctor that is. You need a GP for Caitlan?"

"Yeah, I don't have one. I didn't bother when I came out of prison did I?"

"And talking about prison. Have you told her yet?"

"No, I haven't. I didn't call you for a lecture. I'm just concerned about my girlfriend, that's all."

"Sorry, Aidan. Look, I'll talk to my surgery at Blackheath. So does this mean Caitlan's staying?"

"Sure. She seems reluctant to return to Dublin and if I call Mollie, Caitlan's sister about this, I get the feeling she and her fiancé will be over here post haste to drag her back. There's something else."

"Jesus, Aidan, what's that?"

"This is good news. What are you doing tonight?"

"Tonight? When I leave here I'm going to collect Sammy and Mark from school and soak in a nice hot bath, so I am."

"Look, get your friend Maura to mind the kids. I want you to come to the club tonight. It's my first night as new owner."

A momentary pause. "Come to that den of iniquity?" she snorts indignantly.

My sigh is heavy. "It's not like that anymore. Your brother is in charge now. You can bring Father Mulligan if you want."

I'm sure James, Father Mulligan's scene is hardly a nightclub. He is a priest."

"It's up to you, but I'd appreciate it if my sister was there on my first night and you'll get to hear Caitlan sing."

"So you trying to blackmail me now are you? I told Harry."

"What about?"

"About becoming the new owner of 'The Black Garter' club."

I purse my lips. "So what did he say?"

"All he said was, tell Aidan to be careful and I'm inclined to agree with him. Be careful, Aidan. So where is he?"

"Who?"

"He's tall, lanky and answers to the name of Ruairi."

"I don't know. I haven't seen him." I probably should have confided in Brid that Caitlan had seen, or imagined that she'd seen, someone in our room. Right now, however, it hardly seemed appropriate. "He's not babysitting, Brid. He's coming to the club with me. He's part owner now."

"I didn't tell Harry that Ru was in on it. Harry knows you at least can take care of yourself but Ru, well you know what he's like."

"Oh don't worry about Ru, Sis. He's 21 now. But sure you know I'll look after the stupid wee bastard."

"Just don't… don't…" she hesitates. "If something happens, don't let him be involved in anything unsavoury. He's not like you."

"Jesus, when have I been involved in anything unsavoury, as you call it?"

"My dear brother, sure if you don't have a short memory. As long as it's all behind you, now you've got that sweet girl. She's lovely and Harry's pleased for you, as long as you don't, quote, 'balls it up', unquote from your brother. Perhaps you shouldn't expose her to that kind of life, Aidan, or your brother."

For my own peace of mind, I opt to change the subject. "So you'll come tonight?"

"Och, maybe, I don't know and maybe to keep an eye on my brothers, if nothing else."

*

Caitlan continues to resemble a pale wraith from some angelic painting, although she claims to be feeling better, apart from a slight headache. I counsel her that if she can manage maybe three numbers, that would be enough. She promised to see how she feels. I'd fixed her a cheese salad, plus three mugs of chamomile tea. I'd gone and bought her a new dress and shoes. The dress is emerald green, cut above the knee and fits her perfectly. At 5' 3", she is less than a size

10 and far too thin to be healthy or so I consider. She also eats like a bird. Sometimes I worry that she might be bordering on anorexic.

"Why did you choose green, Aidan?" she addresses the mirror, a trace of annoyance in her voice. "Green shoes too. Just because I'm Irish, it doesn't mean I have to advertise the fact."

"You don't like it?" I attempt to conceal my disappointment.

She does look incredibly beautiful. The dress is fitted at the waist, accentuating her slender figure. To go with it I bought her a necklace, an adornment of pure white pearls. The money has issued from Sorenson. £75,000, aware I should spend it on the club. In truth, I prefer to spend it on her. However, I did buy myself a new suit, a dark pinstripe plus a cream silk shirt and black tie. The way I like to dress. We need to create the right impression, I tell her. I'm a businessman now, owner of a nightclub and dare to wonder momentarily if all this might have gone to my head.

I observe Caitlan regarding me with an odd sort of wistful expression. "When I first met you, you were wearing those old jeans and a check shirt and that old leather bike jacket you looked as if you'd slept in."

"Jesus, was I that bad?"

"I loved the way you looked. I don't want all this to change you Aidan, because if it does, I want my old rumpled Aidan McRaney back."

*

Mike Corman plus two other equally bellicose bouncers are on the door. When I enquire of Corman how his stomach is he makes a face and ultimately steps aside, as if he figures I might deliver another blow to his solar plexus. Caitlan isn't aware of this of course, that I had previously elbowed the big bouncer in the guts for refusing Ruairi and myself entrance.

It is still early. There is at least a couple of hours before the club opens. So I gather all the staff together, without realising that there are so many of them. Jacky Gorman has arrived wearing his customary houndstooth check jacket and light coloured slacks. Sloe-black eyes zero in on Caitlan and I immediately we arrive. His expression appears to be one of disbelief, I guess to observe yours truly actually wearing a decent suit and Caitlan outshining everyone.

The dancers are practising their finishing touches. Suzanne is present of course. I manage to drag Caitlan away to finalise her set. Prior to that, I call a meeting of the assembled staff. My staff now. Barmen. Dancers. The usual acts scheduled to appear on Thursday evenings, plus a young, black DJ and I am finally introduced to Paul Lucas.

I explain that I am content to allow them to continue with their own particular contributions and promise not to interfere unless I'm displeased with their act and if I am, I stress, espying an assorted array of nervously shifting feet, they will be in my office faster than they can breathe.

Ru promised to come by later, with a few friends from Uni. "As long as they aren't under age," I tell him. "That is under 18."

"They're my age, early twenties," he duly informs me.

"Then tell them smart or they're out."

I also outline that if anyone does drugs on my premises, I won't hesitate to contact the police.

The club is finally open and everyone is in place. All I have to do is oversee the proceedings. The punters are already filing in, mostly young people. I intend that the club should cater to all ages as long as they're over 18. I also ascertain that the usual warnings are in place. No drugs. No smoking. No weaponry. That the bouncers are to request ID from anyone who they suspect of being under age. Lamond is true to his word. The electronic search machine is in place in the lobby, attended to by a security guard. I hear someone refer to the fact it reminds them of an airport, but I intend taking no chances. With such stringent precautions in place, nothing can possibly go wrong can it?

By 10.30pm, even on a Thursday, the place is pretty well filling up and I busy myself mingling amongst the crowd in order to ensure there is no trouble.

I am pleased, albeit somewhat surprised, to see James Mulligan, minus his dog collar and soutane, garbed in a dark suit and tie, escorting my sister to a table nearest the stage. Brid has certainly scrubbed up well. Her redish gold curls are piled atop her head. She's wearing a slim fitting black velvet dress, while a black onyx on a chain adorns her throat. I realise that I have never seen her appear more beautiful. Even if he is a priest, it is good to know that my sister has a man in her life again. Although he is 20 years her senior, James Mulligan is obviously what she needs. Mark Collier doesn't know what he is missing and what a fool to walk out on such a lovely woman plus his two children.

Ruairi turns up later with Sandra from 'The Galleon'. Surprise, surprise. He's actually managed to locate a suit from somewhere, even if it is a sort of pale cream colour he wears with a blue tie and black shirt. So he resembles a negative but, needless to add, I refrain from lowering his confidence. His long hair, which is nearly as dishevelled as mine, is freshly washed and he's trimmed some of his beard.

In a blue spotted fifties style dress, her blonde hair upswept, Sandra succeeds in complementing him. The way they are dressed appears reminiscent of the whole fifties jive scene. Or is that the fashion now? Sandra is proud to inform me that she won't be drinking as she is driving.

In turn, Ru quips, "that means I can get pissed then," only to receive an authoritative dig in the ribs from his girlfriend. Several of his friends from the Camden Uni have joined him as he promised.

When Caitlan's set comes on, I join Brid and Father Mulligan at their table, astonished to observe tears in the priest's eyes when Caitlan sings, 'The Fields of Athenry'.

"That's close to where I come from, Bridget," I hear him whisper.

At least the priest is enjoying the singing, but I notice some of the punters have turned their backs toward the stage, are elbowing their way to the bar and engaging in shouting conversation. It serves to infuriate me. I guess I must have declared my annoyance because I entertain the lightest touch of Brid's hand on my arm.

"It's okay, Aidan. People are like that. She has a lovely voice. You have nothing to worry about. I told James that Caitlan is far too good for this dive."

"You're right, Sis." I press her hand in agreement, when I freeze suddenly. I actually, physically entertain the sensation of the blood draining from my face, as the past swiftly begins to unfold before me.

The man at the bar, a thick shock of tawny hair that is equally matched with a familiar tawny beard. The pallor of his features markedly contrasts with the abundance of facial hair. Wearing a grey suit, white shirt, black tie, I fail at first to realise who it is. I've never seen him in a suit hitherto because where he has been there is precious little chance to wear a suit.

The man propping up the bar, nursing a drink is none other than Dennis Mitchell, the guy with whom I shared a cell in HMP Maidstone and, as far as I am concerned, was still inside.

CHAPTER SEVENTEEN

-

WARNINGS

'The Black Garter' club is packed now and I've practically lost sight of Caitlan performing her act. At least those seated around the tables have stopped to listen. She claims to be happiest when she is singing and while she sings, it affords me the opportunity to scan Dennis Mitchell's presence at the bar. A presence which leaves me decidedly uneasy. I have no intention of letting him know I am there. Hitherto he hasn't seen me.

I inform my sister and Father Mulligan that I am going outside for a smoke.

"During Caitlan's act?" Brid frowns.

I assure her that Caitlan will be fine. That she can keep an eye on her while I'm away. Brid manages to whisper to me whilst the priest's attention is otherwise diverted to the stage, "you are treating her right aren't you, Aidan?"

"Sure I am. What kind of question's that, Sis?" I ask. My gaze wanders to the bar where I need to maintain an eye on Mitchell, hopefully without him becoming aware of me.

"She loves you, that's obvious. No other women, okay?"

"Brid." I flick her a disapproving look. "There are no other women, not anymore."

Brid presses my hand. "Good. You go and have your smoke. I'll tell her where you are if she comes across."

Throwing a glance towards the stage, I tell my sister that she won't be finished yet.

The cold night air hits me instantaneously. Soft flurries of snow have already begun to fall. Maybe it will be a white Christmas after all. My first Christmas out of the nick since I was 21. I have a lovely girl, a loving family. A son I care so much about, plus £75,000 in my bank account and one that isn't a loan. I can afford to buy Patrick something decent. With the fifty per cent access, I intend to plead to Judy to allow me to have him with me on Christmas Day.

I'd roll a cigarette, about to ignite it, when a flame flashes in the semi-darkness and a voice I believed I would never hear again, at least on the outside of a nightmare, says wryly, "got a fag, McRaney?"

I freeze, stare into the half-darkness incomprehensibly. His big round face is wreathed in that familiar partially bemused grin I'd come to associate him with, bringing with it a return of the old nightmares. The threat of exposure because he is here. There is a chance that Caitlan will discover the man she loves is an ex-con. I hear her pure, angelic voice emanating from inside 'The Flight of the Earls'.

Here is Dennis Mitchell flaring the lighter to his own cigarette, the red glow pulses in the street lamps.

"What the fuck you doing here, Mitchell?" I am in no mood for niceties. Momentarily I've been allowed to savour the pleasure that having money, love and freedom brings, only for it to be snatched away, perhaps by this man's sudden appearance. "I saw you at the bar. You haven't escaped from somewhere have you?"

"Escaped! Fuck no, and show up in that gaff if I was on the run? I saw your sign outside 'under new management'. Heard Raymondo was in the nick. That Ronnie Engels has moved in on a little joint out Essex way and guess what I was told… that my old pal and cell mate Aidan McRaney had taken over the ownership of 'The Black Garter' now. So how are you, you ould Paddy bastard? If that posh whistle is anything to go by, then I'd say things are looking up for you, mate."

I wasn't to be drawn, though I can't help but remain uneasy. "Things are okay. So what do you want Mitchell, and why did you follow me outside? If it's to catch up on old times, then you can forget it."

"Old times, as in jail you mean? I missed you, you know that."

"Sure y'did. You'll have me in fuckin' tears in a minute."

"Well I did, even if you didn't speak for days and sometimes all I got out of you was 'fuck off, Mitchell'. No, I got out a coupla months back. Last I heard of you, you was having a thing with Charlie Benson's old lady."

Stiffening involuntarily at the mention of Verdi, I glare at him. "That's over. The girl on the stage…"

"The singer. It ain't my cup of tea, but she's got the punters listening. Not the usual kind of bird in this gaff. Where did you find her? Or was she already here?"

"I found her in Dublin."

"So you went home. You always said you would."

"For a few days." I didn't elaborate. I figure it's none of Mitchell's business. "London's my home now. I found her in a bar near the river Liffey and before you say anymore, she's also my girlfriend."

His eyes enlarge. "Fuck me. She's pretty, McRaney. 'Course you always did have that old Irish charm. So what happened to Verdi? You blow her out?"

"It was mutual and I don't want to discuss it. I have a different life now."

"And your kid? You seeing him all right? 'Cos that's all I remember. That fuckin' cow of an ex, you said, got rid of your clobber while you were inside and you was worried you wouldn't get to know your son and he wouldn't call you Daddy."

"Well he does call me Daddy and I see him a lot, thanks to my sister."

"I saw the delectable Bridget. I remember when she used to come and visit you. My old woman used to be rabbiting on but all I wanted to listen to was your sister talk in that soft Paddy accent. Cor' I could have given that Bridget one."

"Shut the fuck up, Mitchell. That's my sister you're talking about."

"I know," he grins lasciviously, "so who's the geezer she's with? Your dad?"

"God no. Just a friend." I have no intention of enlightening the ex-con that my sister is dating a man of the cloth.

"So what do you want, Mitchell? Only I'm going back inside. The club that is, not jail." Finishing the remains of my cigarette, I crush it beneath a boot heel. I'm about to leave when Mitchell grasps my arm.

"I know Lamond's asked you to mind this place while he's in stir." His expression is oddly grave, serious.

Pulling my arm away abruptly, I rasp, "news sure does travel fast in the criminal world, man. Now if you don't mind, my girlfriend will be finishing her act soon and she frets if I'm not there."

"You got an office?"

"Sure," I frown. "But what you have to say, I'm sure you can say out here."

His glances behind him are strangely furtive and guarded.

"What the fuck, Mitchell?" I say.

"I need to talk but it might be less public if we talk in your office. You got a back entrance to this gaff?"

It is obvious he's singled me out for some kind of discussion, one I surmise I'm not going to like.

"Sure. Okay, we'll go to my office but, whatever it is Mitchell, I want you to spit it out and get the fuck out of my life. I have too much to lose. Caitlan, my girlfriend, doesn't know I've been inside and you showing up here is making me nervous."

"You ain't told your bird you've been inside? Fuck, McRaney, that's big stuff. Recipe for disaster mate," Mitchell chortles as he follows me to the rear entrance of the club premises where I have my office and I let us both into the building. Once inside he emits a timeless whistle. "This is nice."

"Just sit down and tell me what you want. Then get out, and the reason why I haven't told my girlfriend is the obvious one."

"You're scared of losing her, right?"

"Got it in one."

He moves around the room as if he's inspecting the place, before his gaze settles on the portrait of me and Frankie Lamond. I'm in the process of reaching for the bottle of Chivas Regal which I figure I'll need, in the filing cabinet. The secret stash of the alcoholic? Maybe it is.

"Driven to drink, McRaney?" Mitchell's gaze latches onto the bottle predaciously, an element of suspicion behind his words.

"You want one?" I have already placed a couple of glasses on the desk.

"Sure, why not? I've been on one beer all evening. It can get kind of boring."

"One beer. That doesn't sound like you."

"Well, I got my reasons. Look, you sure we're alone? There ain't no bugs in this room?"

"Bugs? I take it you don't mean the insect variety?"

"My old lady's telephone was bugged. She didn't know what it was. She kept on about her phone playing up. Her lights going on and off. She had bleedin' BT out twice."

"Not to my knowledge." Passing the scotch toward him, I have drained most of mine without realising.

He plumps his weight into a facing chair. I'm conscious of the bright beads of perspiration breaking out on his forehead.

Dennis Mitchell is in his mid-thirties. Quite a good-looking man I suppose, albeit crime and imprisonment over the years has taken its toll. Being a career criminal is all that Mitchell knows, while his features already testify to the signs of middle age. He sips the whisky slowly, content to observe me above the rim of his glass.

"So, what is it that's so important you wanted to discuss with me, Mitchell? Just because I've given you a drink, it don't mean…"

"Do you remember the boys from Brazil?"

I'd relaxed against the soft headrest of a leather armchair, now I'm compelled to sit bolt upright, draining the whisky in one swallow.

"Not for 10 years now. The boys from Brazil were the guys Frankie Lamond used to buy his drugs from. I tried to advise him against it but I was only his minder. He was paying my wages, not to think for him, to quote Frankie. I used to drive Frankie to the docks, either Southampton or Dover to meet the boat, mostly under cover of darkness. We were wary of the river police."

"Well, there ain't no 'used to', mate. Look, I know you ain't happy I showed up. I knew you was the owner now and I didn't just come here 'cos this was my haunt. We shared a cell. How many years was it?"

"Too fuckin' many," I mutter.

"5 or 6 years and I thought, trust me to share a cell with a moody Paddy, but we looked out for each other didn't we?"

"If you're after a hug and some male bonding, then you've come to the wrong place. When I saw you in here tonight I was transported back to HMP Maidstone again and all the crap that went with it, and there was my girlfriend up there on the stage. The last thing I want is for her to find out. So, is there a point to all this pally-pally, we-looked-after-one-another shit?"

"Still a bleedin' moody Paddy." But his tone is a good natured one. "Well I'm looking out for you now. You've been set up, mate "

Icy tentacles have suddenly begun a rhapsody the length of my spinal column. Half consciously, I find myself pouring another whisky without offering one to the other man.

"What are you talking about, Mitchell?"

"This club. Lamond's been using the boys from Brazil for the last few years, even after Frankie got shot, but Ronnie Engels wanted nothing to do with it. He reckoned, if they as much as darkened his doorstep, he'd contact the police."

"So will I? And nobody sets me up, Mitchell. Lamond's allocated me ownership of this club. I run it my way, understand? And I don't like fuckin' mind games." I'm on my feet instinctively, anger surfacing.

"I'm sorry. I should have guessed how you'd react."

"How the fuck do you expect me to react?"

"Look. Sit down. There's one big difference between you and Engels."

"Sure. He's ugly." I make a futile attempt at humour I'm far from feeling.

"Yeah there's that." Mitchell grins. "But Engels did his time, kept his nose clean. After Ray Lamond was jailed and all his concerns apart from this place were confiscated, it was Engels who talked to the 'suits'."

"I know. He told me. So who are these 'suits' I keep hearing about, Special Branch or something?"

"No. G-men."

"G-men," I laugh. "Jesus, this isn't fuckin' Roaring Twenties America. G-men." I can't help the derision from punctuating my words. "You've been watching too many of those old Jimmy Cagney movies."

"Okay. Government agents then. These agents have this rather high-falutin' idea they can stamp out crime in a more, how shall we say... discreet, less plodding manner than the Old Bill."

"Maybe I've had too many scotches, but I'm not getting any of this Mitchell."

"Let me start at the beginning then."

"Jesus." I heave an exasperated sigh. "If you have to."

"Do you remember how long my sentence was the last time? When we first met in stir."

"Sure. 10 to12 years. So?"

"I'd been inside two years when I was first transferred to Maidstone. I was scheduled to come out in 2014. That's over another two years before my release. That's why you thought I'd escaped."

"So you were released for good behaviour. It happens sometimes. That's why I got out six months early. I studied. Behaved myself."

"The 'suits' got me out, that's why."

His voice sinks to a conspiratorial level.

"You've been working for these 'suits'?" I regard him in disbelief. He nods and I hiss for him to get out. I don't need this crap in my life, not now. Now everything is beginning to fall into place for me.

"So why come to me? To get this place closed down?"

"No. Just to warn you. Lamond has set you up with the boys from Brazil. They're already on their way according to the guys I work for, and there ain't a damned thing you can do about it."

"I told you, I can call the police."

He shakes his head negatively. "You can't."

"Why not?"

"I mean you can, but the 'suits' have the tape."

"The tape?" I drop back into my seat, eyes narrow, as a glacial hand clutches my stomach wall, in spite of the fact I really don't have a clue to what he eludes. "What fuckin' tape? A tape of what?"

Mitchell leans so close and lowers his voice considerably. I am almost compelled to hold my breath in order to catch what he says. "There's a DVD roaming about. Remember Joydens Wood?"

"What!" I swallow and entertain the uneasy feeling that the world is closing in on me suffocatingly. That the few snatched moments of happiness are about to be pulled away. "Wh… what about Joydens Wood?" I demand in a voice I hardly recognise as my own.

"You and Verdi Benson. I ain't saying no more. The 'suits' reckon you did a good job. The Fitzwater's were renegades…"

A loud noise, as if a body has fallen, emanates from upstairs and causes both Mitchell and me to practically jump out of our skins, especially after what Mitchell has intimated, concerning the nightmarish episode at the Joydens Wood farmhouse.

"What the bleedin' hell was that?" Mitchell hisses.

"I don't fuckin' know." I raise my eyes ceiling ward. "It sounded as if it came from the room upstairs. Look, you stay here. I haven't finished this yet and I want you to tell me about this tape."

Clutching my arm all at once, Mitchell urges, "look, McRaney, Aidan, you got a piece?"

"A piece of what?" I ask obtusely. Of course I'm already aware of what he eludes to and I swallow uneasily again.

"A shooter. A pistol?"

"You think I need one then? Only it's life now for firearms possession."

"I know that, but sometimes a man has to protect himself and his family, get my drift? Here…" Reaching to the inside of his jacket, he must have witnessed me stiffen, because his face breaks into a wry smile. "No, I ain't tooled up. What, in this jacket? If you need anything, you know what I mean. I know the merchants man, and I know you're good with the heat. The 'suits' know it too. That's why they could use you. There's a geezer from who you can buy some 'protection' if you want it."

There is a 9mm Browning semi-automatic in a suitcase atop my wardrobe.

Nevertheless, I refuse to confess as much to Mitchell and I shake my head. "Guns only get you into trouble and I have too much to lose. Now, I'm going to see what's going on upstairs."

"You want me to come?"

"I don't need you to hold my fuckin' hand."

Coming on the wake of what he intimated, plus the idea someone has made a tape of what occurred in Joydens Wood, it all scarcely bears thinking about. It also makes me realise that I shall have to obtain that DVD at all costs. If Caitlan ever discovers what I've done, I'll lose her irretrievably. However, I manage a half-hearted quip, "perhaps it's the ghost," to account for the noise upstairs.

"Ghost?" Mitchell arches a speculative brow.

"You know, things that go bump in the night and all that. According to one of the dancers, the room upstairs is supposed to be haunted."

"Blimey. Ghost or no ghost, you'd better go and see what it is. You never know who might be listening and maybe you should take a weapon."

"I don't need a weapon, Mitchell." I am already unsettled by what we'd discussed, namely Joydens Wood, where Verdi and I had taken Stephen Fitzwalter after he'd raped and murdered my sister Laurena. A homosexual, Fitzwalter had had the audacity to try and kiss me after we'd trussed him to a chair. Angrily I'd taken a serrated edged blade and slashed him until he'd died. How could Mitchell have known unless Verdi had talked? Or someone had set up a recording device in the old farmhouse we had set fire to afterward. I doubt if Verdi would have grassed when she had killed Fitzwalter's homosexual partner, Nicholas, and Joanna Sheldon. And I wish that the noise I had heard upstairs really did emanate from the spirit world.

Everything has gone ominously quiet. However, I take care not to announce my presence too readily when I mount the stairs to the upstairs room, where I haven't ventured since having sex with Suzanne and the discussion with Ronnie Engels. On the landing, reaching the white painted door, I twist the handle slowly, about to burst in, until I discover the door to be locked. I'm aware I could have broken it down with Mitchell's help. The silence behind the door indicates that, unless whoever is inside has exited through the window, they have gone noticeably quiet.

"Open this door or I'll break it down!" I demand and wait impatiently for a response. I observe Mitchell has moved to the foot of the stairs.

"Want some help?"

I tell him I'll be fine.

"I said open this fuckin' door!" I rattle the knob vigorously and the door is finally open, albeit gingerly.

Wearing only his trousers, his long hair dishevelled, while a suitably shame faced expression rides his young features, Ru stands there.

"What the fuck you doing here, Ru?" I demand.

"It's not how it looks, Aid," he mumbles feebly.

I burst in to reveal a scared, red-faced Sandra. Her dress is pulled up around her in an inadequate attempt to conceal her nakedness. It's obvious what they've been doing. Somehow, I'm so relieved I could have kissed them. Although when I have time to think things through, I wonder if they've gleaned any information from my talk with Dennis Mitchell. If Ru has heard mention of Joydens Wood, that will take some explaining.

Ru and Sandra had pulled out that divan and Sandra sits bolt upright on it now, her face growing even more crimson with embarrassment. I guess because I'm in the room. In spite of my initial relief, I can't possibly let them off the hook. I close the door, in the main because I have no intention of Mitchell learning anything of their presence.

"So how the hell does it look, Ru?"

"Look, we just needed a place..."

"To fuck," I interrupt.

Quickly locating his shirt, he hauls it on.

"Sandra wants to get dressed, Aid. We... we'll come down."

Instead, I urge him to stay put.

"You what!" Ru regards me, surprised. "I thought you wanted us to get dressed, go downstairs. I'm sorry."

"Sure, it's cool, I told you." My tone softens. "I want you to stay here for..." I pause and flick a glance at my watch, instruct he waits half hour.

"Why? What you up to, Aid?"

"Nothing. Sorry, Sandra." I deal her a watery smile.

"It's okay," she responds quietly.

"Did you hear me downstairs?" I ask Ru.

"Yeah and some other guy. I told Sandra that you were downstairs. So we kept quiet, hoping you wouldn't notice 'til Sandra dropped her bag."

"I'm sorry," she humbly apologises.

"Just do as I ask, okay, and you didn't hear anything of our conversation?"

Ru's brows knit a frown. "I wasn't really listening. What's wrong? You've gone pale. It's nothing to do with us is it?"

"No, Bruv," I assure him, a hand on his shoulder. "It's nothing to do with you. Just try and choose a more discreet place to have sex, okay, and not just above my office."

The years roll back momentarily to 2003, when my beautiful Leanne and I had wonderful sex in the same room. The apartment where I stayed after the club closed, the nights I failed to return to Judy and Patrick.

With Ruairi promising to stay put upstairs for another half hour, I return downstairs. I hear Mitchell shout my name as I reach the bottom of the stairs; discover Suzanne, wearing a figure hugging, scarlet, spandex bikini and outrageous high heels, standing there. Her face is unaccustomedly ashen beneath her make-up. Her words stumble over themselves, "Aiden, it's your girlfriend Caitlan."

"What about her?"

"She's collapsed on the stage. She just fell in a dead faint," Suzanne explains.

CHAPTER EIGHTEEN

-

MANAGING HER CONDITION

Everything appears to be unravelling in front of me after what, ostensibly, had begun as a renewed interest in my life. Having the money, more access to my son and above all, a girl whom I love and who loves me enough to marry me. Then Dennis Mitchell appears like some vengeful spectre from the past, as if to snatch it all away.

Caitlan hasn't recovered from her faint. Brid is a nurse and I allow her to take charge. She called the ambulance and my sister and I travel to the nearest hospital.

I want to forget Mitchell's dire warnings concerning the boys from Brazil. It all appears, in the light of what has happened to Caitlan, to be so unreal now. Simply mind games, that's all.

Brid and I are shown to an impersonally grey-walled visitor's room. I remark how grim the décor is. They could have chosen something more cheerful, less depressing.

Brid hands me a coffee in a Styrofoam cup, with the remark that just lately all we seem to do is sit around in hospitals.

Ru enquired if there is anything he can do and I promise to call him when I have news of Caitlan. Brid is concerned because Caitlan hasn't managed to come around after her faint, in spite of her efforts.

Caitlan was rushed into a side ward and I demand from every passing nurse how she is, only to be informed that a Doctor Marchant will be out to talk to us soon.

When Dr Marchant finally deigns to show himself he extends a hand, and apologises for keeping us waiting.

He's a tall, middle-aged man with greying hair and polished, well shaven features, albeit his eyes are shadow enshrouded, as if he's slept little.

"We were worried that Caitlan hasn't come out of her faint, doctor," Brid says. "I'm a nurse and I was there immediately but she didn't appear to respond."

"She... she isn't in a coma is she?" I ask and shake the proffered hand briefly. She hasn't died as our beloved sister had died the night I brought her in.

"No, Mr McRaney, merely fainted." His tone contains an element of derision and I thought, this guy has no idea what we've been through. "She has now come around and is asking for you. Are you Aidan?"

"I'm Aidan."

"When you've seen Miss McKenna, I'd appreciate it if you'd step into my office." The timbre of his voice has strangely altered.

I freeze, sensing there is something obviously amiss with my girlfriend. "Is... is she okay?" I swallow hard.

"You'll find out for yourself but I'd like to keep her in overnight. Oh don't worry, it's just for a few tests."

"Tests!" Brid and I echo in unison and I ask what kind of tests.

"I'll tell you when you come into my office. Sister!" he signals to a plump, matronly woman wearing a dark blue uniform. "Would you mind escorting Mr McRaney and his sister to Miss McKenna's room please."

At least my girlfriend has a room to herself. However, I can't wait to see Dr Marchant again, whilst simultaneously aware I am also unwilling to discover exactly what is wrong with the girl I love, if it is bad news.

Wearing a less than flattering hospital gown, she's propped up by white pillows, but still manages to resemble some beautiful angel. Her long, dark hair is spread against the contrasting white. I wish for my camera so that I could capture her lovely image for posterity. Alarm courses through me, however, coming in the wake of Dr Marchant's words. Does she have some terrible life threatening illness? It isn't cancer is it, leukaemia? She invariably appears to be inordinately pale. She has been eating little since she has been with me. I consider calling Mollie, informing her that Caitlan is in hospital. She might have some idea what is wrong with her and about any medication her sister is on. Although every time I consider calling Mollie, I am scared she might want to take her back to Dublin. Does Caitlan have but a few months to live then? Is that why Dr Marchant looks so worried? All manner of unwelcome thoughts tumble around inside my head.

She says my name and I join her on the bed, when both women have cause to regard me with concern.

"Aidan, I'm so glad you're here and Bridget thanks for coming. What's wrong?" It is Caitlan who wipes the tears from my face.

"You alright, Aidan?" Brid produces a small packet of tissues from her bag and passes me a couple.

To hopefully take their minds from the fact a 6' 2" guy, who professes to be marginally tough, should be crying like a child, I ask my sister where Father Mulligan is.

"He's gone home," Brid replies. "He knows and respects the fact I have to put my family first. Look, I'll leave you two alone. Grab one of those awful hospital coffees." She smiles awkwardly; I guess witnessing tears in her brother's eyes has distressed her.

"You don't have to go, Bridget," Caitlan tells her.

If I'm not much mistaken, there are tears present in my sister's eyes also. Bridget is renowned for her strength. When it comes to her family, however, I guess she wears her heart on her sleeve. It also makes me realise how much my sister and I love Caitlan. Brid practically flings herself from the room in her haste. "What's wrong with you two?" Caitlan asks with a smile.

I touch a palm to her cheeks. They feel strangely colder than I expected.

"It's nice to know that someone cares," she says.

"Sure we care, sweetheart. If you must know, I was worried sick. So what happened?"

"I just passed out, that's all." Her smile fades all at once. "Actually, that wasn't all."

"What is it sweetheart?" I slip an arm around her.

Her eyes appear oddly distant suddenly, as if they are endowed with some unfathomable light. She stares at something in the room I fail to see.

"The man I saw in your bedroom…"

Not that again, I think to myself but manage to regain my composure and not allow her to witness how her words have disturbed me. "What about him?"

"He was there, in the club. I saw him approach the stage. Then something overcame me and I fainted."

"Look, baby, we'll get to the bottom of this man, whoever he is. I mean it could have been anyone. That place was pretty well packed tonight."

"When you disappeared, I was frightened."

"I… I just went out for a smoke, that's all."

There is no way I can possibly confide in her about my past, certainly none of what Dennis Mitchell has imparted. Worse still, the DVD he's insisted was floating around, of Verdi and me in the Joydens Wood farmhouse. I resolve to obtain it at all costs, determined to contact Mitchell again. I need to discover exactly who is in possession of the DVD, if it exists of course, even if I have to take a gun with me. The anger remains that someone knows about my crime and worse, had the audacity to have filmed it.

"I'm sorry, so sorry, sweetheart. You look so beautiful, like an angel."

"You were crying over me. I've never had a man do that for me before, not even my own father."

"Maybe no man has ever loved you as much as I do. So, I suppose you want me to call Mollie?"

"No! No!" The green eyes snap wide immediately. "I'll call her when I'm feeling better. She'll only want to take me back to Dublin, she'll think the worst of you, I might never see you again and I couldn't bear it if that happened. You don't know what she's like."

"I've got a pretty good idea, but if she did take you back I'd come to Dublin with you. I'd go to Australia, anywhere, Mars if necessary. I'll never leave you, sweetheart. In fact…"

"In fact what?"

"I know it's not the most appropriate place, a hospital and you in a hospital nightie but…" I pause and dropping onto my knees beside her bed, I press both her hands between mine. "Will you marry me, Caitlan Bernadette McKenna?"

"Aidan!" she sounds a little breathless when she speaks my name. "You… you really mean that?"

"Sure I do, baby. A simple yes or no will suffice." My heart is hammering loudly against my chest, in case she refuses me.

"Yes, oh yes I'll marry you. I love you so much." Her eyes shimmer a scintillating emerald. She flings her arms around my neck, as I rise to my feet before dropping back onto the bed again. "I was scared you wouldn't come right out and ask me."

Later, she complains of feeling tired. So I let her rest and return to my sister in the impersonal waiting room to observe she's left me a coffee. I inform her that Dr Marchant wishes to see me.

"Oh!" Brid's eyes round in surprise.

"And there's something else," I enthuse.

"What's that? You okay now? When you started, I started too. I haven't seen you weep since the night Laurena died. Guess it all comes back in these places."

Ignoring her protestations about spilling her coffee, I grab her by the shoulders. "Never mind that, you're going to be a sister-in-law again."

"I am? What's that supposed…?"

"I've asked Caitlan to marry me and she's accepted."

"Oh, Aidan, that's fantastic!" Her arms around me, we hug and I know that Brid is genuinely pleased. "She's a lovely girl," she adds when she releases me. "I was worried you'd never find anyone decent, not after that Benson woman."

"Sure now, that's all in the past, sis. Nothing, and I mean nothing, is going to jeopardise this for me." I realise I have spoken my thoughts aloud.

Not Mitchell, not those so called 'suits' or Ray Lamond, certainly not that fuckin' DVD Mitchell had spoken of. I catch Brid regarding me with a puzzled expression.

"Why should it, Aidan?" she asks quietly.

*

I discover Dr Marchant seated at the desk in his office. On his door, the familiar nameplate declares his qualifications in a veritable string of letters. At my entrance, he raises his head from his computer screen. The screen is partially turned towards me when he motions me into a facing chair. I see Caitlan's name, plus that of a Dr S J Mulcahy, the Merrion Square Clinic, Dublin.

"So why do you want to keep Caitlan, Miss McKenna, in overnight?" I ask.

"Well, her blood count is a little low."

A reptilian something has begun to uncoil itself in my guts. "Is it… has she got leukaemia?"

"Leukaemia? Good God no! Whatever gave you that idea? Are you a doctor now, Mr McRaney?"

I feel foolish now. "It's just that she's so pale all the time and you just said about her blood count. Isn't that something to do with leukaemia?"

"Leukaemia is cancer of the blood, Mr McRaney. Caitlan's blood count is a little low because of the medication she's on."

"For migraine? She takes medication for migraine."

"Migraine is common. This has nothing to do with migraine. I can see she hasn't told you. You're both from Ireland?"

"Sure, but what's that got to do with anything and what hasn't she told me?"

"I'm getting to that." Removing his horn rims briefly, Dr Marchant pauses to scratch at his shock of greying hair, as if he is searching for the right words, before the spectacles are returned. "So how long have you both been over here and are you still attending the Merrion Square Clinic in Dublin?"

"I've never attended this Merrion Square Clinic. I've been in London for 20 years."

"And Caitlan?"

"A few days."

"I see she's been seeing Dr Mulcahy."

"I think so. She does have some medication because I've seen it. I'm trying to get her into a GP here. She wants to stay and I've asked her to marry me."

"Congratulations, Mr McRaney," he enthuses warmly. "I hope she's accepted. You seem a level-headed young man. What Caitlan needs is stability. I can see you're rather in the dark about this. Has she ever mentioned the car accident in which she lost her mother?"

"Sure. She said that's why she has the migraines and all this, whatever it is, has it anything to do with her passing out on stage?"

"Everything, I should say. I've tried to contact Dr Mulcahy in Dublin. I met him once. St John Mulcahy's one of the most eminent neurologists in Ireland."

"Neurologist?" I swallow uncomfortably.

"Apparently, Caitlan suffered a brain injury in the crash."

"You mean she's... she's got brain damage?" No matter, I love her. I'll be there for her, in sickness and health. "It's... it's not a tumour is it?"

Dr Marchant allows himself a small, wry smile. "I'll be treating you for hypochondria, Mr McRaney. No, she hasn't got a tumour or leukaemia but she does have psychotic episodes."

"Psychotic? You mean her mind?"

"The medication she's on is called Teva-Olanzapine. I've managed to patch through a call to the Dublin clinic where she's been treated this last three years. After coming out of hospital, she spent six months in an institution. Her mother's death hit her hard, and along with the injury, she has bouts of schizophrenia."

"Schizophrenia?" In disbelief at the revelation of the illness from which my beloved Caitlan is suffering, I realise I'd begun to repeat every word Dr Marchant says, "you mean dual personality?"

"I'm afraid so. The Teva–Olanzapine helps her to control it. Although all it needs is a trigger to spark off an episode. Of course, the drug has side effects. Weight gain is common, numbness, tingling of the skin, mood changes. I or another doctor would prescribe regular blood tests to monitor the Olanzapine."

"I didn't know any of this."

"Oh don't look so worried, Mr McRaney. It's nothing that can't be managed. It's no different from diabetes. That can be controlled both with tablets and insulin. As I said, the Olanzapine can increase appetite and therefore lead to weight gain. Psychologically, the patient knows this and tends to eat little. So does she live with you and is she planning to stay in England?"

"Yes to both questions."

"When I've had a word with Dr Mulcahy I'll know more. There is some good news, though it'll mean the Teva-Olanzapine will have to be monitored more closely. At least I hope it's good news," he adds.

"What's that Doc? I could use some good news."

"Well I'll need to do a further urine test, but I believe there is another reason for Caitlan's faintness. She's expecting a child, Mr McRaney."

*

All the mind games with Dennis Mitchell are simply that, with no foundation in reality. My forthcoming marriage and the fact she is expecting my baby is all that matters. All I want to do is to put the past behind me. It pains me to leave her in the hospital overnight, although I remained there as late as I possibly could. After Dr Marchant's discussion concerning her medication, she was scared I wouldn't want to marry her.

I occupy the bed beside her, take her hands in mine and promise to be there for her. The way I feel, I would gladly have married her there in the hospital. We are both Catholic. With Father Mulligan conducting the service, Bridget and Ruairi as witnesses, all the pomp and ceremony could go hang as far as I'm concerned.

I tell Brid that Caitlan is pregnant, she is pleased of course. In company with her pleasure and congratulations issues the inevitable warning, "don't start life with a lie, Aidan. Tell her about prison and why you were there. She worships the ground you walk on. She'll understand."

"What about if it sparks off an episode like Dr Marchant said? I don't want to be responsible for making her ill."

"Just talk to her quietly, gently or she might hear it from someone else, and they might not be so considerate. I can't do it. None of us can, only you Aidan, you have to be the one to tell her."

The coward that I am, it all remains unsaid. So it is that Caitlan continues to believe I am an exemplary young man with no criminal convictions, no prison record.

The following morning, I collect Caitlan from the hospital. Firstly, at the consultation with Dr Marchant, he explains how he's managed to contact Dr Mulcahy at the Merrion Square Clinic. If Caitlan wishes him to, Dr Mulcahy will pay her a visit when he is next in London. When I suggest this to Caitlan, she surprises me by adamantly refusing to see the Irish neurologist. I'm also aware she's received several missed calls from Mollie, because Caitlan had left her mobile in the bedroom. There were innumerable texts too. 'Call me, Cait. Are you taking your meds? I'm worried about you.'

*

"So I'm to be an uncle again?" Ru observes at breakfast the following morning.

It is my weekend with Patrick. I'd left Caitlan asleep while I fix toast and coffee. Ru tucks into his habitual cereal.

"Sure y'are and you'll be a father too if you aren't careful." I admonish.

"No way, Bruv, I ain't ready for all that yet."

"Neither was I at 20 but I love Patrick and now Caitlan's expecting."

"It's definitely yours?"

"Sure it is and I've asked her to marry me. Did Brid tell you?"

"She can't stop talking about anything else, her precious Aidan getting married."

I regard him with a frown. I have never heard Ru talk that way before. "What's that supposed to mean, 'Precious Aidan?' She loves you too. Jesus, we're a family."

"I dunno," he shrugs. "I think she remembers what I was like as a kid, when she had to babysit me. I knew she hated it 'cos she'd rather be dating one of those sexy locums from the hospital and I used to play her up, but you were so quiet."

"Sure I was, until I got into trouble, with an almighty chip on my shoulder, hating school and running with the bad boys. You're precious to me, Ru, you're my kid brother." I pause to ruffle his already dishevelled locks playfully. "And if I hear anyone talking negatively about you, they'll have me to answer to and that includes our sister."

My mobile ringing suddenly. I check the call to discover, with a crazily beating heart, it is none other than Dennis Mitchell.

"Who's that? Brid?" Ru asks, raising his head from his cereal speculatively.

"Sure," I lie. "I've got to take this call." Out of earshot of my brother, I move into the lounge, close the door and hiss, "what the fuck do you want?"

"How's your bird?"

"She's fine. Is that all you wanted to know?"

"Look, I've had to call from a payphone."

"Why?"

"I can't use my mobile or landline in case they're tapped. The boys from Brazil have landed. They'll be on their way to the club soon I expect. I thought I'd better warn you."

I freeze automatically. Nonetheless, I refuse to be drawn. "It's nothing to do with me. I'm taking my son out today and Caitlan doesn't need any stress. So call the polis, man and get them arrested."

"I can't do that. How's it going to look? An ex-con with my record going to the filth about drug dealers. You try doing the same. They'll wonder how you knew, for a start. It's drugs, mate, crack-cocaine, the hard stuff. Besides, these bastards are dangerous. If they know someone's called the 'Bill', they might react, you know what I mean?"

"There's something more important than fuckin' drug dealers. This DVD you were talking about, if it exists. Who has it and where did they get it from?"

"Yeah, I got some information on that. Apparently it was seized from Lamond's Maze Hill gaff with loads of other stuff."

"What other stuff and who seized it?" I hear my heart crashing like breakers against my rib cage while he talks.

"It was after his arrest."

"If the polis have it and I'm arrested and go to prison again, it'll destroy my family, just when my life is beginning to get back on track."

"The police don't have it, the 'suits' do. It was them who seized Lamond's stuff. He'd made recordings of murders, prostitutes with their clients. He'd obviously used hidden cameras to spy on them, all kinds of filth, including fuckin' kiddie fiddlers. That geezer was perverted."

"But why should he want to record me and Verdi at the farmhouse? For fuckin' posterity?"

"Maybe to blackmail you into working for him; the Lamond brothers have had a lot of fingers in a lotta pies and not just in England, your country too."

"My country, you mean Ireland?"

"Yeah. Apparently, he's had dealings with some Paddy, O'Malley or something, I dunno. They're all O's and Mc's over there ain't they?"

"Not all of them. Never mind that. Can you get hold of that DVD for me? Or at least destroy it?"

"I don't know who has it. My guess is Lamond wouldn't have sent it to the Bill. After all, he was the one who supplied the weaponry, the safe house. He would have sent it to your family."

"Jesus, what a fuckin' mess."

"Look, I gotta go, McRaney. I'll see what I can find out."

"These 'suits', are they dangerous?"

"They used to be."

"What the fuck's that supposed to mean?"

"Just that most of 'em have been chosen because they have criminal records."

"So, who are they?"

But silence is his only response.

CHAPTER NINETEEN
-
A DAY OUT WITH DISASTER

Caitlan informs me that she is feeling much better now. She will be pleased to meet my son. I ask her if she is sure she is up to having a day out. I like to take Patrick wherever he wants to go.

"Quite sure, Aidan," she enthuses.

Her arms encompass me as she refers to Dr Marchant sorting out her medication. All she hopes is that I won't send her back to Dublin because of her condition. I assure her that nothing has changed. I love her very much and intend to marry her.

Caitlan and I spend the evening planning our future together, while Ruairi looks on concerned. Am I rushing into things? I tell him that I've never been more convinced of anything in my life. Besides, Caitlan is having my baby.

I attempt to dispel Mitchell's concerns about the boys from Brazil arriving at the club. I remember his enquiry - was I in possession of a gun? There is an automatic pistol in my suitcase, above the wardrobe in my bedroom, aware that maybe now is the appropriate time to dispose of it. Not to hand it to the police if I don't wish to risk awkward questions being asked, but into the waters of the Thames under cover of darkness.

On the journey to Esher, even the silence which has sprung up between Caitlan and I seems somehow companionable. I guess she and I are lost in our own retrospections.

As we near Judy's place, I counsel Caitlan she might prefer to wait in the car. My ex-wife can be both fractious and unpredictable. "Like me you mean?" she jokes.

"Not at all like you, sweetheart. Judy is an argumentative bitch most of the time." Her smile fades all at once.

I notice that Judy has added a sort of fountain affair to her front lawn. The hedges are neatly trimmed since I was here last. Maybe she has a man after all.

I leave Caitlan with a passionate kiss and a promise not to be too long.

"Sure, if that's what you want Aidan but I don't mind meeting her honestly."

"I think it's best if you don't."

God knows what my ex might tell her about me.

Judy ushers me into her kitchen when I arrive with an, "oh, Aidan, you're a bit early. I don't think Patrick's ready yet."

She pauses to rake me over pointedly as is her custom. In dark jeans and a blue sweater, I can't help but notice how her nipples, pert and erect, strain predominantly against the garment. She's definitely had breast augmentation. Maybe her plastic surgeon boss performed the operation for her.

"So, how've you been Jude?" I enter the room but without removing my coat.

"I'm fine. I don't need to ask you how you've been. You're looking as good as ever and the beard suits you. I've never seen you with a beard before. Your girlfriend's idea was it?" There is thinly veiled sarcasm in her tone.

"Don't start, Jude. So who told you I had a girlfriend?"

"You did, darling, when you were here last. Oh, not in so many words, but I knew and I've got eyes you know. I saw you pull up in the drive, then saw you snogging her face off in the front seat. Besides, I met Bridget in Oxford Street. She couldn't talk about anything else but you and your little Irish Colleen."

"I said don't start, Jude. I didn't come for an argument. So is Patrick going to be long?"

"He's just brushing his teeth I think."

"So he hasn't had meningitis or anything else you've had him hospitalised for?"

Her mouth tightens and I observe her body tense against the kitchen sink. "No. And I apologised for that and the 50 per cent access. Naturally I was angry at first, but maybe it can work both ways."

"What's that supposed to mean?"

"I'm seeing someone." She pauses to search my face, for what, signs of jealousy? Well, she isn't going to get lucky.

"That's great, Jude. So who is he?"

"Rafe Carswell."

"Your boss?"

"Yes my boss. Oh don't look so holier-than-thou, Aidan. He's going through a divorce."

"So he's still married?"

"Yes, he's still married. You're not my father and if anyone's starting, as you say, it's you. I'm pleased for you and what's her name? Katie?"

"Caitlan."

"So, have you told her that you were detained at Her Majesty's Pleasure? Because, according to your sister, you haven't and Bridget was concerned that it might come out."

"That's none of your business. Look, I'll go and see what's keeping Patrick."

"Why don't you invite Colleen in?"

"It's Caitlan, I told you and she's not capable of standing up to you and your vitriolic tongue."

"What's that supposed to mean?" Her laugh is suddenly shrill and grating. "She needs to be strong to go out with you. When we first met, I was a stupid, naive little nurse and you were the gun-toting minder to that gangster. Now I can give you back all you can throw at me, Aidan McRaney."

"I don't doubt that Judy but I don't want you telling her anything."

"So you haven't?" Her smile is sardonic and she folds her arm across her chest in a defiant pose. "Dear oh dear, a recipe for disaster, my darling." She calls after me when I race up the stairs and I entertain a swift desire to lash out at her, but I dispel the feeling. The trouble with Jude is that she knows how to press all the right buttons. The bitch is still a challenge and knows it. She is also aware that she only has to come on to me and I'll fuck her at the drop of a hat. I don't love her but it scarcely prevents her from attracting me in other ways.

I discover my son on his knees in the process of scrambling around for something beneath his bed.

I enquire what he is searching for.

"Hi Daddy. My other shoe. Am I staying at your flat?" he asks, almost in one breath.

"Is that okay?"

"'Course it is."

"Come on then, let's look for this shoe." I immediately spot it across the room, as if he has thrown it.

"Thanks," he murmurs and slips on the shoe.

"Can we go to the Animal Farm today?"

"Animal Farm?"

"Yeah, it's near…" he searches his memory before admitting that he fails to remember where it is, adding, "Mummy knows. You'll have to ask her. She's got the tickets."

"You have to have tickets?"

Dressed in jeans and a striped sweater, he appears inordinately grown up. "Yeah, to get in. It's cheaper if you have tickets. You can still get in without them, but it's extra. It's a proper farm with all sorts of animals. I went there with the school. I loved it so much, I wanted to go there again. So Mummy got the tickets."

"So how many tickets did you get?" I dare ask.

"Two. For you and me. How many did you want?" He hugs me as I stretch to my full height.

"Patrick," I speak his name quietly, before holding him at arm's length. "It isn't just the two of us."

"Is Mummy coming? Only she said she was going to play golf later."

"Mummy plays golf? Sure, I didn't know that."

"Yeah." His expression is suddenly crestfallen. "She goes with her boss Rafe."

"No, she isn't coming. It's just you, me and Caitlan."

His brown eyes flash a disconcerted look and one that causes my heart to race. "Who's Caitlan?"

"She's my girlfriend, Patrick. Hopefully we're going to be married soon."

Maybe I shouldn't have furnished him with so much information. He is my son. Therefore, I respect his opinion and hope that he will love Caitlan as much as I do.

"She won't be my mother will she?"

"No…" I hesitate. "She won't be your mother."

I encounter my ex-wife on the landing outside Patrick's door. "I was coming to see where you were."

"Patrick wants to go to some Animal Farm place. He said you had tickets."

"Yeah, I almost forgot."

Returning downstairs, she produces the respective tickets and tosses them across the table in my direction. "I'll fetch his coat."

"I didn't know you played golf, Jude."

"Yeah, with Rafe. At Silvermere. It's not far. And the Animal Farm, it's near Brooklands. You know where the old racing circuit used to be."

"Sure." I pocket the tickets. "I know where it is."

"Sorry I didn't get one for your little Irish Colleen, but I didn't know she was coming."

I glare at her. Predictably, she returns the look with her own familiarly seductive smile.

"It's okay, I'll pay for her."

Behind me, Patrick mutters, "I thought it was just going to be me and you. I don't care if Uncle Ruairi and Aunt Brid come."

"How is Ruairi anyway? I heard you and him are running a nightclub now."

"He's fine. Yeah we are, Jude," I say non-committally.

"Rafe and me might come down one night. Your old haunt 'The Black Garter', so Bridget says. She's not happy about it but that was always your thing, wasn't it Aidan?" Shrugging on Patrick's coat and buttoning it, she hugs and kisses him. "Anyway, you both have a good time." She regards me above Patrick's head. "Patrick knows where the farm is, don't you, darling?"

"It's okay, Jude, I'll find it. I know where Brooklands is."

It's a relief to finally exit the house and Judy's sardonic inflections. At the door, as Patrick and I head down the path, she calls, "oh, don't forget to give my love to your little Colleen, darling," sarcastically.

It's enough to make me stiffen, but I control my temper with an effort.

"I'm sorry to have taken so long, sweetheart," I apologise to Caitlan as I slide behind the steering, fasten my belt. I search her face for any signs of annoyance because I kept her waiting. "You okay?"

"I'm fine." Turning her attention to Patrick, she deals him a sweet, welcoming smile because that's the kind of girl she is, as he drops into the back seat.

"He had to find his shoe, didn't you Patrick?"

At least that is partially true. "This is my son, and Patrick, this is Caitlan." There is pride in my voice when I introduce them.

"Hi, Patrick. I'm so pleased to meet you at last. Your dad's talked about you so much, so he has…"

Her words have fallen on deaf ears, however; Patrick has dug out his Nintendo 3DS from his coat and is seemingly more interested in that. His dark forelock marginally conceals his eyes and he refuses to glance up, while his fingers press buttons on his game with an almost nervous agitation. I fire the Cabriolet's ignition and swing into the street.

"Talk to Caitlan, Patrick, or I'll have to confiscate that game."

Caitlan has gone noticeably paler. I guess she feels awkward over my son's irresponsiveness. Smiling her way, I press her knee reassuringly.

"Hi," he mutters, but the greeting is scarcely audible.

"So, Patrick, you going to give your old Dad the directions to this Animal Farm place?"

"Haven't you got a Sat Nav? You only have to put in the directions. Rafe has a Sat Nav."

I bet the fuck he does, although I choose not to vocalise my thoughts. "No, I don't have a Sat Nav."

"He looks just like you, Aidan. It's quite uncanny." Caitlan manages to change the subject, bless her. I am pleased Judy has a man in her life, but what I don't want is my son comparing his attributes and finding mine wanting.

"So everyone says. So, what kind of animals can we expect to see, Patrick?" I ask.

"Just animals." He shrugs.

"You don't mind going to see some animals?" I ask Caitlan, little realising that it is the wrong thing to say because my son chooses to retort, "it's my day out with my dad. It's no one else's business."

I tense, my mouth tightening, but will myself to composure with an effort.

Caitlan has only recently left hospital and is quite sensitive right now with her condition. I reason that although my son might resemble me physically, he has unfortunately inherited something of his mother's vitriolic tongue. I love them both equally but have no real desire to act as mediator between my girlfriend and my son.

"Sure it is, Patrick," Caitlan agrees pleasantly. "It's your day." She touches a slender braceleted palm over mine on the gear stick.

"I'm sure we'll all have a lovely day."

Nevertheless, Patrick remains ominously taciturn while Caitlan and I lapse into a silence of our own, broken only by Patrick declaring excitedly, "There it is. You've just passed it."

*

The Animal Farm, located close to the old Brooklands race circuit, is quite an extensive park and has an assortment of animals ranging from rabbits of all breeds in their hutches, birds in cages, as well as sheep and pigs in sties. I'd taken Patrick to the zoo once but had been duly informed by my ex that our son had no liking for caged animals. Yet here he is enthusing over what we could expect to see, while the smell of the country is definitely in the air.

It is Caitlan who remarks how awful it is to see those poor animals shut up in cages, like a prison, as we walk around. My hand is against her waist while the other clutches my son's. I look at her when she mentions prison but she doesn't return the glance. Her expression remains impassive and she's more interested in the animals.

Releasing my hand, Patrick appears to know his way around and we stop to view a collection of different breeds of rabbit, from Angoras to a small runt Caitlan enthuses over. Because visitors are allowed to pick up the rabbits, Caitlan predictably selects the small, black one and commences to stroke its fur. Half of its hairs have come away on her coat but she appears too involved in cuddling the little rabbit to notice. Patrick has lifted a fat Angora into his arms. When I remind him about his mother fussing over the state of his clothes, all I receive for my pains is, "oh don't be such an old fuddy-duddy, Daddy."

Me, at 29, an old 'fuddy-duddy'? With these two 'children' fussing over bunny rabbits, momentarily I do feel closer to 49 than 29 and if anyone mistakes Caitlan for my daughter, then I'll probably slit my wrists.

"Och, he's so sweet, Aidan!" Caitlan exclaims. "If only we could take him home with us."

"Not in my flat, huh. It would probably crap everywhere."

"You have no soul, Aidan McRaney. He's beautiful."

"How do you know it's a 'he'?"

"You want me to turn him upside down and take a look?" she laughs, green eyes shimmering excitedly. I realise I needn't have worried, both my son and girlfriend seem to be enjoying their day out.

Clutching my hand, Patrick draws my attention to a large pen containing several black and white sheep. "Look at these…"

"You go with him, sweetheart," I urge. All this animal adoration is giving me a tremendous need for a cigarette.

Slipping out the makings from my coat, Caitlan warns, "you can't smoke here, Aidan."

Returning the tin and papers to their home I reason how every scold is so pleasingly delivered but I really can't get annoyed with her and I whisper, "I love you," in her ear.

"I love you too," she whispers back. "Enough to buy me one of David Lennard's cats?"

I rest a hand against her stomach. "We'll have our baby soon," before I catch Patrick's eyes fixed our way and notice how profoundly dark and disdainful they appear beneath his curls. My arm around Caitlan's waist, I follow my son in order to take a look at the unusual sheep in their pen.

"Jacob sheep," I tell him. Both of them regard me in surprise. "I thought they had died out in England. Must be an American import." I read a lot about almost everything whilst in prison, in order to pass the long stretch of time, even on sheep.

"I thought you didn't know your way around animals," Caitlan says, an element of pride in her voice. I have obviously impressed her with my knowledge.

It is early December. The weather is turning even colder and I am conscious of her shivering in her thin coat. "You're cold, sweetheart. Shall we go back to the car?" I suggest.

"I'm fine." She reluctantly allows the small rabbit to return to his pen. "There's a lot of animals to see yet and Patrick's having such a good time. It's his day after all and you still didn't answer my question about having a kitten. It won't hurt the baby, honest."

"My flat's not big enough. It would have to have one of those dirt box things. We had cats in our house in O'Connell Street, but they always went outside to do their business. Maybe if we get a house."

"It'll be good to have a house. Anyway, I think it's you who wants to go back to the car. Come on, you ould grouch." She teases, linking her arm through mine. I cuddle her close, aware that whenever Patrick observes my demonstrativeness towards her, his mouth noticeably tightens and he chews his lip almost through. I guess I should spend more time with him, but I can't keep from touching her all the time. I want her so much. Her closeness, her beauty are all beginning to get to me again. If it wouldn't have caused such disruption amongst the rabbits, I'd have taken her in the straw.

The place isn't too packed at this time of the year, so we are able to move around freely. She appears perturbed by all the caged animals once more.

"That's why I don't like zoos, Aidan, all those poor animals."

"You can't leave them running free, darlin'. They would never survive. The weather's turning colder. Here, they're well looked after. Besides, they might get knocked down by a passing car. You're an old softie, do you know that? You'll make a good mother."

"I hope so, Aidan. As long as I've got you."

"Sure y'have. I'm not going anywhere, sweetheart. I told you I'd follow you to the ends of the earth. Anyway, have you called Mollie yet?"

I'm aware of her hesitation when I mention her sister.

"I haven't told her about the baby yet, in case something goes wrong."

"Nothing's going to go wrong, you funny wee thing." I smile and kiss her cheek. "I won't let anything go wrong, I love you too much."

As if he finds it necessary to distract us, seeing a burger bar at the end of the field, Patrick insists he'd like one. "Please," he implores on witnessing my hesitation. "With fries," he adds.

Now I know why there aren't too many people around the animal park. They are all forming a queue at the burger bar, to which I draw Patrick's attention. "Jesus, that'll take ages." My sigh is heavy.

"Och, come on sweetheart," Caitlan joins, "I'd like some fries too, please and a weak tea will help to warm me up."

"They won't have chamomile," I point out. "They probably haven't heard of it."

"It's cool. I'm okay with a weak tea."

I see her shiver again.

"You're cold." I hug her against me for warmth. "Maybe you do need the food."

"You want my help?"

I shake my head and fish the keys from my coat. Dropping them into her hand, I instruct she sit in the car. "Take Patrick with you. I can manage. They have those wee plastic tray things."

"If you're sure." I note her hesitancy, Patricks' too, guessing he might be reluctant to join her, but she really is cold. It might be good for them to get to know one another without me there as a mediator. "You go back to the car too, Patrick."

He shrugs, "okay," but I hear the reluctance in his voice.

I kiss her before she leaves. To Patrick, I counsel him to be nice, which encounters another shrug from my son. I watch as they move across the grass to where I've parked the Cabriolet before I join the extensive queue at the burger bar. After interminable checks of my watch and a good 10 minutes later, I finally manage to be served. With burger and fries for two, plus a coffee, a Coke for Patrick, the weak tea and fries for Caitlan, all huddled together on a brown plastic tray, I set off across the field.

Reaching the Cabriolet, I'm surprised to discover Patrick alone in the back seat, nonchalantly playing on his game. My question as to where Caitlan has gone, meets with the inevitable shrug and a less than caring, "dunno, she just took off," from my son.

"What do you mean she just took off? Took off where?" I demand, lowering the tray of food onto the seat beside him.

"Thanks, Daddy." He pounces on the food immediately.

"Perhaps she's gone to the toilet, wherever that is," I muse, glancing at the miles of sprawling meadowland. "Did she say where she was going?"

"No." He is more engrossed in unwrapping his burger. "She just dropped me off here, unlocked the door and took off like I said."

"Where's the car keys?" I check the doors, the ignition. "That's odd. Wherever she's gone, she's taken my keys." Dropping behind the steering momentarily, I pause. If she's gone to the loo, she'd be back soon.

"Maybe she forgot she has my keys," I muse aloud. "She shouldn't have left you alone. That doesn't sound like her. Th… there was no one else about was there, Patrick?" I'm invariably on tenterhooks after all the stuff that's happened to me. I thought of Shaun Blackwood, her ex. Has he shown up here, followed us? Is he in London? Has he taken her off?

"No, I didn't see anyone. I told you she just took off."

"I'm getting a wee bit concerned now. Can you stay here? Lock your door. Don't touch anything. I'm going to have to look for her. Besides, we can't go far without the car keys. You eat your food and don't unlock this door for anyone but me or Caitlan, understand?" I hear the urgency in my voice.

"Sure, Daddy," he frowns, before he says almost innocently, "I didn't see any bad guys about."

"Bad guys?" I echo uneasily. "What made you say that?"

"I dunno, but I knew you had some bad guys after you."

"Sure now, those days are over and there's no bad guys around, okay." At least I hope there isn't, although Blackwood's greasy, pockmarked features spring to mind again. "But, just in case," I add.

"I know, lock my door."

"If she's gone to the loo, I'll go and find her. She might have got lost."

My stomach begins to knot a fraction, coming on the wake of what she has been through, so that I can't avoid my anxiety.

People are already heading towards their vehicles. I scan them all in my search for Caitlan. Out of earshot of them, I call her name a couple of times. Suppose someone has snatched her in order to get to me?

Then I see her. She's resting her head against an oak tree. Her coat is pulled up around her, she is shivering uncontrollably. A piece of scrappy tissue is pressed to her face, she appears to have been crying. My senses reel, alerted to the fact that Patrick has upset her.

"Caitlan, sweetheart," I call, before rushing to her side, about to take her into my arms. "What's wrong darlin'? And you've run off with my keys."

Reaching to her coat pocket and pulling out the keys, she tosses them across the grass indiscriminately, so that I am compelled to scramble about in the grass before announcing that I've found them. "We can't go anywhere without these." I slip the keys into my coat and straighten up to confront her. In the process of brushing grass stains from my hands, I observe that her eyes are bloodshot from crying. "Sweetheart, whatever is it?"

A few stragglers crossing the field pause to look. A fact I remind her of.

"Och, I don't know why you're so particular of people looking after what you've done," she snorts hotly. Her voice is husky and she continues to twist at her lower lip savagely.

"What am I supposed to have done? I'm sorry about the queue. You saw how long it was."

"I'm not talking about no fuckin' queue, Aidan. Jesus, how can you stand there looking so fuckin' innocent and pretend to me."

I have never heard her swear quite so much. Now she sounded more like her streetwise sister, Mollie. "I'm sorry. What have I ever pretended about? I don't understand. Has Patrick upset you?"

"You could say that." Although her eyes are red rimmed, they contain a fire, a fury I've never occasioned to witness before. "You... you killed someone. You went to prison. You shot a man. I didn't believe him. Or is he just lying to me because I know he resents me going out with his father? Did he just say it to put me off you? Is it true, Aidan? Don't lie to me, please. Just don't fuckin' lie to me."

She's offering me the turning point, the inevitable borderline. I can lie to her. Insist that my son is lying. Instead, all I can do is nod weakly. "I'm so sorry Caitlan, I should have told you."

The tissue pressed to her eyes again, she begins to sob quietly, her shoulders shaking.

"If you come back to the car I'll take you home. Tell you everything. Why I had to kill that man." I reach to take her arm, but she shrugs me off.

"No one has to die, Aidan. Then... then you must have had a... a gun?"

All I can do at this juncture is affirm her question by yet another feeble nod of my head. "Yes, I had a gun. Please let me explain why I did it. I love you so much. I know I should have told you, but I was so scared of losing you. I did time..."

"How long have you been out?" Her voice is so quiet and self-controlled that I barely hear her.

"A few months. If you must know, I spent most of my twenties inside. Please, Caitlan, sweetheart..." I hold a hand out to her beseechingly. "Please, darlin', I can't lose you. I love you." My stomach lurches when she turns away, refuses to accept the proffered hand.

I'm aware how much I really do love her. Because of it, a hot sensation of tears begins to prick behind my own eyes. For the first time, I regret killing Brian Fitzwalter and going to jail.

CHAPTER TWENTY

-

DOUBLE ENTENDRE

However difficult the situation, I successfully manage to coax Caitlan back into the car, with remonstrations of how much I love her and that it is all in the past. She is my life now. How I was just a kid in the wrong situation at the wrong time.

Patrick has been left alone for a while, but is content to finish his burger. He enquires if I want mine as if nothing untoward has occurred or Caitlan isn't upset. I tell him that I'm no longer hungry and Caitlan manages to shake her head negatively.

"Can I have two then, please?" he asks, his voice small, hesitant.

"No, you can't eat more than one of that stuff," I chide and snatching the untouched food from his hand, toss it out of the window. He lapses silently after that to play on his game. It is as if he's loaded a gun and fired it into a crowd, so nonchalantly innocent. As if he believes that because of my infrequent access hitherto, he can get away with almost anything with me. Now I have a woman I love. If she is hurting, then so am I. Relative to my circumstances, I've had precious little to do with my son's upbringing over the years. Obviously, Jude has implanted things into his head no child should have to hear.

Swinging the Cabriolet into the road, I check on Caitlan. Her back is turned from me, another sodden tissue is pressed to her face. Every time I dare touch her, she shrugs me off. Despondently, I fear that the moment we return to my flat, she'll pack her bags and return to Dublin. I know I should have told her. Guess I was too much of a coward. "You see why I didn't say anything. I knew how you'd react."

"How did you expect me to react, Aiden? I... I thought you were different."

"I am, really, and I do love you. I didn't lie about that."

"So you say."

"Jesus, Caitlan, what's that supposed to mean?"

"What about the other women?"

"What other women?" I almost career the car across the road on hearing the accusation in her voice, the virtual condemnation. Guilt surfaces on recollection of what I was doing when Brid had phoned to inform me that Caitlan had arrived at my flat.

"Once you marry me, you'll have other women because you get bored."

"Is this you talking again, Patrick? Don't you think you've said enough for one day? And there are no other women!" I'm growing angry and I flick a glance in my rear view mirror, alternatively scared that I've said too much and have upset him because of it. His head is lowered over his game. He refrains from glancing up and I can't be certain. I say, "I never loved your mother, Patrick - ever," spitefully. I realise how cruel it sounds but add regardlessly, "now, if no one has anything sensible to add, I can concentrate on getting us back to Shooter's Hill in one piece, huh!"

*

By the time we return home, no one seems to be speaking to one another and all I can dwell on, until the taste becomes almost tangible, is burying myself in a bottle of my favourite Chivas.

Entering my flat, I discover Ruairi in the process of reaching for a beer in the fridge. "Good day, Bruv?" he wants to know. "Didn't bring any animals back then?"

Caitlan has flung herself into my bedroom while Patrick trails behind, his shoulders slumped, his expression downcast, that is until he sees his uncle and then he brightens swiftly. "Uncle Ru!" He's by his side immediately, as if nothing has happened. Ru asks, "what's wrong with Caitlan?"

"Don't ask," I mutter. "You got one of those?"

"Sure. What's wrong, Aid?" Handing me a beer he ruffles Patrick's hair simultaneously. "So, Patrick mate, you have a good time today?"

"Yes thanks, Uncle Ru," he replies politely.

I am about to open the bedroom door in my concern for Caitlan when I hear the lock clicking into place. It's as if she's interpreted my intention.

"Caitlan, sweetheart, I'm sorry. Please let me in, I'll explain everything. Jesus, I love you so much. I hate seeing you so upset. What happened was all in the past. I'm not that man now," I call through the door reminiscent of a pathetic lovesick fool, which is probably what I am.

"What's happened, locked out of your own bedroom? Man, that's a bad sign."

"Fuck off, Ru."

"Sorry, but something's happened, I can tell."

228

"That's pretty observant of you. Yeah, something's fuckin' happened."

Patrick has plumped himself onto the sofa nonchalantly, impervious to it all it seems. He's switched on the TV. "Can I have my DVD's from the car please?"

"Ru, can you get Patrick's stuff from the Cab please. I'm sorry, I didn't mean to snap."

"What happened?"

"Patrick told her," I sink my voice conspiratorially, "about what I did."

"Jesus, man!" he exclaims, his eyes enlarging in astonishment. "She obviously didn't take it too well then. I mean, you did your time for that."

"Sure I did, but she doesn't see it that way. Now I'm worried what she might do behind that door."

"What do you mean?"

"In her delicate state she might do something stupid."

"Like topping herself you mean?"

"Fuck, no, at least I hope not. I meant she might be packing her case."

"What will you do if she does go back to Dublin?"

I shake my head gravely, run a hand, which I note trembles slightly, over my beard, "I don't know, Ru. I'll be the one fuckin' topping myself."

"You really do love her, don't you?"

"What do you think?"

He slips an arm around my shoulder in a reassuring gesture. "Look, Brid's coming over with Sammy later. Brid will talk to Caitlan. If she is planning to return to Ireland, Brid'll talk her out of it. You know how persuasive she can be."

"I can sort myself out, Ru. But Caitlan's having my baby and I wish to God I'd never met Frankie Lamond."

I swig from the beer and feel it warm my insides. I'd prefer a whisky but the beer will have to suffice.

"Sure," Ru commiserates. "I'm sorry, I do feel for you. I'll go back with Brid, stay at her place tonight. Patrick can have my room. Now I'll get his stuff from the car."

"Ru…" I halt him halfway to the door.

"Aid?"

"You're more than a brother to me, do you know that? You're more like my best friend."

"Fuck, man, you'll have me in tears in a minute, but thanks and you know I feel the same way. You going to the club tonight?"

"I wasn't planning to. I can't leave her like that."

Dropping onto the settee next to my son and nursing the beer, I say nothing momentarily. When I slip an arm around his shoulder, a gesture that I love him far too much to remain angry with him, he regards me innocently through the black, curly forelock, as if nothing untoward had occurred.

"I'm sorry Daddy. I thought Caitlan knew about you shooting that man."

"No, she didn't. I was working up to it in my own time but now it's out…"

"Will you go on seeing her?"

"Sure. As long as she wants to go on seeing me. I hope to God she'll still want to marry me."

I half expect Patrick to react badly in the wake of that speech. Instead he says calmly, "if she does, will I live with you?"

"We'll divide the time between your mummy and me."

"You really don't love Mummy do you?"

"I'm sorry, Patrick, no I…" My words trail however, as the sound of my bedroom door is clicked open. I leap from the sofa and race to the door. It is definitely unlocked and I'm not about to take a chance of her re-locking it again.

Bursting into the room, I discover Caitlan lying on the bed. She's undressed, her clothes huddled into a crumpled heap on the floor. A thin sheet pulled over her. I tentatively whisper her name. Beneath the sheet, the outline of her body against the diaphanous material is unmistakeable. She exclaims, "Aidan!" and instantly opens her eyes.

I remain by the door, scanning the room, searching for signs of a packed suitcase. Unless she's stashed the case under the bed, I see nothing.

"Why are you standing there?" She pats the bed invitingly.

"I'm sorry, I didn't know how you'd react." I join her on the bed. "You forgive me, baby?" She allows me to place a hand against her flushed cheeks. "I should have told you, but I was scared of losing you."

"Well, tell me now." Her tone of voice is unexpectedly provocative and oozing sensuality. "So that I can understand what really makes the gorgeous Aidan McRaney tick."

"Sorry," I laugh. "Thanks for the compliment, but I'd hardly call myself gorgeous."

230

"You might not, but it's how women see you, maybe even some men if they're that way inclined. So what happened?" Reaching for me, she begins to trace the outline of my chest through my shirt.

"You sure you really want to know?" I clasp my palm over hers. "And I expected you to have packed your case."

"You want me to?"

"God no! I was scared you were going back to Dublin after what happened this afternoon."

"Och now that was stupid Caitlan talking." Her Irish accent is heavily pronounced suddenly.

"Sorry?" I frown, as a small element of uneasiness pervades my mind. "Why are you talking in the third person?"

"Third person, fourth fuckin' person, what the hell does it matter?" Rolling onto her back, she flings a hand above her head. "So tell me, you fuckin' sexy bastard, what happened to make you kill someone?"

"It's not something I wanna talk about, sweetheart?" All I'm aware of is that I want her. She's thrown off the sheet to expose her perfectly flat stomach. The only contribution to covering her nakedness is a pair of lacy white panties.

Slithering long painted nails the length of her bare flesh, she purrs, "go on, Aidan, indulge me."

I wander to the window turning my back on her, conscious of her breathing a fraction stilted behind me, aware from my peripheral of her fingers inching purposefully in the direction of her crotch.

It all came spilling out. My time as a minder to Frankie Lamond. The upstairs room at 'The Black Garter' club where I fucked Leanne even though she belonged to Frankie. The evening at 'The Copper Kettle' restaurant in Soho, when I'd watched Frankie making sexual advances to Leanne while I sat alone at an opposite table, barely able to contain my jealousy, when a young man entered the restaurant. I learned later that his name was Brian Fitzwalter. That Fitzwalter was the son of the guy whose intended drug deals with Frankie were aborted, at the latter's instigation. Fitzwalter had pulled a gun from inside his jacket. Frankie had chosen that particular restaurant because of its rear entrance. That was what Fitzwalter had also counted on, escaping out the back. When he shot Leanne at point blank range, I was out of my seat, pulling my automatic as I went. The initial shot felled him instantly, but I was too enraged to stop firing and I practically emptied my gun into him before the police arrived and forced me to lie on the floor, where I was handcuffed and my rights read to me.

"Now, if you want to pack your case and return to Dublin I'll be upset, but I'll understand," I add, before her hands are all over me, impatient, almost hurried. Her lips reaching for mine are conducive to taking me by surprise.

"God no, I'd be a fool to do that. You're the fuckin' sexiest guy to come along in ages. Jesus, Aidan, I want you so much."

I turn to confront her and observe that her eyes are enlarged and such an enigmatic green, alive with so much sexuality. She fumbles impatiently to loosen the belt of my jeans, slipping a hand behind it, closing over my erection. Slithering herself down to reach it, she wraps her mouth around it. Straightening up, she pulls off my already unbuttoned shirt, tosses it across the room, the jeans too.

"Lock the door," she hisses.

I move to do as she asks. She moves with me so I am doing it one handed and I click the lock in place before she guides, then half pushes me onto the bed. I'm as naked as she is. My penis is hard and demands entrance into that velvety feminine cavern. Her lips, fitting mine, are passionate, almost violent. When they descend to my neck, she bites the flesh hard.

"Jesus, Caitlan!" But my protests are feeble. She hisses, "who the fuck is Caitlan?" in my ear.

I believe I have imagined it. This is some kind of sexual play-acting on her part.

She is beneath me. I lower myself onto her. "Jesus, I never expected this…" I begin.

"Oh shut up," she spits tensely before closing her lips over mine. "Now," she pauses, regards me speculatively, "what did it feel like?"

"What did what feel like?" I stop moving and stare at her with a frown.

"To carry a gun and shoot someone. Did you carry the gun in a shoulder holster? God, I can imagine you and I can't stop coming when I think about it."

"What are you saying?" About to push my hardness into her, I pause and regard her again, the way her eyes appear so profoundly, oddly glazed, as if aroused by some strange inner light.

"Have you still got a gun?"

I stiffen at her question. There is a gun locked away in this very room. Nevertheless, I explain that it is all in the past, apologise again for her finding out about me the way she did.

"Och, I don't care about all that. People don't change. I bet if someone gave you a gun now, you wouldn't be afraid to use it. I just want you, you fuckin' sexy bastard. I can't stop thinking about it since I found out. We could pull robberies together."

"You what!" I explode in disbelief. This isn't the sweet girl I have come to love. Now she sounds more like Verdi, inciting a man to become a criminal and I really didn't care for the direction this conversation is headed, "what the fuck you saying, Caitlan?"

"And I asked you, who the fuck's Caitlan?"

I'm aware, in stark realisation, this infinite moment of truth laid bare, that Caitlan is in the throes of a schizophrenic episode. That, maybe when it is over, the real sweet natured Caitlan McKenna will emerge and want to leave me. I should stop right there, tell her nothing doing. That she needs help. I guess, however, I'm too far gone. We both are. She urges me to "fuck her harder," when I push my erection into her, pound her, hear her squeals of ecstasy, moans of pleasure. The bed creaks unmercilessly beneath us, but I pay it scant attention, realising I can't stop myself even if I want to. She purrs sensuously, "rape me, oh rape me, you bastard..."

I whisper that I've never raped anyone and wasn't going to start now, huskily. The sexual act is meant to be a consenting union between two lovers.

She raps, "just fuckin' do it!" venomously. "Would you kill for me?"

Too far over the borderline, too irrational. Attaining such unbelievable heights of carnality as I never thought possible, I hear a man respond, "Sure, I'd kill for you, baby," before I realise that the man is me.

The sexual act concludes and I never felt quite as exhausted before, as if I've run a marathon. She lies beside me, cuddles into my arm and runs her fingers the length of my bare torso. I have no idea at this precise moment whether she is my Caitlan or this nymphomaniac, alter ego schizophrenic woman, while I'm also aware that I shouldn't have given into my dominant sexual urges whilst she was undergoing a psychotic episode. The trouble is I was enjoying it far too much.

"I love you so much, Caitlan," I stress her name purposefully, while I practically hold my breath in case she asks who the fuck Caitlan is.

"Why did you say my name like that?"

Lifting my gaze to her face, I'm conscious of the alluring green eyes staring back into mine a fraction non-plussed. She can't remember. "I don't know," I lie, realising that I can't tell her the truth, that she'd undergone a personality change. We'd had sex whilst she was in the throes of it. "So you were upset this afternoon when you found out what I'd done?"

"Aidan," she stresses my own name, "as you said, you did your time. It's all in the past. I was shocked I must admit, but when you love someone it's surprising what you'll forgive and we have this now..." Her words trail when a tentative rap echoes on the door and sends me leaping from the bed. Retrieving my clothes from the floor, I toss Caitlan her own garments, instruct she put them on. Dragging faded Levis over my hips, I call out that I'll be there in a minute. Buttoning my shirt, I watch her dress.

"I could always get back into bed," she suggests.

"I think it's best if you get dressed, sweetheart. It might be Brid, and my sister don't miss a trick, believe me."

"Sure, okay."

We are finally presentable and I crack open the door to discover Ruairi standing there.

The sardonic smile playing the corners of his mouth is effortlessly interpreted as a 'I know what you were doing' kind of grin. I open the door wider on my sister's raised-brow speculation behind him.

"Sorry to bother you 'cos I know you were busy." There's a thinly veiled sarcasm in his words and he steals a glance beyond me into the room where Caitlan is brushing her hair at the dressing table.

"What is it, Bruv?"

"Only old Gormless from the club is on the blower."

"Old Gormless?"

"You know, Jacky Gorman. He wants to talk to you."

My sigh is resigned, reluctant. Not merely that, but my prick feels a little sore. The last thing I intend is to drive to the club.

"Did he say what it was about?"

Ru shakes his head. "He wouldn't tell me. He just said something about 'monkeys and organ grinders'," he grins, "which all sounds pretty painful to me!"

"Especially the bit about organ grinders," I make a face.

"You what?"

"Nothing," I wave a hand dismissively. "So, is he on the phone now?"

"No. He called your mobile. I told him you was taking a shower." He holds his smile, brows elevated.

"I'll call him back. Find out what he wants. It must be important enough to call me. Hi, Brid," I greet her as if seeing her for the first time.

"Aidan, can we talk?" There's an unaccustomed stiffness in her tone.

"Sure, Sis, I was about to take a shower."

"In the kitchen," she grips my arm all at once.

"Where are the kids?"

We enter the kitchen and Brid is about to close the door on Ru shrugging his shoulders. He is obviously put out at being excluded. His, "don't mind me," goes unnoticed.

She sinks her voice conspiratorially. "The kids are in the bedroom. You know Caitlan's having a baby?"

I start to laugh. "Sure, I'm the guy who put it there. So?"

The serious expression on her face renders me sober once more. Turning my back, I opt to fix myself a coffee.

"We could all hear what was going on in your bedroom. At one point I thought the springs would give out on the bed."

"Jesus, Sis, we're not going to live celibate for God's sake. Judy and I had sex while she was pregnant and Patrick's fine."

"I know but just be careful. Besides, Judy was a lot stronger than Caitlan and the early stages can be riskier for losing it."

I am prompted to mention the schizophrenic episode she'd presented when we had sex. Nevertheless, I fail to do so, although I'm certain Brid will understand.

"Ru tell you Caitlan and me had a row today? Patrick had to go and tell her about what I did."

"I told you it would come out sooner or later, Aidan. You should have told her. So how is she now? Though I guess she's forgiven you if all the noise next door was anything to go by."

"We could have been arm wrestling for all you know."

"Och, sure y'were now. You'd have to be both deaf and daft not to know what you and Caitlan were doing…" she allows her words to trail guiltily when Caitlan appears and wraps an arm around my waist.

"Hullo, Bridget," she greets her.

"So you feeling better now, sweetheart?" Brid's smile is affectionate.

Caitlan's gaze, rising to encounter mine, is filled with something akin to adoration. "Sure, I'm fine now, Bridget. How could I not be when your brother loves me so much?"

"That's good then. I'll see how the kids are doing," she says quickly when Caitlan's lips seek mine and crush them to her; it's as if it's her way of dismissing my sister. Brid, obviously feeling awkward exits the kitchen, closing the door. Caitlan asks, "you want it again? I can't get enough of you."

"Maybe later, but my cock needs a wee rest if I don't."

"Am I too much for you, old man?" she teases.

It hurts, as it never has before with other women, when she calls me that. Explaining that I have to call Jacky Gorman and extricating myself from her embrace, I leave her in order to have my shower.

Patching through a call to the club later, I'm surprised to hear Suzanne's voice. Now here's a lady whom I know will never refer to me as an old man.

"'The Black Garter' club, Suzanne Markwell speaking. Oh, Aidan, hi."

I can practically taste the excitement that trills from her voice. I tell her that Jacky Gorman called and wanted to speak with me. "Is he there?"

"He's in the club somewhere. I'll go and fetch him. First, tell me what you're wearing."

I hear the unmistakable sexy purr at the other end and I feel my cheeks flame. Thankfully, Brid, Ru, Caitlan and the kids are not witnesses to my embarrassment.

"You still there?" she enquires.

"Sure."

"You haven't answered my question."

"Just jeans and a shirt. Nothing special."

"I bet the jeans are tight. You've got a great ass."

"Okay, sure the jeans are tight. Now, get Jacky for me will you, darlin'?" I say impatiently.

"Okay, I just wanted to know what you were wearing."

"Jesus, Suzanne, you know I've got someone."

"I know that. I'm not trying to muscle in on anyone's territory baby, and if you are remotely curious, we have this Western evening. I'm wearing this dancehall queen outfit. It's scarlet and purple with high suede button boots and this little slim-fitting tasselled bodice."

It isn't difficult to imagine Suzanne's tall, leggy figure in a scarlet and purple dancehall girl outfit with the boots. With that image in my head, the bitch is turning me on all over again.

"Just fuckin' put Jacky on, darling."

"Okay, gorgeous, I'll get him for you. You know, you'd look fuckin' sexy dressed as one of those old western gunslingers all in black. God, I'm coming just thinking about it."

"Suzanne, for fuck's sake," I can't keep being amused at what she intimates.

"I'll get Jacky, I know. Anyway I gotta go and change my knickers."

I'm still grinning at her impishness, when Gorman growls breathlessly, "McRaney, Aidan," into the phone. He sounds as if he'd been running hard. Guess he is simply out of condition.

"Yeah. What do you want, Jacky?"

He swallows noisily, almost as if he were choking. When I enquire if he is okay, he says, "they're here," in a half whisper, as if someone is listening.

My heart skips a beat instinctively because I know to whom he refers. "Who's here, Jacky?" I pretend nonchalance, however.

"The boys from Brazil, if you get my drift, there's two of 'em. You know why they're here, why Ronnie got out. An' they don't look as if they're gonna take no for an answer. When I told 'em I didn't want no trouble, I was told to butt out. This De Oliveira character asked who the new management was. I told him it was you and he said he wanted to meet this 'Senoré' McRaney."

I attempt to suppress the uneasy hammering of my heart against my chest with difficulty. "Sure, I'll be there. Where are they now?"

"Milling about the club, pawing the birds. You want to see them in your office?"

"Sure, I guess so."

"Be careful, that's all I'm saying."

CHAPTER TWENTY-ONE
-
THE BOYS FROM BRAZIL

After taking a shower, I change into a dark pinstripe suit, black shirt and white tie. In the process of appraising my appearance in the bedroom mirror, adjusting the tie, I almost jump when Caitlan, slipping an arm around my waist, demands to know where I am going dressed the way I am.

Taking her into my arms, I explain that Jacky Gorman has requested my presence at the club. There is some trouble. That might, in all likelihood, contain some foundation if things should go wrong. I could have lied to Gorman that I wasn't feeling well or something, to account for my not showing up. Firstly, I am no coward and secondly, the boys from Brazil are only going to show up again. As Gorman outlined, they won't take no for an answer. Plus, if they are as dangerous as Dennis Mitchell suggests, there is always the possibility my family might be threatened.

"What kind of trouble, Aidan?" she asks, regarding me uneasily.

"Nothing for you to worry about sweetheart, and nothing that I can't deal with, okay?" I kiss the top of her head. Her form is so slight, sometimes she feels like a child in my arms. I realise that I need her so much. If anyone as much as harmed a hair on her head, I will kill them and sod the consequences.

"Be careful, my darling," she says quietly.

"Sure I will, sweetheart. Now, you go and help Brid with the kids."

"I don't think Patrick likes me."

"He's been through a lot. His Daddy coming out of prison. Judy had another man when I came out. Now she's seeing the guy she works for, Patrick's bound to feel a wee bit insecure right now. He'll love you as much as I do eventually. Brid will help. She's accepted you and so has Ruairi. I don't want you near any kind of trouble. That's why I'm here, to protect my family. Tomorrow I'll have a talk with Patrick. Maybe we'll have a kick around in the park."

"Brid's asked me to accompany her to mass."

"My sister sure knows how to show someone a good time."

"I know you don't believe the way Bridget does. Even I'm not so sure after what happened to my ma. I turned my back on my faith and so did Mollie. Maybe I should thank God for sending you to me."

I entertain an urgency to laugh at her comparison. In truth, I consider myself as sent from the devil rather than God. When I shoo her from the bedroom and close the door, I locate the spare key to my suitcase and, lifting the case from off the wardrobe, open it to reveal the 9mm Browning semi-automatic that's wrapped in an old duster. The gun Ray Lamond had given me a while ago. Checking the clip, I discover the weapon to be loaded and lock the safety. Hauling on my coat, I drop the pistol into my pocket.

"Where you going?" Ru intercepts me at the door.

"Aidan says there's some trouble at the club," Caitlan informs him.

"I thought old Gormless sounded worried," Ru says.

"Hopefully I won't be long." I kiss her, adding that I'll look in on the kids before I leave.

I discover Patrick and Sammy seated on the bed watching a 'Shrek' DVD on Ru's portable.

"You going out, Daddy?" Patrick asks.

"For a while." I jangle the Cabriolet's keys absently. "If I'm not back, you go to bed when Caitlan and Brid tell you."

Patrick mumbles, "she's not my…"

"Don't start, please, Patrick. Be nice. I know she's not your mother but I'm your father and when I say you go to bed when you're told, I mean it. Tomorrow if you're good, we'll go to the park, have a kick around."

"That'll be great," he enthuses. "I'll do as I'm told."

"Good. Love you both," I say.

"Love you, Uncle Aidan," Sammy chortles.

Patrick's smile speaks volumes while I ache to cuddle him, but the presence of the gun prevents me. The last thing I want is my family knowing I'm even in possession of one and hopefully, above all, I won't have to use it.

Dropping behind the Cabriolet's steering, firing the ignition, the door suddenly cracks open which almost has me reaching for the pistol. My hand only falls away when Ru drops into the passenger seat.

"Ru, for fuck's sake, what are you doing?" I hear the alarm, intermingled with displeasure, in my voice. "I don't need my family involved in this and that includes my brother."

He has now swapped his old jeans and tee shirt for a pair of black trousers, white shirt and black leather bomber jacket and ploughed a comb through his unruly hair.

"That place is as much mine as it is yours, Bruv. If there's any trouble, at least I can help."

"I don't want you getting involved. I'm used to handling trouble." This is one kind of trouble I'd prefer to handle alone.

"I'm sorry." Leaning his back against the seat, he folds his arms defiantly. "I'm staying put. Anyway, why all the secrecy, Aid? You can tell me. I'm not a kid, you know. I have been in a few fights. Lost most of 'em, but never mind, hey," he grins.

Swinging the vehicle into the street, I shrug with resignation. "Sure, but there won't be any fights if I can help it. You sure you want to come?"

"At least tell me what to expect."

"And you won't tell the girls?"

"God no, you should learn to trust me more."

I explain about the drug dealers, the boys from Brazil, as they were known. "So, you want me to drop you off at the corner?" I ask.

His hesitation is momentary. "If I can't help my brother, then it's a bad job. So what are you planning to tell these boys from Brazil sorts?"

"Nothing doing. The last thing I need is drug trafficking in my club. I also think Lamond's set me up."

"Sounds ominous. So what are you going to do?"

"Truthfully, Ru, I don't know." I expel a lengthy sigh. "Let's see what happens, huh."

"We could run that club couldn't we? You and me. Lamond's in jail. We don't need him."

I'm surprised at his candour, with which I can't fail to agree and the reason why I'm more determined than ever to send the boys from Brazil packing.

*

As attested by Suzanne, the club is in the midst of a theme night. Somehow, the old West seems oddly appropriate.

Mike Gorman and Lew Johnson, the two bullish bouncers, are decked out as old time gamblers, Doc Holliday types in long, black frock coats, hats and those string tie things.

Because I have no intention of entering through the main club area, I fit the key to the back door.

Ru quips that we should have dressed for the occasion.

"I have," I respond. "There's enough cowboys around here now."

I usher Ru inside and request that he re-lock the door, for which I hand him the key. His turned back enables me to slip the automatic into my desk drawer prior to phoning Jacky Gorman. I announce that I've arrived, that I'm in my office and will receive them now. I hear him breathe a relieved, "thank God. I'll send 'em in."

It isn't difficult to surmise that my brother is nervous. He paces the floor of my office before pausing to interest himself in the portrait of Frankie Lamond and myself on the wall, while I hope I'll be able to convince the Brazilians I have no intention of buying their drugs without resorting to anything bordering on violence. I know the score of course. The money wouldn't issue from my pocket. Ray would have that in place. I am merely the go between since the former was otherwise detained.

When a couple of tentative raps sound on the door, I flick a cursory glance at my brother, one that is enough to deduce he is now looking much less self-assured. His face is pale.

At my invitation to enter, Jacky Gorman appears, decked out in a long, black, drape jacket, probably left over from his 'teddy boy' days. The jacket complements a white shirt and string tie. Swiping perspiration from his face, he ushers two men into my office.

The older man sports the sun-bronzed complexion of a South American. Tall, slimly built, I judge him to be in his late forties, early fifties. Conservatively dressed in dark trousers and white shirt, over which he's thrown a tan sheepskin coat, his hands are concealed by the confines of grey suede gloves. The man introduces himself as Senhor Rafael de Oliveira. His companion is much shorter in stature, plumper. His black hair is badly cut, his skin a greasy olive colour. Like Gorman, his brows are ringed by perspiration. I guess it's from their warm clothes and the heat of the crowded club, although I would like to think that I'm the cause of their discomfort. The younger, greasier specimen is introduced by his companion as Eduardo Santos. In all likelihood, Santos is the minder.

"Senhor McRaney." De Oliveira drops both the hand I refuse to shake and himself into the chair facing my desk.

Ru remains standing beside my chair. I hear him catch a breath when the men enter. De Oliveira's English is perfect, with the merest trace of an accent, as if he's been educated over here. Santos nods vaguely, saying nothing.

De Oliveira reminds me of a 'Spanish Don' from the old TV moves I'd seen. I remain on tenterhooks however, as I'm uncertain that the aristocratic Brazilian isn't the proverbial hand in the velvet glove. He's here to offer drugs after all. It is obvious my reluctance to accept the proffered hand has got his back up somewhat. There are tension lines wrinkling his mouth. Jacky continues to mop his brow with a grimy handkerchief.

"I prefer to hear you out, 'Senoré', before I shake hands on anything," I tell De Oliveira. Turning to Gorman, I enquire if the men have been checked out. The only person I need to be armed is myself, I have no intention of disadvantageously staring down anyone else's gun muzzle.

"Ch… checked out?" Gorman echoes anxiously. The frown creasing his brow, his entire air of nervous energy makes me wonder what he is so scared of, me or the Brazilians?

"For weapons, Jacky."

"'Course, boss, they passed through the machine with flying colours."

"Good." But my smile is cold. "You can go Jacky and thanks." Noting his hesitation, I repeat my command harshly. Reminiscent of a subservient bulldog, he backs out of the room, almost colliding with a hat stand in his perturbation, for which he offers a vague apology.

Gesturing to Ru, I ask him to check outside to ascertain that the coast is clear, mainly that Gorman isn't eavesdropping.

Another reason why I haven't entered via the main club area is the fact the gun would have been discovered on my person.

I'd removed my coat and draped it over the back of my chair. Ru's hand rests on the latter. Because he is so close I can hear his erratic breathing, testifying to his anxiety. He need not have come and if something untoward ensues, I'll wish to God he hadn't.

For myself, I feel confidently in charge of the situation. Although I'm relieved the two men aren't armed, I request they remove their coats. In spite of the warmth of the room, De Oliveira seems reluctant to divest himself of his coat. Finally, he does so with a sigh of resignation. "Si, as you wish Senhor."

"Now we've got the preliminaries out of the way, I'm Aidan McRaney and this is my brother, Ruairi."

"Rory?" De Oliveira repeats it parrot fashion.

"Yeah, sure if you like," I say before Ru decides to correct him. "So, 'Senoré' De Oliveira, you wanted to discuss something with me? It must be important to have got me away from my girlfriend at home. So, how can I help?" It is plain that my pretend obtuseness concerning his real business is enough to place him on his guard and he shifts in his seat uncomfortably.

Santos' high promontory of a forehead is effortlessly leaking perspiration. When I have time to study his less than prepossessing features I'm aware of the one-inch long scar that runs from the corner of his left eye to a point just below the same eye, in a sort of diagonal fashion. It is the face of a fighter, a scrapper. It isn't difficult to assess he's probably seen his fair share of pugilism.

"Senhor McRaney, I have been dealing with the Senhor Raymond Lamond…"

"Let me stop you there." I raise a hand, ensuring his silence. "Dealing? As in…" I arch a speculative brow.

"Narcotics, Senhor," he says without preamble.

"And you're asking me to purchase these narcotics for a sizeable sum no doubt? You think because Senhor Lamond has installed me as boss of this club while he's inside, that I'll be an easy touch, a thick Paddy who doesn't know when he's being taken for a ride. Now, tell me if I'm wrong about your reason for being here and if I'm right, then we've concluded our business."

Black eyes suddenly snap wide with a thinly disguised rage. De Oliveira gestures at his sidekick Santos who inches closer. I hear Ru suck in a breath behind me. Feel the pressure of his hand on my shoulder reassuringly. He hasn't so far spoken. I guess he's content to allow me to handle this. For my part, my fingers travel to the drawer where I keep the pistol.

De Oliveira's sun-bronzed countenance appears to have developed a crimson glow. His face is narrow with eyes like dark orbs marginally sunken as to render his features almost skull like.

"I was about to say I've been dealing with the Senhor Lamond for some time," De Oliveira says. "He assures me that you would be, how shall we say, amenable. You have the money I know. You also have to contact Senhor Lamond's lawyer, the Senhor Sorenson. He holds monies. You don't have to do anything, Senhor McRaney. Simply collect money from Senhor Sorenson. Meet me at the club, in your office…"

"What's stopping you from collecting the money from Sorenson yourself? You don't need me in this."

"I need, how do you say? A go between. Besides, Senhor Sorenson, he is no drug dealer."

"And neither am I. Just because I've been inside, I'm no go between or drug dealer. You collect from Sorenson. I run this club legally, that means no drugs. If I were you, De Oliveira, I'd try some other gullible patsy to offload your crap onto."

"Careful, Aid," Ru cautions. I have almost forgotten him. He sounds scared and oddly young.

"It's cool, Bruv. I think 'Senoré' De Oliveira and I understand one another," I stress, but the smile I direct the South American is deliberately chill. I guess Ru has had no occasion to witness his big brother in action. I add, "I have no intention of going back to prison again."

"But you won't, Senhor. Please, it's just a business deal. Senhor Lamond spoke highly of you. He said you would know what to do, the people to sell the narcotics to. He has promise you certain access to your son, has he not?"

Now he really has pressed my buttons. "Fuck, De Oliveira, leave my son out of this." Anger swells inside me and I think impishly, you wouldn't like me when I'm angry. "And you gotta know I don't react well to blackmail."

"I'm not blackmailing you. You see, I have certain contacts, who could, how we say? Make life difficult for you. It's simply a few narcotics. I'm a businessman, Senhor."

"And so am I." Partially concealed behind the desk, the automatic is in my hand. "There's a shooter pointed right at your balls, De Oliveira and if you don't get the fuck out of my establishment, I won't be responsible for my actions."

"Jesus, Aid, a… a gun!" Ru swallows uncomfortably. His face has gone very white and I imagine he is about to pass out. "Where the fuck did that come from?"

"Pl… please, Senhor McRaney, I… I too want no trouble." He blanches beneath his tan. His voice shakes nervously and he hedges back in the chair. Regaining his composure a little, he gestures at Santos once more. The greasy minder is about to inch closer still, until I raise the pistol and stop him in his tracks. I level the weapon on Santos and screw a silencer to the end of the barrel.

The greasy minder stumbles a fraction as he shrinks back to position himself behind De Oliveira's chair, his hands upraised.

"Like boss say, we… we don't want no trouble, Senhor," he pleads.

De Oliveira regards me askance, his eyes narrow and trained on the weapon in my hand. With the silencer attached, he is quick to reason that I might intend killing him. At this juncture I'm not certain what I will do. I have no real interest in shooting either of them. The gun is merely to scare them, let them know I'm not a man to be taken for a fool. The addition of the Carswell is merely an incentive. "Ru," I have to repeat his name when he fails to respond. I guess I can't blame him. He resembles a living statue carved in alabaster and as unmoving.

"A… Aid!" He practically jumps, his voice shakes and I realise he is in shock. I thought, for God's sake, don't burst into tears.

"I need you, Bruv."

"Wh… what do you want?" he stammers. The presence of the gun has obviously unnerved him, as if I've trained the weapon on him instead of the Brazilians.

I instruct him to kill the security cameras.

"How…?"

"Switch them off, Ru," I staccato. "Then pull out the tape, we don't want any evidence."

"Evidence?" Ru looks sick, although he carries out my request without a word. Nevertheless, I observe his hands tremble on the machine.

De Oliveira, however, appears to have regained his composure somewhat, when he enquires if my intention is to kill them.

"That depends on you, 'Senoré'. Just remember I'm the guy with the gun."

"I can hardly forget that, Senhor."

Pulling out the CCTV tape, in his nervousness, Ru lets it slip to the floor. "What do you want me to do with it?" He regards me as he retrieves the tape.

I hold a hand to receive it and he passes me the recording. I tell him that I'll destroy the tape later.

"Senhor Lamond will not be pleased with you pulling 'pistola' on me," De Oliveira warns.

"Fuck to Lamond. Now get up slowly, no sudden movements. Sure now, if it isn't tempting to pull the trigger. Don't make me regret not doing so. Now I need you to leave my club and if I see either you or any of your kind in here again, I really will waste you, I mean it."

It irks me to witness the uneasy expression and anxiety prevalent on my brother's face, doubtless because I've brought a gun into the club. He regards me as if I am a stranger when he says, "just let 'em go Aid, and where did you get that fuckin' shooter?"

I refuse to reply momentarily. I'm more concerned to make sure that De Oliveira and his pal Santos have vacated the premises. When it is obvious I'm not about to kill him, De Oliveira completely regains his equilibrium. Shoot them in cold blood and risk losing my brother?

Notwithstanding I'm aware that these people can make real trouble for me by leaving them alive, the last thing I need is a murder charge sending me back to prison.

When they leave, Ru holds the door open. De Oliveira hauls on his coat and prophesies acidly, "you live to regret this, Senhor."

"Just fuckin' go!" I rasp.

Ru is about to close the door but I follow them out and tell my brother, "you wanted in on this, Ru," in no uncertain terms.

"I didn't know you had a fuckin' gun did I?"

There is both accusation mixed with fear in his voice, plus I haven't mistaken the evidence of tears in his eyes.

"Stay here. Destroy the tape," I instruct him. His hesitation is almost painful.

"Wh… what are you going to do? You're not…" He allows his words to trail. Swallowing hard, he obviously can't bring himself to say the words.

"I'm not going to blow them away if that's what you were thinking, Bruv," I assure him, slipping the gun into the waistband of my trousers, while he regards the action with something akin to disbelief.

Following the two men outside and closing the door, I allow them to leave unharmed. I watch as they disappear into the night to be swallowed up in the darkness, profoundly aware that I'll regret leaving them alive.

Returning to my office, Ru stands there. The tears have dried but he continues to remain pale.

"I thought I knew you… but I really don't know you at all. You wanted to kill those men didn't you? I could see it in your eyes, they looked so cold. You haven't changed have you? I could tell you enjoyed having a shooter in your hand and a fuckin' silencer. Jesus. Nobody carries a silencer unless they intend to kill someone. That's why you didn't want me here tonight isn't it? You knew what they wanted and you intended to shoot 'em."

"Have you quite finished? Jesus, Ru." I run a hand through my hair, sigh exasperatedly. "Those people are dangerous." I grab his arm as he moves to the door. "And you're wrong, I have changed. I've got too much to lose now. I don't want to go back to prison."

"You could have fooled me, Aid." He pulls his arm away abruptly. "If you fool around with guns, that's where you'll end up."

CHAPTER TWENTY-TWO
-
BROTHERS-IN-ARMS

We are all seated around Brid's large dining table. My son has chosen to pick an argument with his four-year old cousin, so I make Caitlan sit between them. Facing me across the table, Caitlan delights in casting me interminably inviting glances from her beautiful green eyes, plus the familiar 'come hither' smiles from sensuous lips, whilst she discusses her sojourn at the mass at St Assumption and Father Mulligan.

Dishing up the dinner, Brid is clearly expressing her annoyance with Ru because he is late. She claims she distinctly told him it would be ready by 1.30. She'd called him, but his phone was switched off.

The meal is finally ready. It's roast lamb with all the trimmings. My sister is an amazing cook. God knows why Mark Collier should want to leave all that.

Predictably, Caitlan requests only a small portion when Brid offers.

"Sure now, if you're not eating for two, Caitlan."

"That's just a fallacy. No one should eat for two," I say.

"And when did you get so health conscious, our Aidan?"

"'Specially as you smoke so much, Daddy," Patrick puts in.

"So what is this? Take it out on Daddy day?"

"Maybe one cancels out the other," Caitlan suggests, probably to be both polite and to spare my feelings.

"Well, tuck in," urges Brid, "there's enough for everyone and where's that brother of ours? Give him a call will you, Aidan?"

But there is no need because Ruairi and Sandra appear in the doorway. He apologises to Brid for his lateness and plants a kiss on her cheek before he introduces Sandra. In a lemon, short-sleeved sweater and short denim skirt which she wears with a pair of black tights, her blonde hair is pulled back into a ponytail and secured with a yellow ribbon, while her arm is interlinked with my brother's as if they are attached at the hip.

"Pleased to meet you, Sandra," Brid greets with a friendly peck on her cheek. "Now you both sit down. I was worried, so I was, with

Aidan left to look after it and you being so late, that dinner would be ruined."

"Sorry, Sis." Ru escorts Sandra into a chair near Caitlan, who he introduces as his brother's girlfriend, while I'm favoured with a brief gesturing nod from Ru.

"And my brother Aidan, who you've already met."

I am about to return my sister's retort about burning the dinner, that it was her idea to go to mass and leave me to look after it, when Sandra who is smiling at me impishly, declares, "Oh, hello, Aidan. Yes, we met. He nearly got thrown out of 'The Galleon'."

Caitlan regards me with raised brows and a puzzled expression and I reason, one more black mark to be added to the ever-growing list of Aidan McRaney's misdemeanours.

"Good Heavens! Why? What you been up to now, Aidan?" Brid asks. She is about to carve the lamb, when I offer to do it for her.

"It was nothing," I shrug. "A mistake that's all. I would prefer to forget it."

"No, go on, Aid," Ru prompts, obviously enjoying my discomfort. "What was it that burly guy said to you at the bar?"

I busy myself carving the lamb, in the main so that I won't have to explain myself. I can't help but be aware of several pairs of eyes focussed my way, making me wish to God that Sandra could have kept her mouth shut.

Before I can say anything in my defence, Sandra adds, "me and the other waitress, Cathy, were stood at the counter…"

She's obviously revelling in the attention she receives from my family around the table. "And Jimmy, one of the bar staff overheard what this guy said to your brother. It was 'effing Micks'. Only he said the actual word, didn't he Aidan?"

I attempt to avoid Caitlan's gaze, although from the corner of my eye, it is plainly obvious that she isn't too happy at the turn this particular conversation is taking. She remarks, "how rude. 'Course we used to get it all the time in The Liffey Bar. Not 'effing Micks' obviously, but the Irish used to say to the English tourists, 'effing Brits'."

"You worked in a bar?" Sandra asks.

"Sure. In Dublin."

"Me too. I mean not in Dublin," she giggles. "I haven't been there."

If she knows where it is, of course. No, that isn't fair. Sandra is merely a chatty, effervescent kind of a girl. I judge her and Caitlan to be around the same age, 19 or 20, except Caitlan is so much quieter and grown up in comparison to the excitable Sandra.

"So where is it you work, Sandra?" Brid asks, as if she hasn't really been listening to the conversation.

"The Galleon pub and restaurant in Esher."

Ru's arm lingers across the back of Sandra's chair so close, he is practically looking down the area of her partially exposed breasts in the low cut sweater.

Sandra asks to whom the children belong, remarking on how pretty they are.

"That's Patrick, he's Aidan's and Sammy's my sister's," Ru tells her.

Sammy giggles and shifts her bum in her seat. Patrick tucks into his meal without raising his head.

"This is good, Sis," Ru compliments, embarking on his own food. "I haven't had lamb in ages. I thought you said we were having turkey?"

"Whatever gave you that idea? We're not American and this is not Thanks Giving." Brid retorts. "Besides, we'll be eating turkey at Christmas. I'll be decorating soon. Can I rely on you boys to help me?" Her gaze encompasses Ru and I meaningfully.

"What do you mean painting and stuff?" Ru teases.

"I was talking about Christmas decorations. So why did you think we were having turkey? I told you we were having lamb," Brid says.

"Oh no reason," he shrugs before he looks directly at me, now that I've taken my seat and commenced on my food. "Didn't you manage to shoot one, Aid?"

I glare at him.

Brid frowns. "What the devil are you talking about, Ruairi?"

An immediate silence reigns. I guess Caitlan understands something of what Ru says, while Brid appears uncomfortable and her eyes narrow on my brother. Sandra frowns at Ru. She obviously hasn't the faintest inkling what he is talking about. I, in turn, refuse to rise to his taunt.

"Och now, Ru, you don't shoot turkeys, you wring their necks," Brid says, "which I'll do to you two if you and Aidan don't stop giving one another those peculiar looks."

It appears that the incident of last night at the club, when I pulled a gun on the Brazilians, refuses to die with my brother, while Brid affords him a frown of puzzlement.

"Did anyone ever read the story of 'Jekyll and Hyde'?" Ru suddenly asks, regarding each person in turn.

"You mean the book by Robert Louis Stevenson?" Brid declares knowledgeably. "What about it, Ru?"

Ru continues, "this doctor. Apparently he was a good guy most of the time, until he took this potion, then it turned him into a monster."

"Is there a point to all this, Ru?" I ask.

"Sure there is, Bruv. I was just saying that somebody can be really nice, you know, good with kids and a good Dad and then become a monster, a killer."

"Are you talking about anyone we know, Ruairi?"

I'm surprised by Caitlan's question, while my gaze fixed on my brother is a glare of reproach from narrowed eyes. I also entertain the sensation of Caitlan's leg, in her high suede boots, brushing mine beneath the table.

"Not particularly," Ru shrugs and looks uncomfortable, as a crimson flush rises to his face. He obviously has not expected the question, certainly from my girlfriend.

"That's alright then, Bruv," I say. "Because if there's no point to this story, then why mention it?"

*

It is only later, when I suggest that Ru, Patrick and I have a kick around in Brid's back garden with my son's football that I manage to get my brother alone.

He is in the process of lighting up a cigarette, hand cupped about the flame. Patrick had gone to retrieve his ball.

"So you think I'm a monster, Ru?"

He regards me somewhat nonplussed above the lighter flare. He edges, "I don't know what you mean?"

Lighting my own smoke, I say, "you've obviously got it in for me after last night. I apologised for that. Like I said, these people are dangerous, plus, you want drugs on the streets of London? Because that's what it'll mean."

"But a shooter… you scared the shit out of me, you know that, but it wasn't just that. I don't care if you've got a whole fuckin' arsenal of weapons tucked up in your flat. I'm just scared you'll go back to prison, I told you and you've got so much to lose. It'd break my heart, man."

"Come here, you stupid wee bastard."

Throwing an arm around his shoulder, I hug him.

"I love you, man," he says when I release him, "so fuckin' much. I have a lot of friends at uni, but none of 'em are as much of a friend as my brother. Since you've been out I like to think we've drawn closer, haven't we?"

"Sure we have, Bruv."

"Don't look now but there are three birds looking at us from the kitchen window."

Brid, Caitlan and Sandra, who have all elected to do the washing up but seem far more interested in what their men are doing, are staring at us. Judging by their somewhat perplexed expressions, I guess they're wondering at our moment of brotherly male bonding.

Patrick says, "get a room," with a wry grin on his face and sounding far more grown up than his years.

CHAPTER TWENTY-THREE
-
MAKING ENEMIES

There is something I've always wanted to do. In fact, it has been my ambition for a while and that is to do a school run. The following Monday I am fortunate enough to see my ambition realised, in the wake of the four-day access I have to my son.

Caitlan accompanies me. We leave early to ensure Patrick should arrive at his Esher school by 8.45 am. Hence, it is the inevitable bustling around I guess parents have to do in the mornings.

I fail to recollect too much bustling about at home in Dublin. Dad had invariably gone to work before I got up and Mum was too much of a placid lady to do much 'bustling about'.

Caitlan obviously recollected her school days. After all, they were but three years ago. She was the one who helped Patrick locate his books, making sure he was dressed properly. She had even ironed his shirt and cleaned his shoes, while I am allocated the task of getting his breakfast. She did allow me to ask that inevitable question all parents are compelled to enquire of their children, "have you got your homework?"

He pats his satchel, heaves an exasperated sigh. "Yes, I have my homework."

"And your lunch?" Caitlan reminds.

"I have school dinners."

I take the utmost pleasure in observing the evidence of gratitude for her in my son's eyes. Maybe if she hadn't made such an effort, things might have been different but it seems she is a proper little mother. As she outlines, it is important that Patrick like her. She isn't trying to take his mother's place, but it's because she loves his father so much. She has no intention of forcing him to love her and she understands how he feels having to reside with each parent in turn.

She confided how difficult it had been after her mother died. Their father had already left and hadn't even come to his ex-wife's funeral. Caitlan and Mollie only had each other. Mollie was 22 when their mother died. She'd lived in a bedsit. When the house was sold, the two sisters were able to afford a better place.

We head out to Esher. Caitlan promises that next time Patrick comes, she and his Daddy will have the flat decorated all Christmassy. She loves Christmas, it is her favourite time, she enthuses, eyes shimmering almost childlike.

I merely mutter, "will we?"

She flicks me a raised browed glance.

"We will," I agree resignedly.

I call Judy to inform her that I've taken Patrick to his school and hear her stifle a yawn. "Thanks, but wait 'til you have to do it on a regular basis, Aidan. School runs are a nuisance."

Even at this time of the morning, with Caitlan sitting beside me in the car, it is with the utmost difficulty that I manage to control my temper. "This is our son we're talking about Jude, and it'll never be a nuisance."

"So how did he get on with Colleen?"

I wish she wouldn't keep calling her that and in such a caustically snide manner. If Caitlan wasn't beside me in the car, I would have admonished her.

I kiss Caitlan on the lips and feeling her respond, I slip an arm around her shoulder, pulling her against me. Naturally, I refrain from giving Judy free rein to gloat by confiding that Patrick had upset Caitlan on Saturday.

"Fine. In fact it was Caitlan who got him ready for school this morning."

Did I imagine she swallows noisily at the other end of the line? "So, Jude, how's your plastic surgeon guy, Rafe?"

"Rafe's fine thank you." She replies somewhat stiffly. "You can ask him yourself. He's fixing me coffee and breakfast in bed right now."

If it is her intention to arouse my jealousy, then she has another think coming. In fact, I'm genuinely pleased for her. With Rafe in the picture, it hopefully means that she won't be re-enacting the Munchausen episode, when she had me hastening back to London believing that Patrick had meningitis.

Returning to the city, I refer to the panic attack Caitlan told me she had experienced in Oxford Street. Would she mind if I take her shopping there? She smiles at me with something akin to adoration. "I don't mind where I am as long as you are with me, Aidan. Any particular reason?"

"You'll see," I tell her and tap her nose affectionately.

The sweet gentle girl that she is, she is almost moved to tears when I take her to one of the most expensive jewellers in Oxford Street and buy her a sapphire engagement ring.

*

With Patrick back at his mothers, I reason it is time I put in an appearance at the club I have now re-named 'The Athenry'. The last time I was there was the night the Brazilians had shown up and I had taken the Browning. It remains locked away in my office drawer. I'm scared that Patrick or Caitlan might find the weapon if I leave it at home. Their reactions would doubtlessly be similar to Ru's.

After Ru and I had hugged at Brid's on Sunday, my brother refuses to be drawn into a discussion of the incident with De Oliveira and Santos. For my part, I hope I have managed to convince them that I have no intention of purchasing their narcotics.

Ruairi has gone ahead to the club. He was being picked up by Sandra, he confided.

"Sounds serious between you two."

"I don't know about that. I like her a lot."

"You like her a lot. Well I suppose that's a start."

I would have liked Caitlan to have performed at the club tonight but having complained of a migraine, she has taken herself off to bed. She is genuinely sorry to disappoint me. She is close to tears, while her eyes appear larger than ever so they almost manage to eclipse every other feature. It is obvious she has not lied. I find her on the bed with the curtains drawn. I inform her that I'm about to leave, although I am loathe to do so while she is ill, and counsel her that if she needs anything she is to call Brid, and to make sure the door is locked and not to answer it, except to myself, Ru or Brid. She wants to know why I'm so concerned and adamant about her not answering the door. The Brazilians and De Oliveira's 'you'll regret this, Senhor McRaney' is never too far from my thoughts.

I called Maxwell Sorenson, telling him nothing doing. That I refuse to have narcotics in my club and he should inform Lamond the same.

"He won't like it," Sorenson warns uneasily.

I retort that it is my club now. Nevertheless, it is my intention to push the memory of the Brazilians from my mind or the fact that Mitchell and Engels have described them as dangerous. A fact which decides me to take the gun into my office, lock the drawer and keep the key on me - always.

*

It is DJ night and I discover that most of the clientele's average age is somewhere around 18 and I'm certain no one is over 25. You have to be 18 to get in. Some of the youngsters look no older than 16. Jacky Gorman assures me they have brought some ID confirming their ages. Now that I've appeared, he claims that his 50-year-old eardrums can no longer tolerate the noise and that he's going home to his missus and some aspirin tablets.

"It can't be that bad, can it?" I grin. He places a hand on my shoulder in a friendly gesture. It seems that Gorman and I no longer appear at loggerheads. In fact, beneath that bullish exterior, I decide that perhaps he isn't a bad guy after all.

"You're young, mate, you'll be fine. Your kid brother's somewhere with his bird, you might be able to clock him in the next hour or two."

Initially I dismiss Gorman as probably being a wee bit past it. I make a beeline for the bar in order to locate a seat and grab a Coke. I much prefer a double scotch but I intend to drive home. Ru has a ride with Sandra so I can't rely on him. Besides, when he and I are in a relationship, we have our own agendas and refrain from interfering.

Jamie Fielding, the young barman, shouts a greeting when I appear but it's barely heard above the loud, thumping music that is already beginning to give me a headache. I order the Coke, leaning on the bar watching Jamie wiping glasses on an already sodden towel. He's a good barman, welcoming and friendly. Shaking his head, he observes, "a bit loud tonight, Mr McRaney, even for me."

Sipping the Coke reflectively, I can't fail to agree and consider it was never like this in The Liffey Bar. I'm beginning to miss ould Flanagan and his stories. I also miss Caitlan not being with me.

The DJ, Paul Lucas, is a young black man who scarcely appears to be much over 20, despite the fact he sports the ostensibly fashionable, if somewhat grotesque, shaven headed look in which the youngsters seem to indulge lately. God knows where that came from. I'm thankful that Ru hasn't opted for that kind of thing. We both have a good head of hair. I like to wear mine long, well, collar length, where it spills black and curly.

Paul Lucas seems compelled to recite a two line poem as an introduction to each song he plays. He rattles the verse off quickly between interjections of 'man' and 'mateys' while his rather plump physique jiggles about so predominantly, it is as if he were on a pivot. Wearing a pair of loose fitting jeans and a sparkly silver tee shirt, he frequently pauses to wipe the beads of perspiration from his brow.

The sound is deafening and if I don't get tinnitus after tonight, I'll be very surprised. The DJ is beginning to grate on my already frayed nerves, making me wish to God that Caitlan hadn't had a migraine tonight. It is tempting to either jump up on the stage and pull the plug or a gun, whichever's easiest. So what am I thinking? This is my club. Lamond has installed me as the owner with the ability to hire and fire exactly whom I pleased. My thoughts are travelling these lines when Ru and Sandra elbow their way through the crowd to join me at the bar.

"There you are. Old Gormless said you was in the club," Ru says.

Sandra giggles, doubtlessly at this reference to 'old Gormless', although I lightly admonish my brother for his rudeness.

"I thought you didn't like him."

"He's okay when you get to know him."

We are compelled to shout above the music. Sandra smiles and greets me shyly. I finish my Coke, lay the glass onto the counter and suggest adjourning to my office for some peace and quiet and to locate some headache pills.

"What's wrong? Too loud for you, old man?" Ru teases.

I hiss, "shut the fuck up, Ru."

"Sorry," he mutters, suitably chastised. Oddly, Sandra seems to shrink from me.

In the familiar lemon coloured top, with a short red skirt, she leans heavily on Ru's arm as if she might fall if he lets her go. She frequently plants kisses on his face, ones that are swiftly reciprocated. It is obvious that Sandra is profoundly attracted to my brother, although his somewhat lackadaisical, 'I like her a lot' speech hardly denotes that the same attraction is overly reciprocated.

"I'd like you to join me," I tell him. The request, which brokers no argument, is solely directed at my brother.

"Sure, Aid. Can I bring Sandra?"

"You two aren't joined at the hip are you?" I hadn't intended to snap. Ru pales, twists his lip. It is an expression he appears to have developed since he was a child when he was reprimanded about something or other. Biting her own lip agitatedly, Sandra tells me that she'll wait at the bar until he returns.

"If you're sure?" he asks her, planting a kiss on her upturned lips.

Sandra nods perfunctorily. There is no mistaking the disapproval in the look she directs my way because I'm responsible for taking her boyfriend away.

The DJ spouts more of his barely legible diatribe in order to introduce another ear bashing, heart-thumping tune.

From my peripheral when we pass, he waves a hand at me, a gesture I deliberately ignore.

Inside my office, the noise fades to something much less deafening, although the erratic thumping still manages to intrude into the comparative silence.

After an extensive search of the filing cabinet and drawers, I successfully locate some paracetamol tablets. Pouring water into a glass from the cooler, I instruct Ru to close the door.

"You didn't have to be so rude to Sandra."

I stare at him in disbelief. "I wasn't rude to her. Jesus, can't I talk to my brother without him having some bird hanging on his arm, as if they were attached like fuckin' Siamese twins?"

"So where's Caitlan tonight?"

"She's got a migraine. Now I've got one too." I pop the pills and drain some water.

"Is that why you're in such a bad mood?"

"I'm not in a bad mood. So this DJ, Pauly…" I ask him.

"He's pretty popular with the punters. You should be pleased. After all, Pauly brings in the custom. I know he's a bit loud, but it is a disco and the music has to be loud."

"Sure, I know that, but does he have to recite those fuckin' poems every time he introduces a song?"

"You what!" Ru laughs. "Poems? It's called rap, man."

"Well, it's far too loud and irritating. It's given me a fuckin' headache, man," I mock. "So, Ruairi, talk to me, did you say you'd done some DJ work?"

"Yeah, at uni. You're not suggesting I do it are you? I mean we had this club out Camden way, near the university. I did a couple of nights, but I only played to my friends."

"Judging by some of those kids out there, they're probably still at uni. What's hard about playing a few CD's?"

"What about Pauly? He won't like me sharing."

"Who said anything about sharing?"

Ru blanches. "You can't get rid of Pauly. He's the breath of fresh air this club needs."

"Jesus, Ru, you call that fuckin' noise a 'breath of fresh air'?"

"What's wrong with you? You really have got some anger management issues, ain't you?"

"Fuck, Ru, just get that Pauly guy in here and you can take over."

"Now, t… tonight?" he hesitates.

"No, next fuckin' year," I can't help but growl irritably. "Now, tonight. And no fuckin' poetry or rap crap or whatever you call it and tomorrow you'll play proper music."

"Proper music? What Caitlan sings you mean? Or maybe you'd prefer fuckin' Beethoven's Fifth."

"Why not? It's better than what your pal's playing out there."

"You're not racist are you, Aid? Only I never figured…"

"Jesus, me racist! I've had enough of being called a 'fuckin' Mick'. No, I'm not racist, just a music lover. Sure, I'd rather hear Beethoven's Fifth played. Now, do as I ask and get that Pauly in here and you take over."

"Suppose I don't?"

My response is merely a reproachful glare at my brother.

"Do you know what…?" He pauses at the door, preparing to exit.

"What's that, Ru?"

"I could swear your eyes give off electrical sparks when you're angry, man."

"Good," I mutter. However, he has disappeared before I can add more.

Do I really have anger management issues? I had undergone some of that whilst in prison. I can't help but get angry sometimes and that crap Pauly plays out there is deafening and can hardly be termed music. It seems an age before he decides to show himself. Maybe Ru has warned him that I'm not happy and he's too scared to face me.

I open the door, hear Pauly prattle something cringeworthy and vaguely interpreted as "I'll hand you over to my mate Rory, enjoy his smile while I go to meet the big boss man from the Emerald Isle."

I thought, for fuck's sake.

When a somewhat tentative rap echoes on my door, I take the opportunity to leap into the chair behind my desk and pretend to be leafing through some files, before I invite him to enter.

He bounces in like a rubber ball on ecstasy, with so much confidence I can't wait to lower. A tacky gold chain emblazons his neck. The sparkly tee shirt liberally suppurates sweat, while he runs a podgy brown hand over the bright beads of perspiration decorating his brow.

"You wanted to see me, Mistah M?"

"It's Mr McRaney. Take a seat, Paul."

I direct him to the chair facing me at the desk and fish for his surname.

"Lucas, but my mates call me Pauly. It's sort of friendly you know, Mistah M, McRaney," he corrects himself quickly at an acid glance from me. "So you're Rory's big bro'? You run this club now, man?" Every word he speaks is delivered with the self-same jauntiness, as if he imagines it is cool to punctuate his speech rhythmically.

"So Paul, how long have you been a DJ at this club?"

He shrugs, considering the question. "How long? Let me put me old finkin' cap on me 'ed." He nods reflectively. "Well, Mistah McRaney, I reckon a year, give or take."

"That long? How many nights do you do?"

"Three nights. Why? You gotta admit I pull in the punters. Better, man, than the junters."

"Sorry Paul, Mr Lucas. D'you know there was nothing about that sentence I really understood."

"I mean, I bring in the punters, Mistah McRaney." The bouncy tone ceases instinctively when I choose to glare at him.

"You see, Paul, unless I have shares in paracetamol tablets, which I don't, I'm going to have to let you go."

"Let... let me go..." He can barely form the words. "B... but, Mistah McRaney..." His erstwhile confidence and cocksureness has swiftly abandoned him. His expression alters from swagger and beaming to crestfallen immediately.

"So, Paul, what's your day job? You do have one?"

"Yeah, yeah, 'course." He shifts in his seat uncomfortably. "I sell music."

I arch a speculative brow. "You mean musical instruments?"

"No. CD's in the Portobello and that pitch don't come easy."

"Sure, I might be a thick Paddy, but I didn't understand a word of that either. I know the Portobello road."

"The pitch. My place in the market. It don't come cheap. A lot of people want to sell in the Portobello."

"Sure they do and is this the only club you DJ in?"

"What the fuck do you care, man? You got it made ain't you? Sitting up 'ere with your smart whistle. With that fuckin' Mick accent the birds go for. I know, 'cos I heard 'em talking about you being fuckin' sexy and stuff. You ain't like Mistah Engels or Jacky. Jacky won't like it, you getting rid of me. He didn't like you changing the name. What's an 'Athenry' anyway? Is it some kind of bird? I mean the feathered kind."

I sigh exasperatedly. "Athenry is not a bird or anything like that. Athenry is a place in County Galway. That's in Southern Ireland, Pauly."

"Fuckin' hell, I might have fuckin' known."

"Meaning?"

"Nothin' and I don't DJ anywhere else. So who's going to do it now then?"

"How much do you get per night for doing this?"

"150 quid."

"150 quid! Bejaysus! Three nights. That's 450 quid a week."

"It pays for my pitch at the Portobello. It also keeps my old lady."

"Your girlfriend?"

"No, my mother. She's disabled."

"Jesus." Guilt begins to assail me now and I run a hand across my beard introspectively. I wonder why I'm behaving like a heel as to let him go when he has a disabled mother. Nevertheless, I really desire to cater for all ages and turn it into a family club, from teens to grannies and granddads.

"Look, Paul, maybe we can come to some kind of agreement. Prove to you that I'm not the heartless bastard you're probably thinking I am."

"What kind of arrangement?" His eyes are narrow with suspicion.

"Change your music and you can keep your job and let my brother take over when you have a break. You'll have to split the profits of course."

His mouth visibly tightens. "Don't do me no fuckin' favours, man."

"Is that a 'yes' or 'no'?"

"Nothing fuckin' doing," he explodes, springing from his chair. "I ain't sharing no profits. That's it, ain't it? You only want your brother doing this, don't you? I'll tell you something, Mistah McRaney, you try turning this club around, you'll lose business."

"I'm sorry, Paul, that's my offer. Take it or leave it."

"I can't play anything else."

"And that awful banter or whatever you call it. What's all that about? It's irritating."

"Oh, sure and maybe you're getting old," he resorts to sneering in his defence. "Although I reckon you're about the same age as me."

"Sure I am. So how old are you, Pauly? 19-20 I'm guessing."

"I'm 25," he retorts indignantly.

"Really? Then I'm four years older than you and the music I grew up on was rock."

"Some people might think you was racist, Mistah McRaney."

"Racist! God no! I know what it's like to be on the receiving end because of my nationality."

"You know fuck all, man. Like I said, the birds reckon you're the bees fuckin' knees around here. None of 'em would say no to hitting the sack with you, 'cos I hear the talk between 'em and that Suzanne bird, she don't give no one the time o' day she's so stuck up, but you come along and she's fuckin' putty in your bleedin' hands. So don't go preaching to me about being on the receiving end 'cos of your nationality or nothing else."

He moves to the door without my express permission. Prior to exiting, he stabs the air with a forefinger in my direction. "You don't know nuffin' Mistah McRaney and I think this interview is over now, don't you? Your brother can have my job if he wants it. I like Rory, he's a nice guy. And I thought his brother was 'til I met 'im." He slams the door violently on his way out.

If Paul Lucas' intention is to make me guilty, to that end he has succeeded. Surely, I'm not alone in my assumption. That music really is far too loud.

I tackle Ruairi about that very subject later as he is on the stage packing up the DJ equipment.

I ask him if he thinks I did the right thing in firing Paul Lucas.

Ru refrains from glancing my way as he works. When I offer to help him, he tells me he'll be fine, he can manage. "Look, for what it's worth, I know where you're coming from, but you have to pander to the punters and not the other way round."

"I know and you, do you want the job as DJ or shall I look elsewhere?"

"Oh, I don't mind, but not every night. I do have a social life you know."

"The lovely Sandra? So, has she gone?"

"Yeah, she left earlier, complaining of a headache. Must be the music," he grins wryly. He is more intent on unplugging the system rather than looking at me when he adds, "she reckons if I do this DJ stuff, she won't have my attention all night. Tell the truth, I was reluctant at first, but you did me a favour Bruv, by giving me something to do. I was pig sick of just milling about. The only thing I regret is you having to get rid of Pauly. He's one of the good guys you know."

"I offered to let him keep his job if he changed his music."

"Jesus, that's like asking the Pope to become a Proddy."

"What do you mean?"

"The banter, the rap. That's his trademark. That's what makes him so popular."

"So what's your trademark?"

"Dunno," he shrugs. "I don't have one."

"Never mind," I pat him on the back affectionately. "You go home. I'll lock up. I need to sort out some paperwork."

I can't help but realise, with something tantamount to disappointment, that Suzanne is noticeably absent. Not that I fancy her or anything, well maybe just a wee bit. When I enquire of one of the girls where she is, I am informed that she doesn't come in every night. That she works for someone but she didn't know who it was. I could have used her secretarial skills.

Ru looks tired. I'm grateful to him for stepping in after I fired Paul Lucas, so I pay for my brother to have a cab.

There is a security guy on duty at the rear of the premises. I don't know him, I haven't seen him before. We merely exchange cursory greetings.

The place is quiet now. Ru had left almost an hour earlier. It is almost 2.30 in the morning. Locking up, I exit by the rear entrance and make my way to my car. I'm about to light a smoke when I hear a foot fall behind me and scarcely have time to turn, when I am confronted by three of them dislodging themselves from the shadows, slowly, almost methodically, as if they have been purposely choreographed.

The lighting at the club's rear premises isn't overly bright and barely serves to illuminate the surroundings, and is not enough to dispel the shadows.

I thought instinctively, it must be Paul Lucas and his mates getting back at me for firing him tonight.

Except, what I have initially believed to have been three black faces, partially shrouded in the half darkness, are actually features concealed behind black wool ski masks. My heart has begun to hammer inside my chest. I've left the automatic in my office.

The boys from Brazil then? De Oliveira. A hit. In seconds, I'll find myself staring down the barrel of a silenced weapon. It seems however, that I'm to be mistaken on all counts. A gloved hand, an arm encased in black leather, swings a knife suddenly and I feel the sensation of cold steel pressing against my larynx. A voice with an unmistakeable Irish accent hisses in my ear, "no sudden moves, McRaney or I'll slit your fuckin' throat, you bastard!"

CHAPTER TWENTY-FOUR

-

THE AGENCY

I have precious little time to react or even think, because that blade is alarmingly cold and serves to deflect any notions I may have of spinning around on my assailant, kicking him in the balls and making my escape, as I'd been trained to do 10 years ago beneath Frankie Lamond's coaching. It all appears relatively useless in this situation. Another of the masked individuals begins to approach, tentatively at first, as if contemplating my action.

The guy holding the knife rasps at his companion, "fuckin' do it man, he ain't goin' nowhere."

The shorter, plumper guy whom he had addressed slams a bunched fist hard into my stomach. I manage to demand what the hell they want. The assault is neither mistaken identity or opportunist. They have obviously been waiting for me to vacate the club. The fist hammers home again, the pain searing through my guts as if they will literally burst. The guy holds the blade tight across my throat. I feel a small sliver of wetness trickle into my shirt. He's fuckin' cut me and I hiss, "what the hell?" and attempt to struggle free.

"You want some more, McRaney, 'cos you will if you move."

I have no intention of giving up without a fight and this time I attempt to spin around despite his rasp of, "no you don't!"

The blade moves into focus, glinting and chill against my already fevered cheek. The third guy approaches. His hands are encased in black, wool gloves. Their faces masked, their clothes all black. It is only their eyes, as piercing and cold as the knife blade that rides the impenetrable darkness.

"You should have left her alone, McRaney." I know who my attacker is now. "You took a long time to find, pal. I knew you'd gone back to London, that she'd found you. Caitlan's mine. She'll never be yours, pretty boy. It's obvious she fell for your good looks, didn't she?" His voice is icy, insidious, culminating in a spiralling explosion of both hatred and venom.

I manage to hiss, "Blackwood!" between clenched teeth.

"Sure, McRaney, your old pal Shaun Blackwood. I ain't forgotten what you did that night in Dublin. I've been nursing a fuckin' grudge ever since, 'cos she was prepared to follow you across the water. We'll see how she likes you now when you ain't so fuckin' good looking, huh."

I stiffen on hearing those words that plunge into my subconscious, aware that pitted against the three of them, Blackwood armed, I didn't stand much of a chance. I wonder where the security guard is, but the streets appear deserted, only illuminated by the shrouded lamps, pallid neon's.

Blackwood is stronger than he looks. His arm remains positioned across my throat, although I know that if he was my sole assailant, I could take him no problem. Now I'm almost resigned to my fate. The more I struggle and attempt to extricate myself from his hold, the worse it is for me because I know that he is just itching to carve up my face. I allow the panic to course through me because if he does, I will no longer be attractive to anyone, forced into the shadows like some poor 'Phantom of the Opera'. In a vain attempt, I guess to protect the features I enjoy appraising in the mirror, I make a feeble plea of "look, Blackwood, we can talk about this. We're both Irishmen…"

"Fuck you, McRaney, action speaks louder than words…!"

From my peripheral, I am conscious of the knife being lowered as if he is about to drop the blade into the confines of his jacket. When the gloved hand appears again I figure, initially, that it is empty, devoid of a weapon. How very wrong can I be? There is something sharp, infinitely lethal. I see a flash of glass, a bottle, its jagged neck, commonly known as a 'barmaid's kiss' as it is slammed into my face.

An excruciating pain shudders through my right eye so vehemently that I am compelled to stagger against the wall. That's all I feel now, nothing but a mass of burning pain as if the eye were on fire. So much so that I'm no longer concerned what they might do anymore, because the pain is so unbearable that I can no longer stand, and pressing a hand to my eye I hear myself scream and fall partially to the ground with the intense agony, as if in a drunken stupor. Unable to see, striking out blindly before I finally slip to the ground, I am almost half-unconscious, in such pain as I'd never experienced before.

Out of my uninjured left eye I observe them run and hear Blackwood hiss, "let's fuckin' leg it. We're done here." They are doubtless satisfied with their handiwork. They'd fucked up my looks, of that I was certain. The damage is done. Suddenly the lead escapee, which I know to be Blackwood, flings his arms up in the air and cries out as if in pain before he crashes headlong. I hear the distinct thud as his body lands facedown onto the asphalt. His companions race as if all hell has broken loose, and I hear one yell in panic, "bastard's got a fuckin' gun," as he stumbles, almost falls, hardly taking time to right his balance after his compatriot.

"Aidan, mate, McRaney, you alright?"

Through what remains of my vision I am astonished to observe Dennis Mitchell, his bearded face inordinately white and anxious, standing above me, as he stashes a silencer equipped automatic in the inside of his coat. Mitchell lowers his hand in order to help me up.

My stomach hurts like hell and my chest affords the sensation that it's caved in. Nevertheless, it's the excruciating pain in my eye that concerns me the most. Ribs will mend eventually. The damaged eye indicates the possibility that I may lose my sight. It is difficult to get my bearings, let alone rise to my feet. I manage to enquire what he is doing here from behind some of the blood I've swallowed. "Jesus!" is all he can manage momentarily.

I'd collapsed against a wall, a hand pressed to my eye, scared that if I move it, the eye will drop into my palm.

"You recognise him?" He's rolled Blackwood onto his back and uncovered his face. Even with the mask, I'm all too aware of who my assailant is. I nod gingerly, give Mitchell his name.

"I gotta make a phone call, then I'll get you attended to. Here…" He passes me a towel and I press it to my face. When I next regard the towel, I note, uneasily, that it is soaked and sticky with blood. "What the fuck has he done to me?" I can only keep the eye closed. It's far too painful to open anyway.

"Like I said, I'll get you attended to. Don't try and talk, Aidan. I'll get the motor, get you in there. Get that eye fixed."

I'm far too tired to argue with him and the terrible pain almost has me gasping. "What about him?" I gesture at Blackwood with a tentative nod.

But Mitchell is already making his call. I hear him informing whoever it is that he has shot someone. "I'm bringing him in now. Aidan McRaney. He's busted up pretty bad."

Mitchell manages to assist me into his motor, a Toyota Auris, and I ease myself into the back, although I can walk unaided. They feel like jelly, I guess from shock, but at least my legs still function. The ache in my stomach hurts as if I've been badly winded. There is a pain in my chest which concerns me. However, I hope that it stems from my injuries and not that I'm about to undergo a cardiac arrest, from which my mother died in her forties. When I breathe out, the pain in my side is even more excruciating and I guess I've sustained a couple of cracked ribs. Aside from all this, despite the possibility of having a heart attack, it's the eye injury that concerns me the most. Whether all the blood issues from that or my face, or both, I have no idea.

Mitchell failed to disguise the alarm in his voice when he first saw me. He concludes his call. I hope it is to the hospital, although whoever he's called, he's hardly likely to inform them that he's shot someone.

As soon as he slides into the Auris' driving seat and pulls out of the car park, his gaze descends to me when I request he take me to the nearest hospital.

"It's 3 o'clock in the morning, mate. You want to spend precious time waiting about for a skeleton staff in flipping A and E?"

I'm about to enquire where I am being taken when a large, black hearse-like vehicle pulls in behind us, its windows ominously blacked out. Two guys, both wearing dark clothing, spring agilely from the front of the van. I guess instinctively why they are there and who they have come for.

As if interpreting my thoughts, Mitchell declares, "cleaners." That is all the information I need. 'Cleaners' indicate that they haven't come there to polish the furniture or hoover the carpets. They are here to collect the body of Shaun Blackwood. When you have lived and worked in this kind of environment, you scarcely need to imagine what the term 'cleaner' means.

It is only when we are clear of the club and that formidable looking vehicle containing the 'cleaners', I realise that I am being driven through the night time streets to God knows where. All I receive for my questions is a closely guarded, "you'll see."

There is so much I want to ask. How had he known to show up at the precise moment Blackwood and his pals decided to ambush me? Why is he carrying a gun? Mitchell has been inside for armed robbery and firearms possession. I guess he isn't the most honest guy I can trust right now. Alternatively, there is no one else and I'm in too much pain and scared that I might lose an eye, to worry unduly about my travelling companion.

"Look, Aidan, mate, you and me go back a long way."

Sure we do. Right back to fuckin' prison, I reason.

"You gotta trust me alright, and you gotta trust the place I'm taking you to, 'cos another reason why I can't take you to A and E is too many questions are gonna be asked. You know that. I could have left you there you know, walked away, not wanted to get involved. But I am involved and you were bleedin' involved from the minute you started working for Frankie Lamond and you shot that Fitzwalter geezer!"

That particular sentence sounds so enigmatic, it leaves me wondering. And I can't avoid the tightening knot in the pit of my stomach. Our destination. The notion that I may be blind in one eye, all serves to afford a prevalent sense of nausea to well up inside me, while my head spins as if I'm dizzy.

"What's that supposed to mean?"

"Don't talk, mate. You'll be fine, honest. Trust me."

"Do I have a choice? You're the one with the gun." I attempt at humour I scarcely feel.

"The shooter ain't there for you, Aidan," he says.

*

Tiredness begins to envelop me. After all, it has gone 3am. I lay there in the back of Dennis Mitchell's motor, a blood soaked towel pressed to my face. As I doze, I wonder if I'll wake up in bed next to my darling Caitlan in a cold sweat, pouring out my heart that I've just experienced one helluva nightmare and she'll comfort me with an arm around my shoulder, placate me that it has simply been just that, a bad dream.

Except however hard I attempt to pull myself awake, I am fully aware this is no dream. I really am here with Dennis Mitchell and we're driving through the darkness to some unknown destination.

I must have uttered something because Mitchell asks me what I said.

"My phone, where is it?" I pat my coat pockets and trousers to no avail. My phone is definitely missing.

"It got busted when those geezers attacked you."

"I need to call my girlfriend. She'll be worried sick by now." The way she is, in all likelihood she'll think the worse. What I have learned about women is that it doesn't occur to them that their man might have had an accident, but that he is with another girl.

"You can do that at the Agency," Mitchell announces and brings himself up sharply. I guess with the realisation that he has obviously given too much away.

"What Agency?" My stomach knots again.

"You'll see."

"Fuck you, Mitchell," I mutter, lapsing back into the upholstery once more.

I lay there in a half-daze before I come fully awake when Mitchell slams the Auris to a standstill and declares, "we're here, Aidan. Do you think you can manage to get out of the car?"

I reason it must be bad if he keeps addressing me by my Christian name when it is invariably 'McRaney'.

I make a vain attempt to open my eye. When I do, an agonising pain crashes through the socket. "I can walk," I tell him, when he offers.

Aided by the illumination of the orange fluorescents and limited vision, I can just make out a grey brick building, conscious of the crunch of gravel beneath the Auris' tyres as we pull in.

The façade reminds me of a large bungalow or village hall. Refusing to accept his hand when he moves to grab my arm, I tell him I can manage and follow him into the grey building. All the while, the towel remains pressed to my face.

The place I initially believe to be no bigger than a large sized bungalow surprises me. The hallway is extensive and is tiled with marble effect flooring and leads towards a long flight of stairs, surmounted by black wrought iron. The vast hallway connects to some nine closed doors. Off to the left of the staircase, (I realise I have been grossly mistaken to imagine it is a bungalow), there is a sign marked 'LIFT' in black lettering. It is to this that Mitchell guides me. Neither of us speak as we ascend in the lift. Only when we arrive at our destination do I enquire if this is a hospital.

"Not altogether. This place is much better than any hospital." Mitchell sounds oddly enigmatic again, so that I am left with little idea what to expect.

In the glow of electric lighting, I see he's wearing a black leather jacket, black trousers and a silk shirt, also black. When he speaks, he sounds as if we've stepped into a church, or library, where silence is necessary.

"Then what is it?"

"We have our own clinic or surgery for injured operatives."

My senses reel once more. "Operatives?"

This time he refrains from giving anything else away. Thus, I receive no response to my enquiry.

The room he ushers me into is accessed by a plush red carpet, either side of which are another half dozen brown-painted doors. He cracks open one of the doors and I'm allocated an initial sight of what resembles a doctor's surgery. The room boasts a single bed, one that is covered by a single white cotton sheet, plus a pillow. A long desk occupies a corner of the room. On the desk, a computer and a 17-inch flat screen monitor. A couple of black swivel chairs reside before the desk.

I turn to Mitchell. "If I wasn't in so much pain I wouldn't have let you bring me here instead of a hospital. So what is all this about? Why should I trust you?" I demand all at once.

"We have to trust one another, mate. Just get onto the bed and you'll be taken care of."

"Taken care of, I don't like the sound of that." I fail to keep the suspicion from my voice. I have come this far. I am injured and the only person I can rely on is a career criminal who is packing heat and obviously knows how to use it.

"Please, Aidan," he urges. His phone is in his hand and flipping the lid, enters his voice into the instrument. "Aidan's here," he says. That's all, before he closes his phone.

I can see the logic in bringing me here, where hopefully not too many questions will be asked concerning my assailants. If I had gone to hospital I guess the police would have questioned me there, and because Mitchell has shot dead one of my attackers, well all manner of awkwardness would undoubtedly ensue.

I may as well resign myself to whatever fate has in store for me, however unexpected or peculiar.

The swing door opens. I guess unexpected doesn't come into it when I see who enters. Tall, leggy, sensuously curvy, she sports a whiter than white nurse's uniform, her red curls piled atop her head beneath her cap. She appears as fresh as if it were three in the afternoon rather than twelve hours later. Her appearance causes me to wonder if I've either stepped onto the set of one of those old 'Carry On' films, or maybe she is a stripogram.

"I'm glad to see you're on the bed, Aidan," she purrs.

Maybe I really have walked onto the set of 'Carry on Nurse' or into 'The Twilight Zone' or this really is a dream as Suzanne, the pole dancer from 'The Black Garter' deposits her weight onto the bed beside me.

CHAPTER TWENTY-FIVE
TREVELEYAN

I am about to enquire what Suzanne is doing in my 'dream'. Sure, if it really is a dream, I must admit it is beginning to improve. She looks decidedly sexy in a nurse's uniform. How much better can it get?

She gingerly removes the towel from my face. The material has adhered to my flesh and I can't avoid emitting an ouch of pain. "I'm sorry, Aidan. Oh, Aidan!" she wails over my injuries, her face paling.

Mitchell sinks his weight into a swivel chair, saying nothing momentarily, although it isn't difficult to read the concern on his face. I ask him why he brought me here, wherever here is. "And why are you here, Suzanne? Or are you the light relief from my nightmare?"

She touches a finger to my lips. "All in good time, Aidan. First, you need a painkiller before we start."

I swallow uneasily. "Start what?"

When she produces a syringe from one of the drawers, I can't help but flinch from the instrument. I ask her the inevitable question, "am I going to lose the sight of my eye?"

Although she refrains from glancing at Mitchell, she assures me that won't happen. "So what's the needle for? You going to put me to sleep?"

"It contains morphine to ease the pain, that's all. The eyelid will have to be stitched, that and the cut below it. That's where all the blood's coming from. Now I've cleaned it up I can see more clearly. Your eye is badly swollen and will probably remain closed for a while, it's nature's way of dealing with trauma, that's all. You'll be the same handsome guy you always were."

I allow her to inject the morphine into my arm. While she does so I ask her how long she has been a nurse. Is that her true vocation with pole dancer and secretary?

"Actually it is. I trained as a triage nurse and I am a secretary. I'm not really a pole dancer." Turning to Mitchell, she asks him, "perhaps you'd fetch Dr Turner, Dennis. Make yourself useful." Her tone is authoritative. I've never heard her speak that way before. Oozing sexual invitations is more her custom, especially where I am concerned.

"Sure." He shrugs compliantly, easing himself from the chair. Exiting the room, he closes the door on his retreating back. "I can tell by your expression you don't trust us," she begins.

"Whatever gave you that idea?" I reply sarcastically. "I saw Mitchell shoot a guy dead. A van came to collect his body. What was I expected to think? Dennis Mitchell, my old cellmate, just happens to turn up the other night and who the hell gave him a gun? Haven't you heard the expression, 'red rag to a bull'?"

The morphine is beginning to do its work and I feel somewhat more relaxed, especially in Suzanne's company. She continues in her customary, gentle manner to clean the wound on my neck, the one on my cheek and around the eye area, often enquiring if she is hurting me. "I know how strange all this must seem to you."

"That's an understatement. Then you show up in that outfit."

"A sight for a sore eye, huh," she laughs. I attempt to join her but my ribs are far too painful for much hilarity. When I refer to them she assures me that rest will heal my ribs. Stripping down to my bare torso I quip that if she wanted to look at my body she only had to ask, to which Suzanne shakes her head regretfully, "the only time I can touch you is to nurse your wounds."

"Meaning?"

"You love someone else."

At the mention of Caitlan, I attempt to rouse myself up in the bed. "I need to call her."

"When we're finished I'll get you a phone. Dennis tells me yours was ruined when those guys attacked you."

The opening door admits a fresh faced young man wearing a white doctor's coat. I judge him to be little more than in his mid-twenties. His features are handsome, his hair is a reddish colour. A wispy beard, similar to Ruairi's, darkens his narrow chin. "Mr McRaney, I'm Dr Turner, Jeremy," he declares. "I'm the physician here. Nurse Markwell been looking after you, has she?" His smile displays the perfect set of almost clinically white teeth, making me wonder, in my now drugged state, if he isn't one of those immaculately turned out good looking doctors from every medical TV drama I'd seen, and have these people been chosen for their good looks? Their beauty? I wonder also, by her constant smiles his way, smiles that almost border on adoration, if Suzanne and Jeremy Turner might be having an affair.

"We've given Aidan a morphine injection to help with the pain," she volunteers.

"Good." His gaze settles on me thoughtfully. "Let's see what we can do with that eye. I think it's more a question of the healing process. It's very swollen. I guess you can't see out of it at all."

"I can't even open it." Panic seizes me, incensed by his concerned expression. "I... I won't lose it will I?"

"Nobody loses anything on my watch. I look out for my people," he says, whatever that means. "So Dennis tells me he thinks those villains used a jagged necked bottle, commonly called 'a barmaid's kiss'. It would certainly account for the damage sustained. A fist would merely result in a black eye, but looking on the bright side, I can give you much better attention than any A and E department. The waiting times at most hospitals can cost, as in your case, the sight of an eye, even death in more serious cases. I trained in one, I should know, then Mr Treveleyan, or should I say Sir George, appointed me as medic here."

"Jerry," Suzanne admonishes him, "I haven't mentioned Mr Treveleyan yet. I think it's better if we attend to Aidan's eye first."

"Who's Mr Treveleyan?" I ask, curiously.

Jeremy Turner clears his throat a little embarrassedly, coming, I guess, in the wake of Suzanne's chastisement. "He's our boss. The head honcho. Now, let me attend to that eye and then you can get some rest. After breakfast Mr Treveleyan will explain everything."

"But I can't possibly stay the night, Caitlan will be..." I start to protest.

"Night, Aidan?" Suzanne echoes. "It's morning. Anyway, you're in good hands. Jeremy's the best. I should know."

"Is there something between you two?" I dare to enquire.

"God no! Whatever gave you that idea? Jeremy is my brother."

Recollecting once again Dr Turner referring to 'my people', I wonder what this can possibly mean. He is in the process of stitching me up. One slip and I could lose my sight irretrievably. He warned me of that. While he works, he reminds me that they can't be certain of anything until the healing process is underway. When it has begun to heal, he advises that I should have the pressure checked. He enquires how my vision is normally. I respond that my vision has always been perfect, 20/20, according to Frankie Lamond's optician in 2003.

"Then, Aidan, we'll get it back to 20/20 again or I'm rubbish and should be sweeping roads instead of being a surgeon."

I have begun to like the guy. He is friendly and confident. He discusses Suzanne favourably, even though she is there assisting him.

I enquire as to why someone with her obvious medical skills should feel the need to moonlight as a pole dancer.

Dr Turner and his sister pause to exchange raised browed glances and enigmatic smiles. "You really don't know do you, Aidan?" he says.

"What my brother means is I'm not actually a pole dancer. That was just my cover." She passes him the required instruments, the oh so professional nurse.

"Cover? I don't understand."

"You'll have to tell him now, Sis."

"You see, we've had our eye on 'The Black Garter' club for a while before Ray Lamond was arrested," she says.

"Why?" I ask.

"I'll let Mr Treveleyan explain everything. He won't like it if Jerry and I tell you everything now. He's top dog and he likes to stay that way. Besides, I think you should rest. We've finished now," Dr Turner says.

While they talk, both my interest and curiosity is aroused concerning this Mr Treveleyan, plus the morphine has managed to dull my pains to such a degree that not only can I not feel any, I entertain a strange lightness of spirit. Maybe it stems from the faith I have in Jeremy Turner's medical skills.

He pauses to admire his handiwork. "You'll have to wear a patch for a while I'm afraid. It'll help the healing process. I must warn you that all operations carry a degree of infection. You'll judge yourself how it's doing. Feel free to treat this place as your own, Aidan. I'll leave you in Suzanne's capable hands," he says, the smile never once leaving his face.

"Jesus, I must look a mess," I moan when he's gone and she and I are alone. "What's Caitlan going to say when she sees me with a patch over my eye? She'll go to pieces, I know she will. She's sort of fragile y'know."

"If she loves you, which I know she does, it won't bother her. Anyway," she places a hand against my cheek, "I think you look pretty sexy."

"Don't start, Suzanne. You'd say I looked sexy with a paper bag over my head."

"With that body, 'course I would."

"I still can't get over you being a nurse. So who's this Treveleyan guy you and your brother keep mentioning? And Dennis Mitchell, where the hell does he figure in all this?"

"Don't try to work it out. I want you to rest now, try and get some sleep and please trust us."

"Sure, I guess I have no choice."

"You ask where Dennis figures in all this. I can tell you that at least. He knew you were in trouble. That's why he was sent and he's your minder."

She prepares to move away from my bedside and I latch a hand onto her arm. "What makes you think I need minding, Suzanne? I can take care of myself," I stress.

"The way you did tonight, Aidan?"

I catch myself stiffening at her remark. "There were three of them. One had a knife blade held to my throat, but point taken. I don't think they actually planned to kill me and robbery wasn't their motive. I think they came across the water simply to spoil my looks. I know who it was, Caitlan's ex, Shaun Blackwood."

"We know," she admits quietly.

I regard her in puzzlement. "How could you have known who he was? I met the guy when I was in Dublin. He was about to beat up on Caitlan, so I sort of rescued her. That's how we met."

"We knew he'd been looking for you. That he caught a flight from Dublin to Heathrow a few days ago. He'd obviously been looking for you since then."

I stare at her in disbelief. "How could you possibly know that?"

"We do, that's all. I'm sure you'll want to call Caitlan, so I'll fetch you a phone. I'll also leave you with some water. Then get some rest. You've been through a lot."

"Sure, nurse." I make a vain attempt at a smile, but am unable to avoid emitting an ouch of pain when my eye starts to throb again. "So, if Dr Turner is your brother and your surname's Markwell, then you must be married."

"I didn't think you cared."

"Just curious that's all."

"I was." A note of regret permeates her voice. Moving to the door, a hand on the knob, she pauses.

"Was?"

"To a surgeon, Alan Markwell, we have a daughter, Lucy. I'll go and fetch the water and a phone."

She exits before I can say more. When the jug of water, glass and a phone are delivered to my bedside, it is by an elderly man in a white starched jacket. His taciturn exterior is unresponsive to my question of where Suzanne is, before he vacates the room.

So there is no chance of either Caitlan or my family contacting me. It is up to me to ring them. Rousing myself up in the bed with further tortuous pain from my bruised ribs, I observe that bruises are beginning to develop around the lower half of my torso.

I pick up the mobile and stare at it contemplatively, to ring or not to ring. Alarm Caitlan by trying to explain that I've been attacked and by who. That Blackwood has been shot dead by my ex-cell mate. A hearse like van had appeared and taken his body away. As I told Suzanne, in Caitlan's delicate state, both with her triggered psychotic episodes and with the baby coming, she would probably go to pieces. With little else to do but lie here and reflect, I wonder what have I taken on? No. I love her. She's consented to become my wife. I'd bought her an expensive engagement ring. I'd be nothing without her love. However, I return the phone to the cabinet. Pour water into the jug. Maybe she won't want me now. The morphine has helped both to ease the pain and to think. Suppose I have lost the sight in my eye? Maybe I'll be scarred and have to wear an eye patch for the rest of my life. I will myself to calmness with an effort and manage to regain some semblance of equilibrium. Dr Turner is a good surgeon. He is confident I'll be fine.

I guess I must have dozed. The room is quiet. Although it is morning, the sun barely penetrates the thick dark curtain at the window. I am awakened by a tentative rap on the door, but feel too weary to respond.

The door opens to admit a man whom I judge to be well into his fifties, maybe even his sixties. The man is in a wheelchair, one of those high-powered electrical jobs, which he guides across the room towards me. His hair is grey, short and balding from a high narrow forehead. His deep-seated eyes are oddly perspicacious and as grey as his hair, all in perfect accompaniment to a neatly trimmed spade beard. His features are quite heavily lined, as if he has suffered pain in his life, but are somehow kindly reminiscent of a favourite grandfather's. The suit he wears is also grey, with a grey marl pullover. Only the addition of a white shirt with a dark blue tie manages to throw the sombre ensemble into relief. There is nothing particularly remarkable about this man, yet I detect an indefinable something, even before he speaks, that commands people to attention. He also has either Army or Police written all over him.

"Mr McRaney, it's good to meet you at last." His accent is synonymous with an Oxford or Cambridge educated man. "It's a pity it is under such upsetting circumstances, at least for you. I'm George

Treveleyan. Although I was actually knighted for my services to the Metropolitan Police, I feel it too presumptuous of me to be called 'Sir' all the time."

"Thanks for what your doctor did for me. I take it Dr Turner is your doctor."

"Absolutely. We searched high and low to find a surgeon of Jeremy Turner's magnitude."

"As you're probably not with the NHS, I guess here comes the part where you hand me the bill for a grand or whatever. I mean, sure now, if this place isn't a wee bit grand for just any hospital."

"My dear Mr McRaney, Aidan, I can see your injuries haven't prevented you from losing your sense of humour. We aren't going to charge you for treatment. As Dennis rightly said, if you'd gone to A and E at almost any hospital you'd probably still be there, untreated and with the possibility of losing the sight of your eye."

"It's serious isn't it? My eye I mean?"

"I don't think so, but it could be if left untreated for too long."

"How long will I have to wear the bandage?"

"I'm not a doctor. I have to rely on Dr Turner to help me get through the day. You'll have to ask Jeremy."

"And Suzanne, the last time I saw her she was a dancer at my club."

"Suzanne Markwell. Beautiful isn't she? Suzanne's a remarkable woman. She has many skills, but I believe that nursing is her primary one. She told me she explained about the pole dancing. That it was her cover."

"You mean like a spy?"

"In a way."

"Jesus, I thought I'd stepped onto the set of a 'Carry On' film, now it's more 'James Bond'."

His smile is a thoughtful one. "I suppose it is a little. I guess you deserve some explanation. That you have several unanswered questions."

"Jesus, man, that don't cover it."

"Perhaps we can talk at breakfast."

"Sorry, Mr Treveleyan, explanations first, breakfast later. Besides, I gotta go home. Give my fiancée a fright. She's gonna freak when she sees my eye all bandaged up and the bruises. She's a wee bit delicate. She's on medication and stuff and I could use a smoke."

"All in good time. Your fiancée, is that Caitlan McKenna?"

"Sure. What do you know about her?"

"Oh don't get excited, Aidan. You don't mind if I call you Aidan?"

"Sure." I shrug. "You can call me what you like, but Aidan's as good a name as any."

"As I said before, you have a good sense of humour, if a somewhat, how shall we say, sarcastic one. You can call me George."

"First names sound a wee bit too pally and I ain't ready to be your pal just yet, Mr Treveleyan, not until I know what the fuck's going on." I swing my legs over the edge of the bed in an endeavour to search for my clothes. I ask where they are, that I have to go.

"There was blood on your clothes. Our laundry lady has taken them to be washed."

"You have a laundry lady? That's cool, man, my laundry lady is called Bridget. She's my sister. Your Doc has patched me up. I really do have to go."

"I thought you wanted explanations. I don't understand. Haven't we made you welcome? Attended to your wounds?"

"Sure y'have and I'm grateful, Mr Treveleyan, you know I am. So my ribs still hurt, you've patched up my eye and I think you've told me enough. It's just that…"

"You're worried about your girlfriend. I do understand that, but I'd still like to talk for a while. Suzanne will get you some clothes. Rest is what you need."

"I'll get that when I get home."

"How will you get home?"

"I'll call a cab. Just tell me where this place is."

"We're in South Lambeth. Anyway, I want you to apologise to Caitlan for me."

"Sorry?" I regard him with a frown.

Still seated on the edge of the bed, I feel somewhat embarrassed because I am only wearing my shorts and I pull the sheet around me. "What have I got to apologise to Caitlan for?"

"I'm afraid I gave her rather a fright a few nights ago."

"A fright? I don't understand."

"Let me start at the beginning. As you can see, I'm wheelchair bound. I was a police officer in the late seventies, early eighties. In 1983, there was a shoot-out during a bank robbery. I managed to pop off a couple of villains, but then I myself was shot and my spine injured leaving me like this. I had only just got married. My wife couldn't handle the way I was. I was your age, Aidan, 28 years old and left a cripple. She wanted a child you see and the way I was…" he shrugs disconsolately, "she finally left me."

"So what's that gotta do with my girlfriend?"

"When Margie left I buried my head in books, not the usual brainless fiction but factual accounts, books about other countries. I received a sizeable pension. Apparently, it wasn't the money that meant anything to Margie but having a baby. She met someone else and did just that." The sadness that appears in his eyes is conducive to affecting his voice. He continues regardlessly, "I had a newfound interest in Tibet, a most fascinating country. You really should go there. So, I was a cripple and I hired a nurse, not the lovely Suzanne, I doubt she was no more than a child, but the nurse I hired enjoyed travelling as much as I did. We journeyed to Tibet. There I met the Lamas, the monks. They taught me a lot, Aidan." Interlacing his rather elegant, if somewhat liver-spotted fingers against his mouth, he adds thoughtfully. "They taught me how to get out of this chair, not as a physical body of course, but in my etheric double."

At this juncture in his rather unbelievable narrative, I wonder if Sir George Treveleyan, who is probably on so much medication to dull the obvious pain he is in, might be high and hallucinating. "How?" I ask in a husky voice.

"By astral projection, my friend."

Now I really am certain that he is on some hallucinogenic drug. "Astral what?" I start to laugh despite the pain of my injuries.

"Astral projection. Out of the body. I have learned from the Tibetan monks how to project my etheric double to anywhere I wish. That's why, I'm afraid, as I contemplated what Suzanne had told me about you, how she found you an attractive man and couldn't stop talking about you, how she would enjoy the job if it meant getting close to you, that I suppose I was thinking along those lines when I involuntarily projected myself into your bedroom in Talbot Place, Shooters Hill. Your girlfriend caught my reflection in the mirror. You have one facing your bed. You were asleep, but she happened to see me. I cannot speak while I'm in that state. I'm not entirely solid either. Again I apologise."

I stare at him disbelievingly. So this is the man with the grey beard Caitlan had seen. "Jesus!" I run a hand across my face, at a loss for words, while the hand comes away damp with perspiration. "If what you're saying is true, we could have been..."

"Having sex, is that what you were about to say?"

"Sure. Something like that, but you can see when you're in this astral what's it? It all sounds too far-fetched to be believable."

"Astral projection. Oh yes, I can see perfectly. There is so much I can teach you, Aidan."

"Why me? And why Dennis Mitchell?"

"You're both ex-cons. It's called self-preservation."

"I still don't understand."

"I can see that. You and Dennis both have certain skills and who knows the criminal world better than ex-cons? The people in my employment have dabbled in crime at some point in their lives and for their own reasons. I take it you have heard the expression, 'fighting fire with fire'?"

"Sure." I continue to regard this man in both astonishment and disbelief at the things he has intimated.

"You mean use criminals to catch criminals?" Treveleyan says, "We all live in our own little worlds. Go about our daily lives obliviously, blinkered if you like. So blinkered in fact that we really don't want to know what's going on, and maybe we don't want to remove the blinkers, because if we do we'll realise that this country, and not just this one but others too, is slowly being pulled into a state of decay and oblivion." His voice becomes almost agitated. He makes me listen, unwittingly I admit, but as I initially conjecture this man instils so much command you can do no other.

"Crime is on the increase. The police are undermanned because of the cuts. People like Ray Lamond, a man who has more branches in the criminal world than you'll ever know, have to be stopped before they become the rulers. Mitchell explained about the tapes that were seized in his Maze Hill house after his arrest?"

I nod perfunctorily, my heart hammering because I'm all too intrinsically aware to what he is eluding.

He adds quietly, sotto voce. "You know I have seen a DVD of you and that Benson woman?"

My senses reel. I grip the bedrail so vehemently I imagine my hand will be cut right through, while an inherent anger courses through me once more. "You know I'm prepared to get that DVD at all costs. So you have it?"

"No, but one of my operatives does. He'll give it to you. I'll issue a signed note. He's an exception to the rule; he hasn't been to prison but has other uses."

"So, who has it? Dennis Mitchell? Suzanne?"

"No." He shakes his head. "But you know him."

I demand to know who it is.

"He's a neighbour of yours. David Lennard. I believe he has taken up residence in the basement flat. Now shall we go and have some breakfast, Aidan?"

CHAPTER TWENTY-SIX

-

SUZANNE

At least I am marginally presentable again. Suzanne has found me some clothes. A rather tight pair of black jeans, plus a black muscle tee shirt she decides I'll look good in. Because she is unable to contact me, I reason that Caitlan will probably have had an episode by now. I hadn't been home at all last night. Now I wish for nothing but to be out of here. It seems, however, that Sir George Treveleyan has other ideas.

The facility, or that's what Treveleyan terms it, appears to cater for everything. There is the surgery of course. A kitchen and dining room fashioned with black granite Parisian style tables. There are two cooks; one a mature lady in her fifties, the other is younger. When Sir George arrives, the two women practically bow their obeisance.

He's been a cripple for 30 years, he explains but, as he assures me, renewed his education towards all things relative to a mystic nature. Plus, the setting up of the Agency has afforded him a new lease of life, one he probably wouldn't have had if he had not sustained the spinal injury which had seen him invalided from the police force. He would have had children with his wife Margie, he says. Whenever he speaks of her, an inevitable wistfulness appears in his eyes.

Part of me continues to believe that Treveleyan is nothing but a nutter, albeit a rich nutter, with an eminent doctor and a pretty nurse to attend to his every want. I'm aware that now my wounds have been attended to I should leave, except there's a reluctance in me to do so. I want to listen to more concerning this man and his Agency and there is an unwillingness to observe Caitlan's reaction when she sees my eye patched up. Notwithstanding I'm also interested to discover that my neighbour, a man I believed to be nothing more than an eccentric homosexual with a more than overzealous love of cats, is actually one of Treveleyan's operatives.

The young cook, introducing herself as Emily, wears a starched white uniform while her short dark hair is enveloped within the confines of a less than flattering equally white cap. She presents herself at the table where I sit opposite the 'great man'.

"A full English, Aidan?" He cocks a speculative brow.

"Jesus, no, I don't eat all that stuff, man." I direct a solitary eye at Emily. "Just toast please sweetheart, and coffee, plenty of coffee, black, no sugar."

Interlacing those speckled brown, almost effeminate fingers that rest on his bearded chin, he pauses to observe me diligently. "You really are a man who likes to take care of himself."

"Sure I was, until I got this." I point to my bandaged eye.

"Beauty is but skin deep Aidan, but it's good that you eat properly. You are, shall I say, wiry for a man of your age and height."

"I've always been wiry, like my dad. He's nearly 70 now and he's like an emaciated old spider or at least that's what I call him behind his back." I offer him a somewhat lopsided smile.

Returning his attention to Emily, who is shy and blushing, waiting attendance on us, Treveleyan requests she brings in some toast. "With butter please, my dear. Oh, and I'll have a pot of Darjeeling. Thank you." He smiles at her politely, his manner both gentlemanly and considerate.

"Of course, Mr Treveleyan." Emily practically curtsies.

"Oh, and a cigarette," I add.

"You smoke, yet you like to take care of yourself otherwise."

"Sure I smoke."

"Have you ever tried to quit?"

"Jesus, what is this? No, I've never tried to quit. My old man smokes. He's smoked all his life. As I said, he's nearly 70. If I live that long I'll be fuckin' grateful. My mother didn't smoke and she died of a heart attack in childbirth in her forties."

"And some cigarettes, my dear. Any particular brand, Aidan?"

"I roll my own, just some tobacco, darlin' and the makings, please." I smile her way.

"Certainly, sir." She returns the smile and colours, heightening her rather plain features.

"See, you've still got it, enough to make a young girl blush. People react differently to injury. If you're concerned about Caitlan, if she loves you, it won't put her off. I always believed Margie loved me. In sickness and health and all that, but when I got shot and the doctors told her that I'd be confined to a wheelchair for the rest of my life, she left me. Sadly, she was the one who died first. Cancer, so her husband told me. Never mind. Here is our breakfast..."

"Your tea and toast, Mr Treveleyan and your black coffee, Mister..." still colouring to the roots of her hair, Emily fishes for my name.

"Aidan. Thanks, Emily."

Her colour has heightened to such a degree, I half expect her to pass out.

When she'd gone, Treveleyan says, "you shouldn't tease, my boy. I can see why Suzanne was so enamoured of you and why your girlfriend should wish to leave her native Dublin to be with you."

"Look, you've spent most of this session talking about me. I'm more interested in you, Mr Treveleyan, and David Lennard. I know he's a homosexual. Not that I've got anything against them as long as they don't come onto me." I recollect Stephen Fitzwalter. After Verdi and I had tied him up. How his attempt to kiss me had ultimately cost him his life.

"That's just his cover. The homosexual thing," Treveleyan imparts, spreading butter onto his toast. He also checks his pot of Darjeeling before replacing the lid.

"You're saying he isn't really gay?"

"What David? He has a wife and a child in Streatham."

Why is it I catch myself shivering involuntarily in such a way that has nothing remotely to do with my injuries? "So why the fuck did he pretend to be gay?"

"I told you, it's his cover. Look, Aidan, I don't expect you to believe any of this. You see, David Lennard used to be an actor. Not TV or the movies, mostly theatre, and because of the way he speaks, in that soft, almost effeminate manner, he always played homosexuals. His agent said if ever they got a part for a gay they would always think of David, until he'd had enough. Other parts weren't coming his way. He wanted to do straight stuff. It made him so depressed; he even tried taking his own life. Acting was his life. Then I suggested he come and work for me. Like you, he was suspicious, distrustful when I told him I could use his talents. He hated it at first but the money was double what he was getting in the theatre and waiting for parts to come his way. With that kind of money, you should see his house in Streatham, Aidan; he even relented on playing the homosexual parts. You see... I... ahem," he clears his throat uncomfortably, a gnarled hand to his mouth, "I wanted you kept on ice, so to speak." He coughs awkwardly, I guess the surprise must have registered on my face.

"What!" I explode and almost choke on my toast. "What's that supposed to mean? Why should you want me kept on ice?"

"Alright, I'm sorry, I'll come straight to the point."

The bruises are growing painful again, while my eye has begun to throb so much behind the bandage, I am compelled to place my hand there.

"You in pain?" Treveleyan asks with concern.

"You could say that. My eye is fuckin' killing me."

"The morphine has probably worn off."

"I don't want another injection."

"You won't. I'll call Suzanne, she'll give you some pills." Treveleyan makes a call from a phone he takes from his jacket. "Can you come to the dining room, please, Suzanne? Bring some painkillers for Mr McRaney. Thank you my dear."

She appears within minutes. Her nurse's uniform is exchanged for a slim fitting red wool dress and red high heels. Her hair spills around her shoulders.

"Sorry, were you about to go out, my dear?"

She shrugs, "not particularly" and sets a bottle of white pills onto the table in front of me. "You guys look cosy. Sorry you're in pain, Aidan." She presses a hand over mine commiseratingly. I refrain from pulling away, although I'm aware that I should. "Thanks," I tell her and swallow a couple of pills with some water from the jug. It is plainly obvious that Suzanne's intention is to join us.

Treveleyan says, "I was telling Aidan about David Lennard."

"Oh yeah, David," her laugh is subtle. "He does drag as well sometimes."

"As an act?" I ask.

"As a cover, he's such a good actor. He manages to convince everyone."

"He definitely managed to convince me," I say.

"Jerry said you'd beat about the bush, Georgie."

"Please, Suzanne." Treveleyan appears oddly embarrassed all at once. Perhaps it's her reference to him as 'Georgie'.

Interlacing my fingers, arms resting on the table, a familiar inflection of Treveleyan's it seems, I say, "so I'd have to be a thick Paddy not to know what you really want, George." I stress his name. "You want me to work for you. You sent David to act the homosexual to 'keep me on ice' as you put it. And Dennis Mitchell. He works for you too, right?"

"Yes, Dennis works for me. You see, Aidan, we catch criminals by using criminals. I believe you already know this, as Dennis explained to you that most of my operatives have served time in prison. Unlike David, not everyone is an actor. If someone is sent undercover, as clean as a whistle, how can they possibly understand what it's like to be a criminal? No one knows that better than someone who has, how shall I say, gone astray, as it were."

"But surely the police…" I allow my words to trail because Treveleyan sports an oddly enigmatic smile.

"The Bill stick out like a sore thumb, darling," Suzanne purrs. She's now positioned herself behind my chair so that I can hear the steady undulation of her breathing, which leaves scarcely little to the imagination, inside the red wool dress.

This tableau. What had happened to me last night, all appears so distant and a world away from my family and Caitlan. I think Suzanne is beginning to believe this too, because I'm aware I had tasted her once, she is probably hoping that I will do so again. I have Caitlan now, or do I?

"The business of the DVD, I hasten to apologise for that." Treveleyan interrupts my retrospection. He spoons a single sugar into his tea, while I sip my own beverage thoughtfully. My heart has begun a somewhat erratic pounding against my chest, doing nothing to alleviate the soreness of my bruises, when he refers to that DVD.

Suzanne is certainly aware of what Verdi and I did. I run a hand over my face, hardly daring to glance her way, when guilt assails me so predominantly. A hand is suddenly placed in mine and Suzanne, uncaring that Treveleyan might wish to talk to me alone, has pulled up a chair and sits down at our table.

Treveleyan adds, "you did a good job, my boy. The Fitzwalter's were renegades and deeper in gangland than you'll ever know. They were evil people who used soft targets, like your poor sister, to get to their intended targets. We don't work that way."

I recollect Ronnie Engels referring to 'the suits' abducting his daughter in exchange for Engels handing over Lamond. I wonder if these were 'the suits' he'd spoken of. Nevertheless, I refrain from mentioning that fact. Instead, I ask him about my family ever discovering what's on that incriminating DVD.

"Your family need know nothing," he replies.

"Then you're not going to use it to blackmail me into working for you?" I push aside the plate containing my half-eaten slice of toast. "I suddenly don't feel hungry anymore." Somehow, a cigarette appears more inviting. Beneath Treveleyan's reproving gaze, I roll and light one regardlessly.

"Of course not," he retorts. "Please, Aidan, my boy, trust me." There is an unaccustomed begging intimation in his voice.

"For a start, I'm not your boy."

"I'm sorry." Treveleyan bows his head momentarily.

Suzanne flicks me an amused smile. I wasn't smiling, however. "Then why have you kept the fuckin' DVD if it isn't to use it against me in some way?"

"Oh please tell him, Suzanne…" Treveleyan pauses, runs a palm across his grey beard wearily. "He needs to know."

"The fuckin' hell I do, Treveleyan." I make a vain attempt to quell the rising tide of inherent anger. "If you took that tape to the polis, Jesus, I could get banged up for fuckin' life, man. Think what it would do to my family, my girl, my son. Caitlan's expecting my baby. She also has psychotic episodes that only need a trigger to spark one off. She don't need no fuckin' stress. So you destroy that fuckin' DVD or I swear to God." I bunch a fist against my leg vehemently.

"Or you'll what?" Treveleyan's question is challenging while his expression, those oddly perspicacious grey eyes, are strangely hooded, guarded, reminiscent of a bird of prey. Momentarily I have the utmost difficulty in tearing my own gaze away and realise, with acute uneasiness, that it's as if the guy is trying to hypnotise me. Nonetheless, I manage to stand my ground, defying that oddly compelling gaze. "I'll fuckin' kill you and you know I can. I can handle a gun, man."

"I don't doubt that." In spite of my angry outburst the narrow mouth, thin lips crease into the semblance of a self-satisfied smile. "That's why we need you and yes, I won't deny it, I would like you to work for me."

"What as? Some undercover operative?"

"As… as…" Why is it, whenever I ask him what perhaps passes for an awkward question, he has to go through the motions of clearing his throat.

"Oh for God's sake, Georgie!" Suzanne interrupts with exasperation. "Talk about beating about the bush. As an assassin, a trigger man. What else, darling? The way you…"

"Jesus, for fuck's sake!" It is my turn to interrupt and I leap to my feet instinctively, despite the fact my ribs hurt like hell. The sensation of my eye throbbing so profoundly I feel the wetness, like water, drizzling behind the bandage. At least I hope it is water. "I have a family. Being a good father to my children, that's all I care about. Get Dennis Mitchell to do your fuckin' dirty work, man."

"Oh he does, Aidan," Treveleyan's response is nonchalant. "Now I'm tired and Suzanne will take you home. I could almost predict how you would react, but there is precious little work out there for an ex-convict. What I'm offering you is security."

"It may have escaped your notice, Treveleyan, but I already have a job. I happen to own a nightclub now."

I observe Treveleyan visibly blanch. He shifts in his seat uncomfortably. "That iniquitous dive, if that's what gives you pleasure, but you must know it comes at a price."

"And what's that, Treveleyan?" I pretend obtuseness, but I already know, and maybe I paid the price the night De Oliveira and Santos showed up and I threatened them with a gun. Again, I refrain from confiding in Treveleyan.

"That place is gangland owned. Then again I don't suppose I need to tell you that, or that no good will come of it."

"At least I won't be seeing iron bars and a fuckin' slop bucket," I retort. "And I will if I kill again."

"You won't go to prison, Aidan. No one can touch you. Things are so bad in this country. Gang rule is on the increase, the police are losing control. Maybe you don't watch the news. Riots on the streets…"

She shrugs haphazardly, as if I'm a lost cause.

"We have to protect honest citizens and if blowing away a few bad guys can do that…" Again, she allows her words to trail.

It is Treveleyan who smiles, the proverbial father figure once more. "Exactly, I'm on first name terms with the Chief Constable. He sanctions what we do. Archie is a canny Scot with a penchant for good quality Scotch whisky, but I do understand, Aidan. Now, you'd better go home to your family. Also, remember, there is so much I can teach you. Have a final check with Jeremy Turner before you leave and if that nightclub business turns sour, as everything does where gangland is involved, then you know where I am."

"I won't change my mind and I'm planning to make that club legit…"

"Good luck with that, Aidan," Treveleyan mouths behind that annoying clinical smile.

"I don't need luck, just savvy. Now if you'll sign the paper to show David Lennard, so that I can get that fuckin' DVD and destroy it."

"Of course," Treveleyan says simply.

*

As she drives me toward Shooters Hill, Suzanne seems oddly preoccupied and I ask her if she'd ever been one of Treveleyan's assassins.

"I'm strictly medical, Aidan, but if the opportunity ever arose, I wouldn't be scared."

"To kill someone?"

"If you like. Like Sir George says, the money is amazing. We have clients who want someone out of their lives, but mostly it's the bad guys. Really, Aidan, you could do worse. You know how to handle a gun. Why not use it for good?"

"Why does everyone want me to do this stuff? I just want to lead a normal life. What does it take to make people understand that? What happened at 'the Copper Kettle' was ten years ago. All I want to do is forget it and Treveleyan seems rather bitter. All that crap he was talking about, that astral what's it."

"Astral projection. The other stuff he does. Remote viewing, have you heard of it?"

"Sure I've heard of it but I'm not sure what it is."

"The method we use is a viewer has to get hold of an object belonging to the person they are trying to locate. Psychics have been able to do it to find missing persons. The object is usually held over a map. Treveleyan is able to locate anyone in the world, even if they've changed their features, no matter where he or she is or how safe they think they might be. The police don't have that kind of skill."

I find myself shivering involuntarily at what she hints. "Does it work?" I swallow hard.

"If it's perfected properly, but it takes a great deal of concentration. As I said, some of the assassins use remote viewing to track their targets. People bury their heads in the sand, that's the trouble."

"Meaning?" My eye unwittingly descends to the long, shapely legs where the red dress has ruched up a fraction; observe her delicate white palm as it grips the gear stick near my leg. Whether it's because of the residue of the remaining morphine or my own erstwhile male sexuality, suddenly I want this woman. She is beautiful, she oozes sex, it suppurates from every single part of her. Of course, she isn't exactly the kind of woman I could settle down with. Guiltily my thoughts return to Caitlan. Suppose she reacts badly when she sees my bandaged eye. I am now wearing a black patch over the dressing.

Concentrating on the streets through which we drive, Suzanne says, "this country's in a poor state, Aidan. Criminals and muggers are allowed to roam the streets. Oh, don't get me wrong, I'm not knocking the police, they try their level best, but this dreadful deficit the politicians have thrust upon us. How they've had to cut the services. The police, the military. You can't deprive a country of its defences. I love England. I was born and brought up here. Alan, my ex, owned a beautiful house in Buckinghamshire until he started playing away, as they say. I still live there, he has allowed me that much.

"After I had Lucy, my daughter, I returned to nursing. It was Jerry who told me about Sir George's agency. I wanted to see for myself what it was all about. I love the undercover work. When you took over that club George wanted me to see what made you tick, as it were. Of course, we knew about the Brazilian drug dealers and if you do work for the Agency, you won't end up in prison, honestly. The Agency is no different from Special Branch or MI5."

"But it'll still be killing people, won't it?"

"If that's what it takes, but you'll be preserving the good people. The old ladies who get mugged out of their life savings, the children who are abused by perverts and paedophiles."

"I don't know, Suzanne. I just want to see my family, that's all. Suppose I did what Treveleyan asks and they found out? It would destroy them."

"They need never know…"

"Jesus, Suzanne," I interrupt. "Caitlan's bound to ask where I'm going. What do I say, 'oh, just going to blow someone away, darlin', shouldn't take me more than an hour.'"

"I do understand," she laughs. "When I lived with Alan he had no idea that I was living a double life. Why should he? As far as he was concerned, I worked in a clinic in London."

"That isn't why you separated then?"

"No, Aidan, it wasn't. He had an affair with another doctor."

"So your daughter, Lucy was it? Does she know who you work for?"

"Sure she does. She's still a child and she doubts nothing that I tell her. Anyway, she calls him Uncle George. This is near your flat isn't it?" she reminds and swinging her Citroen against the kerb, brakes the car to a sudden halt.

"You sure you'll be okay?" she asks solicitously. "How's your eye, still painful?"

"Not so much with the painkillers."

"It shouldn't take long to heal. My brother's a good surgeon. He's taken bullets out of operatives and no one has died yet."

Placing a hand against my cheek, she brushes a kiss to my lips. "I like you a lot, Aidan. Maybe if we'd met before Caitlan, I don't know…" She allows her words to trail on a wistful note.

Initially I had no intention of responding but suddenly I can no longer help myself and I'm crushing my mouth to hers because I need her. I know I shouldn't think it, but since I've been out, I realise how much women dominate my thoughts. How difficult it is to go without sex now that I have discovered it again. I'm uncertain how Caitlan might react to my injury. Suzanne is a nurse, injury scarcely bothers her, aware how easy it would be to persuade her, despite my injuries, to have sex with me. As if interpreting my thoughts, she whispers, "if you need me and I mean for anything, you know where I am," when I release her.

"You'll be at the club tonight?"

"Of course, I can't have my cover blown just yet can I? And you, you should rest you know."

"I've rested all day. I'll see you later."

"Okay and don't worry about Caitlan. She loves you, in sickness and in health and all that malarkey." She smiles and blows me a kiss when I alight from her car.

CHAPTER TWENTY-SEVEN

–

INCRIMINATING EVIDENCE

Reaching my flat, I have no intention of returning inside immediately. I have to see someone first. Scanning my surroundings, a cigarette signposting my lip, I wait patiently before David Lennard appears at his door and I catch his outline in the upper panel of frosted glass. I kill the smoke before he cracks open his door and he exclaims, "Aidan!" I guess at my appearance, "oh dear, whatever's happened to you?"

"I got jumped didn't I?" I mutter unwilling to explain and, I thought, you can cut out the 'pouf' act. You're no more of a homo than I am. I refrain, however, from accusation momentarily. I need to get into his flat to locate that condemning DVD. I wonder if he's watched it.

He regards me, oddly imploringly as if he is attuned to the fact, as testified by the coolness of my demeanour, that I am onto him and if he has seen that tape he will be aware of what I am capable.

"She's here," he says finally.

"Sorry? Who's here?"

"Caitlan."

I stiffen. "Wh… what's she doing here?" With Caitlan's presence in Lennard's flat, I can hardly retrieve the DVD.

"I found her walking up and down the street. She looked so worried that I went out to see what was wrong. Moo's had her kittens so I asked Caitlan why didn't she come in and see them. I gave her some chamomile tea which managed to calm her down. She was looking for you. Come through, Aidan."

This is the first time I've been inside Lennard's flat. The layout is similar to mine. The hallway leads off to the kitchen. The master bedroom is located adjacent to the lounge, except in marked contrast to mine, Lennard's flat smells badly of cats.

He ushers me into his sparsely furnished lounge where I observe Caitlan kneeling down to the small, fluffy kittens curled up in a wickerwork basket. One of the kittens is sucking her finger. She coos at it with an almost childish delight causing my heart to perform an agonised somersault. She is so innocent, so sweet and gentle with her love for children and animals she scarcely deserves a villainous bastard like me. Caitlan is the reason why I have no intention of working as one of Treveleyan's assassins.

"Look who's here, Caitlan," Lennard declares.

"Sweetheart," I breathe raggedly.

"Aidan!" Her eyes light up instinctively when she sees me, her pleasure evident, only for the same light to extinguish in the beautiful green eyes, almost as if a candle were being snuffed out. She jumps to her feet instantly, stammers, "wh… what's h… happened to you?" She can barely speak and there's a rise of hysteria in her voice. "Your… your eye." She begins to physically tremble and practically falls onto Lennard's sofa. "I was so worried about you. You didn't come in all last night."

"Sweetheart," is all I can say. I realise how much I love and need her. Whatever I'd felt for Suzanne was merely sexual. It is Caitlan who I truly love, enough to marry, to spend the rest of my life with.

Catching sight of my reflection in the mirror I am astonished at how truly villainous I really appear. The black patch over my eye stands out markedly in accompaniment with my unshaven features, the black beard, wild dishevelled hair, all black clothes, with the realisation that I hardly deserve a lovely girl like Caitlan McKenna, that pole dancers and prostitutes are more my thing.

"Would you like a coffee, Aidan?" Lennard offers, his voice small and anxious, he disturbs me from my unwelcome reflections.

"No thanks." The coldness evaporates and in its place, I inject an enforced politeness. "Caitlan, baby, I got mugged when I came out of the club last night," I attempt to explain, in the knowledge that I can't possibly confess that I was attacked by her ex-boyfriend. "I… I went to the hospital. You know how long they keep you waiting there." More lies, McRaney. "I had to have my eye stitched and I couldn't call you 'cos my phone got smashed. I'm so sorry. It's not as bad as it looks. I have to wear the patch 'til it heals, that's all."

Her face remains ashen. Initially, I believe she is about to faint.

"Did you see who did it, Aidan?" It is Lennard who asks the question.

"No, they were masked. One of them had a knife. I didn't stand a chance. There were three of them and one put the boot in. My ribs are pretty painful." I make a face with indication.

"You tell the police?" he insists.

"Sure." I lie. "But I couldn't give 'em an adequate description. Like I said, they were masked. Balaclavas." At least that part was true.

"Any money taken?" Lennard really is concerned, so that I am beginning to warm to the guy and I wonder the best way to obtain that DVD without getting too Andy McNab.

"Yeah," I respond non-committally.

"Dear oh dear, but I must say, the patch does nothing to detract from his good looks does it, Caitlan?" Lennard says.

While I am compelled to congratulate him on his acting skills I reason that he is wasted working for Treveleyan. Maybe the money is better.

We regard each other, she and I, simply making eye contact in Lennard's less than prepossessing room. I guess he really doesn't need many fripperies when the flat is merely used as a cover. As Treveleyan outlined, he resides in a nice house in Streatham with his wife and child. For now, I decide to go along with the pretence in front of Caitlan.

"Oh Aidan," she wails, her voice catching, "I worry about you so much. I was worried sick when you didn't come in last night." Tears spill unchecked from her eyes as she places her almost childlike palm into mine. Then suddenly the tears are blinked back and the enthusiasm driving her words takes their place. "Now come and look at Moo's kittens, Aidan. They're grand aren't they?"

"Sure, grand," I mutter, unable to muster a great deal of enthusiasm.

"Can I have one? I mean when they've grown up a wee bit." She regards me imploringly before turning to Lennard. "Is that alright, David?"

"Of course, but it's up to Aidan," he responds quietly.

"Look, sweetheart, we'd better go. I need to catch up on some sleep. I didn't get a lot last night." I help her rise. My heart hammers in case she chooses to pull away. She accepts the proffered hand however, and continues to clutch it as we move to the door. I thank Lennard for looking after her, that we'll discuss the kittens later.

"Well it is nearly Christmas," Lennard states in his best Oscar winning tone.

Upstairs I am greeted by the sight of a tall 5ft Christmas tree, which is in the process of being decorated by my brother. Nursing a beer in one hand and a string of fairy lights in the other he starts to exclaim, "oh, Caitlan, I wondered where you'd…" his words trail all at once when he sees me and he almost drops his can of beer. The lights he has begun to arrange around the tree dangle unheeded through his fingers. "Jesus, Aid, what the fuck's happened to you?"

He quickly deposits the beer and lights onto the nearest table and is by my side immediately. "Wh… what's happened to your eye, man?"

I half expect Ruairi to display tears as Caitlan had, I can tell he is close to them. She clutches my arm as if she never wishes to let me go.

"It's not as bad as it looks." I start to explain; that I'd been ambushed after leaving the club, omitting the part where Mitchell shot my attacker dead and who the attacker was of course.

"I should have fuckin' stayed, I knew it," he spits, tight lipped. Shaking his head regretfully, he bunches a fist against the leg of his jeans. "You was okay when I was packing up the DJ equipment." He is about to give me a sympathetic hug when I warn him off with an ouch of pain.

"I've got bruises on my stomach and my ribcage hurts like hell."

"It wasn't that DJ, Pauly and his pals was it, Aid?" Ru asks uneasily. "I know he wasn't happy when you told him you didn't like his music."

It was definitely not Paul Lucas and his pals who had attacked me, but how can I confess in Caitlan's presence that it was Shaun Blackwood who had deemed it necessary to cross water just to fuck up my looks.

"It might have been," I say non-commitally, "I don't know, Ru, they were wearing ski masks. Anyway, you got one of those beers man?"

"Sure, Aid." After briefly disappearing into the kitchen, he returns with a Becks beer and hands it to me. Caitlan guides me to the settee as if I were blind, makes a fuss of me by straightening cushions around my back, while enquiring if I'm okay. I enjoy the fuss of course, especially when it's made by a pretty girl. I might only be able to see out of one eye, but I'm not ready for a white stick yet. I ask her if she finds the patch a trifle off putting.

"It worried me at first, when I was so concerned for you, thinking the worse that…" she hesitates.

"That what, sweetheart?" I drain the beer and sod to the fact I'm on painkillers. "You didn't think I was with someone else did you?"

"No," she says somewhat uncertainly. "But we should be honest with one another." Clutching my arm she lays her head on my shoulder and I attempt not to blanch at her words because everything I have told her, hitherto, has been nothing short of a lie. I feel such a heel. I kissed Suzanne simply because I need to keep her 'on ice' in case Caitlan rejects me and I desire to know where my next screw is coming from. Sure if that doesn't make me out to be the heartless bastard that I probably am.

"I'm sorry, Aidan, it did occur to me that you might have been with someone else."

Coming on the wake of what I am thinking, her words allow the guilt to wash over me once more. I really do love her, so much, aware that if she left me I'd be finished yet I can't help thinking the way I do.

"We really was worried sick, Aid," Ru enjoins, dropping his weight into the facing chair.

"I haven't asked how you're feeling, sweetheart. You had a migraine," I remind her.

"Och, I'm much better now, thanks. You didn't mind us decorating your flat for Christmas did you? Ruairi says you wouldn't have bothered and this is your first Christmas since…" her words falter and she averts her eyes as if she's spoken out of turn.

"Since I've been out. It's cool, darlin'. I'm glad, even relieved that Patrick told you, that it's out in the open." I thought of that DVD again. In all likelihood, it is sitting on David Lennard's lounge shelf. I realise that I'll have to make an excuse to go down, retrieve the damn thing somehow. Or all this, my brother and girlfriend's concerns for me, will become null and void if they should happen to see what is on that tape.

Here they are, like two children enthusing over the coming festivities, while I have so many concerns and worries on my shoulders that make me suddenly feel older than my 29 years.

"You told the police, Aid?" Ru breaks into my thoughts.

"Sure I did," I lie.

"And your eye. You haven't lost it have you?" They both regard me in concern again.

"It's cool, Ru, I told you. It looks worse than it is and no, I haven't lost it."

"When I saw you with a patch over your eye, I didn't think it was a fashion statement." Ru quips. "Anyway, I almost forgot, Brid's been phoning practically all morning."

"Because I didn't come home? Jesus, I'm not 12 anymore."

"She was calling about Dad," Ru says.

"Dad? What about him? He hasn't been taken into a home?" I fail to keep the suspicion from my voice. Brid is convinced that our dad has early onset dementia, but he is my dad. So he can be a miserable old grouch at times, but I love him and don't wish to see him go into a care home.

"It's not about that. Apparently Mrs Jenkins phoned," Ru says.

"Mrs Jenkins?" I arch a solitary brow.

"Yeah, she's the woman who's been looking after him. She's a neighbour. Brid thinks Mrs Jenkins believes Dad's got money from when he sold his decorating business."

"That was 20 years ago. Anyway, what's wrong with Dad? Is he ill?"

"Bridget said he's been having palpitations, didn't she Ruairi?" Caitlan interjects.

"He's not in hospital is he?" All this and now the possibility there is something wrong with my father.

"No, but the doctor had to be called out. That wasn't what Mrs Jenkins was calling about. The palpitations happened afterwards."

"Afterwards?"

"According to Mrs Jenkins, to quote her own words, 'some coppers from Ireland want to talk to him.'"

"Coppers from Ireland? You mean the Gardaí? What do they want?" As if I didn't know. How can I confess to these two young innocents that our father killed someone, the reason why we left Dublin in such a hurry in 1993? According to Harry, Dad had killed the man who'd been having an affair with his wife Marie, our mother. Harry had helped Dad to bury the body of one Michael Docherty somewhere in a wood outside Dublin. I'd only learned of this recently. After all, I was only 9 and a half at the time and Ru was a toddler. I wonder how much Brid remembers. She'd been 14.

Ru says, "why would the Gardaí want to talk to Dad? Jesus, we left Ireland 20 years ago. Apart from a wedding and a couple of funerals, we haven't been back since. You have though. You didn't do nothing untoward when you were there?"

"Jesus, Ru, I won't even dignify that with a response," I retort.

Caitlan clutches my hand. Both of us, I guess, recollecting the business with Shaun Blackwood, but why should the Gardaí feel it necessary to talk to Dad?

"What does she want me to do about it? Only I've got enough on my fuckin' plate right now."

"They said they'd come back," Ru says.

"We know nothing. Jesus, man, we were kids."

"You'd better call Brid then, 'cos she was worried about you not coming in last night or calling us," he says.

"Later maybe, I'm going to get some sleep first. You coming?" I ask her, slipping an arm around her shoulders.

"But your injuries," she remonstrates, aware I guess of what I'm after.

"First, a trip downstairs to see David Lennard. I'll call Brid when I return," I tell Ru.

"What do you want to see him for?" he enquires with a frown.

I slip a finger beneath her chin and kiss her without glancing at my brother. "To discuss the kittens, what else?"

"Oh, Aidan!" she throws her arms around my neck, her eyes wide and shimmering, in her enthusiasm she reminds me of a kitten herself, gentle, soft. Despite the pain in my ribs, I pull her into my body.

*

David Lennard comes to the door immediately I press his bell, the blue Persian in his arms.

"Oh, Aidan! I'm surprised to see you again quite so soon. Has Caitlan forgotten something or did you want to discuss the kittens? I know how much she would like one."

"Can I come in?" I begin politely. It is far from the way I'm feeling when I think about that condemning DVD which he has in his possession. Nevertheless, to alert him as to my real reason for calling on him might result in his refusing me admittance. He opens the door, ushers me inside.

"Of course, we are neighbours after all." Closing the door behind us and depositing the cat somewhat protestingly on the floor with various cooings of "Daddy loves Moo," he adds, "you wouldn't think the little minx had just given birth a few days ago would you? In about four weeks, the kittens should be ready to leave their mother. If Caitlan wants one for Christmas…" he continues his prattling.

Brushing cat hairs from neatly pressed grey trousers, he smiles. "You know you really do look quite piratical and villainous, like Blackbeard…"

"I know what I look like," I snap.

"Of course you do." He stammers now, reproved by my rather acerbic response. He also begins to back away a little. I suppose I do appear intimidating, doubly so when I slide the bolt across his outer door before following him into the lounge.

"What's wrong, Aidan? Look, if it's because I've befriended Caitlan you don't have to be jealous. You know I don't have any interest in women."

"Don't fuck with me, man!" I rasp. "The play acting's over. I know all about you."

"Wh… what on earth do you mean?" He pales, shrinking back against the door, when I pull the signed paper from Sir George Treveleyan from my jeans and thrust the note into his startled face. I hear the Persian hiss behind me because I might be threatening its master. I pay the cat scant attention, however. "Treveleyan says you have a certain DVD featuring me and a woman called Verdi Benson. I want it."

He swallows noisily, while his Adams apple bobs like a buoy on the ocean. "Wh… what DVD? I don't know anything about any DVD."

"Come on, for one of Treveleyan's operatives you're sure behaving like a fuckin' wimp."

"You… you've met Mr Treveleyan? How… how?"

The homosexual act. The cooing. The coming onto me gestures all abandon him now and David Lennard reveals himself in his true persona. Despite all that, maybe he could still be acting. Treveleyan reckoned he was good at his craft.

"Sure. It was Suzanne and Dr Turner who attended to my wounds. You know them I trust?"

He nods painfully. "S… so they told you about me?"

"That you were sent to spy on me?"

"I… I was simply instructed on what I had to do. I'm just a j… jobbing actor. Mr Treveleyan said I was to find out as much as I could about you."

"And what did you find out, David? If that's your name?" I stress coldly.

"Yes, my… my name is David Lennard. They hadn't lied. You… you were the man they wanted. I saw the D… DVD. Wh… what you did?"

"So you watched it then?"

He swallows uncomfortably again. "I… I saw what you did to that man. I… I didn't know him, but you and the red haired woman…"

"So where is it?" I demand. "I'll get it somehow."

Barely conscious of what I am capable of, I catch him by his shirt collar in a half stranglehold and pummel him belligerently against the wall. My mouth clenches and I hiss into his face angrily, "how do you know I'm not carrying a blade now? You saw the film."

I really do sound like a villain, but this time I've been pushed too far. He struggles in my grasp and I slam him back against the wall before deciding to release him. He adjusts his clothes with nervously shaking hands.

One day Caitlan may discover this other side of me, the side I want nothing better than to turn my back on. I'm not that man anymore. If only people wouldn't keep trying to make me the way I was 10 years ago. All I want now is to do school runs, honest work, be a father to my children, an ideal husband to my future wife, while the pain of my injuries does nothing to lessen my temper.

"It's in the drawer in my bedroom," he says, on reading Treveleyan's note.

"Go get it then," I urge him irritably. "And remember, no phone calls or funny business. When I'm gone you keep quiet about this, understand?"

"You really are capable of killing someone aren't you?"

"Yeah sure I am," I edge. "You in a minute. Now do it!"

He half jumps at my command and scuttles like a frightened spider in the direction of his bedroom. Because I fail to trust him not to make a call to the police I follow him into the room in time to witness him pull open a drawer in a bedside cabinet, clock something metallic that glints amidst a sheaf of papers inside. His intention is to reach for a small automatic pistol, but I leap towards him instinctively and forcibly close his hand in the drawer. My ribs ache like hell and I am half winded by my action. Releasing the drawer and the weapon inside, I push him away with his rasp of, "you fuckin' bastard!" hissing in my ear. I grab the pistol. "You're hurting me, you bastard," he half sobs, particularly as he now finds himself facing the muzzle of his own weapon.

"So where's the fuckin' DVD? I don't have all day." I gesture with the gun. Checking the clip, I discover it to be loaded. "Do it!" I command at witnessing his hesitation. "Why don't you want me to have it? Get off on it do you, man?"

"Look, I… I didn't ask for this. I didn't want to have that DVD 'cos I knew you'd come looking for it one day."

We return to his lounge. He locates the DVD in the sleeve of a film called 'Love Actually', before passing the tape to me. "So what will you do with it?"

"I'll destroy it of course, and don't mention any of this to Caitlan."

"She doesn't know what you've done does she? Your greatest work."

"What I've done is in the past. I have my family now and you can go back to Streatham with yours."

"He told you everything then? Mr Treveleyan."

"So what do you know about Treveleyan?"

"Nothing much. I do know he's a bitter man since he was shot and confined to that wheelchair when he was in his late twenties."

"I know, he told me. Anyway, I hope this is the right DVD because if it isn't, I'll come after you."

"Oh don't worry it is. I want no more to do with this."

"I believe he was going to use the tape to blackmail me into working for him."

"So are you going to work for the Great Man? The money's good."

"Look, I'm going to check this out. Then I'll destroy it and I suggest you get out of Dodge, if you know what I mean. Now I'm going to be with my girlfriend. She's having my baby. They need me. Since my release from prison I've had folk on my back, either using me for target practice or wanting me to work for them like I'm some fuckin' Old West gunslinger or something. Well I'm not buying. Now, it's over, and in answer to your question no, I'm not going to work for Treveleyan."

"Mr Treveleyan won't like it."

"Fuck to Mr Treveleyan. I have my own life to lead, okay?" Slipping the gun into my jacket, I tell him that I'll get rid of it. He nods his head perfunctorily, an expression I interpret as disbelief etched on his face.

CHAPTER TWENTY-EIGHT

-

BE SURE YOUR SINS

On my return upstairs the presence of the small automatic, which I discover to be a .32 Walther, affords me an idea, notwithstanding I debate within myself whether or not I'm doing the right thing. Loving my brother the way I do, his ostensible innocence, I reflect on how different he is than I was at his age. At 21, Ruairi's age now, practically since leaving school really, I always knew how to take care of myself. With inherent anger management issues plus a proverbial 'chip on my shoulder' as far back as the age of 14, at 15 I'd been in fights and won most of them. I'd learned how to stand up to the bullies. Maybe it was because of the way I was attracted to like-minded youths who swiftly grew to realise that Aidan McRaney was no pushover. I learned my trade on the back streets of London, but Ru is different. His world consists of Uni, lectures and books, a world that had not been for me until I'd gone to prison. Although I try to shake it off, danger is tenacious and appears to follow me. Last night I'd lost my first round and almost my right eye in the process, something I am determined should not occur again, either to myself or my brother.

The incriminating DVD is still inside my jacket when I return to my flat. I take care that neither Ru or Caitlan are around when I secrete the tape into the suitcase in my bedroom and I resolve to watch it when I'm alone, merely to ascertain that it's the right one of course, before destroying it.

Ru is in the process of putting the finishing touches to the Christmas tree, placing the ornaments and tinsel carefully around the branches before he checks the lights. He stands back to admire his handiwork and I ask him where Caitlan is.

"Taking a shower. I swear that bird seems to spend half her life in the shower. So, you pleased with it?"

"Sorry?" I barely hear him. Lighting a cigarette I go in search of a beer in the fridge.

"The tree. Caitlan and me took a lot of trouble over it." He sounds put out by my inattentiveness, but I'm preoccupied with more pressing matters than a Christmas tree. "Sure, it looks great, Ru." I mutter absently. "Anyway, it's just for the kids, the tree and stuff isn't it?"

I wonder if after the age of 12 I was really a kid at all. Straight from childhood directly to manhood with nothing in between but anger and resentment. "Anyway, can I talk to you? In your bedroom."

He continues to fiddle with the tree, rearranging the baubles with a practiced care, as if he hasn't heard me.

"Now!" I rasp and blanch at my own impatience.

He looks up from what he's doing with reproach. "Okay, okay, I'm coming. There's no need to shout, man. What's so fuckin' important anyway?"

"Quick, before Caitlan comes out of the shower."

"We got plenty of time then."

It is my turn to glare at him reproachfully. "That's my girlfriend you're talking about."

"Sorry, Aid. So what do you want to talk about?" He lowers his voice to a half whisper. "Is it about those kittens?"

"Kittens? Jesus, no. It's not about fuckin' kittens. Just get in there."

"Okay, okay," he shrugs. "Keep your shirt on, man."

Ushering him into the bedroom and closing the door I motion him to the bed where I join him.

"What is it? Why don't you want Caitlan to hear? Has it got something to do with old poufdah downstairs?" he grins.

"Just listen to me Ru, and what I tell you is just between you and me, okay? You're my brother, I love you and I trust you."

"That sounds ominous." He regards me uneasily. "I love you too and I trust you, but something's happened ain't it?"

"That 'poufdah' as you call him isn't."

"What? He's not a pouf?"

I shake my head. "Sure now, it's time I put you in the picture, Ruairi."

"Jesus, Aid, something's wrong. You only call me Ruairi when you…"

"When I need to talk to you seriously."

He sits on the bed, confronting me. His mouth opens, closes, as if it's his intention to interrupt. He refrains as I relate everything concerning the 'mugging' of last night and who had really attacked me, while his expression of curiosity is punctuated by occasional frowns. His occasional 'Blimeys' and 'fuck me's' are his only response.

"You mean this Blackwood character came all the way from the Emerald Isle to fuck up your boat?"

"Sure now, they didn't take my money." I also dare to refer to the incident when Dennis Mitchell, my ex-cell-mate, pulled a pistol from his coat and shot Blackwood in the back as the latter is making his escape. I relate how the black hearse-like limo had rolled up to remove Blackwood's body. I talk about Doctor Turner and Suzanne stitching up my eye in the Agency building in South Lambeth. Everything came pouring out and Ru's youthful features with his wispy beard, wild curls like mine, transforms to something fashioned from alabaster.

"So this Treveleyan geezer. You're not going to work for him are you?"

"No, sure I'm not. What do you think?"

"And that Suzanne sort. Blimey, so the pole dancing was just a cover and old David downstairs is really an actor playing at being a poufdah. Well, he fuckin' fooled me, man. Jesus..." He runs a hand through his tumbled hair indiscriminately.

"I know it all sounds pretty incredible, but it's true. Sure I can hardly believe it myself."

"They must want you real bad though, Bruv." He sounds worried. "Suppose they don't take too kindly to you refusing 'em?"

"The only thing that matters to me is my family. I realised that when I was in prison. I'm about to be a father again and I don't want anything to upset Caitlan. I also want you to be safe."

"You don't think I... I'd be a target do you?" His voice shakes a fraction on the question.

"We lost a sister, I don't intend to lose you too, but I can't be there for you 24/7. That's why I want you to have this..."

A hand inside my jacket produces the .32 Walther and I hold the gun out to him.

He couldn't have reacted any worse if I had physically struck him. His face, already pale, has turned a sort of chalky colour. His eyes widening, I read the disbelief reflected in their depths when they regard the pistol.

"Wh... where the fuck did you get that? I... I..." he stammers, and I watch as he swallows noisily.

"That doesn't matter. Take it please, Ru. Like I said, I want you to be safe."

"Does Brid know all about this, the guns? And I thought you'd changed, man."

"Jesus, Ru, I have." I heave a prolonged sigh. "For God's sake, don't go talking to Brid about any of this."

Easing himself from the bed he wanders to the window, hands plunged into his jeans pockets. "I don't know you anymore, Aid."

"What's that supposed to mean? I'm trying to offer you some protection. The pistol fires seven shots. Even if you don't hit the target the first time, you can't miss."

"Target?" He spins around on his heel angrily. "I ain't like you. I ain't no fuckin' gunman and if I take that thing I'll probably end up in jail, the way you did, and I ain't ever fired one of those things in my life. All I know is Uni and stuff. So don't fuckin' pull me into your world."

Before his wide-eyed gaze, I slide out the clip, show him the gun is loaded, before slamming the clip back with a practiced hand. "It's small enough to conceal in your jacket, Ru. These people are dangerous. At least you'd stand an even chance."

"If someone decides to shoot me you mean? It won't fuckin' happen, Aid. Now fuckin' get out of my room and take that thing with you. You say these people are dangerous. If you didn't involve yourself with them in the first place, they wouldn't touch our lives. Jesus, man, you have a nine-year-old son, a kid on the way, a delicate girlfriend. What about little Sammy and Mark? Fuck you, and I'm fuckin' scared of those things, I'll admit."

"There's nothing to be scared of, really. Look, I need you to pick up my motor from the club," I add, changing the subject.

He fails to respond momentarily. It is only when he moves to the door that he suddenly says, "I want my brother back. Or were you always going to end up being some fuckin' cheap gangster who enjoys carrying a gun, Aid?"

I scarcely have much time to reflect on what Ru infers because the buzzer sounds on my door indicating that I have a visitor. I shove the .32 out of sight in my bedroom drawer. Caitlan answers the door and tapping on Ru's announces that Bridget has arrived. I hear her demand, "is Aidan here?"

Caitlan responds, "he's in the lounge."

Bridget sports a dark green corduroy coat over her ward sister's uniform, her red/gold curls are piled atop her head in her customary style. Predictably, she stops in her tracks when she sees me and her naturally healthy complexion transfers to ashen instinctively. "Oh, Aidan, what's happened to your eye?"

"It's nothing, Sis," I shrug. "It looks worse than it actually is."

"It doesn't look like nothing to me, not with that patch over your eye. Ru said you were mugged leaving the club last night. I told you that place was cursed. I said you shouldn't have taken it over, didn't I Caitlan?" She is compelled to bring my girlfriend into the conversation.

"I'm beginning to believe you're right, Bridget," Caitlan agrees.

"What's this?" I laugh in an attempt to pass it off. "My sister and my girlfriend ganging up on me. Look, I was mugged, that's all."

"And you contacted the polis?" Brid insists.

"'Course," I lie.

"What did they say?"

"Nothing much." I shrug. "The guys who jumped me were masked. Anyway, what's all this about Dad and the Gardaí?"

Although I am compelled to change the subject in an endeavour to steer it away from myself, I already guess what the Gards might want with our father. Only Harry and I know the truth. That Dad had killed his wife's lover.

"What is it with this family?" Brid tuts and rolls her eyes heavenward. She removes her coat indicating that she intends to stay. "Where's Ru?" she scans the room.

"I think he's in his room isn't he, Aidan?" Caitlan says. She's changed into tight blue jeans, a white sweater with the jeans plunged into her familiar black suede boots. No one would believe that she is pregnant. Her figure is still so boyish and slender. I can't wait for Brid to leave so that I can have Caitlan all to myself and it is growing increasingly difficult to control the erection that pulses against my jeans when I look at her.

When Brid says, "it seems they found a body," the erection plummets to earth faster than a suicide from a 20-storey building.

"Oh my God!" Caitlan has a trembling hand to her mouth.

"Jesus!" I almost drop the beer I'd taken from the fridge. "A… a body? Who found it then?"

"Some guy out walking his dog. Apparently, there had been a terrible storm the night before. The body was in a shallow grave in a wood just outside Dublin. This woman, a Mrs Docherty, had reported her husband missing from South Armagh about 20 years ago."

Regaining my composure, I demand to know what it has to do with Dad.

"Nothing I'm sure. According to Mrs Jenkins they were merely eliminating people from their enquiries."

"It must have been important for the Garda to come to London though. So who was this Docherty guy? I've never heard Dad mention anyone by that name," I say.

"You were nine at the time. You probably wouldn't remember. There was a man named Docherty. He was a travelling book salesman. Sure if the body hadn't gone to a skeleton by now. 'Course they can tell by the dental records I suppose," Brid says. "Actually the Gards wanted to know where Mrs Marie McRaney was. When they mentioned Mum, it was then, so Mrs Jenkins said, that the palpitations started. Mrs Jenkins called the doctor and she called me. Och, I really don't think it's anything to worry about. The Gards, she said there were two of them, one was an Inspector Callaghan."

"It wasn't Harry Callaghan by any chance?" I quip and hear the nervousness present in my voice because of the guilt. Guilt because of what I know and cannot bring myself to confide to my family. "You know 'Dirty Harry' Clint Eastwood. Wasn't he Inspector Callaghan?" I deal them a lopsided smile, to which I receive nothing but blank obtuse stares. Brid says, "it's not funny, Aidan."

I guess my sister fails to realise that my vain attempt at humour is in a brave endeavour to conceal my anxiety.

"They need to conclude their investigation with us, so I said we'd be there next time," Brid adds. "We can't expect Dad to be on his own in this."

"Sure, if I can help. Anything for Dad, but I was only a kid, I don't know much." I slip an arm about Caitlan's shoulder in the realisation how Dad must have felt, that the woman he loved, the mother of his children, should have had an affair and got pregnant. In his position, I would have killed also.

"Anyway, you…" Brid addresses me so authoritatively that's it's conducive to pulling me out of my unwelcome retrospection, while the tone of her voice matches the starchiness of her uniform. "Let me take a look at that eye."

"I'm not one of your patients," I retort.

"Is it painful?" she asks, concerned.

"I think he's in a lot of pain with it. I know he's been knocking back the painkillers and I am worried," from Caitlan.

"I am here you know, ladies. Look, make it quick will you? I've got to take a shower and go to the club." Wishing that women didn't fuss quite so much, I hand my beer to Caitlan with a shrug and a promise not to be long, when Brid suggests we go to the bathroom. Ru appears and greets her with a, "hi, Sis. Where you two going?"

She informs him, "to check out Aidan's eye," and ushering me into the bathroom, she closes the door.

My sister has been a qualified nurse for more than 15 years, so I suppose she knows what she's doing.

Removing the patch and the dressing she starts to examine the eye with various exclamations of, "oh, Jesus, Aidan," amid considerable head shaking punctuated by occasional tutting.

"So where did you have it stitched? At A and E?"

"Yeah, sure, at the hospital near the club." How can I possibly tell her the truth? She might understand. Alternatively, she may not. Either way I decide against taking the chance. "I don't know what the hospital is called; I was losing a lot of blood. My ribs are bruised as well."

"I'll take a look at the bruising in a moment. Bruising will heal on its own but that eye is infected, Aidan."

My stomach rolls nauseatingly. "Wh… what do you mean infected?"

She asks me to open it slowly, but not to worry if I can't. I can't. The eye has stuck down fast. There is no way I can prise it open.

"Don't do anything now," she counsels. "No wonder it's painful."

I'm astonished at her words and am now beginning to concern myself, perhaps for the first time since I received the injury. There is a small residue of greenish yellow pus emanating from the closed lid.

"Jesus, Aidan, you need to go to hospital, now."

"Hospital! I can't go to hospital," I protest in panic.

"Sure you can. You want to lose the sight of your eye?"

"You know I don't, Sis. Is it as bad as that?" I hear the desperation in my voice. Now I'm growing scared, anxious that I might lose my eye.

"Don't worry." She hugs me briefly. "I'm no expert, I'm just a general practice nurse, but the stitching's fine. I'll get you seen by Leo Sutcliffe. He's one of the best eye doctors in the business. I'll give him a call. Get you seen tonight. He owes me a favour." She smiles inwardly but without elaborating.

I replace the patch without looking in the mirror and observe Brid biting savagely on her lower lip, she drags her teeth right across it. "This Dr Sutcliffe won't see me tonight will he?"

"Don't worry, he will. Like I said, he owes me a favour. Leo will sort you out. Your Sister Collier's brother. Whatever did they hit you with? Because whatever it was, was harder than a fist. It looks like glass, a jagged bottle maybe. I've seen this kind of injury after someone's had a fight. I'm not going to ask you who you've upset with that Irish temper of yours Bruv, but I think if it is a jagged bottle, it is probably the cause of the infection. Dr Sutcliffe will be able to tell you more."

*

The name that is engraved on the door bears testimonial to the fact that Lionel J Sutcliffe is an ophthalmologist with a veritable string of letters after his name.

Dr Lionel, or rather Leo, Sutcliffe is a handsomish, middle age man I judge to be somewhere into his late forties. His features are quite plump, fleshy, while his hair is a thick blond thatch, almost too blond I deduce, for a man of his age, without a streak of grey as if, dare I think it, Dr Leo dyes his hair. He also sports a thin blond moustache. I wonder again what Brid meant when she related that he owed her a favour.

"Come in," his welcome is enthusiastic. "Bridget!" His arms are extended as if she would permit him to hug her before piercing blue orbs settle on me. His, "how's my favourite Irish colleen today?" Scarcely prevents the suffusion of colour from rising to her cheeks. "And this must be your brother Aidan?" He shakes my hand before introducing himself.

"Thanks for seeing my brother at such short notice."

"Anything for you, Bridget." Sutcliffe is charm itself. "May I call you Aidan?"

"Sure, you can call me what you like if you can get this eye fixed." I wish for a smoke right now as I take in the room, which contains the usual ophthalmologist's paraphernalia, the medical instruments, eye charts plus two black leather armchairs. However, my interest is suddenly distracted by the presence of the two large wall charts. One of the posters depicts the interior of an eye and reminds me of a giant peach, the other of an orange, because the latter appears red and fiery, obviously an injured one. "The peach coloured eye is the healthy one, right?" I ask.

"Absolutely." He talks in a sort of sweeping tone.

"The other is an injury?"

"Not unless you're diabetic, Aidan." Sutcliffe's smile is wry. "You haven't been diagnosed with diabetes have you?"

"God no!"

"That's alright then. Now, take a seat both of you while I jot down a few particulars." He motions Brid and I into the leather armchairs. He sinks his own weight into the chair that is pulled up at his desk.

The latter is cluttered mainly with papers and files, which he is compelled to ease aside in order to get to this computer.

"Your name is Aidan James McRaney?" he asks, his gaze riveted on the screen.

"Sure."

"Date of birth, Aidan?"

"21st June, 1982."

"Okay, so let's take a look at that eye, Bridget said it was quite urgent over the phone. First I'll need to put some drops in."

"He can't even open it, Leo," Brid says anxiously. "I was worried."

Sutcliffe raises a dismissive hand. "It's alright Bridget, leave it to me. You know, I swear your sister probably fusses over you as much as she does her patients. In fact, I think I knew you already before I'd even met you. Bridget's always talking about her brothers, especially you…" He smiles at me.

All I can think is please get on with it, Doc, so that I can get out of here. I already know what my sister's like.

Because of the strong lighting in the room, in marked contrast to that in my bathroom, when Dr Sutcliffe removes the patch, I almost scream with pain when the light hits my eye. Regardlessly, he requests that I open the eye carefully, that he needs to administer some drops. He stands by with the glass containing the drops because the eye has stuck fast, it is difficult to open it, but I'm aware it is imperative that I try.

He enquires if I can see anything out of the eye.

Everything is merely a blur with no definite outline. He holds up a hand, but I can barely make it out. The drops are cold and cause me to recoil.

"It's okay, leave them in a while, then I'll take the pressure."

"The pressure?" I echo warily.

"The intraocular pressure will indicate any damage that might have been done. Usually we check this pressure for glaucoma," Sutcliffe says. "I'll also check the veins in the retina to make sure they are not blocked."

"You think my eye might be damaged, that I might have to wear a patch for the rest of my life?" I hear the anxiety akin to panic in my voice and deliberately ignore Brid's, "Jesus, Aidan, I'm sure it won't come to that, though it would put paid to your appeal to other women a wee bit."

"Dear me." Sutcliffe sweeps a hand about him indiscriminately, tuts and shakes his head. "We are in the 21st century and not in

Nelson's Navy when limbs and eyes were removed without preamble, and I'm not some old sawbones. Now, let's be optimistic and relax young man. If you hold this pad against your eye, just to make sure the drops go in, then I can take a better look. On the bright side, whoever stitched up the wound certainly knew their job. If you do everything I prescribe once I've examined the eye, you'll be dating in no time with both wonderful brown eyes intact."

I allow Brid to take this one. "He's got a girlfriend. She's expecting his baby," she retorts tartly.

"Oh, I do apologise. There I go again putting my size elevens in my mouth. Do you know that your sight is affected by what you eat or drink? The old saying, eating carrots can make you see in the dark. That's true you know. Vegetables, fruit and fish are wonderful for vision, but too much alcohol, red meat and spicy foods can affect your vision quite detrimentally over the years."

We both sit in some kind of frozen silence while Dr Leo lectures us on his obviously favourite subject, eyes. It is almost as if he possesses a kind of fetish, making me wonder if perhaps he keeps all kinds of different coloured eyes in glass containers in his house.

"So, Aidan, Bridget tells me you were mugged." He returns me to the present and I'm surprised by his question.

"Yeah I was," I answer non-comittally.

"So, you called the police?"

"Sure." Now I sound evasive and am uncertain whether he believes me or not.

"The police will find out who did this and you know you can receive compensation," he says.

"You mean a claim, Leo?" I might have known Brid would pick up on that.

"Indeed." Clasping fleshly brown hands together and pressing his fingers against his nose, his expression is thoughtful.

"I would suggest it was something jagged, a glass bottle perhaps, but it's the surgery, although expertly done, which has caused the infection. All surgery, no matter how perfect, carries a risk of infection. The eye is a delicate instrument. So, Aidan, did you know your attackers?"

"No, I didn't know them and they were wearing ski masks." How can I possibly confess I had known my attackers, or that one had been shot by my ex-cell mate?

"So you went straight to A and E?" Sutcliffe pursues. I nod and he asks, "so who did you see?"

I merely shrug at his question. "I have no idea. It was nearly 3 o'clock in the morning. I was in agony, okay? I barely noticed the hospital I was in."

"Never mind. The important thing is sorting out that infection." He motions me into a chair in front of the tonometer machine and I am instructed to place my chin on the rest.

"If you've never had the pressure in your eyes checked before, I see you have no optician's prescription, so I'm guessing a young man of your age probably hasn't, you'll feel a couple of puffs, like a breeze, in the eye."

The puffs of air injected into my eye cause me to recoil a fraction. Afterwards he examines the eye with a small torch light. By now the eye is beginning to feel really painful. The light filtering into it is half blinding me.

He returns to his computer explaining that he's concluded his examination for now. I want to know if I can replace the patch.

"I think that would be best, especially if the light is causing you pain. You can always get prescription sunglasses, although these types are quite thick and heavy and it means the vision in the other eye is limited," muses Sutcliffe. His tone is quiet, maybe too quiet. It is left to Brid to tentatively enquire what his findings are.

His expression remains thoughtful. He appears to spend an age studying his screen, as if he is composing himself how to break the news I guess will be bad. That I'll never see out of that eye again. "The pressure is a little high," he begins finally. "It's a fraction over the normal. What I was looking for was ocular hypertension. There's a little, but no risk of glaucoma. The surgery was well done. It's that which has probably saved your sight. The drops I'm going to prescribe are to be administered three times a day. There's a Boots across the street. They have a midnight pharmacy so you can purchase the prescription now, this evening, because I don't want you to delay. I'll give you a prescription for two weeks supply of antibiotics. They'll take you through the Christmas period. Once the infection clears up we'll know more. The infection is the main problem. The antibiotics are rather strong I'm afraid. So that means no alcohol, Aidan."

"No alcohol!" I echo flatly. No alcohol, but it's Christmas.

"So what's your favourite tipple?" he asks.

"Chivas Regal whisky." I tell him.

"You like the good malt then? Well, there's some non-alcoholic beers on the market. Non-alcoholic wines. From what I know, Chivas hasn't come up with any non-alcoholic whisky."

"Well, sure now, if that isn't all to the good," Brid interjects.

"What if I take an alcoholic drink while I'm on these antibiotics?" I ask.

"As I said, they are quite strong."

"Would it kill me?"

"No, it wouldn't kill you, unless you overdosed of course, but alcohol will diminish the potency of the antibiotics. They won't clear up the infection and I believe, from my examination of your eye, it's the infection that's causing the problem. A neglected infection could cause you to lose the sight in your right eye."

CHAPTER TWENTY-NINE

-

SINS OF THE FATHER

Hitherto, the eye is the least of my problems. I imagine that it is something that will heal itself in time. Losing the sight isn't something I'd bargained for. So the prognosis isn't good, particularly as I will have to abstain from alcohol for at least two weeks during the Christmas period. Naturally, both Ru and Caitlan are anxious to know how I fared. I merely shrug, pass it off that everything is fine. Unfortunately I'll have to wear the patch for a while until it heals, I explain to Caitlan, and hope that she won't find it too off putting. She placates that we both have our crosses to bear, even if hers aren't physical. I love and hug her for that.

Her gaze encompassing both my brother and my girlfriend, Brid says, "if you want to bury your head in the sand, Aidan, then it's up to you."

I blanch at her words, while Caitlan regards me with a frown. His face whiter than his tee shirt, Ru wants to know what she means by the remark. "Is it worse than you're letting on?" He twists his lower lip with his teeth.

"There's some infection, nothing a few wee antibiotics won't clear up." I smile awkwardly. "The only trouble is that while I'm on the antibiotics I can't drink, 'cos if I do, the infection will take longer to clear up, that's all. It's nothing. Jesus…" Extracting myself from Caitlan's arms my initial instinct is to fetch a beer from the plentiful supply that I keep for myself and Ru in the fridge. As if interpreting my intentions Brid positions herself in front of the fridge.

"Jesus, Sis, I might want some milk to make a coffee," I tell her.

"You normally take it black," she counters. "I know you want a beer. Och, if I don't know you too well, little brother."

At 6' 2" tall, I hardly describe myself as 'little'. "Don't you have some churchy stuff to do? You haven't been to confessional for 24 hours. I suppose you're all confessioned out." I know my sister means well, but does she have to treat me more as a wayward son, rather than her brother." I hear Ru stifle a girly giggle from behind me.

"If you want to be blind in your right eye for the rest of your life, Aidan."

"What!" Ru and Caitlan echo in unison. "You... you could lose your eye?" Caitlan's face whitens. "Then we'll make sure you don't drink, won't we Bridget?"

"Jesus, save me from bossy women," I mutter and reluctantly move away from the fridge. "I suppose a coffee's out of the question. Too much caffeine. What about a cigarette? I might get lung cancer." Brid's mouth tightens shrewishly. "Don't joke please, Aidan, we shouldn't play fast and loose with our health. You might only be 29 but no one's invincible and if you lost the sight of your eye, what about driving?"

I guess it's the kind of bombshell I need to jolt me from an erstwhile complacency. Driving is my passion. After being incarcerated for almost eight years, not being able to get behind the wheel of a car is hard. Prior to that, I'd been Frankie Lamond's driver as well as his minder. I fail to imagine what it would be like not being able to drive.

"Even with one eye, I can still drive," I remonstrate.

"You'd probably have to have a special test and stuff. I don't know. Not being able to see to your right will be rather inhibiting I should imagine," Brid says. "Another thing, using one eye all the time can put a strain on the other one."

"You always were a little ray of sunshine, weren't you?" I mutter grimly.

"Perhaps you should listen to her, Aidan," Caitlan says, taking my hand.

"Sure. Maybe I could have that coffee now, please darlin'" I ask her.

"Sure." When she moves away to prepare it, I follow her. Slipping my arms around her waist, I whisper in her ear, "I love you, baby."

"Get a room you two," Ru jokes.

I tell him that we have one.

The phone ringing in her bag, Brid, flipping it out, speaks her name, her face going pale. "I'll have to get Maura to look after the kids."

"What's wrong, Sis?" I ask.

"They've arrived."

"Who has?" Ru wants to know.

"The Gards. They're at Dad's house. If you feel up to it, Aidan, I need you."

At the mention of the Gardaí calling on Dad, my senses reel. I hope that Caitlan hasn't detected my body stiffening against hers

315

because I am the sole member of my family, apart from Dad and Harry, who know what the Gards want, but Harry is in Italy.

"It's cool, you don't need to ask Maura. I'll sort it out, see what they want," I tell her.

"You were only nine when we left Dublin. What will you know?" Brid remonstrates.

"Sure now, I remember more than you think I do. You want to come, sweetheart?" I ask Caitlan. "You haven't met Dad yet have you?"

"The only trouble is, Bruv, you'll need a designated you know what," Ru suggests, dangling the keys to my Cabriolet.

"It's okay. Caitlan can drive can't you?"

She shakes her head. "I don't know my way around London."

"I can give you directions," I say.

"Well I want to come," Ru insists. "See what the Gardaí want that's important enough for them to come from Ireland. Besides…" He clears his throat uncomfortably.

"Besides what?" I arch a solitary brow.

"You won't lose your temper will you? I know what you're like with the cops."

"Aidan won't lose his temper will you?" Brid says. "You'd better not, Bruv. This is a very delicate matter."

*

On the journey to Billet Road, when she sees that my intention is to smoke my lungs out, Caitlan opts to sit in the back seat of the Cabriolet. I smoke, in the main because I hate not being able to drive my car and because both my eye and my ribs are growing increasingly painful again.

Arriving at Dad's house, I clock the unfamiliar vehicle parked in his drive. I guess Caitlan is relieved to escape the polluted confines of the car. Ru helps her alight, while I sit there momentarily and wonder what I should say to the police.

"Come on, Aid," urges Ru. "Let's get this over with. I don't really know what it's all about. I don't remember much about living in Dublin anyway."

"Well you wouldn't, would you? You were only two when you left, but I do. Quite a lot as it happens." Heaving a reluctant sigh, I vacate the Cabriolet, kill my umpteenth cigarette, and realise that I'm stalling in an endeavour to collect my wits; if necessary, to act my socks off.

Linking her arm through mine, Caitlan and I follow Ru up the path. It is left to my brother to ring the bell. The door is immediately answered by a short, quite plump lady I judge to be somewhere in her early to mid-seventies. She sports a neat old-fashioned perm. A flowered tabard is thrown over a grey knitted top she wears with an equally grey skirt. Sensible grey brogues plus round owl-like spectacles serve to remind me of all old-time and stereotypical grandmas I had ever seen. Behind the spectacles, piercing blue eyes encompass the three of us with thinly disguised speculation. "Mrs Jenkins is it?" I ask. "We've come to see Dad. I understand the police are with him, the Gardaí from Ireland."

"You'd better come in." She sounds a fraction breathless and holds a fleshy liver-spotted hand against her chest. "Where's Bridget?" She looks beyond us in to the road.

"She had her children to attend to," I tell her. "So she sent us instead. My girlfriend Caitlan, my brother Ruairi and I'm Aidan."

"It's okay, we've already met, haven't we Mrs J?" Ru enthuses.

"That's right, Rory," she deals my brother an exclusive smile before ushering us into the hallway.

For a one time painter and decorator, our father has scarcely bothered much with the place since he's been there. Some of the wallpaper is peeling and the paint is cracked and grimy.

Dad sits by the window in his favourite brocade armchair. His fingers scramble around in the stuffing that protrudes from the arm.

There are two officers present, both plain clothes. What had I expected? For them to have 'Garda' emblazoned on the backs of their uniforms? I guess that's what I recollect about the police as a child.

Bustling ahead of us, Mrs Jenkins introduces us to the officers. The latter remain standing and turn at our entrance and so does Dad, who half rises from his chair. Predictably, it is on me that his eyes initially rest and he regards me a little nonplussed. So we've had our differences in the past, the old guy and me, but I love him. After all, he is my dad.

"Why you wearing a patch over your eye, Aidey? You ain't been fighting have you son?"

"No, Dad, I haven't been fighting." How can I possibly tell this dear old man the truth? "It's an infection."

"So what's all this about?" Ru asks, regarding the officers warily. "And what's it got to do with Dad?"

"I'm DI Callaghan." The senior officer introduces himself and displays his ID before mentioning the shorter, slighter man with him as DS Wonnacott.

DI Callaghan is tall and solidly built. In his mid-forties, I guess. "It's nothing to worry about, Mr McRaney," he addresses Dad. "It's as I said, merely to eliminate you from our enquiries."

"It can't be nothing if you had to come across the water," I said stiffly. Our eyes lock, his and mine. I observe both Ru and Caitlan have deposited themselves onto the matching brocade settee. Sinking my weight next to them, I slip my arm around her shoulder.

"Who's the wee girlie, Aidey?" Dad wants to know, ignoring the officers, while I wish he wouldn't call me 'Aidey' as if I were 12.

"Caitlan, my girlfriend," I inform him proudly and with a smile her way, one which she reciprocates.

"Pleased to meet you, Mr McRaney," she flashes a smile on Dad.

"An' you an Irish girl," he observes, purposefully ignoring DS Wonnacott's sigh of impatience.

"Whatever questions you need to ask, you can talk to me," I suggest.

"Perhaps you can make us a cuppa, Dolly," Dad addresses Mrs Jenkins who stands idly by and, I can't help but notice, is listening attentively.

She nods her acquiescence. "You all want tea?"

The officers nod. Ru and I opt for coffee. Caitlan wants to know if she has any herbal infusions, to which Mrs Jenkins responds with a puzzled frown and an obtuse, "don't know what that is, duck."

"Sure now, it doesn't matter, I'll have a weak tea please," Caitlan says, smiling politely.

"Well, if I ain't ever seen so many Irish people collected together in one place," declares Mrs Jenkins as she heads off in the direction of the kitchen, while Dad reminds her about the tea. I reason how much she seems to have made our dad's house her own, recollect Brid's assumption that Mrs Jenkins might be after some of the money he received from selling his decorating business when he pops his clogs and I thought, not if I can help it. That's if he had any of course.

Callaghan is saying, "as I told your father, a body, or rather a skeleton was discovered in a wooded area just outside Dublin."

"Well it ain't nothing to fuckin' do with me," mutters Dad. Lapsing back into his seat, he has a hand over his heart region.

"What's wrong, Dad?" Ru asks, sympathetically moving to his side. Dropping his weight onto the arm of the stuffing protruding chair, he places a hand on his shoulder. "Dad's memory ain't what it was, is it Aid?"

To which I nod my agreement.

"It's just routine that's all," Callaghan adds.

Neither of the officers have sat down. Dad hasn't chosen to offer them a seat. "So what's it to do with Dad?" I demand.

"Nothing we hope. The dental records on the corpse identified him as a Michael Docherty," Callaghan consults the notepad he produces from his jacket.

"I don't know anybody of that name," Dad says. "Don't know why you come to me."

"We have to check up on all leads, that's all," Wonnacott explains. "Mrs Docherty reported her husband missing 20 years ago. They lived in South Armagh. Mr Docherty was a travelling salesman in books. His route took him south, to the Dublin area. The company he worked for had a list of Mr Docherty's customers," Wonnacott pauses to consult his own notebook, "in 1991. I wouldn't have thought any of you…"

His gaze encompasses Ru and Caitlan, "…would have remembered much. Mr McRaney," he zeroes in on me, "you were how old in 1991?"

"I was almost 10. Sure, I remember living in Dublin, O'Connell Street. My brother Ruairi was only a toddler, so he won't know anything," I retort. "So what do you want to know, 'cos there's no point in questioning our dad, he has early onset Alzheimer's…"

"Mrs Marie McRaney was on his list," Callaghan interrupts.

I glare at him. "That was our mother. Ma never mentioned anyone called Docherty."

"So what happened about his decorating business?" Callaghan continues to address his questions to me.

"What about it?" I challenge. With Dad's permission, I roll and light a cigarette.

"According to a Mr Padraig Keenan, one of your dad's employees," Callaghan begins, only to be interrupted by Dad, "how's Padraig? He was a good boy, a good worker." He shakes his head sadly. "I miss him y'know. He's about your age, Aidey."

"Mr Keenan's in his early fifties, Mr McRaney," Callaghan says, "I was going to say, according to Mr Keenan, the decorating business was thriving in the late eighties, early nineties."

"That's not true, Inspector," I cut in, maybe because I am used to talking, or is it lying, to the police? The mere fact of their presence in my father's home is conducive to getting my back up. It's almost as if I'm the one accused of killing Michael Docherty, in the main because I too have killed. The recollection of Dennis Mitchell shooting Shaun

Blackwood in cold blood remains with me guiltily. "I'd heard Mum and Dad talking, well arguing really, 'cos Dad reckoned the decorating business wasn't fairing too well, that he was losing customers. That was right wasn't it Dad?"

"Sure it was, Aidey," he agrees. "You look like a pirate, especially with the beard," as if nothing has penetrated.

His brown eyes have grown smaller, almost sunken and rheumy. His body is pipe cleaner thin, his features narrow, badly shaven.

Mrs Jenkins announces that tea is ready, that she can do with some help. I gesture to Caitlan and whisper in her ear for her to stall Mrs Jenkins in the kitchen. I have no intention for this to be gossiped to with her neighbours, because Mrs Jenkins ostensibly has gossip written all over her.

"Thanks, Dad," I mutter and grimace at his reference to my resembling a pirate and wonder do I really look like that?

"You ain't gotta wear it all the time have you?" he asks uneasily.

"No Dad." I sigh, attempt to reassure him, although I'm not certain of anything at this stage.

Sighing impatiently, DI Callaghan reminds me once again about Dad's possibly failing business back in Dublin.

"I told you that the business folded as businesses do. People can no longer afford to have painting and decorating done. So what's that got to do with Mr Docherty or whatever his name is?" The timbre of anger must have asserted itself in my voice for Ru, who continues to perch on Dad's chair arm, issues a look of warning from beneath his fringe of hair.

"We're simply chasing up some leads, that's all Mr McRaney," Callaghan relates. "The reason why you all left Ireland in such a hurry, practically uprooted from your school, almost a wee moonlit flit was it now? And you were what? 9½?"

"Fuck no!" I'm on my feet instinctively, temper surfacing. "It was no moonlight flit as you call it. If our ma knew this Docherty guy then you'd better have a fuckin' séance and contact her on the other side hadn't you?"

"Aid," Ru whispers uncomfortably, his face whitening. "Look, Inspector," he turns to confront the Gardaí officer, "Aid don't know any more than I do and you can see our dad's memory ain't what it was. He obviously don't know what you're talking about. Aidan's right, if our mum knew this guy then she's taken the secret to her grave. She's been dead for 19 years giving birth to our sister, who's also passed. We've had enough tragedy in our lives, man. Look…" he
320

pauses on witnessing Dad's eyes filling with tears, obviously at the reference to his beloved Marie, "so please go back to Ireland. I know you've had to check things out, we appreciate that, and if my brother says Dads decorating business was going bust, then it was."

Ru and I exchange companionable looks, while mine is one of gratitude. Dear Ru, I want to hug my brother. For all his stupid jokes, his boyish antics, he can be quite grown up when it suits him. His palm covers Dad's hand and I feel quite touched by it all.

"I don't know nothin' and I can't help you with your enquiries. As my boys said, it's been a long time since I left Dublin. I didn't want to leave. Fair broke my heart, so it did. O'Connell Street was my home, but I had to look for work 'cross the water. I had me kids to look after and my Marie was pregnant. That's why I left, I had to support my family. Should I have left them to starve then? Now I'm tired…"

In response Dad slumps back in his armchair indicating this interview is terminated. Framed in the doorway, armed with a tray containing the tea things, Mrs Jenkins wants to know why the two officers are leaving. She's just made the tea.

CHAPTER THIRTY

-

SEEDS OF DOUBT

The Garda have gone, for good I hope, back to Ireland. Their arrival has naturally upset Dad. Despite that, he has his tea and dunks his biscuits. Afterwards Ru helps him to bed regardless of Dolly Jenkins looking down her nose. We are his sons. If anyone's going to look after our father, it is Ru and I.

Dad is pleased that one of us, he has seemingly forgotten who, is dating an Irish girl and I have to remind him that it is me, that I've asked her to marry me. It is obvious that she's been accepted by my family. All I hope is that my son will also accept her as readily.

Ru has taken Dad to his room. Caitlan is finishing her tea, taking time over the ingestion of one small biscuit, as if the biscuit is a three-course meal.

Left to my own devices, in the wake of the Gardaí's departure, I seek out Mrs Jenkins and find her washing up in the kitchen.

"Mrs Jenkins." I say her name sharply, causing her to jump involuntarily, and she allows the plate she is washing to drop back into the bowl sending cascades of soapsuds into her face.

"Oh, you gave me a fright," she exclaims, patting at her upper regions. "It's Aidan ain't it?"

"So, Mrs Jenkins." I maintain a deliberately cold tone. It is the kind I invariably used in the days I worked for Frankie Lamond, the voice which denotes that I mean business and brooks no argument. "Tell me, what is your relationship to my father?"

"Me and Dermot... well, I expect your sister told you, I come in and clean for him. I only live next door and when I cook I usually cook for Dermot too. You sound disapproving. I don't know what all that business was with the Irish coppers, but I know for certain that Dermot wouldn't do anything wrong, not like killing someone."

Leaning my weight against the door and rolling a smoke, my eyes never once leave her face. My expression is deliberately hard and she is compelled to avert her attention. I believe she means well and it's good that my dad has someone to look after him, but I need to make her understand where I'm coming from.

"You're right, Mrs Jenkins, our dad wouldn't kill anyone, but I don't want any of this to get back to your friends. So that means you don't speak of what you heard, that it stays within these four walls. Do I make myself clear, Mrs Jenkins?" I approach closer.

She regards me warily and I observe her give an involuntary shiver. Maybe she finds me intimidating, and not just from the tone of my voice. I am quite dark with the addition of the beard and the eye patch.

When she fails to respond, I place a gloved finger beneath her chin, lift it, so that she is compelled to stare into my face. Behind her spectacles there is fear in her gaze. As if I have hypnotised her, I force her to face me and answer my question.

"I…. I won't say nothin', honest I… I won't," she stammers, too scared to move her head until I release her, and I witness her shiver again.

Caitlan slips an arm around my waist and the spell is broken. "I wondered where you were. Your dad's nice isn't he?"

"Sure he is," I stress, mainly for Mrs Jenkins' benefit. I pull my girlfriend into my arms, crushing her lips with mine.

"Jesus, you two…" Ru appears, grinning like a Cheshire cat. "Every time I see you, you're always at it. You alright, Mrs J?"

"Fine thanks, Rory," she replies, but there is an unmistakable tremble to her voice, as if she is close to tears. Her head lowered, she carries on washing up without glancing our way.

"Anyway, Dad's having a lie down. He says I was to tell you he'll have some tea later, Mrs J, and thanks for what you're doing for Dad, hey Aid?" He slips an arm around her waist affectionately. "We're grateful ain't we?"

"Sure we are, Mrs Jenkins," I respond. Still she refrains from raising her head. There you go again, upsetting people McRaney. Guilt assails me and I entertain an urgency to slip an arm about Mrs Jenkins shoulder and tell her how sorry I am. Somehow, I can't bring myself to display the same kind of affection toward her as Ru has.

We return to the Cabriolet and Ru wants to know what all that was really about with the Gardaí. That it must have been important enough for them to journey to London.

I dismiss it with a shrug, mainly for my own peace of mind. "You heard what they said. It happened 20 years ago. We were kids. Maybe our mam knew this guy, but it was obvious that Dad didn't, neither did I. Nothing to worry about, Bruv, honest, he just happened to travel to Dublin to sell his books, that's all, and nothing to blacken mam's name, okay?"

I suppose I'll have to contact Harry to inform him about the Gards arriving in London to question Dad.

Right now, there are more pressing matters to attend to. I have a DVD to watch. A DVD that not only can destroy my family, but also contains enough incriminating evidence to send me down for a lengthy stretch.

*

Caitlan has gone with Ru to the shops. They asked me if I'd like to join them but I tell them there is stuff I need to do. Caitlan is concerned that I'm feeling self-conscious because of the patch. Truthfully, I'm not self-conscious about it at all, apart from what lay behind it. Momentarily I have too much else to occupy my mind. In fact, as David Lennard outlined, it detracts precious little from my looks and being unable to see out of the eye is merely a nuisance, nothing more. Perhaps thought of that incriminating DVD has managed to eradicate all other anxieties.

Ruairi and Caitlan inform me that they are going Christmas shopping. I explain that I'm not really in the mood.

Maybe I shouldn't allow Caitlan to be with my brother quite so much. I often see her laughing at my brother's jokes and sometimes I'm so preoccupied that I haven't paid her as much attention as I should. Brid had warned me not to throw them together too often. Just because Caitlan is expecting my baby doesn't mean to say that she might not enjoy another man's company. Brid also reckons that she'd seen Ru ogling Caitlan when he thought I wasn't looking. Nevertheless, I trust my fiancée. We love each other.

I locate the damning DVD in the 'Love Actually' case, about to slip the tape into the machine when the phone rings. I'm surprised to discover the call is from Harry, coming on the fact I was about to call him but hadn't known how to broach the subject of the Gardaí coming across the water to see Dad.

He begins by referring to the fact that I was to tell Bridget he can't make it for Christmas, that he'd try and come to London for the New Year.

"So what's wrong, Bruv, too scared to tell her yourself?" I joke.

"No, 'course not. I just thought you could pass the message on, that's all. So, Aidan, how are you? It seems ages since we spoke. I heard the Gards came to talk to Dad about you know what. What did you tell 'em? Nothing I hope."

324

I relate all that had occurred, concluding with the fact Ru and I had managed to convince them and add, "at least I think we did."

"You haven't told Ru what I told you. Jesus, you know what he's like."

"He knows nothing. They left. So I think I managed to convince them we knew nothing and without any arrests being made."

"I hope so, I really do." I hear Harry sigh.

"And if they're not convinced?"

"Then Dad'll be in the shit and so will I. They'll extradite us both back to Ireland and maybe even prison."

"It'd kill him. We can't let that happen."

"Don't worry it won't. They can't prove nothing. So, I hear you've got a steady girlfriend then," he says, changing the subject.

"Brid talks a lot, don't she? Sure, I have a girl. Her name's Caitlan and she's Irish."

"So Brid said. Apparently Caitlan's got a few issues too."

"Meaning?" I attempt to suppress a familiar acrimony.

"That she's on medication. She suffered some brain damage when she was in the accident when her ma died. You sure you ain't getting serious over her just because she's Irish?"

"Jesus, Harry, trust you to say stuff like that," I retort angrily and am almost prompted to conclude the call. "Why do you always think the worst of me? Ever since that incident with Gina. That I can't hold my women. Jesus, I love her. She's having my baby and we're engaged."

"Fuck me!" he exclaims, an echo of disbelief in his voice. "Brid said you had a lot going on in your life right now. That you were the owner of that low dive in Soho 'The Black Garter' club, is that true Aid?"

"Sure it is," I edge. "Anyway, it's not called 'The Black Garter' now. I've re-christened it. It's called 'The Athenry'."

"From that town in Galway?"

"Sure. So what else are you going to reprimand me about?" I demand defensively. "Or do I fuckin' finish this call?"

"I'm sorry, I didn't mean to get your back up. I'm sorry too that I accused you of dating the girl just because she's Irish. Bridget thinks a lot of her. Reckons she's good for you. She also said something about you having an eye injury, that you're wearing a patch. What's all that about Bruv? You were mugged, she says. Is it true? Or did your anger get the better of you? I know you, Aid."

"I was mugged, okay," I snap. "Look, Harry, is that all you're calling about? Is this, 'have a go at Aidan day'?"

"Keep your shirt on. I just wanted to know how it went with the Gards that's all. So, when are you coming out to Milan? Bring Caitlan with you. I do miss you all, y'know. Look, you take care of yourself. Hope the eye gets better soon. It isn't permanent is it? I mean you haven't lost the sight?"

"No, it's not permanent," I stress vehemently, maybe too vehemently, because I hope to God that once the infection clears I'll be able to see out of the eye again. I add, "thanks for your concern Harry. I really do have to go now. Caitlan will be home soon and I promised to get tea for them."

More importantly, I need to watch that DVD before they return and I'm growing impatient with my brother.

"Them?" Predictably, he pounces on that one word. No way will I give him the satisfaction to learn that my girlfriend has gone to the shops with my brother.

"Caitlan, I mean."

"You're getting domesticated then Bruv," he says, before I finally conclude the call.

Now for that DVD. I am about to play it when the doorbell buzzes and the moment dissipates yet again and I curse exasperatedly. The tape is already poised over the opened tray. Fuck. I close it again, shove the DVD back inside 'Love Actually' and race into my bedroom where I lock the DVD away, while my heart pounds erratically inside my chest.

Aware that Caitlan enjoys these romantic movies, she might find it and watch it, if I leave it in plain sight. It is inconceivable what her reaction would be if she had occasion to witness the man she loves, in company with another woman, thrusting a serrated edge blade up through the stomach of a guy helplessly bound and gagged to a chair. It was out of retaliation for what he'd done to my sister, but Caitlan might not understand any more than perhaps the other members of my family would.

Caitlan breezes in ahead of Ru. My brother trails in her wake, overloaded with shopping bags which he deposits, with a sigh, onto the nearest chair. If there's one thing that I've learned about my girlfriend, she's like other women who enjoy nothing better than spending money. Luckily, we have some remaining from the 75 grand Max Sorenson had allocated me.

"You'll never guess what, Aidan?" Caitlan enthuses. It is obvious she is bursting with some news and she kisses me on the lips.

"You won the lottery?" I joke.

"I bleedin' wish," Ru mutters, collapsing onto the sofa wearily.

"No, but David from downstairs has gone," she adds.

"Gone!" Sure he has darling. At my suggestion and at the point of a gun. Naturally, I feign surprise.

"Yeah, just had it away on his toes," Ru takes up the narrative. "There's a 'To Let' sign gone up already."

"I really wanted one of those wee kittens. They were gorgeous, weren't they, Aidan?"

"Sure. Gorgeous, sweetheart," I agree absently. "If that's what you want." Pulling her into my arms, I placate her that I'll buy her a kitten for Christmas.

Throwing her arms around my neck she gushes, "oh, Aidan, I love you so much. That's what I really want," in her familiar childish innocence.

"Cats need looking after. Don't ask me to change its nappy," Ru quips.

"Cats don't wear nappies, Ruairi," giggles Caitlan, a palm to her mouth.

"Ignore him, sweetheart," I tell her. Hear Ru mutter to himself mockingly, "ignore him, sweetheart."

∗

Christmas Eve is the first time I have occasion to watch the DVD. Ru is out. Caitlan's in the shower; again. As Ru identifies, she does spend a lot of time in there, although I refrain from questioning her. She's entitled to her privacy.

Slipping the tape into the player in Ru's bedroom and closing the door, I settle on the bed in order to watch it. Except when it plays, cold disbelief shoots through me; my heart hammering much too fast to be healthy. The DVD really is 'Love Actually'. With impatient fingers and more expletives than Caitlan's delicate ears should have knowledge of, I fast forward and rewind, countless times. No, the fuckin' movie really is 'Love Actually'.

Needless to add, I fail to recollect any murdering bastards slicing up anyone with a serrated edged knife blade in it. It means that the damned thing is still out there, if it exists of course. According to Dennis Mitchell it does.

I attempt to contact him by sending him a text to call me, stressing that it is urgent. However, his phone appears to be permanently switched off. I consider trying to locate the Agency HQ, but that idea is thwarted when Caitlan emerges from the shower.

Tonight we will go to the club. She is going to sing. The trouble is, that missing DVD is never far from my thoughts. I manage to shelve it, at least temporarily, when I perceive the way she looks in the dress I bought for her. Cut a fraction above the knee, the dress is semi-fitted black velvet, which she wears with a pair of black stilettos. Her dark tawny hair has grown longer, is freshly washed and cascades past her shoulders, the way I like her to wear it. Just a little touch of make-up, her finely chiselled features scarcely require any adornment. Nothing that makes her appear like either Suzanne or Verdi, women of the world which Caitlan definitely isn't. She's sweet, innocent, this childwoman. That's why I love her so much. Tonight I've never seen her appear more lovely or alluring. We're in the bedroom. My arms encircle her waist and I compliment her on her beauty. I remain half-dressed, wearing only my suit trousers. I purr in her ear, "if only we didn't have to go out. I want to make love to you, sweetheart."

"Aidan." She says my name rather sharply, almost as if it is a reprimand. "Can... can I ask you something?" She sounds hesitant and I wonder what's coming.

"Sure, baby, you can ask me anything."

"Och, it's... it's just that I'm worried about the baby."

I freeze. "There's nothing wrong is there? We had a scan and it was okay."

"No, it's not that." She pauses, clears her throat, as if what she's trying to say is difficult. "I... I think we should abstain from sex until it's born j... just in case."

"Abstain from sex!" I explode, surprised. Then, softening my tone slightly, although I'm trying to recover from her bombshell, I say, "I've been gentle with you haven't I?" I smooth a hand over her stomach, the new life that barely shows. "Jesus, Caitlan, I'd never hurt our baby. I'm looking forward to the birth as much as you are, but it's another 7½ months yet."

"If you love me, sex doesn't matter does it?"

No drink. No driving. Now, no sex. I may as well slit my wrists now. "Sweetheart, sex is all part of love and I do love you, very much." I attempt to cajole her into changing her mind.

Suddenly she is out of my arms, green eyes enlarging and snapping wide.

"I love you, Aidan, you know I do, but sometimes I think all you want is sex."

"Jesus, Caitlan, that's not true." I remonstrate "What's got into you? You know the way you look turns me on all the time. Like now, in the clothes I bought you." Every word is the truth. So I need sex with her all the time. It serves to take my mind off that damned DVD and the uneasy sensation there is someone out there who is holding my freedom in their hands.

I slither a hand around her waist, the other inches toward those velvety nether regions she is trying to deny me. I ignore her protests and pull her hard against me. Her breasts slam into my bare torso, my lips close over hers, crush them demandingly, my tongue reaches to the inside of her mouth.

Her remonstrations of, "Aidan, what are you doing?" fall on deaf ears because I have guided her toward the bed. Lifting the dress, my hands sweep every inch of her. The dress is in the way of what I want and I yank down her panties, unzip my trousers with a free hand, fumble with the button. Already erect, my hardness is about to enter that membranous paradise.

"Aidan! Aidan!" she screams my name.

Still I ignore her protestations. Swinging herself from the bed, she pushes me away with her slight strength and sheer determination. "I… I told you."

"Jesus!" Left with no other choice than to collapse back onto the bed I regard her incomprehensively. Easing up my zipper, I make a vain attempt to suppress a surfacing anger. "What's wrong? I'm not going to hurt you, for Christ sake. I just want a little sex that's all."

Her shoulders shake. She confronts me when I raise myself from the bed.

"Sometimes you scare me, Aidan." Tears stand in her eyes. I wonder at the reason for them.

"What the fuck's that supposed to mean?" I can't help my anger now. Dare to appraise my reflection in the bedroom mirror. Long wild black curly hair sweeps around my neck, the dark beard outlines my jaw, the black patch that covers my right eye, all serve to remind me of some ruthless marauder, debaucher of women.

"I… I don't know." She refuses to look my way.

"Then why did you say it? I'm sorry, I didn't mean to scare you. I'm sorry about what just happened, but you turn me on something rotten and I want to touch you all the time."

I slip an arm around her shoulder once more. She shrugs me off and eases herself from the bed. "I'll wait in the other room until you're dressed." Her tone is so stiff that my heart plummets.

Donning my best dark pinstripe suit, cream silk shirt and a black tie, I decide to conceal the patch behind impenetrably dark shades.

Exiting the bedroom, I discover Ru and Caitlan on the sofa; they are laughing at some comedy show on television. Ru is ready. He's not a suit person. In black trousers and shirt, he's added a white tie and more resembles bar staff. Nevertheless, he does appear inordinately smart and handsome. His long hair freshly washed and his beard trimmed.

They're sitting close together on the sofa. The woman, who's just accused me of scaring her, is the laughing child again in my brother's company. I hoped it might have stemmed from a psychotic schizophrenic episode, this 'let's abstain from sex' business but she is undergoing regular checks, and is taking her medication. Dr Marchant is pleased with her, he assured me.

"You ready, Aid?" Ru asks. "The whistle looks good, man."

Caitlan says nothing.

Brid's words surface to torture me. How she's seen Ru ogling Caitlan. Judging by the affectionate smiles that she directs him, I wonder if maybe his attention toward her is reciprocated.

The nurse reassured us that if we are careful, sex shouldn't be a problem. The baby is well cocooned in the mother's womb.

Is she having sex with my brother? No, of course she isn't, I'm simply being paranoid, though I could have sworn that his arm, slunk across the back of the sofa, had Caitlan's head resting on it only for the arm to be withdrawn the instant I appear.

CHAPTER THIRTY-ONE
-
BETRAYAL

The club is heaving by the time we arrive. Caitlan's spot isn't scheduled for another half-hour thus she retreats to the backstage area to prepare herself. We decide she'd do five numbers. Afterward Ruairi would take over as DJ.

The place is decorated and Christmassy. I've never seen Caitlan, almost six weeks pregnant, looking more radiant but wonder why she should suddenly suggest that we abstain from sex. Seven months is a long time. Again I can't help but wonder about Ru. Not wishing to alienate him if I accuse him of anything, I opt to remain quiet. I am simply being paranoid. If I accuse them, I might end up losing them both.

The bar is crowded, overdressed bodies of both sexes grouped around it, all shoving, pushing to be served. I order a Coke. No whisky unfortunately, although tonight I would have enjoyed nothing better than getting thoroughly pissed. Because of the antibiotics, this isn't going to be likely.

A feminine arm, numerous bracelets jangling like keys on a jailors ring, slithers around my waist and causes me to stiffen because I'm aware that the arm does not belong to Caitlan, who is on stage. Also, that perfume isn't something I'd approve of Caitlan wearing. It assails my nostrils with its pungent sweetness.

"Hullo, I thought that was my gorgeous ex." Leaning an elbow onto the counter she rakes me over pointedly and with raised brows.

Dressed in a short black number, shapely ankles encased in high equally black stilettos, black stockings, her outrageously augmented breasts heave provocatively toward me. It's plainly obvious she is also bra-less. The breasts are the first thing I notice. Only when I've had enough of plunging flesh do I raise an eye to her face, conscious of the familiar seductive smile when she sees me. Tonight her blonde hair is piled high. As she wears it quite short, I figure the rest is a hairpiece.

"Jude!" She is the last person I expect to see. "So what you doing here?"

"You don't have to sound so offhand, Aidan. I'm here with Rafe. He's sitting out there." She gestures around the room indiscriminately and somewhere in the direction of a table in the corner, which is all that I can make out amidst bodies, dancers, waitresses milling around dressed in short red mini dresses. I have never seen the club quite so packed. I guess we should make a fortune tonight. After all, it is Christmas Eve. From what I can make out of Rafe, he is, I judge, in his early or mid-forties. His hair is thick but greying at the temples. In a black dinner suit, bow tie, white shirt, I imagine he epitomises an extra from one of those old fifties B-features. Plus the redoubtable Rafe resembles the actor George Clooney.

She orders a white wine spritzer plus a martini with ice.

I say, "I thought the guy is supposed to get the drinks, Jude."

"Oh, he offered darling," she oozes. "Then I zeroed in on you at the bar wearing those black shades and in that suit. The last time I saw you, you could hardly afford one." She touches my shoulder with a slender palm. Wondering if she can actually see me at this distance with all those bodies, Caitlan, beautiful, sexy, has kicked off her shoes as she had in The Liffey in Dublin. Her confidence restored as it had been the first time I'd seen her. Then she'd wanted sex, couldn't get enough of it with me. So whatever has changed causes me to entertain the uneasy feeling that it might not altogether be because of the baby.

Caitlan sings my favourite, 'The Fields of Athenry'.

As the bar is located a considerable distance from the stage, amidst the crowd I hope I can remain unobserved by her, while I'm with Judy.

"Things have changed a wee bit since then. Anyway, hadn't you better return to your table? Rafe…" I stress his name, "might get anxious."

She waves to him from the bar. His head is turned and he doesn't appear to notice. Caitlan's music is fairly quiet despite the strength of the sound system, so we are able to make ourselves heard.

"So you're having Patrick on Boxing Day. Is that right?"

"Sure, that's right." I commence sipping at my Coke without glancing her way.

"So what's with the shades, gorgeous? Is it some image thing or something?"

"Don't call me that, Jude," I hiss.

"What. Gorgeous? But you are, you bastard. And the Coke. I thought you preferred whisky or has your little Irish colleen got you well trained?"

"Don't start, Jude. I'm on antibiotics if you must know."

"Then you must have an infection. Jesus, it isn't an STD is it?"

Anger surfaces because of her audacity to travel along those lines. "Fuck you, Jude. No it isn't."

"I'm sorry. So what's wrong?"

"The infection is in my eye."

"Poor baby." Sympathy rolls off her tongue. For once, she appears genuinely concerned. "So that's the reason for the shades. You look pretty hot. Take them off."

"Why should I?"

"You're wearing an eye patch."

"Yeah, go on."

"Go on what?"

"Gloat. 'Cos I know that's what you're doing."

"Well then you'd be wrong wouldn't you? I know you don't believe it but I do care and this infection, is it catching? I mean if it's conjunctivitis that is contagious. I can't possibly let Patrick..."

"No, it isn't catching, okay. If you must know, I was attacked, my eye was injured and it's got infected. So why don't you go back to Rafe or whatever his name is and leave me alone."

"Jesus, Aidan!" She exclaims in astonishment. "Who attacked you?"

"I don't want to talk about it and certainly not to you."

It seems, however, she isn't about to let it go. "You call the police?" Her eyes fill with concern again.

"Sure," I shrug. "Don't you tell Rafe or Patrick, okay?"

"If you don't want me to, but Patrick will be worried when he sees you wearing an eye patch."

"Just tell him that it's an injury, that's all."

Caitlan launches into another number, and one I haven't heard before, something about 'Deportees'.

"Goodbye to my friends, goodbye Rosalita.

Who are these dear friends who are scattered like dry leaves?

The radio said, they were just deportees!

All they will call you will be deportees."

"She's got a beautiful voice, Aidan," Judy says. "You're a lucky guy and she's a lucky girl to have you and I hope your eye gets better soon. So can you drive?"

"Not at the moment. I'll get Caitlan to drive me when I pick Patrick up. She'll stay in the car if that's what you want."

"It's okay. She can come in. I'd like to meet her. Don't worry, baby, I won't bite." Her laugh is sultry. "I'd better get back to Rafe…" She allows her words to trail when I catch her arm.

"So is it serious, you and him?"

"He's just obtained a divorce from his wife and he's asked me to marry him. Why? Because you still want me? Even if it's just for a fuck, I'd give up Rafe, that clinic we're planning to buy. Everything. 'Cos you know I still want you." She pauses, touches a palm to the side of my face, traces the length below my injured eye.

"I'm sorry, Jude, it is over. You know I have Caitlan now."

"Sure you do," she shrugs. "A girl can't help but try can she? I still love you, you know that. I guess Rafe is more dependable and she's a sweet girl, Aidan. Love her as you never loved me."

"Sure, that's very magnanimous of you Jude, and good luck with your clinic and stuff."

"And you, darling," she smiles tenderly. "I'll marry Rafe, but I'll always have a place in my heart for Aidan McRaney."

She leaves, walks away without a backward glance. I'd been a bastard towards her from the outset, having an affair with another woman while she remained at home with our son. She'd had a crush on me since I was 18, when she worked with Brid at the hospital and my sister initially introduced us. All I'd wanted from Judy was sex. She deserved better and I'm genuinely pleased for her. Now I have Caitlan, a wonderful girl whom I scarcely deserve. She is far too good for this place, I reason, as she launches into another number.

*

It's the first time I've seen Suzanne since she dropped me off at my flat the other night. Her auburn hair is pulled back into a ponytail. She wears a red silk shirt with a pair of sexy black leather jeans. Catwoman epitomised. A black leather bolero style waistcoat is thrown over the shirt. She hasn't seen me hitherto. I see her, clock her as she heads in the direction of my office, making me wonder if she is actively seeking me out.

Finishing a now rather tasteless Coke, I decide to follow her. Not for any other reason except I need to locate the whereabouts of that DVD. Lennard has done a bunk. The tape he has given me in the 'Love Actually' case really is 'Love Actually'.

I pass the stage and blow Caitlan a kiss to which she responds weakly, doubtless because I'm leaving the room. I only hope she won't get the wrong idea as to why I'm pursuing Suzanne. Needless to add, I can hardly confide in her about the DVD or why it's imperative that I find it before someone either hands it into the law or sends it to my family.

Suzanne walks straight past my office, heads to the 'Ladies'. The toilets are located nearby and are the private ones reserved solely for the staff. Waiting patiently it isn't too long before she appears. She's still unaware of my presence, so I say her name.

"Aidan!" Her eyes widen and light up. Her pleasure is evident. She has no idea what I want yet. "I wasn't sure you'd be here tonight. How's your eye?"

Ignoring the question, I command her to go into my office. The surround of thick mascara that darkens her green eyes affords her the impression they eclipse every other feature in surprise, at my request no doubt. In the leather outfit she's wearing, skin tight jeans encasing nubile hips, I'm getting a hard on, one I really don't need but, with Caitlan's 'let's abstain from sex' deal, plus the fact I haven't had it in a while, I can't help it.

"Wow! That sounds like the kind of invitation I like to hear," she purrs and reminds me of Judy all at once. There is really something inordinately feline about this woman, it oozes from every sensuous body movement, every inflection, so that it wouldn't be difficult to propel her up against the wall, peel off those tight jeans and thrust my hardness into her. Instead, all I can manage is to hiss, "don't fuck with me, Suzanne." I hold the door open, motion her inside, close it again. "You know what I want."

"Jesus!" she giggles, undulates her hips in those jeans provocatively. In those jeans, her legs appear even longer. "And your girlfriend doing her numbers on stage." She directs her gaze ceiling ward. "'Course we could always go upstairs."

"I'm not talking about sex. I'm talking about that fuckin' DVD, Suzanne. Treveleyan said David Lennard had it. So I went to his place, where he pulled a gun on me."

"I expect he was scared, but I don't understand."

"Sure, he gave me a DVD. He palmed me off that it was a 'Love Actually' case. When I looked at the DVD, it really was fuckin' 'Love Actually'. You know what's on the fuckin' thing, if it exists at all, or is all this some kind of fuckin' mind game? Because I've had enough. I want to live a normal life. I have a beautiful girlfriend whom I love and who loves me, a baby on the way, a son. I don't need all this crap, understand?"

"The tape exists," she's stopped smiling.

"Then you know where it is?"

"You'll have to talk to Treveleyan."

My heart hammers erratically, while my senses reel with surfacing anger. Right now I could use a drink and I don't mean a Coke. "What the fuck's that supposed to mean?" I remember the bottle of my favourite Chivas in the filing cabinet. Pulling open the drawer I observe the bottle is still there, it beckons to me invitingly. All I have to do is reach for it. Sod to the antibiotics. I remove the dark glasses and slip them into my shirt pocket.

"Treveleyan doesn't tell me everything. I'm just the nurse, I'm afraid."

It isn't difficult to conjecture by the sheer evasiveness in her tone, the agitated worrying of her lower lip with her teeth, she is stalling for some unaccountable reason, indicating that she probably knows where the tape is. As my hand closes over the bottle and glass, my eye alights on the object next to it. Afraid to leave it at home, in case Caitlan ever discovered it, I'd deposited the .32 Walther pistol I had confiscated from David Lennard into the locked filing cabinet.

Suzanne paces the room, her lips pursed, wearing a thoughtful expression. While she is doing so, it enables me to slip the pistol into my jacket.

Beneath her watchful, reproving gaze, I pour a neat whisky into the glass; imbibe a swig before topping it up.

"Are you still taking medication for your eye?"

I shrug. "Sure I am. My sister, she's a nurse too…"

"I know," she interrupts. A flame of colour negotiates her face and she bites her lip again, doubtless at her faux pas.

"'Course you do. You know everything about me don't you?" I retort acidly. "I was going to say my sister took me to see this eye doctor and he prescribed antibiotics."

"Then I'm guessing he also warned you not to drink."

"I have enough with my family on my back, my girlfriend and my sister telling me I shouldn't do this, shouldn't do that."

"It's because they care, Aidan."

"Upstairs!" I gesture ceilingward. "Now!" We can talk if you want…"

Fuelled by both the whisky and my anger, I grab her forcibly around the waist. "I said upstairs. You're right, we can talk and you're going to tell me where that fuckin' tape is."

She really is a beautiful and caring woman, who doesn't deserve my anger. Her overly made-up features have transformed to ashen as she attempts to extricate herself from the tight grip I have on her waist.

"You're hurting me, Aidan. You can be so cruel sometimes."

My senses reel with the impact of her words. Am I cruel? It isn't the way I want to be and if I am cruel then it's because everyone seems to get a kick from playing mind games with me. It appears that Suzanne Markwell is no exception. Nevertheless, I release her with a shrug. She moves ahead of me up the stairs. Once inside the room I close the door and, catching her arm, half push her a fraction brusquely onto the divan before I slip the Walther from my jacket.

"Jesus, Aidan!" Large mascaraed eyes widen in disbelief, a hand runs, visibly trembling, to her mouth. "If you want to have sex with me, you don't need a gun."

And still she teases as if it's second nature to her. I guess she thinks this is some kind of game, because she starts to rise from the divan, until I command she stay put. Locking the door I rasp, "sex isn't going to happen, darlin'. I love my girlfriend."

Keep telling yourself that, McRaney. I'm beginning to get hard again at the way she looks, a fraction scared, uneasy and suddenly, so incredibly young.

"So, what is it you want, Aidan?"

Her tone is composed. I guess she really isn't scared of me and she complacently believes that I won't shoot her.

"Some answers, darlin'. For instance, there's something that's been bugging me. We torched that farmhouse in Joydens Wood. The place was practically burned to the ground. I'm sure a digital versatile disc wouldn't have survived such a fire. So stop all this fuckin' playacting Suzanne and confess, that DVD really doesn't exist, does it? Treveleyan sent me on a wild goose chase to see David Lennard. I had to intimidate him into telling me and this shooter belongs to him. Now, tell me why you think it's some kinda sport to play games with me. Maybe you think I really am some fuckin' thick Paddy who doesn't quite get the connection 'cos don't underestimate me, sweetheart, you tell me the truth or I might just have to disfigure that pretty face."

Her face pale, she pushes herself away from me, further onto the bed, as if for some kind of sanctuary. "Please, Aidan, I... I'll tell you anything you want to know."

"Then talk, darlin'." I level the Walther directly in line with her eyes.

"All I know is the tape wasn't burned in the fire. Someone rescued it, only for the Agency to seize it from amongst Lamond's nefarious little collection of porn and paedophilia, plus all the murders he had his men did and filmed. So, I suppose Lamond had the tape taken out before the fire started."

"Then someone must have set the tape running and took it out before we torched the place. I saw no one else and I sure didn't want anything recorded, so it must have been Verdi." I swallow uncomfortably at the very idea that Verdi Benson could have betrayed me in such a way. For Lamond? A cold reptilian tentacle slithers around my inside until I feel almost physically sick.

Wild, free spirited Verdi, offering me her sexual favours, the joints, the knowledge of the criminal underworld, how to destroy dental identification.

As if in response to my uneasy retrospection, Suzanne says, "Verdi worked for Lamond. She has since her son was blown up in your car, but I don't know what she does now Lamond's inside, and I resent you threatening me. All I can do is tell you what I know. I haven't seen the tape personally. I don't think I really want to. You're basically a nice man, one of the good guys, and I do understand how angry all this must make you when you're trying to make a go of things with your family, since you come out of prison, and the only reason you're running this place is because Lamond has set up a drug deal with the Brazilians. He was counting on you to go along with it, that he'd probably blackmail you into doing it. Dennis said they were at the club. You must have seen them. So did you set up a meet?"

"God no! Who the fuck do you think I am? I've been taken for a ride long enough. I know, Mitchell warned me. So I sent them away with a flea in their ear or rather at the point of a gun."

"Jesus, Aidan!" Her eyes widen once more and she clamps a hand over her mouth. "You... you pulled a gun on them?"

"Sure I did. They won't be back," I say with conviction, maybe with too much conviction because somehow, I don't believe it myself.

As if to confirm it, she says, "you don't know them. The idea was to set up a meet."

"Why? The last thing I want is drugs in my club. That's what I've been against from the start."

"I know that. But if you'd set up the meet, Trevelyan's men could have taken them out. As it is, they'll be back. This time they won't be so easy to get rid of. They are dangerous people, Aidan, you don't know how much. Anyone else witness you pulling a gun on them?"

"What do you mean?"

"Was it just you and them?"

Ruairi was present. Nevertheless, I have no intention of involving my kid brother in any of this.

I lie, telling her there was no one else. "Now you're changing the subject. I need to know where this tape is. Why Treveleyan should lead me on a wild goose chase to see David Lennard."

"Treveleyan didn't lie. Lennard does have the tape."

"Then the bastard's gone and taken the fuckin' thing with him and Verdi is no angel, believe me. She's killed too, maybe more than I have and if I go down, I'll take that bitch, fuckin' kicking and screaming if necessary, with me."

"You won't go down and the DVD was given to David because he wanted to see it, find out the kind of man he was entrusted to observe. He's essentially a civilian, just an actor, that's all. After he'd seen the tape, he told Treveleyan he was shit scared of you and wanted Georgie to pull him out. Maybe David's destroyed it, I don't know. Don't worry, whatever happens, the police will not see that tape, okay?"

"Then who else? My family?" I'd begun to entertain a physical sickness imagining what that would do to them. Caitlan, Ru, Bridget, Patrick. At thoughts of my precious son witnessing 'that'. For answer, she merely favours me with a perfunctory nod. "That wasn't Treveleyan's idea, I can assure you. He wouldn't do that, none of us would, but I can't say the same for Verdi Benson, especially as maybe you've scorned her love. It's common knowledge how she feels about you."

"Verdi hated me that much? How do you know all this?"

"Because the Great Man makes it his life's work to know exactly who the bad guys are and Charlie Benson was always high on his list. Luckily that bastard's still enjoying Her Majesty's Pleasure. Verdi took pains to blab it around how much she hated Aidan McRaney, vowing that she'll make 'that fuckin' Irish bastard suffer'. You left her bitter, Aidan. I can see why. You have that way with women."

All I can dwell on is the 'make him suffer' part until anger has become a living, breathing entity and I hiss at her, "the fuckin' bitch." I gesture with the Walther. "You, sit over there, in the chair."

She remains unmoving momentarily, although Suzanne begins to display a real fear when her eyes alight on the gun.

"What are you going to do, Aidan?"

"You'll see. Just do it. The chair," I staccato impatiently.

"Okay." She drops her weight onto the hard wooden chair near the window, a fraction hesitantly.

Dropping the pistol into my jacket and removing my tie, I pull her arms back against the chair rungs unceremoniously amidst her protests of what did I think I was doing. "I'm not going anywhere."

Maybe I should be taking my anger out on Verdi. Since she's not here, I guess Suzanne is forced to take the brunt of it. I've been duped by women before. Is Caitlan the only genuinely sincere one in my life, apart from dear Bridget of course? I wonder what she'd say if she were present?

"No, you're not, sweetheart." I fasten the tie securely about her wrists and around the chair.

"What did you do that for? Are you going to gag me too?"

"Not at the moment. I need you to talk. Maybe when I get fed up listening to you I might, or if you decide to scream or something. Now, where's your phone?"

"It's in my bag. Who are you going to call?"

"Fuckin' Ghostbusters. Now, you're going to make the call."

"If you haven't noticed, you've tied me up."

"For Chris sakes, woman!" The gun is out and closes in on her face. "I'll dial the number. I want you to speak and you're going to tell Treveleyan, if he don't bring the fuckin' tape in less than two hours, he's gonna find you dead."

"You wouldn't kill me, Aidan?" Her beautiful eyes remain defiant, while her voice issues a challenge, although it isn't difficult to detect the evidence of a tremble in her words.

"My patience is wearing thin. I told you, I've got a lot to lose if my family see that tape."

"I told you Treveleyan wouldn't do that."

"Well, sure now I'm not taking any chances. If I refuse to work for the bastard, there's no telling what he might do."

"But murder. Even you…"

"Wouldn't stop at murder. I'm sorry, Suzanne, you gotta know I'd kill to protect my family. Now, the number…"

I believe that Suzanne realises, finally, that I'm not bluffing. She vouchsafes Treveleyan's number which I dial and place on loudspeaker.

"No tricks, okay?" I warn. The gun is at her head as she speaks into the mobile. I hear Treveleyan's composed velvet tones.

"Suzanne my dear," he enthuses, surprised. "I wasn't expecting you to call today."

"George, listen, I… I need a favour." She pauses to regard first me then the gun warily.

"Are you alright, dear? You sound upset. It's not Lucy is it?"

She flares me a look; one which almost has me recoiling from the sheer venom in it.

"You know the DVD, the… the one." She clears her throat painfully, "from the farmhouse at Joydens Wood?"

"Mr McRaney's tape? What about it, my dear?"

"I want you to get someone to bring it to 'The Athenry' club."

"'The Athenry' club? Why?"

"Please, George, just do as I ask. He… he's holding a gun to my head."

Again, I receive another venomous look from mascara-darkened eyes.

"Oh, for fuck's sake! Listen to me, Treveleyan."

"Aidan?"

"Sure, Aidan. Just do as she says and yeah, I'm holding a pistol to her head and if you stall over this, I'm fuckin' angry enough to kill her. If you send any of your men in to try and take me, then I really will fuckin' waste her, understand?" I rasp. "All I want is the tape and I'll let her go, I promise. I don't want to hurt her, that's not who I really am, but you've all pushed me too far and I don't fuckin' like being pushed. Get my drift, Treveleyan. That means no double cross either."

"Of course, my boy, I understand perfectly."

Why does he have to sound so goddamned conciliatory? So unfazed? Instead of putting me at my ease, his friendliness only serves to place me on my guard. He adds, "I really haven't underestimated you have I?"

"Meaning?"

"I'll get Dennis to bring the tape. You really are the kind of man we're looking for and no double cross, I promise, because I know you will carry out your threat. I know I'm not dealing with some nervous wimp who wouldn't have the guts to pull the trigger."

"Sure I have the guts, Treveleyan. So get that tape or I will kill her, understand?"

"Perfectly. Oh by the way, Happy Christmas to you, my boy. Do you know it's Christmas morning, Aidan?"

I wonder momentarily why he hasn't mentioned the reason for David Lennard not giving me the DVD but shrug it off. I guess it isn't important in the scheme of things. Lennard was merely a scared wimp and the solicitous voice really is making me uneasy now.

Suzanne murmurs, "you have your family you'd murder for. I have my eight year old daughter." Tears shine in her eyes. The mascara has run and my heart goes out to her so that it would take little effort on my part to release her. The trouble is, that damned tape has haunted me ever since learning of its existence.

I conclude the call to Treveleyan, turn to reassure Suzanne that once I have the tape in my possession she can go and join her daughter for Christmas, when a couple of sharply impatient raps echo on the door.

The pistol I'd dropped into my jacket is now in my hand and I mutter, "Jesus, that was quick. What did he do? Fly?"

Because I believe that it is Mitchell, my heart hammers erratically when a familiar voice calls out, "you in there, Aid?"

Ruairi sounds angry. Momentarily I make no move to answer the door. Ru is the last person I expected.

"I know you're in there, and you're with that bird."

"Just a minute," I tell him.

"I'll give you enough time to put your trousers on."

Ignoring that, I locate a bandana handkerchief in my jacket and fashion a gag across her mouth shutting off her hiss of "bastard," behind it.

"I'm sorry Suzanne, but I can't take the chance of you making a sound. I'll remove it when I come back. Oh, and don't try to untie yourself with any stunts you might have learned with the Agency. The sooner I get this over with, the sooner you'll be with your daughter."

Behind the gag, she has no choice but to lapse into silence. I unlock the door and encounter my brother on the landing.

"What the fuck do you want, Ru?" is all I can growl at him. "Whatever it is, we'll take it downstairs. I thought you were out there deejaying or whatever you do, only I'm in the middle of something."

"No fuckin' change there then. No prizes for guessing who that something is."

He precedes me downstairs into my office, while I hazard a cursory glance to the door behind where Suzanne is bound and gagged, with the uneasy knowledge that at any moment Dennis Mitchell will arrive with that damned DVD. I vow inwardly to get rid of Ru before then.

"If you're spoiling for some kind of fight, Ru, I'm not in the mood. So what's wrong?"

"I've taken Caitlan to Brid's. She was having one of her migraines, Caitlan that is. It came on when she saw you with that Suzanne."

"Is Caitlan okay?"

"No, she fuckin' isn't. I told you, she saw you with Suzanne. If you really want to lose Caitlan, you're going the right way to do it. What the hell's got into you, Bruv?" His words tumble over themselves all at once. "You wanted me to take her shopping just 'cos you couldn't be bothered."

"Look, Ru, I'm really not in the mood for this," I remonstrate wearily, my eye alighting on the half-empty bottle of Chivas on the desk. I pour myself a glass.

"What the hell you doing? That Doc told you not to drink with them antibiotics."

"Nobody tells me what to fuckin' do. So you took Caitlan home. Thanks, Bruv. I want you to go home too."

"Don't it bother you that your girlfriend's so upset she was crying? You know, with her condition and that, and I don't just mean her pregnancy, you don't seem to care a fuck."

"You know I care Ru, and it's not what you think. There's nothing between me and Suzanne."

"Then why is she still upstairs in your love nest if you're not screwing her? Caitlan doesn't deserve a bastard like you, and she's having your kid."

"Don't you think I don't know that?" I drain the whisky, pour another.

"Fuck you. You wanna lose that eye?"

"And I told you, don't tell me what to do" I wag a finger at him meaningfully. "Maybe Caitlan is better off without me." Now I'm feeling sorry for myself. "Is the club still open?"

"It's about to close. Caitlan met up with Judy. Judy didn't waste any opportunity to tell her that she'd seen you with Suzanne. Judy said that Aidan won't change. He'll always chase anything in a skirt, that he sees women as a challenge. I know your ex and me don't exactly see eye to eye but I'm beginning to believe she's right about you. You really can't stay true to one woman, can you Aid? Not even a lovely girl like Caitlan."

He bunches a raised fist, one I am swift to intercept before he can strike me, as I see that's his intention. I push the fist as far back as it will go until Ru expels an ouch of pain. Only then do I release him. His eyes are cold, radiating an anger I've never had the occasion to witness before, making me realise that maybe I might have lost the best friend I ever had. My own brother.

"But I can. You see, I think I'm falling in love with Caitlan," Ru says quietly.

I regard him in disbelief. "Jesus, Ru, what are you saying? Caitlan doesn't love you."

"You was the one who pushed us together. She reckons you scare her sometimes."

"What the fuck's that supposed to mean? How do I scare her?"

"Your anger, your violence. She told me a lot of stuff tonight. That's when I told her I loved her."

"Jesus, Ru, if you're trying to goad me, I'm not fuckin' buying, okay? Look at you," I deride him. He is a good-looking boy but he's too skinny, ostensibly undernourished with his long gangly limbs, wispy beard. Wearing tight black trousers, black shirt, he reminds me of Dad.

"Look at you. It works both ways. Your long curls, the beard. All the birds falling over themselves to get into your bed. I hear the talk around the club even if you don't. The guy who thinks he's got it all. Fancies himself as a ladies man. They reckon even the patch over your eye don't make you any less desirable. Your world really is gangland isn't it? The women you find attractive are pole dancers and call girls…"

I flick a glance to my watch, barely listen to his 'let's insult Aidan' diatribe and hope that Suzanne hasn't decided to perform any Houdini style stunts and escaped her bands.

Ru obviously hasn't finished his lecture, "maybe those sorts of women, like Verdi Benson, like to be with the kind of man who carries a gun."

"Oh, for Christ's sake Ru, shut the fuck up will you and leave me alone."

"Oh, yeah, I'll do that alright and with pleasure. Like I said before, I want my brother back. Oh, by the way, Caitlan's sister and her fiancé are in London and they're coming to see Brid tomorrow. If Caitlan's got any sense she'll go back to Dublin with them."

I regard him, surprised. "I didn't know that."

"'Course you didn't 'cos you're too preoccupied with yourself, man."

"So what did she say when you told her you loved her?"

He shrugs, mutters almost inaudibly, "I tried to kiss her too," before he moves to the door, prepares to exit, until with the anger spilling out of me I grab his arm, force him to confront me.

"You did what!"

He smiles so defiantly, self-assuredly, prompting me to bunch a fist in readiness to strike. "Yeah, I tried to kiss her and she fuckin' responded." I bring my face up close to his, jealousy coursing through me when I imagine them together. My worst fears confirmed that my brother and my girlfriend might be having an affair. Ru is right. I have been too preoccupied with myself and that DVD. Ruairi and Caitlan are relatively the same age. I am almost 30. I've been to prison, committed murder.

"You ever try to kiss her again and I swear to God I'll…" I allow the sentence to trail, mainly because there are tears in his eyes at the expression of cold threat in my voice.

"You'll do what, Aid? Kill me?" Tears slide unimpeded down his cheeks. Moving to the door, his hand is outstretched imploringly. "I really do, I want my brother back…" His words ending on a broken sob he practically flings himself from my office, slamming the door after him.

I open it again after he's gone to discover Jacky Gorman standing outside in the corridor. His black eyes are almost on stalks below that inordinately overhanging brow, I suspect because my brother and I have had an argument.

I hiss, "piss off, man," before closing the door on his puzzled expression.

CHAPTER THIRTY-TWO

-

HOSTAGE

Her arms are strapped to the chair. With the rag bound about her mouth, she is hardly likely to scream. Suzanne hasn't done me any harm and I almost feel sorry for her because of the way I'm treating her.

My brother Ruairi confessing his love for Caitlan. That he had kissed her. His erstwhile outrage with me. Of course, it is all well deserved. If it wasn't for that damn tape that Treveleyan and his acolytes delight in dangling over my head like the proverbial 'Sword of Damocles', I wouldn't now be holding a woman hostage, and I wouldn't have practically thrown my girlfriend into my brother's arms. In my preoccupation, I realise that I haven't got Caitlan a Christmas present.

I check my watch. Note that Mitchell is taking his time. Almost an hour and a half has passed since I made that phone call. As it is, I've left her too long. Another lengthy swig of whisky, straight from the bottle this time. Like a gnawing rat, anger rises again to eat away at my insides. A more than latent rage prompts me to unlock the drawer of my desk. The Browning is still there. I check the clip. It remains full. Adjacently, lying there also, the silencer. I slip the latter into my jacket, the Browning into the back of my trousers belt. This time she will realise that I mean business.

I let myself into the upstairs room, re-lock the door. She remains in the same position, which indicates she hasn't made any effort to free herself. She deals me a frantic entreaty from behind the gag, and makes an attempt to move the chair.

Moving to the window, I ignore her and turn my attention to the street below. It is silent, empty. A soft, wet snow has begun to fall. I ease the Browning from behind my jacket, fit the silencer and observe her eyes round in alarm. The running mascara surrounds and blackens her eyes. No wonder they call it 'the panda look'. She's been crying and it makes me want to placate her that things will be okay, assure her my threats are empty. I trace a finger beneath her left eye, wipe away a tear. Despite the fact I fitted a silencer to the automatic, I want to explain that I am merely bluffing. Nevertheless, I refrain because

346

I'm aware that if I am double-crossed, I would be left with little choice than to pull the trigger.

Behind the gag, she murmurs inaudibly and edges away from the close proximity of the gun.

"What did you say, sweetheart?" I adopt a gentler tone and lower the bandana far enough from her mouth in order to enable her to speak.

"Please Aidan, take this off now, I won't scream, I promise."

"Maybe not, but you talk too much and I need time to think." I replace the gag. "All this fuckin' crap I've been put through has probably cost me my girlfriend and my unborn child. That was my brother. He reckons she might return to Dublin because she saw us together and thought the worse. And Mitchell's taking his time. He's risking your life, so he is."

Reaching for her phone, I patch a call through to Dennis Mitchell again. It seems an age before he deigns to respond.

"You're stalling, Mitchell. What's happened?" I rasp. "If this is more mind games, I've had enough. I'm mad enough to kill her. There's an automatic pistol pointed at her head and I've got a silencer. Do I need to say anymore? So you get here within the next half hour or she dies, understand?"

"You really think Treveleyan won't have you killed when he finds out what you've done?" Mitchell retorts.

"Then you'd better get here fast, hadn't you? Look man, I don't want to kill her. She's pretty and she's got a wee daughter waiting for her. So you want her death on your conscience do you?"

"I'll be there, McRaney."

Concluding the call, I turn my attention back to Suzanne. She sits there numbly, unwilling to raise her eyes to look at me. If only she realises what a heel I feel; hating myself for putting her through this, but I'm desperate, scared of that tape falling into the hands of my family. Suzanne reckons Treveleyan wouldn't do that but I've gone too far. The only person I can trust now is myself.

"I reckon you're looking forward to spending Christmas with your daughter, Lucy is it?"

Tears slither down her cheeks again.

With so much guilt coursing through me, I'm unable to look at her any longer and I begin to pace the floor, to continue this one-sided conversation. I could remove the gag. She's a spirited kind of woman who doesn't scare easily, and I know she won't scream. Nevertheless, I entertain a kind of perverse pleasure from seeing her trussed up like this. It would be so easy to have sex with her because an erection is never too far from the surface, despite everything.

"I was looking forward to spending Christmas with my family. Tonight Caitlan and I were going to become officially engaged. Instead, I'm here with you, a pistol in my hand, waiting on my ex-cell mate to bring me a DVD that could alienate me from my family forever. Since my release from prison, I've never stood a chance."

She mumbles something behind the gag again. I lower it slightly to enable her to speak. "What did you say?"

"You're a bastard, do you know that? To think I thought you were a gentleman with your charm and that soft Irish accent. I also think you're getting off on it." She is about to release a globule of saliva into my face.

Anger getting the better of both myself and my better judgment, I crash the back of my hand into her face. It's the first time I have ever struck a woman. The whisky, this interminable waiting is beginning to take its toll. In spite of the fact that her lip is bleeding, I yank the gag back into place tighter than before. I secure the tie about her wrists forcefully, uncaring that I might lacerate them. There is nothing more I can say to her. So I don't. She is right. I am a bastard and, checking my watch for the umpteenth time, I curse and remind her that time is running out. She is aware, judging by the sheer terror in her eyes, that I am not bluffing, that I am mad enough to kill to keep my family from discovering what I really am, although I believe that Ruairi already knows.

I'm alerted by a sound from downstairs. My nerves are so highly strung now, adrenaline pumps through my veins at the thought of Treveleyan sending in some of his men to take me. A couple of tentative raps sound on the outer door. Raising the pistol, I warn her to keep still. Her only response is a chilling regard from angry, frightened green eyes. Hopefully it's only Mitchell with the DVD.

Wedging the Browning behind my jacket, I move onto the landing, closing the door on Suzanne. I descend the stairs cautiously, my heart palpitating hard against my ribs. Hitherto, I have no idea if I'm to be the victim of a double cross. I have no reason to trust Treveleyan and his people, even Dennis Mitchell. At least I am armed, which gives me an even chance. Although the automatic is out of sight, my hand is never too far from the weapon. I crack the door open gradually, gingerly.

The collar of a dark wool coat pulled up around his face against the cold, Mitchell regards me dubiously. His eyes are hooded, guarded with unease. Snow follows in his wake. Soft, snowy whirls have settled on his shoulders, a khaki knitted hat is pulled low over his ears.

"You going to let me in, McRaney? It's fuckin' cold out here."

"Sure." I shrug, ushering him inside. "You bring the tape?"

He says nothing momentarily, brushes snow from his coat and rubs his gloved hands together.

"The coat, take it off," I instruct him. "I want to make sure you're not packing heat like you were the other night."

"Sure. Regular little gangster aren't you?"

Shrugging out of his greatcoat reveals a black leather jacket, which he opens slowly beneath my discerning gaze, in case he's reaching for a gun. Instead, he produces a brown wrapped parcel, which is small enough to be a DVD, and places the package into my hand.

"So why didn't I get this in the first place? It could have avoided Suzanne's predicament. Now, upstairs," I command him and pull the Browning from behind my jacket.

"Jesus, mate, I've brought you the DVD, and in answer to your question, no, I'm not packing heat. Treveleyan said you was tooled up, so I didn't want to risk it. He also said you was as jumpy as a kitten. I thought you might be somewhat trigger-happy. So, you going to let her go?"

"Not until I'm satisfied."

"Okay." He moves ahead, up the stairs. "She alright?"

"What do you think? Another half hour and I would have had to call my bluff."

He regards me warily, his gaze descending to the gun. "Would you really have killed her?"

"Not without wrestling long and hard with my conscience. It wasn't something I wanted to do. Now, inside. There's a DVD machine in there. Put the damned thing on. At least I want to make sure."

"We are on your side, McRaney. I know you don't believe that."

Mitchell, preceding me into the room, clearly shows his astonishment when he sees Suzanne. He asks if she's okay. "You didn't have to truss her up like that, McRaney."

All she can do is nod, while tears of obvious relief at Mitchell's arrival course down her cheeks, disappearing into the bandana which he is about to remove.

"Not yet!" I command. "I want to see that tape first." Mitchell looks uncomfortable and he runs a hand across his beard with agitation, or so I imagine. "I've had enough of this fuckin' game and when this is over I never want to see either of you again. As for working for the Agency, I'd have to be crazy and if this turns out to be 'Love Actually' or '51 Dresses' or whatever it is, then you really have signed her death warrant, man." I gesture at Suzanne with the gun noting how huge her eyes really are, probably because they are incensed by her fear of death, now that the make-up's been washed away by her tears. My heart somersaults with conflicting emotions of both guilt and longing for this woman in spite of loving my girlfriend.

"'51 Dresses'. What the fuck's that?" Mitchell growls.

"I don't know. One of those romantic comedy things isn't it? Now, the tape." I jam the gun into his back. My stomach crawls as if a thousand live worms have burrowed their way into my intestines at being this close to discovering the truth of what's on that tape. If it isn't starring Verdi and me, then what? Blow Suzanne away? I'm aware that's impossible. I can't kill this woman. It's easier to concentrate the weapon on Mitchell who raises his hands resignedly. I direct him to where the DVD player rests on a glass shelf beneath the TV. He slips the tape into the machine and levels the remote. We slump onto the bed. Suzanne has closed her eyes.

All that appears on the screen, momentarily, is static and my heart races because I wonder if it will ever clear. The static does so, eventually, although the picture is still very grainy and almost too hard to distinguish. I get Mitchell to do something with the picture, although he shrugs and looks uncomfortable again before explaining that's the best he can do. From what I can make out, I'm standing over a trussed up Stephen Fitzwalter. The Browning is levelled into his terrified face. At least that's as much as I can make out, even then I have to get up close to the screen. With the limitation of having only one eye, it's difficult. At the moment when Fitzwalter moves in to kiss me, I switch the damned thing off.

"So that's it," Mitchell muses. "You ashamed, McRaney?"

"I'm not ashamed of what I did. I was angry after he killed my sister."

"You did a good job, I'll give you that. Sir George really could use a guy like you, McRaney, Aidan."

"No one uses me." I realise I could use a smoke. It has been a long night and I haven't had a cigarette in ages because of the fire alarms. Guess I'll have to wait a while longer.

"Pity. Now release her please. Dave Lennard really did have the DVD. He was scared to give it to you, in case the note you gave him was bogus and Sir George got angry."

"What was wrong with Treveleyan phoning ahead to say I was coming?" I'm in the process of untying Suzanne's bonds.

"Dunno," Mitchell shrugs, blanches for some unaccountable reason. "I don't know how the Great Man's mind works."

The instant I slip off the gag, she hisses into my face angrily. "You really were getting off on this, McRaney, you bastard. I bet you had to wank yourself off didn't you? 'Cos you're not getting it with me again."

Colour warms my face and I can't bring myself to look at Mitchell. "'Course I wasn't getting off on it." I'm swift to defend myself at her accusation. Was I getting off seeing her tied helplessly to a chair? Yeah you were, McRaney.

I smash that DVD beneath my heel, collect up the fragments and commit them to my jacket beneath their searching gazes. I can't even bring myself to throw the smashed article into a bin. It concerns me that Suzanne, an ostensibly law-abiding citizen, knows what I've done. Mitchell, on the other hand, has precious few scruples when he was jailed for several armed robberies and the attempted murder of a Securicor guard. Of course, Treveleyan is aware of my secret and somehow he appears oddly proud of it, rather than disapproving. Now, however, there is no evidence that the incident at Joydens Wood ever occurred at all.

Suzanne reaches for her bag to lift out a packet of tissues and runs one over her black encircled eyes where her mascara has run. She's also determined to have her say at my expense. "I swear to God, McRaney, you were enjoying holding a gun on a woman tied to a chair and you promised to remove the gag. You knew I wouldn't scream but you kept it on. Turned you on didn't it, you perverted bastard."

Mitchell sports a grin a Cheshire cat would be proud of. "Christ, girl, you can't blame him for that. Any man would get off on it. A pretty woman gagged and tied to a chair."

"No decent man would think that way." She rubs her hands in an endeavour to restore the circulation.

"Well, we ain't decent men are we, McRaney?" Mitchell holds his grin.

"Speak for yourself, and sex was the farthest thing from my mind, I was more concerned about that tape."

"'Course you were, mate," Mitchell mocks. "Anyway, I got something for you in the motor."

I regard him narrowly, failing to trust either one of them. All I hope is I'm the only one with the gun. "What is it? A bomb? More games?"

Suzanne continues to rub at her sore wrists, and then wipes her eyes. Perspiration sullied the underarms of her blouse. Her eyes remain bloodshot from crying and she blows her nose vigorously with the sodden, black smeared tissue. "You really don't trust anyone do you, Aidan? Or have you always been paranoid?" she taunts.

"The only people I trust are my family. So whatever it is, lead the way Mitchell and don't forget, I have a gun."

"Where did you get the shooter anyway?"

"Believe it or not, from Ray Lamond, Verdi gave it to me. You know me well enough to know I can use it."

"You ain't the only one who's fast with the heat, McRaney."

"When you boys have decided who's faster on the draw, perhaps we can get out of here," Suzanne retorts and I observe her shiver.

Downstairs Mitchell lowers his coat around Suzanne's shoulders. She shivers again and grasps the coat tightly about herself, murmurs a grateful thanks to the ex-con. Her face is so pale without make-up. She is no longer the teasing girl with her sexual innuendos, as if, dare I think it, I have broken her spirit? This is a new side to Suzanne Markwell I've never occasioned to witness before. My heart misses a beat guiltily. Now, with the relief of destroying that condemning tape, I really am ashamed of what I put her through.

"I'm sorry," I apologise to her, my throat dry and husky. She allows me to slip a finger beneath her chin as I attempt to explain how much my family mean to me. I feel certain that she understands and has accepted my apology. I move in to kiss her on the lips when the crash of her hand, hard against my cheek, almost sends me reeling in surprise. "Jesus, you've got a dangerous right hook, darlin'." I regard her above the hand I hold to my face.

"I've been wanting to do that since you tied me up, you bastard," she hisses.

"You deserved that, McRaney," Mitchell mutters.

"I told you I was sorry."

"That doesn't fuckin' cover it, McRaney."

"Sure now, let's get this over with, what you have to show me," I remind, holding the door.

Mitchell dons his jacket, shrugs up the collar as he regards the darkness. The air is cold with frost, while the snow flurries have become heavier.

"A White Christmas," Suzanne mutters, and there's a tremble in her voice, as if she is about to break down again.

Now it's over, the way I feel, overcome with such guilt that I might have left her scared and neurotic, I hope it is a bomb. For doing what I did tonight, I deserve to die.

We head in the direction of Mitchell's Vauxhall Auris, Suzanne's Citroen is parked close by.

Mitchell brings me out of my uneasy reverie with, "Dave reckons your bird wanted one of his kittens."

Hitherto, I'm still not certain, in the aftermath of tonight's events, that this isn't one of those peculiar, 'Twilight Zone' moments. "Kittens?" I echo absently, uncertain that I heard right. So commonplace, so ordinary.

"He might have acted the 'pouf' but him and his missus breed cats. They even have their own cattery in Streatham. He thought you could give your bird one for Christmas as she seemed so taken up with them, and by way of apology for what he's put you through."

The burly ex-con cracks open the Vauxhall and lifts out the small cage that rests on the back seat. I'm permitted my first sight of the small, black, furry feline, it's big round eyes staring up at me from the confines of the cage. I guess I'm too stunned to utter a response momentarily.

Mitchell asks if I want a lift to anywhere, while Suzanne, who seems to have regained a semblance of equilibrium now, mouths something about returning to the Agency, mainly to get some sleep. Her mother is staying at her sister's for Christmas Day and Lucy is with her father. It's as if she hasn't just been held bound and gagged, at gunpoint, by a heartless Irish bastard who had threatened to shoot her. Mitchell adds, "might be a peace offering if nothing else."

I regard him blankly.

"The kitten. Your bird. You stayed out all night, remember, and birds get kinda funny about things like that."

"Sure," I agree, surprised by the ex-con's solicitousness. Turning to Suzanne, I enquire if she's okay to drive.

"Piss off, McRaney," is all I receive for my concern. "I'd rather take my chances with the weather than you."

"Women," Mitchell grins and shrugs into his coat.

Aided by the snow that falls around us, the fact this is Christmas morning, everything seems to have taken on a strange kind of surrealism.

Suzanne has driven away.

"Merry Christmas, McRaney. So where you staying?" Mitchell asks. "With the delectable Bridge is it?"

CHAPTER THIRTY-THREE

-

RUAIRI'S ABSENCE

An interminable silence has sprung up between us. All Dennis Mitchell and I seem to do is smoke so that the interior of the car is thick and acrid. Concerned how the smoke will affect the kitten, I cover the cage with a blanket from the back seat. The snow really has begun to descend heavily.

"A White Christmas," he remarks, serving to distract me from my thoughts, most of which stem from guilt feelings concerning the women in my life. Suzanne and the way I had treated her, simply because I was angry, the self-same anger that had sent me to prison. The anger that appeared to have begun after leaving Dublin and one that seems not to have lessened.

Caitlan, whom I love so much. Because I hadn't come in all night, she'll naturally assume I was with another woman, obviously Suzanne.

"Penny for 'em," Mitchell says, but he refrains from glancing my way. In this weather, the road demands his full attention as we head out toward Shooters Hill.

"Sorry?"

"You was deep in thought. What you thinking about McRaney?"

"Women."

He grins to himself. "I think about 'em all the time, but that's all I do. Not like you. You never seem to be short of birds. Not since you come out anyway."

"Actually, I was thinking about Suzanne. I wish I didn't get so fuckin' angry all the time. Maybe I should buy her some flowers or something. Sure, I know I acted like a bastard but I was worried about the DVD falling into the wrong hands, but Suzanne didn't deserve how I treated her. It's not the way I want to be with women."

"Well it bleedin' turned me on you know, seeing her all trussed up like that. I bet you were getting off on it. Go on admit it?"

"Jesus, Mitchell, what are you?" Nevertheless, I feel the guilty colour flame my face again. Not that I'd admit as much to Mitchell but I'd had a fuckin' erection practically throughout the entire time she was trussed up. All I say, however, is "no, I was angry. I told you. I just wanted to get hold of that DVD and destroy it."

A cigarette, an omnipresent signpost stuck to his lower lip, he concentrates on the now rapidly whitening stretch of road, with his wipers on. The sign for Blackheath looms.

"Anyway, you going to show me where the lovely Bridget lives? You know when she used to come and visit you? I don't know how she managed to get so many orders. It seemed like every other week. I reckon she spent as much time in Maidstone as we did. My old lady used to come. She'd be rabbiting, 'oh Dennis, you never listen to a word I say'." He makes a show of mimicking his mother's cockney accent. "No, I was more interested in what Bridget was saying in that lovely Paddy accent. 'They looking after you in here, Aidan?' 'Course they are, Sis, it's a prison'." He affects an exaggerated Irish accent while I can't help but smile at the interpretation.

"So, is she seeing anyone, I mean, since her old man walked out? What a fuckin' idiot. She's gorgeous. I wouldn't walk out on a woman like that."

"Sorry, but she wouldn't look twice at you unless you wore a dog collar."

"A dog collar?"

"We don't know for sure but she spends a lot of time at church, does my sister. Ruairi, my brother, thinks she has a crush on her priest."

"I'd change my religion if I got a date with her. Not that I got a religion. Catholic isn't she?"

"She's Catholic, sure, but don't mention anything about asking her out. You know far too much about me and you might let it slip to my sister, some of the stuff I've done, and I don't like people knowing too much about me." Tossing the cigarette from the wound down window, into the snow, I add impishly, "I might have to kill you."

Mitchell brakes the car suddenly as if he's skidded and I warn him to be careful. I hear him swallow noisily. "And I don't take kindly to threats, McRaney."

"I was just kidding. I have enough blood on my hands. It's over now. New Year's just around the corner. New Year resolutions, and all that, and mine is to look after Caitlan and my son. We're having a baby and I want to do school runs, be like other Dads and no fuckin' crap."

"Then you won't change your mind and come and work for Treveleyan?"

"God no!" Cupping a hand about my lighter flame, I flare it to yet another cigarette, expelling twin smoke wreaths ceilingwards. "I told you and I meant it, I don't want to see any of you again."

"Talking of babies," Mitchell's tone is surprisingly subdued as we draw near to Brid's house. I instruct him to park adjacent to her Saab, now pretty well snow covered where it has been left in the drive. "Verdi's pregnant you know."

"What!" The cigarette almost slips from my mouth in disbelief. "Get outta here. So she found herself a fella then? I'm pleased for her."

"She ain't got no fella."

"Don't tell me it was an immaculate conception," I quip. "So who's the Daddy then?"

"I'm looking at him," he declares, his eyes profoundly boring into mine.

I stiffen. My stomach rolls. I regard him in disbelief again, "me?"

"Hey up…" He changes the subject quickly. "If I'm not much mistaken, there's the lovely Bridget. Even with her pinny tucked around her waist she still looks fuckin' sexy."

I swallow uncomfortably without directing my attention to my sister heading, as if she's on a mission, our way. "I'm not the father, I can't be." I say it almost to myself.

Mitchell merely smiles enigmatically, his interest is already zeroing on my sister. He cracks the door open on his side, mutters, "she reckons you are but she don't want you to know where she is. Oh don't look so worried, McRaney. She's in Kent somewhere, that's all I know. I shouldn't have told you. So forget it, hey?"

"Forget I'm the father of her kid." I always believed that Verdi had known how to take care of herself in that department and besides, we'd always used condoms.

Mitchell eases himself from the car insouciantly, as if he has not moments before dropped his bombshell that I have fathered another child. I vacate the car and Brid rushes toward me. Her hair is piled atop her head in her customary style, loose redish gold tendrils fall about her face, a face flushed I guess from her Christmas cookery.

Predictably, she scans a disapproving eye over my companion, despite the persistent smile on his face.

"Och now, Aidan, where have you been all night again?" Before I can get a word, in she is determined to have her say. As for me, I remain in shock after Mitchell's revelation that Verdi is expecting my child.

"Sorry, Bridget, it was my fault for keeping your brother out all night," Mitchell's tone is conciliatory. "Although he is well over 21."

I thought, don't push it, while Brid glares at him stonily. This serves to remind me when she'd come to the door, the self-same affronted expression negotiating her face, to reprimand my friends when I was in my early teens, about keeping her brother out late. "And you've upset Caitlan. Seems she saw you with that lap dancer or whatever she is. So what you got there?" she gestures to the small cage I lift from the back seat of Mitchell's car.

"It's a kitten. Caitlan wanted one for Christmas," I explain.

"Sure now, if it isn't a peace offering more like." Her Irish accent is overly pronounced when she's angry about something, as she obviously is. "So who are you again?" She eyes Mitchell suspiciously. Guess he should be used to that. "I've seen you before haven't I?"

"Prison. Maidstone. You visited your brother nearly every week. I was his cell mate, Dennis Mitchell." He extends a hand for her to shake. She does so briefly, while he's practically bowing over her palm before she swiftly withdraws it. "Look, it's freezing out here. Can we talk inside?"

"You were just going weren't you, mate?" I remind him meaningfully.

"Was I? I was. Look, Bridget, me and your brother had a few jars last night."

"He shouldn't be having a few jars. He's taking antibiotics for his eye," she scolds, as if I'm not present. Then, as if aware of my presence for the first time, she admonishes, "what about that lap dancer, Aidan? Caitlan was in tears when Ru brought her back here."

"The lap dancer," Mitchell winks at me, an inflection I pretend to ignore. "I dumped her and she was upset. We both knew her at the club."

"Och, never mind. It's none of my business what you wee toe rags get up to but it is Caitlan's. You have responsibilities, Aidan, and don't forget, Mollie and Niall are coming this afternoon. You'd better have a good explanation otherwise, they'll be taking her back to Dublin. So how's your eye? You're still wearing the patch I see."

If it isn't for the presence of the patch, the pain has lessened somewhat, I can almost forget about the injury. There are other things serving to dominate my thoughts, including the news that Verdi Benson is expecting my child. "It's okay, Sis."

"So, Mr Mitchell…" Brid is obviously in no mood to allow either of us off the hook.

"Yes, Bridget," Mitchell enthuses.

"So where are you having your Christmas dinner? Since you're a friend of my brother's, you're welcome to eat with us."

Mitchell's eyes round, tawny brows shoot up in surprise at her invitation. A broad grin spears his face. The last person I want to sit down to eat Christmas lunch with my family is the man who knows far too much about me to be healthy.

Before he can respond, I guess it will be in the affirmative, I put in quickly, "he's going to his mother's for Christmas lunch, aren't you, man?" I mouth the single word, 'yes' behind Brid's back.

"Yeah, I'm going to my old lady's for Christmas lunch." His disappointment is almost tangible but Brid's attention is already diverted to the small kitten in its cage.

Taking the cage from my hand, she says, "I don't like seeing animals in cages. I'll take him in. You really do need to talk to Caitlan, Aidan."

Taking me by surprise, Mitchell says, "do you like seeing men in cages, Bridget?"

I mutter, "Jesus, Mitchell," in exasperation.

"Maybe some men deserve to be put in cages, Mr Mitchell," Brid retorts haughtily. I can't avoid a grin at his expense.

"I take your point, Bridget. So I'll be moseying along then, as they say in the old westerns." He sounds reluctant to leave but no way is he staying.

"You don't want to keep your mother waiting on your lunch," she reminds.

"Thanks for the offer anyway."

"I'll join you in a minute," I tell her as she turns to head back into the house.

"Don't be long, Aidan. Dad's here by the way."

"He is? Tell him I'll see him shortly. I've got to see Dennis off the premises." Immediately Brid disappears into the house, I follow Mitchell to his car. I want to know where he is really having his lunch.

Dropping behind the Auris' steering, he rummages around in his pockets for cigarettes, and I offer him one of mine.

"It's okay, McRaney, I don't wanna cramp your style with your nice little family. You're a lucky bastard, mate, so don't balls it up and I am going to see my old dear. She's on her own. It's the least I can do. That sister of mine can't be bothered. It's probably because she knows I'll be there, her ex-con brother. They ain't all like the lovely Bridget."

"Look, take this…" I entrust him with the automatic and silencer I pull from my coat. "I can't allow my family to see that. Take it. Oh, and buy Suzanne some flowers. Say they are from me by way of apology and you sure Verdi's expecting my kid?"

"I'm not sure, to be one hundred per cent. 'Course, I just heard it from Mal Smith. Do you know her? Only I dated her a couple of times, Mal that is."

"I've never heard of her and I thought you didn't have a bird. You're a dark horse, man," I tease with a grin.

"Mal ain't a bird. She's a scrubber. Look, I shouldn't worry too much. You got your little Irish bird."

"Does Verdi know about Caitlan?"

Mitchell fires the Auris' engine. "She won't hear it from me and if you don't go and join your family, smooth things over, you won't have Caitlan either. Merry Christmas McRaney and if Bridget fancies a real man instead of a priest, anyway I thought they were celibate, tell her I'll take her out."

"Fuck off, Mitchell," but my expletive is good humoured. I watch as he plunges into the slush of the street until he is lost to view. Only then do I head toward the house where the welcoming smell of roast turkey assails' my nostrils and reminds me that it really is Christmas and that the events of last night might never have occurred.

Instantly I appear, little Sammy flings herself into my arms exclaiming, in childish concern over my eye, that I resemble a pirate because of the patch. Dad occupies an armchair nearest the telly, a bottle of beer sentinel on the table at his elbow. His eyes light up when I appear and we hug in a father and son embrace.

Caitlan is a small figure with her hair in bunches. I wish she wouldn't wear it that way. The style makes her appear closer to 16 than nearly 20. She's so young, so beautiful. I murmur quietly, "hi, sweetheart. I'm so sorry about last night," before I hand her my present. Green eyes shimmer and she's a child again.

"Oh, Aidan, thank you so much." Her pleasure is evident when she sees the kitten. Then, as if she remembers, the light is swiftly extinguished, she demands, "where were you? You didn't come in all night."

So much guilt washes over me again because of the lies I can't seem to help. Yet how can I possibly explain to this delicate woman what I have done, without revealing my past. Instead, I say, "I… I got a wee bit pissed and Dennis Mitchell brought me home."

"I thought you weren't supposed to drink with the antibiotics? And who's Dennis Mitchell?"

"He's an ex-con, sweetheart," Brid interjects, with a tut, eyes raking the ceiling.

"Yeah okay, Sis," I mutter with exasperation, aware of disapproving female eyes, including my niece Sammy, who queries, "is Uncle Aidan going to wear a patch over his eye all his life?"

I lift a beer from the fridge, which results in further tutting and head shaking from my sister. "He will if he don't stop boozing. 'Course, it's all men can do is booze, so it is."

Caitlan, however, appears more interested in stroking the small animal in her arms. "Thanks again for my present, Aidan. He's lovely. I should be angry with you. I was last night when Ruairi brought me home. I saw you going up the stairs with that woman. I felt as if I'd lost you and I really wanted to go back to Dublin. Anyway, I've bought you a present." She selects a very small wrapped parcel that huddles amidst all the other brightly coloured presents beneath the tree, and places the parcel in my hand. It looks too small to be a watch. "Well, go on, open it," she urges.

I do so and reveal a set of cufflinks engraved with the letter 'A'.

"Caitlan, sweetheart, you shouldn't. This must have cost you…"

"Nothing for the man I love."

My arms come round her and I fit my lips to hers, uncaring that Brid is bustling about in the kitchen. "Thank you, sweetheart. That woman meant nothing. I… I just wanted to ask for her help in buying your present." Nice one, McRaney. I hate myself for lying to her. Coupled with the present, I scarcely deserve this girl, that's for sure.

"So you drank despite being on antibiotics?" There's a subtle reprimand in her voice.

"I'm sorry. Guess it's because it's Christmas and Mitchell came along and we sort of got talking about old times."

"In jail?" sneers Brid, while she continues her bustling, her face crimson from cooking or is it temper? My sister invariably likes to give the impression if you're not helping, then you're probably in the way. Ignoring her, I ask Caitlan if she forgives me. I lay on all the smouldering charm I can muster and, grasping Caitlan by the shoulders, gently tilt her chin to face me. "I love you so much and I'm here now. I… I had some business to attend to at the club, that's all." Hear the hesitation in my voice. "Like I said, Mitchell came along and we got a wee bit hammered. I know I shouldn't with the antibiotics."

I've been so engrossed in placating Caitlan I hadn't realised, hitherto, that Ru is noticeably absent. I ask Brid where he is.

"I don't know. I thought he was with you. I haven't seen him since he brought Caitlan home last night. He went out again. He said he had to see you."

"I'm afraid Ru and I had a wee bit of a falling out. Have you tried his phone?" I ask the obvious.

"Sure, several times but he's not answering. Perhaps the wee bastard's still in bed. So what did you fall out about?" Brid asks.

"Nothing much." I am unwilling to confide in her. "I'll give him a call. I need to take a shower first. Have you got any spare clothes around? I want to get out of this suit."

"Sure, there's a couple of my skirts that might fit," Brid offers, deadpan.

Caitlan giggles.

"I mean men's clothes. I don't cross dress y'know," I grin.

"There's some jeans and stuff of Ru's in the back bedroom that'll probably fit you."

"I'll help with the dinner, Bridget," Caitlan offers.

Before taking the shower, I call Ru only to receive the inevitable, 'the person you have called is unavailable. Please leave a message.' So I do, before texting him. 'I'm sorry. Where are you? Call me. Aidan.'

After a thorough search amongst the men's clothes at the bottom of the drawer, I manage to locate a pair of black corduroy jeans. While I hope they aren't Mark Collier's cast-offs, I also find a white shirt and a black waistcoat, which somehow looks cool, even for me, and add the cufflinks she bought me to the shirt.

Minus the patch, I note the eye is finally beginning to heal. I can at least open it and it's less swollen, albeit things are still a fraction blurred. A tentative rap issues on the bathroom door, and on opening it I admit Caitlan into the room. Returning to the washbasin, I concentrate on trimming my beard and refrain from glancing her way. "Lunch nearly ready?"

"I think so," she replies quietly. "Your eye's looking better. You don't have to wear that patch now, do you?"

"I'll see how it goes, if you'll pardon the pun."

"We need to talk, Aidan."

"Sounds ominous, sweetheart?" I assume a nonchalance I don't really feel because her tone is oddly self-controlled, the kind that brooks no argument. "I'm glad you're pleased with the present. Mine's nice too." I show her that I'm wearing the cufflinks. She flicks me a wan smile, a mere flirting of her lips, while her face has gone noticeably paler, making me wonder that whatever she wishes to discuss, I may not like.

"Sure it's lovely."

"So what do you want to talk about, baby?"

"It's not very private downstairs, not with Bridget bustling about the way she does and your da…"

"What is it, Caitlan? It sounds important and you don't want to take notice of Brid. It's her way, to bustle about…"

"As important as our baby, Aidan?"

I cover her hand with mine when she smooths it over the barely discernible new life inside her.

"Nothing's as important as our baby, sweetheart. So what's wrong?"

"I couldn't talk to you in front of your sister. She means well and we get on grand but she just gives you those snide remarks about that man being your cell mate."

"You mean Dennis Mitchell?"

She nods and I add, "och, you don't want to worry about him, darlin'. You worried that we've met up again?"

"Yes. I saw you get out of his car. Bridget said he was in prison for armed robbery and GBH. He can't be a good influence on you. What I'm saying is, if you have to be friends with someone, can't they at least be honest? I… I'm so scared you'll go back to prison again."

My hand hovers around her shoulders with the intention of cuddling her close but she moves deftly away, adding, "I'm not strong like Bridget. She told me how she used to visit you inside, take in photos of Patrick growing up. I'd faint away if I had to do that."

"Sweetheart." My sigh is heavy and I attempt to prevent the exasperation from creeping into my voice. "I promise you I won't go back to prison." Although I mentally cross my fingers. "Is this 'cos me and him had a few drinks last night?"

"Amongst other things. You seem different when you've been with him and that woman Suzanne, were you and him with her?" she tugs her lip agitatedly.

"Are you asking, did we have sex with her?"

When she refuses to respond, I continue in defence of myself. "No, we didn't have sex with her, at least I didn't and there never was anything between Suzanne and me, I told you that." I attempt to dispel the familiar aggression at her persistence. How can I possibly remain angry with this lovely girl who is carrying my little baby inside her? I long to hug her, kiss her, promise that we'll go away somewhere, anywhere we can be alone without these awful outside influences. No ex-cons. No long legged redheads. No demanding wheelchair-bound ex-coppers. Above all, no incriminating DVD's. This is all I wish for, more than anything, when Caitlan says, "I don't know you anymore, Aidan. I don't know what to believe and because I don't want to lie to you the way I know you lied to me."

"When have I ever lied to you?" I thought, oh you really are a bastard, McRaney.

"All the time probably."

I am about to interrupt in defence of myself once more until she raises a hand halting me mid-sentence with, "no, please listen to me because I won't lie to you. Ruairi took me back to Bridget's last night. I was upset when I saw you go upstairs with that Suzanne. You had your arm around her and don't tell me you didn't, or you haven't had sex with her at some time. I might behave like a scatterbrain at times but I'm not stupid. I know it's because I asked you to abstain from sex a while because of the baby. I know that it's hard for a hot-blooded male like you to understand, but when you love someone the way I love you then that's all we need. Sure, I miss it too. I'm not a nun y'know, but I really want this baby so much and I don't want anything to go wrong. Mollie got pregnant with Niall's baby a wee while ago and because they continued to have normal sexual relations, she miscarried. I really thought you would understand how much I want this baby, because it's yours, but you were so desperate for sex you had to turn to another woman."

"Jesus, Caitlan, that's not true." My heart performs a double somersault and I move to approach her, my hands outstretched in pleading. If only I have the courage to confess the real reason why I had taken Suzanne upstairs. Alternatively, how can I possibly do that? If I do I'll lose her for sure, yet I can't help the feeling that she's already slipping away from me or shall I allow her to leave? To find herself a decent man to take care of her and the baby. Verdi is more my type. She could be a bitch but it's because I hurt her too, the way I'm hurting Caitlan, the self-same way I hurt everyone who loves me and Caitlan is hurting, I can tell. It is reflected out of those beautiful, alluring emerald eyes. "I really didn't have sex with her," I attempt one last desperate plea. "I know I don't expect you to believe it but it's the truth. And… and we were discussing the present to buy you. And let's abstain from sex. Anything you want until the baby's born…"

"Och, I know you too well, Aidan McRaney. I can tell when you're lying because you hesitate over your words as if you're thinking up an explanation but as I said, I won't lie to you, that Ruairi kissed me."

Now the live worms that are hatching in my stomach are really having a party. "What!" The exclamation is practically choked out of me. Initially I believed that the little toe rag was lying in order to provoke me into some kind of fight. So it was true.

"He was angry with you. I think that's why it happened. It was because of the way you were treating me. When he took me back to Bridget's, he stopped the car and put his arm around me. I thought at first it was a comforting gesture because he could see how upset I was. Then he told me he'd fallen in love with me. That's when he kissed me."

"And?" I prompt, and now I can no longer avoid my ever-surfacing temper as it rises to an uncontrollable level. "And?" I snap. My heart plummets when she shrinks from me as if she fears I might physically strike her.

"And… and…" Her hesitation is painful and delivered on a choking sob. "I… I responded." The last word almost screams from her.

Jealousy is a maleficent demon inside me and I rasp, "you did what?" Barely conscious of my actions I grip her by the shoulders belligerently.

"Please, Aidan, you're hurting me…" Tears spring to her eyes; she regards me so imploringly it serves to instil tears in my own eyes.

"But you gave me a present and one you obviously took care over. So why… why are you doing this? I love you."

"I love you too, Aidan, and I bought the present because there was so much love in my heart for you when I did, but you seem to be pulling further away from me. I don't love your brother. I love you so much that it feels like an actual physical pain every time I see you with another woman, as… as if you've stabbed me in the heart. After Shaun, I thought you were different but you're not, not really, and maybe… maybe…" the words seem to adhere to her throat momentarily, "even if I don't love him now, knowing that Ruairi loves me and won't cheat on me."

"Jesus, Caitlan!" I tousle my hair with a trembling hand. "This is Ruairi we're talking about. He's fuckin' 21 years old with hormones permanently on turbo and asking him to abstain from sex would be like asking for the moon, and I'm not cheating on you. How many more times have I gotta tell you that? You… you're not going back…" I swallow uncomfortably, as if something that refuses to move has stuck in my throat, "to Dublin with your sister are you?" I manage to ask finally.

"I… I think it's for the best, don't you?" she speaks almost stoically, as if she were reading unfamiliar words on an autocue. "If I don't see you, maybe I'll forget you after a while. Sure, if it won't break my heart. But… but Ruairi says he'll be there."

"What about that?" I indicate her swollen stomach angrily. "Won't that remind you of me? And you think that scatter brained brother of mine will take care of your kid? He probably won't know how to change a nappy for fuck's sake…" I'm storming at her now too, angry and outraged, uncaring how I hurt her. It is only because I love her so much, aware that the only two options I have left, if Caitlan returns to Ireland, is to follow her there or turn to the drink.

"Aidan!" My name is shouted through the door and Brid returns me to the present.

"What!" I snap irritably. "What do you want, Brid?" I observe that Caitlan is crying quietly but I make no move to comfort her.

"You're phone's been ringing for ages. I think it might be important. Aidan, are you listening?"

My tone fractious, I inform Caitlan that we'll talk later. That if she returns to Ireland, I'll follow her and add, "don't forget my aunt and uncle are over there."

She fails to respond, however. I open the door to Brid with a mix of both irritation and relief.

"Everything alright with you two? Only lunch will soon be ready. I still can't raise your brother but your phone's been ringing for a while. I go to answer it but they ring off when I do. Then it rings again. No name other than 'withheld' comes up."

"I'll come and help you dish up, Bridget," Caitlan pushes past me as she exits the bathroom, while I ache to pull her into my arms and kiss her but the moment has gone and I am left alone, thus I resolve to attend to the impatient caller.

The voice on the line causes a sense of cold foreboding to possess me.

"Senhor McRaney, you have exactly 12 hours. It is now precisely 2.15pm."

"What the fuck!"

"Listen carefully, Senhor. By 2.15am tomorrow, you bring me, I give you pick up point closer to time, £300,000 sterling. Senhor Sorenson has money. He expect your arrival, we give you drugs and this time you distribute them from club as we previously ask. Also this time, I not be staring down barrel of your pistol. You should not have done that, Senhor."

De Oliveira. The last fucking person I expected to hear from. After Caitlan's threat to return to Dublin, informing me that my brother kissed her, that she had responded, my anger really knows no bounds now.

"Nothing's changed, you bastard." I lower my voice in case I'm overheard. As soon as I hear his voice, I fling myself back into the bathroom and close the door. "No fuckin' drugs, I told you. So where are you? And I can't promise you that you won't be looking down the business end of my gun," I hiss.

"Please, senhor, don't try being tough guy again. I tell you where near dropping time."

Raphael De Oliveira's tone is softly spoken, without raising the timbre, yet it is filled with such menace it practically freezes the blood in my veins.

"No fuckin' deal, De Oliveira. Next time I won't just point a fuckin' gun at you, I'll pull the trigger."

"And let your brother die?"

"Sorry, what!" My limbs have suddenly frozen. Momentarily I am unable to move and it's as if the phone has now become an insidious viper in my hand. "What are you talking about? What about my brother?"

"Rory is it? You double cross us and Rory die - and no polizei or your brother will die anyway. You have 'til 2.15 tomorrow. I will call."

"Can't Sorenson deliver the money?"

"And be struck off as lawyer? You are dispensable, Senhor McRaney. You ex-convict. You always were."

The crash of my heart is painful against my ribs and I have a problem catching my breath. I am dispensable, I always was.

"The fuck I am," I spit. I regain an equilibrium of sorts and demand, "how do I know you really have my brother?"

I hear De Oliveira's voice, as if he is issuing orders and my brother sobs, "Aid, Aid, you gotta do as they ask, please. They… they're gonna kill me…" before he is abruptly cut off. I shout his name down the phone in panic.

"Please, Ru…" I'm half crying now. Despite everything that Caitlan has confessed about her and Ruairi, I love my brother too much to allow him to die.

De Oliveira says, "we call you, Senhor. You won't find us. Big city. No deal. One dead brother. Pity." He clucks with a pretend despondence. "He so young too."

I listen for any clues as to their whereabouts but the Brazilian has already rung off.

CHAPTER THIRTY-FOUR

–

PAST LIFE REGRESSION

It is a while before I am able to collect my wits. In my sister's bathroom, I stare at the phone as if the instrument really is a poisonous reptile that's about to sink its fangs into my hand. I know that De Oliveira isn't bluffing. £300,000 in exchange for the drugs. That's a lot of fuckin' cash. 'The Athenry Club' the collection point. Ray Lamond nominating me as the collector. Maxwell Sorenson as the 'go between', the 'bagman' as it were. If I fail to deliver, Ru will undoubtedly be killed.

I slide to the floor, bury my head in my hands, wonder if I can do this anymore as I allow my emotions to take control and I bang the wall with bunched fists, beyond anger now, a wild, uncontrollable outrage and one that I ultimately release in tears. Here I am almost 50 years old, over 6ft tall and crying like a child before I swipe my eyes with the back of my hand, light a smoke, blink back the tears in an attempt to both compose myself and discover an escape route from this predicament. Everything is ostensibly so normal. Festive. That 'wonderful time of year'. Flurries of snow outside. A perfect white Christmas. My father, my sister and my girlfriend downstairs. The nostalgic aroma of Christmas dinner, the inherent memories of a Dublin childhood. This my first Christmas after spending nearly eight in jail. It should be a happy time. I've brought this on my brother. Because of me, his life now hangs in the balance. I hear them bustling about downstairs preparing lunch. Brid calls up, "where are you, Aidan? Lunch'll be cold…"

Hitherto, all I had to concern me was Caitlan preparing to dump me and return to Dublin with her sister. All of which I have brought on myself. Nothing has really seemed normal since leaving prison. Now this. So who can I possibly turn to for help? My sister? My girlfriend? Dad? Hardly. Knowing my family as well as I do, they'll obviously suggest contacting the police. It is the most logical step after all.

London is a big city. The chances of locating my brother are decidedly slim. The proverbial 'needle in a haystack'. I need help. Treveleyan. The last person I should appeal to, but who else do I have left? 'No polizei', he said. Harry would have known what to do, but Harry is in Italy. That leaves just me, fuckin' on my own with less than 12 hours to find my kid brother. Of course, I can do as De Oliveira requests. Go to Sorenson for the money. Hand it over to the Brazilian for the drugs. Swamp the city. Eventually get lifted as a drug dealer because, to all intents and purposes, Sorenson is a squeaky-clean lawyer, whereas Aiden McRaney is simply a dispensable 'Mick' who already has a criminal record. I reason there is nothing left and the longer I stall the closer the time gets to Ruairi's death. I will have to contact Treveleyan.

What about my family? How safe are they? I've tried so hard to protect them but all I've succeeded in doing is endangering their lives.

I still have the gun. The .32 Walther automatic. Hauling on my coat, I slip the pistol into the pocket.

Downstairs, Brid is dishing up the dinner. A huge roast turkey rests on a ceramic oval plate. The vegetables so perfectly cooked, stuffing, cranberry sauce. Crackers neatly laid adjacent to the plates.

She reminds, "dinner's ready, Aidan," before swiftly regarding me askance. "Why are you wearing your coat? Don't tell me you're going out. It's lunchtime."

"Brid. Sis…" I catch her by the arm forcibly.

"Aidan, what is it? You look as if you've seen a ghost."

"Put that down, please." She is in the process of mixing a bowl of bread sauce.

"But I'm…"

"I said, put it down, Sis, please."

"Aidan, whatever's wrong? Who was that call from?" she regards me uneasily.

"Where's Caitlan?"

"She bought Sammy a doll and wanted to give it to her before lunch. They're in the lounge. Why?"

"Leave that and come with me. It won't take long."

"What's happened, Aidan?"

I manage to usher her into the downstairs toilet. The only room where I figure we'll be safe from anyone intruding and wondering what my sister and I have to discuss so urgently. The room is small, but I squeeze myself in with her.

"All this sounds very mysterious. They'll be wondering where I am, and where are you going?"

"I have to be somewhere and I need you to listen. I don't want you to scream or cry or set fire to yourself."

"Aidan, what is it? Why should I scream?" she sounds really worried now.

"If you scream I'll have to put my hand over your mouth, understand?"

"You're mixed up with something unsavoury aren't you? I knew it as soon as I saw you with that Mitchell character."

"Listen and shut up, for God's sake!" I bring myself up sharply for the way I have spoken to her and I hug her briefly. Releasing her, I observe her mouth is tight, her eyes narrowed with suspicion. "Look, there's some people I've... ahem," I clear my throat hesitantly, "sort of upset. Some dealers okay..."

"Drug dealers?"

I thought, how perceptive of her and I nod. "They want some money and they... they've..."

"They've what, Aidan?"

"They've fuckin' snatched Ru and I have to find him," I blurt finally.

Her eyes are suddenly rendered dark, frightened above the trembling hand with which she clasps her mouth. "Oh my God! N... Not Ru. It's happening again isn't it? First our poor sister, now Ruairi. It's all because of you, the people you mix with."

Regaining a marginal composure, she wants to know what I'm going to do. "Call the polis I hope," she adds narrowly.

"No polis, Sis. They've threatened to kill him if I do." I slip an arm around her shoulders because she looks so scared.

"What about if you do as they ask?"

"Flood the city with £300,000 worth of crack-cocaine and whatever else those bastards are supplying. I can't do that, I really can't."

"But why you? It's to do with that club isn't it?"

"Yeah, sure it is. It's obvious now why Lamond was so keen for me to run it."

"The bastard. That man is evil. I hope he rots in jail, so I do."

I pull her into my arms, cuddle her into my chest, hear the erratic pounding of her heart, aware she is close to tears but aware she's managing to suppress them with difficulty. "Listen, Sis, I don't want you to call anyone. It's my problem, it's up to me to sort it out. That means no phoning Harry either. He'll only worry and blame me for what's happened, which is true I know, but the last thing I want is my big brother putting his size 11's in... And say that Ru is meeting his friends from Uni, that he'll be in later."

"But I... I can't lie." She raises her eyes, dark and tear filled, to my face.

"You'll have to, Sis. Say a few 'Hail Mary's' afterwards. I'm sure the church will absolve your conscience in this case."

"Who... who are you going to see, Aidan? Because I'm scared of losing you too, either to prison or... or worse."

"Just some people," I tell her quietly.

"What if you don't come back? Oh, Aidan, can't you call the polis? Let them deal with this." She clutches my arm imploringly.

"No, I told you. If I do, they'll kill him for sure. These people are dangerous."

"Oh, Jesus, dear God in Heaven!" She crosses herself hastily.

"Now, I want you to do something else. I'm not sure how safe any of us are."

She swallows hard. "You... you mean they could come here?"

"They snatched Ru didn't they? That's why I want you to take this."

"What is it?"

I produce the Walther and she crosses herself again, her face ashen before a hand clasps her mouth once more. "A... a gun, Aidan? Oh my dear Jesus. Where did that come from? Now I know you really are mixed up in something criminal. Those eight years you were inside almost cost me my family. I don't think I can go through it again."

"Please, Brid, it won't come to that. Just take the gun for me, I need to know you're safe. Look at Caitlan and Dad. They're not strong enough, but you are. You've always held it together for all of us."

"But... but I have never used one of those things. I'd be too scared to even touch it."

"Hopefully they won't come here and you won't have to use it, but if they do, look."

I demonstrate the weapon, pull out the clip, explain that it's loaded, that's where the bullets are, before I slam the clip into place with a practiced hand. "It fires seven shots. Keep it somewhere safe, particularly away from the children."

"If Caitlan knew you had that thing it really would be the end of your relationship."

My sigh is dispirited. "I think it already is, Sis."

"Oh?"

"I'll explain later. I have to go." I watch her take the .32 and slip it into her apron pocket.

"I'd put it into your bedroom drawer if I were you." I kiss the top of her head. "I'll sneak out. Tell them I've gone to pick Ru up and I will return with him. Try and show you're not scared, okay?"

"Just come back, Aidan." Her voice breaks. She follows me to the door. I hug her again, counsel her to behave as normal. Tilting her chin with a forefinger, I assure her that I'll bring Ru back with me. If only I can reassure myself so effortlessly.

I let myself out of the house, pull on shades and maintain a discreet distance before I call Dennis Mitchell.

"What do you want, McRaney?" he asks in his customary growl. I can also detect the fact that he's eating, he chews quickly and sounds annoyed at being thus disturbed. The rumbling of my own stomach indicates I too could use some lunch. I could have remained to eat with my family but Ru's imploring sobs of 'they're going to kill me, Aid,' prevent me.

"I need your help." I cringe at the begging note in my voice. "I want you to take me to Treveleyan." I dive in because his line at the other end has gone ominously quiet as if he's rung off, until he mutters, "what the fuck, McRaney? What's so fuckin' urgent? I'm eating…"

"Shut the fuck up and listen."

"You want my help, mate, you mind your manners. We ain't here at your bleedin' beck 'n' call." Mitchell sounds angry. I can't blame him after the way I treated him and Suzanne.

"So what's so all-fired important you gotta see Treveleyan on bleedin' Christmas Day, mate?"

"I know what day it is. The Brazilian's have snatched my kid brother and I don't know who else to turn to." I feel tired, exhausted all at once. It has been one helluva night and I listen to the broken sob punctuating my words.

"Jesus, McRaney, why they snatched your brother?"

"I can't discuss it over the phone. Can you meet me at the end of my road?"

His sigh is filled with resignation. "Okay, I'll be there. I'm sorry about your brother but Mr Treveleyan ain't gonna like it, disturbing him on Christmas Day."

*

Mitchell pulls the Vauxhall Auris to the side of the road and I drop in to the passenger seat. Lighting an umpteenth cigarette, my hand trembles on the Calibri. Only when he swings the car into the street do I opt to relate everything that De Oliveira has intimated during the phone call. That he has kidnapped Ru as insurance, until I collect the cash from Sorenson to purchase the drugs.

"Why couldn't he have asked Sorenson himself?" Mitchell asks the obvious.

"Because Lamond doesn't want anything to connect to the oh so exemplary lawyer. Apparently, I'm dispensable."

"So Sorenson can keep his hands clean? Lamond needs him, obviously. The last person he wants banged up is Max Sorenson."

"Something like that."

"You really should have let the Agency handle this instead of pulling a shooter on this De Oliveira character. He obviously took umbrage to that. Look, I'll take you to Treveleyan but you can't just go using people the way you do."

I stare at him in disbelief. "Do I really do that? I feel so fuckin' guilty all the time."

"She'll make you feel guilty."

"She?"

"Suzanne. She'll probably be having lunch with the old boy about now. When we get there, I'll call him to let him know we're coming."

"Suppose he tells me to piss off when you tell him who you're bringing? Maybe we should surprise him."

"Surprise Treveleyan! Jesus, you gotta be crazy. Nobody surprises Treveleyan. He'll have more security crawling out of the woodwork than you've had fuckin' hot dinners, mate. They'll force you to the floor with automatic shooters trained on you. You never see 'em but they're never far away, believe me. Don't look so worried. Treveleyan likes you."

"Even after what I did to Suzanne?"

"Suzanne's another story, McRaney."

*

This time I am able to ingest more of my surroundings. The somewhat nondescript, facaded, bungalow-like building. From the exterior, it appears more like a block of offices. Heading up to it a rough gravel driveway, it's circumscribed by a sprawling area of dark wood fencing. I also take a particular notice of the street where I now find myself. No blindfold. No security. I will certainly be able to locate the place again. I am fairly adept at finding my way around. I had to be as Frankie Lamond's minder.

Mitchell makes the call, all the while chewing at his lower lip with agitation at having to contact the Great Man sitting down to his

Christmas lunch, on my behalf, when I'm doubtlessly no longer flavour of the month, certainly not with Suzanne.

"Yes, Sir George. Of course, Mr Treveleyan."

Three bags full, Sir George. Mitchell instructs I'm to accompany him to Sir George's private quarters.

"I never had you figured for a 'yes' man, Mitchell."

"I'm not, but when Sir George commands, you obey."

"Why? No one commands me to do anything."

"If I don't, I'm back behind bars faster than you can spit."

"Jesus, man, that's blackmail."

"I've got a good life here. I don't intend going back to stir whatever happens, understand?"

"Keep your hair on." I am in no mood to argue with him and I follow my ex-cell mate up the path. Now I am able to focus on my surroundings, I observe the entrance hall is fashioned from Italian marble complete with roman gods on stone plinths strategically placed at all four corners of the room, near the stairs. At the end of the hall is the lift which Mitchell and I step into and he presses the button marked, 'Penthouse'. Mitchell explains that is Sir George's private rooms.

The rumble in my stomach again reminds me how really hungry I am. Guess it is to take second precedence to my brother's fate, while I have no idea whether or not Treveleyan can or will help me. After all, it is Christmas Day. I voice my thoughts to Mitchell, who merely shrugs.

"You've come to the right place anyway. He has ways of finding anyone he wants in this city or anywhere else." Something I find particularly comforting.

I have no idea of the kind of reception I can expect to receive. Upstairs we enter another hallway, this one is carpeted with thick burgundy pile. Mitchell speaks his name into an intercom in the wall, inserts a code into the keypad before we are finally given entrance, but not directly into Sir George's quarters. There is yet another room, an intercom is here as in the other, but this time we have to press our hands into a pad that, Mitchell explains, records our fingerprints. The machine obviously recognises me although we still have to say our names separately.

"That's to record your accent. You talk differently to me. The machine is unfamiliar with alien accents."

"I'm from fuckin' Ireland, not Mars," I mutter.

"Just say your name," Mitchell responds impatiently.

"Aidan McRaney to see Sir George Treveleyan."

A buzzer sounds and the door is immediately flung open by an elderly grey haired man who is dressed, surprisingly, in a black tailcoat plus equally black, sharply pressed trousers. Obviously some kind of factotum or manservant.

Mitchell greets him, "Harland, is Sir George having his lunch?"

"It's alright, Mr Mitchell, you can go in." The grey head nods his acquiescence while his gaze zeroes in on me.

"Send them in please, Harland." Treveleyan's warmly velvet tones issue from behind the door.

Partially bowing from the midriff, Harland ushers us inside. The sensation of his eyes boring into my back when I enter the room serve to leave me uneasy.

Treveleyan is dressed in a black dinner suit. The suit, a fitting accompaniment to a bow tie, frill white shirt, into which he's tucked a spotlessly white napkin, the Great Man feasts on a plentiful supply of roast duckling with orange sauce, roast potatoes plus an assortment of vegetables. A bottle of Chablis rests on the table, and at his elbow, a half emptied wine glass.

Across the table that is decorated by a Christmas patterned cloth, Suzanne is in the process of biting into the piece of meat attached to her fork when she sees me. "What in God's name is he doing here?" she exclaims acrimoniously.

I thought, pleased to see you too, darlin'.

Her top lip is still slightly swollen where I struck her. Did I really inflict that amount of damage to her beautiful face?

The penthouse suite is lavish with olde worlde charm and dominated by a magnificent ceiling-high bookcase. A dark brown, leather, chesterfield settee appears both expensive and comfortable. Behind where Suzanne sits, resting on an antique sideboard, a plain white vase contains the largest bunch of lilies I have probably seen. Their aromatic scent serves to play down the smell of the food somewhat. When she catches me looking at them, Suzanne's mouth tightens and she swiftly rises from her chair. Removing the lilies from the vase, she thrusts them at me, exploding, "Lilies! I hate goddamned lilies, McRaney. What did you think they were? Some stupid bloody peace offering? They remind me of funerals." Alluring, sexy in her red knitted dress, a narrow tie belt is secured about her slender waist. A skein of pearls adorns her sculptured white throat. Red hair upswept. Despite my anxiety over my brother's predicament, I wish for nothing better than to grab her around the waist, pull her to me and fuck the

376

ass off her. It's odd but her anger, although directed at me, somehow turns me on.

"Please, my dear." Sir George appears uncomfortable by her outburst, "now is not the time." And to me, "I apologise for Suzanne."

"I'm sorry," I tell her. In spite of the swollen lip, she does look particularly lovely today. "But the lilies had nothing to do with me." I flick Mitchell a raised brow glance. He pales but chooses to say nothing in his defence.

"That's typical of you, McRaney." Suzanne is still determined to have her say, only dropping back into her chair when Sir George lays a placating hand on her arm.

"So you got Mitchell to buy them?"

"I thought you would like lilies. He told me to buy some flowers as compensation."

Looking suitably chastised, he gestures at me.

"Please, Aidan, my boy, sit down." Treveleyan directs me to a vacant chair at the table. "And you too, Dennis. Let's attend to the business in hand. Oh, and Harland, will you please put those flowers back that Mrs Markwell has taken from the vase. I've got pollen over my dinner now and Mr McRaney's wearing black. Pollen's a nuisance to shift."

Mitchell and I sit facing Sir George Treveleyan at his dinner table, while the perspicacious grey eyes regard me so critically that I am compelled to avert my gaze momentarily.

"Your brother has been kidnapped, I understand," he says at length, as if every word is to be savoured.

All I can do is nod my response, for suddenly this grey haired granddad figure regards me with such concern and sympathy that I'm practically on the verge of tears. As it is, I feel the wetness that slithers from my eyes, which I quickly brush away, although I might have known the perceptive Suzanne would pick up on it.

"Shall I get a camera or am I seeing things? You crying, McRaney? Jesus, the big tough guy can't be crying can he? You know it don't excuse what you did to me." She points to her lip meaningfully. "Look at my face."

"I said I was sorry." I say, quietly.

"Suzanne, please." The softly spoken voice conveys a subtle reprimand. "You were, as they say, out of order Aidan, for what you did to Suzanne. It is our fault of course. We should not have put you in the position where you were forced to subject one of my operatives to a rather intimidating experience."

"Intimidating don't cut…" Suzanne flares again. She reminds me of a firecracker, the kind that you light before it goes out, but you know it'll reignite as soon as you approach and go off in your face.

Treveleyan has but to raise a hand, it is enough to silence her mid flow, while her mouth works tirelessly in an endeavour at controlling her temper. I suspect if she and I were alone in the room, I would incur a slap across the face again. Somehow I wish we were alone, Suzanne and I, because it is this erstwhile anger which, despite my love for Caitlan, continues to turn me on. If she and I were alone, I would have given into my insatiable male urges and, pushing her down onto that inviting chesterfield, entered her.

Having concluded his lunch, Treveleyan eases his plate aside. "I'll get Harland to fetch you some food or have you boys eaten?" The grey eyes encompass Mitchell and I speculatively.

Mitchell informs him that he has eaten at his mother's. Shaking my head, I admit that it's been a while.

I hear Suzanne mutter, "let the bastard starve," beneath her breath. The men choose to ignore her, including myself. I merely flick her a wry smile, one to which she predictably refuses to respond. I tell Treveleyan I'm too concerned over my brother to eat.

"But you must eat," Treveleyan remonstrates. "Just a small amount. Not too much. You'll need to keep up your strength. So, what makes you think I can find one young man in a city the size of London?" Steepling a bridge with interlaced fingers he circles his lips with a lean brown hand.

"Sure, I don't know," I reply wearily. "I didn't know where else to go but to you for help."

"That's good, Aidan, because with your help I can find your brother, but I do need more information. Tell me everything you know."

I heave a relieved sigh and blurt out everything that De Oliveira has intimated over the phone, including the part concerning the £300,000 he wants in exchange for the drugs. "The drugs he intended I should buy to flood the city."

"And this Sorenson character, the solicitor. I know him. It's an obvious question but instead of involving you…"

"Sorenson's the guy who lends me the money."

"The bag man?"

I regard Treveleyan in surprise.

378

"Oh don't look so astonished, my boy. I was once a DI in the Serious Crime Squad. I know the terms, believe me. You know, Aidan, you really should have let us handle this business with the Brazilians. That's why I suggested Dennis warn you, but that's the impulsiveness of youth," he muses.

"They don't say the Irish are thick for nothing," Suzanne is a still small voice at Treveleyan's elbow.

This time my initial amusement transfers to one of reproach and I direct her a withering glance. Sure, if she isn't fuckin' begging for it and I will if she doesn't…

But Treveleyan is speaking and I am compelled to shelve my thoughts about what I would enjoy doing to Suzanne. "Pulling a gun on them has obviously angered them."

"He's as fast with a gun as he is with his…" Suzanne cuts in again but is silenced by Treveleyan who sports an injured air and reprimands, "please, Suzanne, this persistent sniping at Mr McRaney smacks of the school yard, my dear. You're 28 not 12, please."

So she's 28, but looks younger.

Treveleyan continues, "I was young once. A long time ago." He shakes his head wistfully as if in an attempt to disregard the memory, while Mitchell grins wryly. "I can help you, Aidan, yes, but you have to help me." He regards me again and I feel myself being drawn or would drowning be more apt, into those deeply seated, hypnotic grey orbs. It is as if he and I are the only two persons present in the room.

I hear the manservant, Harland, bustling about clearing the dinner things. Imagine I can hear Mitchell practically holding his breath so as not to disturb the rapport the Agency boss is attempting to align with me. Even Suzanne remains unaccustomedly silent.

"So what do we do?" I'm the first to break the silence. "Scour the city?"

"What would that achieve, to scour the city? We could do that until doomsday," Treveleyan says. "By then your brother, I'm sorry, but he could be dead. What we know of the Brazilians is, if we don't find your brother, I wouldn't trust them, even if you do hand over the money, not to kill him?"

"So what do we do?" I shrug haplessly.

"First, just a little food," he persists. "Ah, Harland."

The manservant enters, carrying a tray on which rests a small plate that contains little more than a child's portion of roast duck slices, two potatoes, a handful of vegetables. A meal Caitlan would be pleased to enjoy.

Seeing it, I realise how really hungry I am. I'm a 6' 2" tall man and could have scoffed the lot in one mouthful. The manservant deposits a singular cup of black coffee in a white china cup at my elbow.

"I can tell by your expression you expected more." Treveleyan's thin lips contain a peculiar smile, one I fail to understand the reason for. "Too much food spoils the concentration, makes the body sluggish and for what we have to do, we require both the body and mind to be in tiptop reception."

Whatever that might mean. "So what are we about to do?" I ask.

Something with weapons probably. Training. No stranger to guns, I'll enjoy blasting those bastards who've snatched my beloved brother, with a high-powered assault rifle. I can taste their death until it almost becomes tangible.

Treveleyan says, "Suzanne and I will help you make contact with your brother."

"Contact?" I echo, hear the derision in my tone because they all appear so serious. "What do you mean by contact? You make it sound as if he's already dead and we're going to have a séance." My heart races because no one, not even the down to earth Mitchell, appears to think it odd that Treveleyan refers to 'making contact' with my brother. I only hope that the latter means by telephone.

"In a way, that's what it is," Treveleyan says.

"Can't… can't we sort of wait until the pick up?" Mitchell sounds uncomfortable, which doesn't help me any.

"From what I've learned about these kinds of people, Dennis, they will, in all likelihood, choose a crowded place," Treveleyan infers.

"If there's the remotest hint that you are armed, the police will swoop on anyone carrying weapons. If Aidan is willing to do this, then I will help him all I can."

The hawkish grey eyes settle on me once more.

"So what do I have to do? You mentioned I had to contact him. Of course, you mean by phone. For a minute I thought you really meant a séance." I allow myself a half-hearted smile despite the way I feel and the gnawing ache in my guts when I think of the danger, the fear a sensitive boy like Ruairi may be in.

"No, I don't mean by telephone, Aidan. Please trust me, but you have to help me."

"Sure, that's why I'm here but I still don't understand."

"I don't expect you to. You remember the man your girlfriend saw in your bedroom?"

Treveleyan brushes his hands over his thinning scalp as if in embarrassment. I merely nod. Suzanne grins, raises the perfectly sculpted brows. She makes a face at my expense or maybe Treveleyan's, I've yet to decide.

"The man with the grey beard that we spoke of before."

"Sure. But as far as I know Caitlan was merely dreaming." I recollect how terrified she had been, traumatised enough to urinate in the bed. Not that I'll confess it, of course, and risk more of Suzanne's sniping. I make a mental note to introduce her to Judy when this is over. The two women can form a 'mutual snipe at Aidan' society.

"Caitlan was not asleep, Aidan," Treveleyan breaks into my thoughts. "It was no dream. I told you, the man you saw was me."

"How? I mean that's not possible."

"Believe me, there are worlds of possibilities out there you can hardly conceive," Suzanne declares.

"I was lying on my bed," Treveleyan explains. "As I said, I thought of you and how we could use a man of your talents when I suddenly discover myself in the bedroom of your Shooters Hill flat. Your girlfriend caught a glimpse of me in the mirror. Of course, I appear little more solid than a ghost. Even I'm not adept enough to appear solid. A late friend of mine did have that ability. When another friend of his passed him in Piccadilly, he spoke to him but was ignored. When he was accused of snubbing his friend, my friend was actually lying on his bed in his house."

"Jesus!" I run a hand over my beard disbelievingly. "Is all this for real?"

"As real as you and I, Aidan," Treveleyan replies quietly, the kind grandfather again.

"So, if you are willing to work with me, we have procrastinated long enough. We have a young brother to find, held hostage by the kind of people who obviously don't wish to be found."

He is either a highly intelligent individual or as nutty as a fuckin' fruitcake. Hitherto, I have not decided which description actually applies.

Suzanne instructs me to follow them when Treveleyan wheels his chair from the table. I divest myself of my coat.

"By the way, Dennis, make yourself at home. I believe the games room is open," Treveleyan tells him. "There's a TV."

"You have a games room?" I echo in surprise. "What kind of place is this?"

"A haven if you like, Aidan. If you'll follow me. Now that you've eaten. Not too much, just enough to keep the wolf from the door, as it were. Don't worry, we'll find your brother."

"So, is this what you call 'remote viewing'?" I enquire.

"In a way, but this is a little more intensive. Remote viewing can take longer and because we're not psychic, even I don't have that ability, merely my knowledge, as I say, from the monks of Tibet. I'll also need several of my operatives in order to unionise concentration."

"You lost me after the first sentence," I tell him. "Then, hopefully we find him, what happens then?"

"Then you and Dennis will know where to effect a rescue won't you?" Treveleyan states.

"With this psychic stuff?"

"Oh dear me no," Treveleyan laughs, "with guns, my boy, with guns."

Now that is the kind of language I do understand. All the other stuff he sprouted belongs, as far as I'm concerned, to the realm of fantasy and mumbo jumbo.

Treveleyan wheels ahead, Suzanne opens the door and I am ushered into a bare white-walled room where I am allocated my initial insight into the kind of place where I now find myself. I wonder again, how far I can trust these people.

Apart from a single bed, the room is completely devoid of furniture and approximately 8ft by 8ft square. The bed itself is fashioned in a sort of teak with a white headboard and covered by a single sheet, one solitary pillow, also white.

"I still don't see…" I allow my words to trail, simply because I'm uncertain what to add and because there's an uncomfortably cold and scared feeling in the pit of my stomach. I've been trussed up on beds before, feet and hands secured to the bedrails, gagged, my eyes covered. The memory remains. Luckily, there are no bedrails. Nevertheless, I am reluctant to climb onto the bed at Treveleyan's instruction.

"Please, Aidan. I can understand your hesitancy but we don't have much time. I need you to get onto the bed. I promise you won't come to any harm as long as you listen to my voice."

Warily I ease myself onto the bed. He counsels me to lie still and flat so that my hands rest against my sides in a relaxed pose. "Are you comfortable? Your jeans."

"What about them? I'm not taking them off," I say, purposely not looking their way.

Suzanne stifles a giggle.

Treveleyan's expression is impassive, however, while he actually asks me if my jeans are too tight. "I'm not asking you to take them off, Aidan. It's important that you're comfortable enough to be completely relaxed."

"You sure the jeans aren't too tight," Suzanne teases.

"Och now, you'd like to take them off, wouldn't you, baby?" I tease back.

"Please, enough of that!" It's the first time I've heard Treveleyan raise his voice. "If you're going to behave like it's the school yard again then I'll dispense with your services young lady! You've been in this kind of mood since Aidan first appeared."

"Well, he brings out the worst in me. And I'm sorry, Sir," she adds, suitably chastised.

From my position on the bed, I observe for the first time, there is only one small window in the room, through which I can see the soft flurries of falling snow outside.

"The room is sound proofed," Treveleyan informs me.

"So that my screams can't be heard," I say.

"Good Heavens no. There shouldn't be any screams. You really do have an over active imagination, young man. You should be a writer. No, the room is sound proofed because it shuts out any exterior noise so that it makes it easier to concentrate. The only sound you will hear will be my voice."

His tone is so infinitely quiet, soothing, that his placating voice manages to invade my subconscious. "You are the only link to your brother Ruairi. You are the same parentage?"

"Sure we are."

"Close your eyes. Relax. Put everything else from your mind except your brother. Remember the first time you saw him. He was a baby, right? Do you remember him as a baby?"

My senses reel. What the hell has all this to do with finding him? "We're wasting our time here," I retort, a familiar aggression begins to rise again.

"Please trust me, Aidan." There's an element of exasperation in his voice. "Or we'll never find him."

"Sure I remember him as a baby. I was eight when he was born."

"The first time you saw him you developed a close bond. Think about his growing up years."

"He was 13 when I went to prison…"

"That doesn't matter. Think of the bond between you. How much you love him. Link your thoughts. Imagine you are hugging him. Any petty squabbles you have mean nothing now. Imagine what he must be going through."

Suddenly, inexplicably, my thoughts, my very reason, somehow moves away from Ru. I search blindly for where he is… it's then I actually entertain the notion that I can reach out to him, but it is as if someone or something has plucked him away from me or at least that's how it feels. My mind drifts… drifts, my subconscious is no longer my own. There is the faintest breath, like the wind, in my face and I discover I'm in someone's house. It's an unfamiliar place. It smells of a curious mix of stale cooking and baby's urine. A tired looking, young woman, dark auburn hair upswept, is washing up at her sink. A small child I judge to be about 18 month's old plays on the floor. The woman continuously swipes loose tendrils of hair from her face. The tall, raw-boned man with her sports a mass of black curly hair. A man I have seen in the mirror so many times because, in shock, I realise the man resembles me and I hear the crazy rhythm of my heart pounding inside my chest. The woman who appears to be in her mid-twenties, I fail to recognise. The man looks a couple of years older. A black beard, similar to mine, shrouds his chin. He wears rough patched jeans, a check shirt and is about to slip an arm around the woman when there's a sound, a sharp, staccato rap on the door. The man withdraws his hand while the woman's eyes suddenly fill with fear when she looks at him. A shaking hand runs trembling to her mouth.

"Hide! Hide!" she hisses at him in panic.

Requiring no second bidding, the man swiftly disappears into an adjacent room leaving the woman to scoop the infant into her arms. The man has concealed himself behind the door to the lounge and watches with bated breath as the woman moves to the outer door, the child in her arms. In the hallway, my eye is drawn to a wall calendar where I notice that the year is 1982, the month February.

There are three of them standing on the threshold. They wear masks, black balaclavas, camouflage clothing. I see that the armbands decorating their jacket sleeves read 'UVF' in black. Ulster Volunteer Force.

"Where is he, Mrs McMartland?" rasps the leader, the accent an unmistakable Northern Irish. "Tell us!"

The first two men tote Armalite rifles. The lead guy holds his weapon upraised as if in readiness to fire and I think, oh God, no, please let me wake up, but realise that I can't, my limbs no longer seem to move, as if someone has strapped me to the bed, so that I'm forced to witness what... that the man who is screaming is me.

"Tell us where your husband is, Mrs McMartland!"

"I don't know where he is, I... I haven't seen him," she stammers.

Barely has she uttered the words, such pleading in her voice, than the Armalite roars into instantaneous life. The man fires, hits the trigger repeatedly. The weapon blasts the woman and child. Blood. There is so much blood, exploding, blistering their faces, their bodies, viscera, scarlet, glutinous, mother and child unrecognisable, dying in a hail of bullets. The woman and child's screams will haunt me forever, I'm certain.

I can hear a man screaming, guttural, bitter. The husband of Mrs McMartland, an unwilling eyewitness to that terrible, sacrilegious bloodbath, the destruction of his wife and child. It's odd, but the man's screams seem to fill my head and I realise I am awake, because I'm certain I hear Suzanne hiss, "you've regressed him, Sir, you've regressed him!" an element of panic in her words.

But all Treveleyan wants to know is what year it is. Still in my hypnotic state, I tell him that it is 1982.

CHAPTER THIRTY-FIVE

-

THE SEARCH FOR RUAIRI

Because of what I witnessed while I was in a hypnotic state, I remain so disorientated. I wonder if I have returned to full wakefulness or am I still labouring beneath Treveleyan's hypnosis? It is only when I hear a gasping sound, as if someone is choking next to me, that I realise my hands are wrapped around his throat and I'm practically pummelling the life out of him.

"What are you trying to do to me? Dear Jesus!" I am crying in both anger and horror at what I had witnessed. The poor woman and child blasted in the face with an Armalite. The bands on the killers' arm denoting them to be members of the Ulster Volunteer Force, the place, somewhere in Northern Ireland. Why had such a vision come to me? And why have I had other experiences of being in the IRA? Twice while I was in prison and once just after my release. Then it had been the same dream, of being chased by soldiers through the streets of a Northern Irish town. Of turning to fire on them only to discover that my gun clicks on empty. As it is with dreams, you run but seem to get nowhere fast. My family has had no connections with the IRA and why, oh why did the man whose wife and child were killed resemble me so much? In my anger and desperation, I had involuntarily gripped Treveleyan around the throat. I only come to when I hear Suzanne screaming at me. I realise what I'm doing and mumble an apology and all I can do is bury my head in my hands when I release my hold on him. Raising my head I can't help but glare at him reproachfully, "what the fuck was all that about? The dream I've just had was fuckin' horrible. I... I don't want to continue this farce. It isn't helping to find Ru. That poor woman and baby." I shiver involuntarily. "The look in their eyes. I'll... I'll never forget that. I don't know why I saw what I did. My guess is it's another of your fuckin' tricks, Treveleyan. And you ask me to trust you. Fuck you." I am off the bed and waving my arms around angrily. "Then forget it, man!"

Treveleyan is in the process of straightening his collar while Suzanne, the dutiful nurse, has a glass of water standing by and I watch as he pops a couple of white pills before swallowing the water.

386

The withering looks she directs me indicate that I've obviously upset the boss, but if he had seen what I had…

"No trick, Aidan." Treveleyan's voice remains harsh and rasping where I tried to strangle him.

"What Sir George means is he regressed you by mistake. What you saw was probably a stored memory," Suzanne attempts to explain.

"Regressed me," I scoff. "More mumbo jumbo and that was no memory of mine. There was a calendar on the wall in that house. It said February 1982. In February 1982, I was still in Mummy's womb for another four months. So, like I said, it was hardly likely to have been a memory of mine."

"Do you recollect any names during your experience, Aidan, my boy?" His tone is benevolent, as if I haven't attempted to snuff the life out of him moments before, while a peculiar light seems to emanate from those piercing grey orbs.

As if he is capable of plucking the names from my brain, I tell him there was someone called McMartland, and about the UVF officers coming to the door searching for Mrs McMartland's husband. The terrible outcome that I can barely bring myself to discuss.

"I'm sorry you had to witness that. I really can't apologise enough," Treveleyan says.

"It's him who should apologise Sir George," Suzanne reminds. "He almost killed you, Sir. A man of his height and youth."

"And me a helpless cripple," he finishes for her, before patting the delicate palm that rests on his shoulder with affection. "And I should not have regressed you. I hadn't realised that you were such a receptive subject. Not everyone can recollect placed or stored memories, they must be very strong. Now, let's find young Ruairi shall we? Back on the bed please, Aidan."

My body continues to be suffused with a cold sweat, in awe of what I have seen. I am too scared to fall beneath Treveleyan's hypnotic spell in case I have occasion to witness that terrible vision again.

"I'll have fuckin' nightmares for weeks after seeing that poor woman and her child."

"Please, Aidan, I'll be more careful this time." He lays a reassuring hand on my shoulder when I reluctantly return to the bed. "Now lie back, relax and concentrate on your brother. Contact him mentally," he instructs.

"How do I do that? All this seems so hopeless." I am beginning to feel sorry for myself and so damnably guilty because it is my fault that the Brazilians have snatched Ru. If I hadn't got mixed up in all this, my kid brother would be at home enjoying his Christmas. We both would, and I wouldn't be lying on a bed listening to a guy I still consider to be a 'fruitcake' regressing me, as he terms it, to witness a woman and child in 1982, somewhere in Northern Ireland, getting blasted by a UVF Armalite.

"Please." That familiar softly spoken voice compels me to lie back on the bed. "Relax, relax," he repeats. "Now, Aidan, bring your brother's face into your mind. Think about him. Forget everything else. Shut out all other memories and fears. Nothing will happen to you. The harder you concentrate on Ruairi the sooner we'll be able to find him, effect a rescue and return him safely for Boxing Day, and those terrible drug dealers will be no more. Now concentrate." His tone is soporific, gentle, so that I discover myself drowning, sinking deeper, profoundly deeper into the comfortable and placating softness of the single white pillow. There were no more visions. Concentrate on Ru. Sorry we argued. I'll make it up to you.

"Concentrate. Good. Good." Treveleyan's kind old granddad voice drifts into my subconscious until it blots out all other sounds. I have no idea how long I lay there simply listening to that voice, the gentle cajoling. "Relax. Feel it. The pull. The connection," he continues. "The contact…" He repeats the words like a mantra. The connection. The contact. What does that mean? Then I realise, because something is beginning to occur deep down in the pit of my stomach. Something pulls, tugs, as if someone is trying to remove my appendix but without an operation.

"What are you experiencing, Aidan?" Treveleyan urges.

"I… I don't know what it is." My hand automatically descends to my stomach where I feel the tugging sensation. "What the hell's happening to me?"

"Let it go, Aidan. Release it. Don't fight it. Let it go. There's nothing to be afraid of. I know how it must feel. I was terrified the first time it happened to me. Once you master it, it's a wonderful feeling. I'll talk you through what is happening to you. The pulling sensation you are experiencing is emanating from your solar plexus. It means that the etheric double is about to be detached." There is an element of excitement underlining his words. He might be getting off on it but I am fuckin' scared because I am powerless, helpless in his hands. All this could be stupid mind games for all I know.

"Aidan!" My name is spoken sharply. "Clear your mind of negativity. Please trust me. If you do not trust me, we'll never find Ruairi and he'll be lost to us. Now please, relax, concentrate. Tell me what you are experiencing." His tone softens. I realise that, nutty or not, is Treveleyan capable of reading my mind? I refer to the tugging.

"Give into it."

Give into it. So I do.

I am floating, or at least that's how it feels, as if I'm on some weird and wacky LSD trip. I am no longer in the room, while I dare to glance back to perceive the man on the bed, his hands by his sides as if they are strapped. The man is me. Treveleyan occupies his place beside me in his wheelchair, Suzanne in close proximity. She looks anxious, continues to tug at her bottom lip. I thought, tell me about it and I am the one experiencing this.

"Concentrate." Treveleyan's voice slips into my mind again. "Let it go," he urges. "Everything will be fine. If you return to your body too quickly, we'll have to give up, try later, and there's too much to lose, your brother will be lost to us by then. Concentrate Aidan, your brother's life depends on it."

It isn't so bad now. Am I a ghost? Have I died? My body isn't flesh and blood anymore. It seems effortless to simply move through the streets. I note the road signs yet continue to wonder where I am. When I dare myself to look at my body, I freeze, because I don't have one. I don't have a body and yet it feels real enough. Is this what a ghost is? Disembodied, a matterless nothing. I am dead and I am a fuckin' ghost and… and… Panic sets in. Again, I hear Treveleyan's voice, he says my name sharply and causes me to jump, startled in my strange, ethereal state. "Aidan, concentrate, don't go off on a tangent, please."

Aidan James McRaney, Born: 21st June 1982 - Died 25th December 2011.

"You are not dead." Treveleyan again. The guy really can read my thoughts. Jesus. "Where are you, Aidan? Tell me where you are."

Can I talk? From what I've read about ghosts, they point because they can't speak. Well, they do in the movies anyway. So is this death? Purgatory. No. According to Treveleyan, I am not dead. The sensation I'm experiencing consists of this peculiar lightness, weightlessness. I guess without a body you would be able to lift off the ground like a bird.

Although I seem incapable of physical speech, I read the street names, without actual words. I am sort of holding a conversation in my head. I'm not certain how he does it but Treveleyan says, "it's how I communicate with you. I can hear your thoughts. You can't speak. You have no vocal chords. They're in the body of the man on the bed. He is not dead either, merely in a suspended state until the etheric counterpart returns to your body."

Suspended. Now all this really does smack of Science Fiction. "Suspended animation you mean?"

"If you like and it's not quite Science Fiction, Aidan." I hear the amusement prevalent in his words. "It's called telepathy. ESP, whatever you like to call it."

"But I am a ghost?"

"In a manner of speaking."

"Is this how I'll be if I really die?"

"Let's not get maudlin, my boy. But yes, I believe this is how you and I will be when we die."

"What if I decide to haunt someone? It would give my sister…"

"You leave the etheric double too long on this plane to 'haunt' someone as you put it, you really will die. Now lets concentrate on finding young Ruairi shall we?"

"Will Ru be able to see me?"

"No. But those in the room may be able to sense something. I can project my double almost solid because I am an adept and can control my own astral form. I'm the one who is controlling yours. That's why it's difficult for me to maintain too long. Once I relax, you're out on your own, and you could become a wandering soul in purgatory, forever."

"So this is purgatory?"

"No, it isn't purgatory. I'm just trying to explain what will happen if I don't connect you with your physical. There are other things too…"

"What other things?" He sounds anxious, which doesn't help me any.

"An untenanted body can fall prey to all sorts of evil entities. All I'm saying is, you get too cocksure over this, Aidan, and all will be lost." Suitably chastised, I apologise.

"Now, think of Ruairi, the brotherly love you share, the blood ties." His voice is weary and I'm beginning to grow uneasy by thoughts of being a wandering soul indefinitely. "Aidan!" But his reprimand is as sharp as ever because I forgot, momentarily, that he can read my thoughts.

"Don't let your mind wander. Call to him."

I repeat his name over as if I am calling him physically. Suddenly, before I realise, I find myself standing outside what appears to be a kind of lock-up, the façade of which is partially galvanised, similar to a garage. Adjacent to the lock-up, a battered grey door. All of which I manage to relay telepathically to Treveleyan.

"Now where are you? The street, Aidan."

And I search my disorientated state for a name. I see it. Deptford Strand. Running alongside the lock-up is a river with numerous trees and vegetation surrounding it. The street is unfamiliar, although I've been to Deptford, aware I would not have found this place if I scoured the city for weeks. The place is very isolated.

"Enter!" Treveleyan's command rasps in my mind.

"What?"

"Enter! Go inside. Make certain Ru is there."

So I enter.

Raphael De Oliveira watches television in the small uncluttered room. His torso is bare, he is clad in dark trousers. A Taurus automatic rests on a small table adjacent to his bed.

Santos is there, of course, and drinking from a beer. The small aperture of a window, high above their heads, is the only form of natural light. A shadeless bulb hangs suspended from a badly mildewed ceiling.

His hands are securely bound behind him to a lattice framework chair, his mouth is taped and they have covered his eyes. My dear brother. If I had been able to, I would have untied his hands. As it is, my hand hovers over the Taurus on the nightstand.

I breathe Ru's name.

"There is fuckin' draught. Close the door." De Oliveira snaps at his companion irritably.

"Ruairi," I whisper his name. Of course, the word is only in my head, I have no power of physical speech. Although, do I imagine it, that he turns his head in my direction?

"Get out! Now!" Treveleyan is almost screaming in my brain. "We have the location. You have to return to your body now."

"But my brother…" I protest and realise that I am crying.

"There is nothing you can do for him as you are."

Rising from his chair, De Oliveira lifts the Taurus, brings it close to Ru's face and twists the muzzle belligerently against his right temple. Ru's gasps behind the gag are heartfelt and tears slide behind the rag bound around his eyes. I want so much to untie the ropes and yell, "bastards, fuckin' bastards!" angrily.

"Shut fuckin' door, I tell you," De Oliveira growls again.

"The door is shut."

The door is shut. I realise, with a start that I've only walked straight through it.

"Yes, Aidan, so we've established you can walk through doors, now…" his voice has suddenly drifted into nothingness. I am propelled with infinite intensity and an incessant buzzing in my ears, the sound reminiscent of an ocean's roar crashing against the rocks, unceremoniously back into my body. I feel it jerk spasmodically as I enter and as if I've been injected with a thousand volts of electricity. The roaring filling my head begins to ease, thankfully.

"Sorry it was such a rough landing, Aidan," Treveleyan sounds relieved. Somewhere in the distance, I can't pinpoint exactly where, I can hear a choir singing 'Silent Night'. I don't mention it, however, in case it's all in my head.

"I'm feeling incredibly tired now." Treveleyan moves a palm across his forehead indicatively. "Maintaining someone else's etheric double is similar to guiding a novice to land an aircraft. So I hope you won't mind if I get some rest now."

"You okay, Aidan?" Suzanne asks solicitously.

At this juncture, I am uncertain how to respond. All I can do is nod.

"At least we have the location. Look, you rest for a while. As soon as you're able, I'll send Dennis in. The rest is up to you."

I can but regard her nonplussed. Still in a daze, I attempt to recover from the experience of what has occurred. All I can envisage is my beloved brother held hostage by the Brazilians in that lock-up near the river. Ruairi bound, gagged and blindfolded.

"At least we've found him," Treveleyan says. "You were a marvellous subject. After you rescue your brother, we'll talk. I'll explain more of what you've experienced later. Now, I really must lie down. Dennis will come in shortly. You and he have a great deal to discuss."

CHAPTER THIRTY-SIX

-

DELIVERANCE

Moving off the bed, I swing my legs over the edge. The door opens and Dennis Mitchell peers his head around it. Suddenly, nausea wells up inside me until I feel physically sick. To Mitchell's enquiry, how do I feel, all I can manage to blurt is "bathroom." He promptly presses a button for a connecting door, which thankfully turns out to be a bathroom, where I fling myself and vomit my guts into the toilet bowl. Catching my reflection, I observe how dark my eyes are. The injured one has begun to heal at least, although it remains a fraction blurred and a little bloodshot, but I am now able to open it and realise when I was out of the body how perfect my vision was and now I have time to reflect how good I felt, as if I had been administered some exhilarating 'happy' pill. A further inspection of my features reveals that the beard has grown thicker, the hair longer. Has time progressed then? And Ru. Oh God, I hope he is still alive. And that poor woman in the eighties. Just a horrible vision surely, all part of the process of this psychic stuff. No different from a movie, it didn't really happen did it? It couldn't have.

I return to the room to discover Dennis Mitchell toying with my phone and I believe, hope, that those unwitting 'twilight zone' moments have disappeared, until he greets me with, "the top o' the mornin' to ya'" in a peculiarly exaggerated Irish accent. No, maybe I have now entered a parallel universe where everyone has an Irish accent or is he just taking the 'Mick', if you'll pardon the pun.

"Why are you talking like that, Mitchell? I'm not in the mood for your stupid Irish jokes, okay? Not after what I've been through."

"While you was – erm – indisposed as it were, I had to be you," Mitchell explains. "I hadn't realised how difficult it is to talk the way you do. I think the accent sounded more Belfast than Dublin. The pick-up…"

"What!" I exclaim, coming fully awake now.

"I just hope I manage to convince 'em I was you."

"Jesus, Mitchell, if they didn't speak to me, they'll think…"

"That you'd talked to someone, I know. Most of the time all I had to do was listen."

"I hope to God you didn't say 'top o' the mornin' did you? 'Cos I don't speak like that."

"No, no, 'course I didn't. I think I convinced 'em they was talking to you…"

"Never mind that. You said the pick-up." I grab the phone as my stomach heaves again but manage to avert the rising tide of sickness. "Where is it?"

"Like the old man says, a crowded place. Tonight 9pm. There's a Carol Service in Trafalgar Square and from what I know, there'll be lots of people there. They usually have a candlelight procession. There's no chance of taking these bastards in that crowd. They know it. Their plan is for you to leave the dough in a trashcan; they'll replace it with the drugs. Sir George sent me in. You made contact, he says."

"Oh I made contact." I allow myself a secretive smile when I think about it.

"We do what we do best, McRaney."

I'm still trying to come to terms with the wonderful sensation I'd experienced when I was out of my body and wish I too could become, what is it Treveleyan said, an adept, so that I can experience it again. That sensation of floating is far better than any drug. "And that is?" I ask absently.

"Break out the weaponry, man. All we gotta do is run over a map, locate the place, Deptford, Suzanne says. When you're feeling up to it, we move in," Mitchell enthuses. "That astral stuff takes a lot out of a geezer or so I've been told. So how do you really feel?"

"A wee bit strange, I guess. I've never experienced anything like that before."

"Would you do it again?"

Oh yes, definitely I would. I have never felt so fantastic, although I respond, "maybe," non-committally.

*

Less than four hours to go. Almost 6pm. Boxing Day. Is it only yesterday that I had left Brid and Caitlan to collect my brother? I guess they'll all be frantic by now, aware that I have to call them. Explain. What can I explain? That I've taken a wander on to the astral plane in order to locate my brother, kidnapped by Brazilian drug dealers? Jesus, I wouldn't believe it myself. I'm convinced I've lost Caitlan, but what else could I have done? Rescue my brother, then lay everything at my girlfriend's feet in an attempt to win her back?

I manage to contact Brid, to inform her that I've found Ru but that we, I refrain from saying who else, have to effect a rescue.

"Aidan, if I call the polis," she begins.

"You haven't have you, Sis?"

"No, I haven't but…"

"Don't. They'll kill him for sure."

"But if you know where he is, why don't you tell the polis. I can do it…"

"No polis. I'll handle it my own way, okay. They'll just arrest 'em, probably deport them and the guy we're dealing with is a slimy bastard, but worse than that, get him down to the nick, he'll incriminate me and you'll be applying for a visiting order again. You want that, Brid? And it won't just be for eight this time. I'll be lucky to get out of jail before I'm 60."

"You know I don't want that but please be careful, Aidan. Are you going to be armed…?"

But I have already hung up on her because Dennis Mitchell has hefted an Uzi semi-automatic SMG rifle onto his shoulder and is in the process of checking its action. I feast my eyes on the assortment of weaponry Treveleyan has in the spacious oak-panelled room he calls the Armoury. Even Suzanne has strapped on a belt holster about her waist and drops a big P238 into the leather.

"Are you coming in on this?" I ask her in surprise. She's hauled on a dark wool coat over black trousers and a grey sweater.

"I'm just the driver, but in case something should go wrong and you bozos fuck up, then I'll need some back up." She pats the big Sig Saur resting on her hip.

Mitchell is obviously in his element. He's changed into camouflage, a black knitted hat covers his tawny hair. I continue to remain in a daze, remember the place where Ru is being held, aware of my anger but alternatively aware that what we are doing is risking all our lives. Obviously, there is no other way and if anyone suggests to Mitchell there is he'll probably sulk, like a child who has his favourite toy taken away, if he is unable to tote that Uzi he's so lovingly inspecting. I do, however, refer to what my sister suggested about calling the police.

"Fuck, McRaney!" Mitchell's mouth drops open as if I've just informed him that he has a terminal illness. "I hadn't figured your sister for an idiot. She ain't called the law has she? What did you wanna tell her for? Her being so fuckin' religious an' stuff…"

"Relax, man, I managed to talk her out of it," I tell him. "I wouldn't want to deprive you of using that baby." I gesture to the weapon his big fist is wrapped around.

Treveleyan, who appears as excited about all this as Mitchell does, says, "I'm sure your sister means well, Aidan but, as I told you, the police leave lots of things up to us these days. They are aware of the situation with the Brazilians. 'Course, it's all a question of politics, which I won't bore you with. We have people in place who, should a drugs war break out, can handle things in South America. There are, unfortunately, but the three of you here today. It is Christmas after all and my operatives have families they prefer to be with. I would love nothing better than to come with you but as you see," he gestures to the wheelchair haplessly, his useless legs resting on the plate, "I can't, and although I was a policeman once, I'm afraid they didn't get called 'plod' from dancing the pirouette, Aidan."

Mitchell and Suzanne smile at his quip. My heart races with adrenaline when Sir George reaches for a Heckler and Koch sub machine gun, which he explains is a MP5KA4, that it fires 15 short round bursts and has a four position selector trigger, before he passes the gun to me. "Now, your brother is waiting. Because if you allow much more time to roll by, the Brazilians will expect you in Trafalgar Square with the money, that's if Dennis' pseudo – Irish accent has managed to convince them we'll meet their demands."

The weapon slips into my hand. I tell Treveleyan that I'd never used one before. With expertly practiced fingers, he demonstrates the Heckler and Koch, slamming the clip back into place before handing the gun back to me. "If I couldn't use the weapons in my Armoury then it wouldn't make sense me keeping them. Now you try it my boy and no more mention of the police, hey."

Performing a similar operation as Treveleyan I'd mastered the weapon in minutes. "You gotta know I'm not working for you yet."

"We will be pleased to welcome you, Aidan. There is so much you and I have to discuss." Treveleyan's smile is fatherly again. "I hope you get your brother back in one piece, not to mention yourselves. We know the location."

"So what happens when we find the Brazilians?" I dare ask.

"Jesus, McRaney, do we have to draw fuckin' diagrams now?" Mitchell retorts with a grin.

*

There is no turning back now. Not that I have any desire to. Whatever happens, I cannot lose another member of my family. In my trance-like, out of the body state, I have seen Ruairi bound to a chair, gagged, blindfolded. De Oliveira and Santos in the dingy lock-up, all of which I describe in detail to Treveleyan, Mitchell and Suzanne.

I guess the three of us, Suzanne in the driving seat, her glorious titian hair covered by a black wool hat, are lost in our retrospections. Even Mitchell says little. Like me, he smokes to excess while Suzanne coughs indicatively and winds down the window. What we are about to do is dangerous to say the least. They need not have helped me, particularly Suzanne after what I put her through and her desire to be at home with her daughter at Christmas. I can only entertain both respect and admiration for this woman.

And Mitchell. When I enquire why he has chosen to help me rescue my brother, he merely shrugs, growls that he hasn't anything better to do. That he'll only be sitting at home listening to his old lady rabbiting on. That if he has to choose between the former and blowing away some drug dealers, well there's no comparison. Besides, he finally admits, I'm the only friend he has and if it means getting into Bridget's... I stop him there.

"Good books, I was going to say," he quips with a familiar wry grin.

As aforesaid, Mitchell has changed into camouflage. I'm no soldier. Besides, I hate camouflage. It serves to remind me too much of my brother Harry, the ex-squaddie, of what he'd probably have to say if he knew what I was doing. "He'd probably be pleased," I hear a masculine voice inside my head say. "Did someone say something?" I look to Mitchell for confirmation.

"No, I didn't say nothing, mate. You must be hearing things, McRaney."

Of course, I am fully aware it isn't Mitchell who has spoken. I purse my lips, drag hard on my cigarette and wonder if Treveleyan isn't still reading my mind. I could have sworn it's his voice I have heard. So I am fuckin' telepathic now, Jesus. I am dressed in black and a Browning automatic, my favourite weapon, is strapped on inside my jacket.

The sign for Deptford looms, the place I remember seeing in my astral state, Deptford Strand. Exactly as I have witnessed, the river runs alongside the grey building. I see the lock-up garage with the galvanised roof. The closest we can get to it is the riverbank.

"This is it," I mutter. She kills the engine and Mitchell is the first to crack open the door, step from the vehicle. Killing an umpteenth cigarette beneath my boot, the Heckler and Koch SMG is cradled in my arms and I attach the silencer. Rolling a black ski mask down over my face, I follow Mitchell and he urges we get this over with.

Suzanne whispers, "Good Luck," before settling down to peruse a magazine in the front seat.

Everything is exactly as I had seen it. The battered grey door adjacent to the garage is locked. At my instruction, we move into position either side of the door, our weapons raised, ready to fire, hoping there will be no passers-by. Two masked men toting assault weapons might just appear a wee bit suspicious. In that eventuality, Treveleyan has drawn up fake ID's, with Special Forces on a laminated card, to account for our presence. Tapping gingerly on the door with a gloved hand, I hear my heart beating far too loudly now that the moment has arrived. Although I can't see his face, I guess Mitchell is equally as anxious; his eyes dart back and forth and his mouth in the narrow slit is compressed and tight. Of course, my worse fear is endangering my brother's life. Thus, Mitchell and I both agree we should open fire on the Brazilians, leaving them little chance to return fire and recollect the Taurus automatic De Oliveira has in his possession.

The battered door cracks open after what seems an age. We move as far away from the door as possible so that when it is finally opened, they'll probably think it's kids messing around because we haven't shown ourselves hitherto.

"Who is it?" Santo's voice.

"Shut fuckin' door, no one there," De Oliveira snaps.

Santos is obviously not satisfied, for the fleshy sun-bronzed face peers around the aperture, before he's about to close the door again. His hand remains on the door so when I slam it hard against the wall he ouches in pain and disbelief, terror too is etched in his black eyes. Cracking my boot hard against the door, the SMG upraised, I burst into the room and Mitchell joins me. My eyes zero in on my brother. All he can do is turn his head in the direction of the sound with his bound eyes. Duct tape wraps his mouth, his hands and feet are fastened securely to the chair.

Aware of De Oliviera reaching for the Taurus, Mitchell and I open up in unison. I haven't reckoned on those 15 short burst rounds spitting quite so much lead, and so fast that I can barely control the weapon, and I am scared of hitting Ru. Mitchell and I just let her rip. The staccato-delivered slugs shatter the hand with which De Oliveira clutches the Taurus and he has no choice but to let the gun slip from his grasp. Mitchell seizes the pistol, slips it into his jacket. Santos drops face down on the dirty tiles with blood pouring from a gaping hole in his head. Despite the possibility that Santos is already dead, Mitchell rains more bullets in his direction. De Oliveira's mine and 10 Heckler and Koch slugs tear into his expensively tailored clothing. Flesh, blood and brains from his splintered skull decorate the filthy room. Before he gasps with the barest iota of life left in him, I imagine the sign of recognition in De Oliveira's eyes, the half whispered, "McRaney…" before he slips to the floor, his body writhing and jerking like an out of control marionette.

Blood and viscera spill across the floor beneath the couple of pieces of old furniture. Still bound to the chair, unable to see or understand what has really happened, Ru appears like someone stranded at high tide in the chair. There is so much blood, and two Brazilian drug dealers floating face down in it.

The assault rifle anchored across my shoulder, the first thing I do is untie the ropes that bind my brother's hands, peel off the blindfold and remove the tape as carefully as I can. Mitchell wants to know if he's okay. I murmur that I don't know. Ruairi is free but he remains unmoving in his chair. He is obviously traumatised. His face is the colour of chalk and when his eyes rake me, he recoils all at once. Pulling off the mask, I whisper his name huskily. "Ru, it's me, Aidan…" but he continues to stare at me as if I am a stranger. He hasn't spoken or even blinked to adjust his eyes to the light.

"Shock. He's in shock," Mitchell is a distant voice behind me.

"Oh, Ru, I didn't think I'd see you again." I'm crying, hugging him tightly, feel the stiffness of his body against mine almost as if he's frozen. I release him and still he regards me unseeingly.

Then he mouths, "Aid." That's all.

"Sure, it's me, Aid. It's all over. I'm taking you out of here, get you cleaned up."

There's blood everywhere, on our clothes, saturating the surrounding walls. Ru sees the two dead men for the first time but cradling him against me, I counsel him not to look. Bursting into tears, Ru sobs uncontrollably on my shoulder and I cry with him.

"Carnage," Mitchell mutters. "There's so much carnage." But I refrain from glancing his way.

CHAPTER THIRTY-SEVEN
-
REVELATIONS

Suzanne appears relieved but concerned when she vacates the car and rushes to help Ru. Dropping into the back seat, I cradle my brother as if he were a child. His body continues to be wracked with sobs while I feel the wetness of my own cheeks, because we have rescued him and this is over.

Sometimes he looks at me in puzzlement and as if I'm a stranger and it screams out of me that, although I rescued him from his captor, he continues to blame me, making me wonder if I've lost him.

I turn my attention to thank Suzanne and Mitchell for what they've done.

"That's alright, McRaney, I didn't have anything better to do, I told you," Mitchell says, but his voice is oddly subdued and he stares ahead of him unblinkingly, as if he too is in shock. I believe that neither of us realised how powerful and deadly those weapons actually were. For my part, all I feel is relief that I have my brother back safe and sound and I'm glad those bastards are dead. I ask, what happens now? About the bodies.

"Oh, don't worry, Georgie'll send in the 'cleaners'," Suzanne assures me. "As soon as you appeared, I called him. Can't have someone stumbling on that, can we? So, Ruairi, how do you feel?"

"Okay, I think. I really believed I was going to die. They said they'd kill me. I couldn't believe that was you, Aid. What you did…"

"Ru, it's okay, don't talk about it. It's over." I hand him a cigarette, light one for myself. His hands continue to shake and I am compelled to do it for him. "You're safe, that's all that matters. And I've got to make a phone call, if nobody minds," I tell them.

"No, go ahead, mate. Who's that? The lovely Bridget?" Mitchell says.

Ruairi regards him in surprise. I regard him with pursed lips but say nothing. Easing my jacket aside, in order to reach the phone, I unwittingly reveal the Browning riding leather strapped across my chest and receive a disbelieving stare from my brother. Nonchalantly, however, I put the call through to Brid.

"Where the hell are you, Aidan? I was worried sick. Is Ru okay? Are you okay?"

I'm compelled to hold the phone away from my ear because when she is angry and upset, I swear my sister lapses into Gaelic. "It's cool, Brid. We'll be home soon. Just calm down, Sis."

"Is Ruairi with you? They… they haven't… He isn't…"

"No, he's perfectly safe. It's over."

"Oh, thank the dear God…" Her words trail and I realise she is crying.

"Sis, it's over sweetheart, we'll be coming home soon."

"I'm sorry." I hear her attempt to control herself. "But I was so relieved. Patrick's here. Judy brought him because you hadn't picked him up from her house and she promised you could have him today."

"Tell Patrick I'm sorry but something came up." I regard my brother with a smile, but one he fails to return.

"That's what I told him. How could I explain anything to Patrick? Do you know what he said?"

"No, but I guess you're going to tell me. So what did he say?"

"He said…" She makes a show of clearing her throat, as if she finds it difficult to formulate her words and I catch myself stiffening. "It always does with Daddy."

I blanch, but enquire about Caitlan. Is she okay?

Brid clears her throat awkwardly again before replying. "She… she's gone, Aidan." A sob escapes her once more.

"She's what!" I explode so loudly.

Ru jumps, Suzanne swears, "Jesus, Aidan, whatever's happened?" Mitchell merely regards me with upraised brows.

I swallow uncomfortably and my stomach crawls with a thousand live worms all over again. "You… you mean back to Dublin?"

"Their plane doesn't leave until tomorrow, but that bossy sister of hers took her off before the wee girl could protest. I pity that fiancé Niall. He's really nice. They were sorry to have missed you but Mollie is on the warpath. She reckoned you was no good, she said, the first time she saw you."

I thought, how perceptive you are, Mollie.

"So where did she take her, Sis?"

"To a hotel."

"What hotel?" I stress.

"Don't cause a scene, Aidan."

"What hotel?"

"It's called 'The Belmont'. It's in Greenwich. Aidan, when are you coming back?"

"Soon, Sis, soon," I say quietly and favour Ru with a transient smile when he regards me with a frown. I conclude the call thoughtfully, my heart racing because my worst fears are confirmed. Caitlan has left me. Yet, somehow, after all that has happened, the fact I have been forced into a situation where I've had to kill again, maybe she is safer, better off without me, except all I can think is she's carrying my little baby inside her.

*

I would have preferred to have taken my brother home but Sir George, (God knows why I pander to that man) instructs that he wishes to talk to me. Unwilling as I am to return to the Agency, I am aware I should at least show my gratitude.

I can feel Ru's eyes boring into me when he believes I'm not looking. Sometimes his regards are incomprehensive, as to why I behave the way I do I suppose, and as if he deserves some kind of explanation for it.

In the Agency's spacious Italian-tiled bathroom, complete with busts of Plato and Aristotle on marble plinths, I divest myself of my jacket and wash my hands. It's just Ru and I, we are alone and I stupidly don't know what to say to him.

"You didn't know what it was like, Aid. I was so fuckin' scared, man. I mean really scared you know."

Do I detect a note of accusation in that speech? Or is my guilt so profound that I imagine it? "I know," I murmur sympathetically, I'm washing his face, his hair and hands in the bath, as if he is my son rather than my 21 year old brother. If it hadn't been for my involvement with these people, my brother would not now be standing there, shivering and afraid and appearing so ridiculously young. I believe I have lost Caitlan, have I lost Ru as well.

Suddenly he pushes my hand away as I run the flannel around his wet, perspiring face. "I can fuckin' do that. I'm not a kid, so don't try treating me as one. Just go, Aid, please..." Averting his gaze, he twists at his lower lip savagely, tears welling up in his eyes, "I was right wasn't I?" he says strangely.

"About what, Ru?"

"If you aren't enjoying all this. This tough guy image. You fuckin' enjoy carrying that shooter, gangland and all that stuff and those drug dealers. I wouldn't have been in the position I was in and you wouldn't need to have acted so fuckin' Jean-Claude Van Damme, you and that

Mitchell geezer. I bet he was enjoying it as much as you. Brid told me he was in jail for armed robbery. Is that your next venture?" he spits angrily between broken sobs and swiping at his eyes.

"What is, Ru?" I'm too weary to raise my voice, also because I'm aware he is right.

"Blags."

"Ru, don't do this please. No, of course it isn't. It's over, I told you."

He sits on the edge of the bath. I move to the door, inform him that I'll leave him alone if that's what he wants, but it's plainly obvious I'm not going to be let off the hook.

"All the time I was trussed up and blindfolded and those fuckin' Brazilians were jawing away in their own language, I thought of you, and it wasn't that De Oliveira character and his greasy sidekick I was angry at, it was you. You... you who I was blaming for all this and if Caitlan's gone..."

"How did you know that?"

"I ain't fuckin' deaf, man. I heard what Brid was saying when you called her. She wasn't exactly speaking quietly and you use Brid, she does your washing and stuff, she can't do enough for her precious Aidan, especially since you got out. And Caitlan. I don't blame her if she has left you. She fuckin' worships the ground you walk on, like Brid, and that Suzanne, she can't keep her fuckin' eyes off you. Is it because you know you can get any woman you want that you ride roughshod over 'em, Aid?"

"I don't do that, Ru, not intentionally." I stretch a pleading hand toward him. "I'm so sorry..."

He ceases his sobbing, runs the flannel around his face, shrugs as if it's of no more concern before he approaches me and I tell him how sorry I am, again, and how much I love him. Before I realise, or I can prevent him, he's pulled the Browning from my holster and I find myself staring down the barrel.

"Ru, what the fuck are you doing? Give me the gun. It's loaded." I hold my palm out toward him uncertain, as he is in this particularly acrimonious mood, whether or not he will pull the trigger.

"I just want you to know what it feels like to be on the receiving end of one of these things. I love you. You're my brother. I've always looked up to you, Aid..." he's sobbing again, "but I'll kill you for what you've done to me."

"But, Ru, I rescued you. You don't know what I had to go through to do it."

"Oh sure you did. Being gagged and blindfolded, tied to a chair and threatened with a shooter every few minutes was a fuckin' breeze, Aid. I thought I was on holiday…"

"Okay, Ru, I can't begin to say how sorry I am. I'm a bastard, sure I am. If you hate me so much," I raise my hands, invite him to shoot me. "Go on pull the trigger, Ru. Maybe I deserve to die…"

Three sharply delivered raps on the bathroom door is conducive to startling the pair of us and my heart somersaults because I'm scared Ru will pull the trigger out of sheer panic. But, caught unawares, I take the chance, when his attention diverts, to grab the gun and drop it back into the holster.

Ru merely slumps into the chair that is placed adjacent to the bath. I call, "who is it?" whilst maintaining a wary eye on my brother and remain uncertain of his reaction in the kind of mood he is in.

"Sir George wants to talk, Aidan. He says it's important. You two okay?" Suzanne calls through the door.

"Sure. We'll be out in a minute." I lay a hand onto my brother's arm but he shrugs me off abruptly.

"Treveleyan wants to talk. You coming? I don't want to leave you the way you are."

"I ain't gonna fuckin' top myself, if that's what you're thinking. I'm glad to be alive. I'll take a bath. You just go and see your people."

"Ru, I… I love you. Please…" I feel the tears well up unbidden in my own eyes now, and once again, I ache to put my arms around him and hug him. "Do you really hate me so much? You oughtta know I was worried sick, Bruv."

Raising his head finally, his eyes are so large, filling with tears again beneath his long forelock of hair and, looking much younger than his 21 years, he is in my arms suddenly and we finally hug one another, crying on each other's shoulders like a couple of girls.

*

I have precious little time to dwell on all that has occurred, for I swiftly discover myself joining Sir George Treveleyan in his opulently furnished living quarters. 'The Great Man' is seated before a laptop at his table where previously he and Suzanne had enjoyed their Christmas lunch. He is alone and he invites me to take a seat while he pours us both a neat whisky from a 50-year-old Chivas Regal, or so he informs me, "I hear that's your favourite tipple, Aidan. I would have thought you were a beer man myself."

"I like a beer but I've always had a penchant for Chivas, although I don't know why."

"Maybe something from your past. I believe everything we enjoy in the present stems from our past lives."

"Sorry, Sir George, but I still don't buy into that stuff, okay."

"If you say so," he says enigmatically.

"So, how's Ruairi after his ordeal?" Before I can tender a response he continues, "of course he'll require careful observation. How old is he? He looks very young. 18 or 19?"

"He's almost 22."

"Really?" Treveleyan raises a surprised brow.

"Look, Sir George, I'm grateful for what you did…"

"I did nothing, my boy. You did all the work, you, Dennis and Suzanne. I merely acted as your guide. You certainly knew how to use that weapon. Have you used an assault rifle before?"

"God no… Look…" I drain the whisky in one smooth swallow. Sure if it doesn't taste good and I could use another. "I really have to go, and my brother will be fine. I need to see my girlfriend. If I don't manage to convince her to stay, she'll be leaving for Dublin tomorrow and she is expecting my child. I really can't let her go."

"Always the women hey?"

"Sure." I rise to my feet. "Thanks for the drink. It was amazing. Now I'll go and fetch my brother. He was having a bath."

Treveleyan chooses that moment to swing the laptop screen around to face me. What I see there halts me in my tracks and brings a return of the memory of what I had experienced when Treveleyan supposedly regressed me. The woman whom I saw blasted to death on her own doorstep, with her baby son in her arms, is now staring at me from the screen. This time she appears much less bedraggled and tired with long dark auburn hair spilling around her shoulders and green expressive eyes. She really is very pretty and I regard Treveleyan incomprehensively.

"That's the woman you saw wasn't it, Aidan?"

All I can do is nod my agreement dumbly. Something in my throat prevents me from replying.

"Catriona McMartland and the man," he changes the picture and I am looking at it as if I'm staring into a mirror. "Connor McMartland, her husband. Connor McMartland was suspected of being an IRA terrorist. He drank in Republican bars, was guilty of associating with known Provos. But, until February 14th, 1982, McMartland was a simple plumber."

A newspaper, 'The Irish Times' appears on the screen and depicts the headline 'EVIL VALENTINE'S DAY MASSACRE'.

"The Parliamentary Ulster Volunteer Force in County Armagh were hired to seek him out. When his wife and child were murdered, Connor McMartland joined the Provos. From February until June, he went on a murdering rampage of bombings, doorstep assassinations and robberies. He was gunned down with two other Provos at a Crossmaglen checkpoint," Treveleyan relates. "Now, Aidan, does 21st June, 1982, mean anything to you?"

Whether it stems from the chilling yet animated tone of his voice when he says it, I merely nod my head in a sort of frozen agreement. "It's the day I was born. So what's all this, Treveleyan? I don't understand. You said County Armagh. I've never been to County Armagh in my life. Remember I've been in England for 20 years."

"Do you remember the hour you were born?"

"Sure, I was out celebrating my birth," I can't help my sarcasm.

"Please, Aidan, indulge me."

"I think my mother said it was around midnight. What has all this to do with me?"

"Midnight on the 21st June, the eve of the Summer Solstice," he enthuses, his voice, so normally subdued and stoic, now becomes animated, his excitement mounting.

"The transition from spring to summer and the time that Connor McMartland was shot was midnight on 21st June, 1982. The night his soul was transmigrated."

"You're saying some IRA guy has taken over my body when I was born?" I'm doing my utmost to stifle my laughter at this stage.

"A simple interpretation, but yes, basically."

"Please, Sir George. I've seen and done some stuff which seems about as real as a dream or maybe a nightmare, but I have no interest in the IRA, and no one has taken me over or transmigrated or whatever you want to call it. Now, right now, on December 26th, 2011, I have a pressing engagement with a girl I really don't want to lose." I have already moved to the door when he says, "have you ever had flashbacks? Visions of being in the Paramilitary. Maybe in the last couple of years."

It is odd but I feel a little faint momentarily, probably because I haven't had a decent meal in a while, not that Treveleyan's question has touched a raw nerve. "They were just dreams, that's all," I shrug. "Why the last couple of years?"

"Connor McMartland was 27 when he was killed. Two years ago you were 27."

"So what?"

406

"What happened to your wife and child might account for some of your anger."

"For fuck's sake, Treveleyan. I'm sorry to swear but they weren't my wife and child. They were Connor McMartland's. I'm Aidan McRaney, son of Dermot McRaney." I throw my arms up in the familiar gesture of anger. "And if I don't go now, I'm going to lose my potential wife and child. So we're done here."

"I'm sorry, Aidan, there is so much I can teach you. Please will you come to work for me. I can't force you…"

"Then don't. Maybe if I can call a cab." I'm about to reach for my phone. "Anyway, why is it so important I come and work for you?"

"Because, just because," he edges, clears his throat as if he is embarrassed. "And there's no need to call a taxi. I don't wish for uninvited strangers to come to this place." From a drawer where he sits he lifts out a set of keys.

Selecting one from the ring, he suggests that I'll find his Mercedes in the car park downstairs. "And you haven't answered my question. Will you come and work for me? Get rid of that wretched club. It'll only bring you trouble, hasn't it already? You'll have more money than you've ever dreamed, a nice car, a nice home for your wife and children. More clothes than you'll have room for."

"As an assassin?"

"Why not as an assassin? So you kill people. Haven't you already done that? There are some evil people out there, Aidan, and I feel also, that even though Lamond is in prison, there'll be someone to take his place. You only have to search some of those forbidden websites to know what terrible things some people are doing."

"Then you must have looked at them."

"On occasions, I'll admit, but only to brief my operatives. So?"

"So, I'll think about it."

"Don't take too long, Aidan."

I wonder where I've heard that before.

Needless to add, I mention nothing of the rather strange conversation I had with Treveleyan to Ru. I also swear my brother to secrecy about what has occurred. In turn, he says that if he talks about it, he'll have to relive it and that isn't something he's prepared to do. Occasionally I observe him shiver. I promise to take him home to Brid. That I need to be at the Belmont Hotel in Greenwich in order to persuade Caitlan that I want her to come home. That I love her, and not merely because she's expecting my child.

Ru apologises for pulling the gun on me. I leave the Browning at the Agency for obvious reasons. I wonder again, what all that guff Treveleyan was sprouting about this McMartland guy transmigrating his soul to mine, whatever that meant. The old boy is definitely two sandwiches short of a picnic. Just because I'm Irish for Chris sake. I also can't help wondering why he should want me to work for him quite so much and if I do, and do what he asks, what about Caitlan? I hardly think she'll approve of my killing people for a living, even if they are the bad guys. When I drop Ru back at Brids, I head out to the Belmont Hotel in Treveleyan's Mercedes. I wish I had a motor that handles so beautifully and I guess I would if I worked for him.

The Belmont Hotel is an opulent glass building. I move across the red-carpeted foyer to the polished reception desk where I enquire of a middle age lady as which room Miss McKenna is staying.

Demure in a neat blue suit, white blouse, spectacles perched on the end of her nose, she consults the register before announcing that there are two Miss McKenna's, Miss M and Miss C."

"It's Miss C McKenna I wish to see."

To which she duly informs me that Miss C McKenna is in room 246. "Second floor, Mr…"

"McRaney. Thanks." I smile at her politely. I'd reached the second flight of stairs, about to ascend the landing, when a man I judge to be in his early thirties pauses, on his flight down, to stare me out almost to the point of embarrassment. His hair is thick, unkempt and of a reddish colour, as is his beard. He is a much larger man than myself. When he bars my way on the landing, my inherent self-preservation instincts take over. After all that I've experienced, I wonder if this is one more obstacle I have to face because all I have to do is grab his arm, propel it unceremoniously behind him until it almost snaps and demand what the fuck he's doing standing in my way?

Garbed in a brown tweed hacking jacket, neatly pressed black trousers and cream shirt, in spite of his age the guy doesn't appear to be overly fashion conscious.

I hiss, "Let me pass, pal." There is a command in my tone which brooks no argument from the red haired man.

My intention is to pass him with the minimum of trouble, at least that's what I hope when, taking me by surprise, the man grabs my arm suddenly.

CHAPTER THIRTY-EIGHT

-

RUMBLINGS AND REUNIONS

Before I can either shrug him off or demand what the hell he thinks he's doing, he swiftly releases his hand on my arm. "I'm sorry," he extends the hand and enthuses, "I'm Niall Brierley."

The name fails to ring any bells although I detect a familiar Irish accent. "Sorry?"

"You're Aidan. I'd know you anywhere. All the pictures your sister has of you."

"Sure, but I still…" I continue to remain suspicious because he seems to have the advantage.

"I'm Niall, Mollie McKenna's fiancé." Still I refuse to accept the proffered hand and he allows it to drop to his side. "Mollie sent me to intercept you when the call came through to Caitlan's room that you were downstairs and wanted to see her. Apparently, that's what they do now, and…" he brushes a hand across his beard awkwardly, "Mollie was… was a little worried you might cause t… trouble." His voice is soft, uneasy and he averts his gaze from mine in discomfort. On our initial meeting, I'm already beginning to feel sorry for him and, judging by what Brid had related, how Mollie bossed him about, I'd never let a woman do that.

Finally, I extend my own hand and he flicks a hesitant smile before shaking it warmly. "Pleased to meet you, Niall, and I'm not here to cause trouble of any kind. I just want to see my girlfriend, that's all. My sister told me she's here. Is she in room 246? That's what the lady downstairs said. It's just there," I realise we've been standing directly outside 246.

The door is cracked open and the two sisters step out. Mollie is the first to appear, Caitlan behind her and my stomach lurches because I'm uncertain of her reaction after what I've put her through. She breathes, "Aidan!" when she sees me. Mollie grabs her arm, retorts, "if you don't leave, Aidan, I'm calling security." Her eyes are as snapping as her words. She appears cold, unremitting.

"At least can I talk to her?" My arms outstretch imploringly and I think, although she's a smaller figure retreating behind her sister's back, how beautiful Caitlan is. She wears jeans and an emerald sweater. Her hair is pulled back into a ponytail and she looks so incredibly young. "I won't cause any trouble."

"It wouldn't hurt surely, Mollie," Niall remonstrates. His colour heightens when several people pass and afford us their attention. "Only if we don't do something," he adds, "they really will call security and we'll all get thrown out."

"Och, don't talk so ridiculous, Niall," Mollie snaps.

Niall blanches and appears as if he wishes to sink into the flooring. Poor guy. And I flick him a commiserating smile, to which a response merely flirts around his lips indecisively. There is but a six-year age difference between Mollie and Caitlan but the former's shrewish attitude is conducive to affording her a much older appearance.

"Okay, I suppose you better come into the room but mister," she pauses to wag a finger at me, "you cause any trouble or anything, I really will call security."

Yeah right, piss off, Mollie. "Me cause trouble?" I smile at her sweetly to which I receive a predictable cold-eyed response from Mollie McKenna. To think, that if I ever do get far enough to marry Caitlan, this creature will be my sis-in-law.

Once inside room 246, Mollie folds her arms, retorts peevishly, "I really don't like this city. If my sister wasn't here," as if it is all Caitlan's fault, "and she wouldn't be here if it wasn't for him." Crossing the room and wandering to the window, she glares at me as if I'm contaminated.

"If you mean me, Mollie, why don't you say what you have to and get it over with." The familiar aggression is building. She somehow manages to bring out the worst in me so that I can't help but realise that if she were a man, I'd fuckin' sock her one.

It is as if Niall and Caitlan are not present. The latter has slumped into a chair, bites her lip and looks close to tears. I ache to comfort her, pick her up, bodily if I have to. I've done it before. Practically she weighs little and I long to carry her off defiantly, though I guess if I did Mollie really would call security, and the last thing I wish to incur is an arrest.

"You've got to know, Aidan, I'm taking Caitlan back to Dublin with me, after the way you've treated her." Mollie insists.

I look at Caitlan but she's turned her head away. Niall mutters, "Mollie, you shouldn't…" but his words are silenced instinctively at a withering glance from his fiancée.

Mollie continues acid tongued, "I bloody knew it, so I did, what you were like. What all men are like."

"Mollie." Niall beseeches.

"Well maybe not you, but you've been with me a while," she admits.

Long enough to break his spirit, hey Mollie? I thought. I'd really like to get to know this guy. Get him away from the 'dragon queen' and have a few jars one night while he's still in London.

"I love Caitlan and if I didn't, I wouldn't be here and I'm sorry," it's to Caitlan whom I turn, my anger subsiding as it invariably does in her presence. "Sorry for what I've put her through. Not being there, but I had a lot of things going on in my life."

"Oh yes, with other women?" Mollie positions herself between Caitlan and I. Like a referee on the sidelines, Niall, hands outstretched, attempts to calm his fiancée with a half-hearted, "let him explain, Moll, please."

"There are no other women. It's always been Caitlan. My sister said you'd gone and to which hotel."

"Och did she now! I swore her to secrecy. She wasn't to tell you," Mollie retorts.

"My sister tells me everything. Anyway, I would have got it out of her. I needed to know and if I didn't love Caitlan, I would have let her go without a word. It's up to her now," I regard her directly, hopefully, my heart hammering in case she refuses. Despite all the things I've done, the violence I have exerted, when it comes to this woman I really can't afford to lose her.

Caitlan speaks for the first time. "Perhaps Aidan and I should talk, Mollie, and please don't call security. Because if you do," she pulls herself from the chair to stare her sister down defiantly, "I'll never speak to you again."

Both Niall and I exchange surprised glances that Caitlan has the courage to stand up to her bossy sister.

My arm slips against Caitlan's waist and I am pleased because she doesn't pull away. Notwithstanding, Mollie's shrewish features become even more thunderous, "Alright, we'll leave you alone but you trust him again, Caitlan McKenna, sure now you'll only be a fool, but it's your life."

"It is Mollie," Caitlan says simply.

When Niall moves to take his fiancée's arm, she shrugs him off. "And you're worse than useless," she admonishes. I deal him a commiserating shrug. Poor Niall. He really is a doormat.

When they've gone and Caitlan and I are left alone she says, "I know you probably don't believe it but she means well."

"It's Niall I feel sorry for. That guy really should move on. No woman's ever going to boss me around like that."

"Niall loves her I suppose," she muses thoughtfully. "And no, I can't imagine anyone bossing you around."

"So what's with the suitcase?" I notice there's one resting on her bed. "Does that mean you are going back home?"

"It's all up to you. If you hadn't come today... because I hoped Bridget would tell you where I'd gone, even if Mollie did swear her not to tell. I was scared you wouldn't know where I was until after I'd left London."

"So, I would have turned up on your doorstep in Fenian Street. No matter where you were in the world, I'll be there stalking you. That's if you want me to of course."

"I love you, Aidan, and I don't want to go back to Ireland, at least not without you. It's just..." She moves to the window.

"It's just what?" I'm almost holding my breath, scared of what she is going to say.

"It's just that some of the stuff Mollie said was right. I mean, where were you for so long? I asked Bridget but she was acting so evasively, I knew she was covering up for you. She just said that I wasn't to worry, that you did things like that. Disappeared sometimes. That you must have had a good reason. She's your sister. She's bound to stand up for you. Like Mollie," she flickers a smile briefly, "but where were you, Aidan? Were... were you..." she struggles to form her question, "with that Suzanne? Because if she's in the picture with you, then I really will go back home without a second thought. It'll break my heart, so it will, but I can't share the man I love with another woman."

"Sweetheart, look," I implore. "Suzanne is definitely not 'in the picture' with me, as you call it. She never was. You want the truth. You deserve to know and, as you said, people who love one another should have no secrets."

"Sure, Aidan, yes I would like to hear the truth."

"Then you'd better sit down, my sweetheart."

She plumps herself onto the bed next to the suitcase, her attention riveted on me, and I am compelled to avert my gaze from those beautiful trusting eyes. I compose myself, expel a breath and stare out of the window instead of at her, at the bustling streets below, the darkening snow-laden sky, as I relate all that has transpired, beginning at the club with the drug dealers, De Oliveira and Santos. Dennis Mitchell warning me about them. My pulling a gun on them. Yes, I've had a gun for a while. Ruairi's kidnapping by the Brazilians, although I refuse, mainly to spare my own embarrassment and guilt, to tell her about tying Suzanne to the chair for the return of the incriminating DVD. I explain how Treveleyan had put me into some kind of hypnotic state, omitting the part about the McMartland's, believing that to merely being a dream, even if Treveleyan did have evidence to prove they existed.

I relate how I had seen, in this hypnotic, trance like state, my brother bound and gagged and blindfolded in the lock-up, held by the drug dealers. That Mitchell and I had rescued Ru by bursting into the lock-up garage with Heckler and Koch assault weapons and blasting away at the two dealers. I conclude my narrative and hold my breath momentarily, wait for the hysterics, the angry, frightened tirade. Maybe she'll beat at my chest, tell me what an evil murdering bastard I am. How she's definitely going back to Dublin now. All these things probably.

Suddenly, unexpectedly, in the comparative stillness, in the aftermath of my laying bare my very soul, she starts to giggle in a sort of high pitched, slightly nervous, kind of school-girlish laugh, making me swirl around from the window to regard her in utter disbelief.

Has my narrative triggered off a psychotic, schizophrenic episode?

A palm covers her mouth as she attempts to stifle her laughter.

"Jesus, Caitlan, I wasn't expecting a reaction like that. Did you hear everything I said?"

"Sorry, Aidan, I didn't mean to laugh. It is Aidan McRaney isn't it?"

"What do you mean?" I frown.

"I mean it isn't James Bond is it? You're such a fantasist."

"A fantasist! Jesus, Caitlan, what's that supposed to mean? It's not a fantasy, it's the truth. That's what you wanted."

"Look, if there's another woman, Aidan, you don't have to make up stories about drug dealers and stuff. I mean that pole dancer Suzanne…"

"There is no other woman. Jesus, why do women naturally assume because their man is away, he's with another woman?" To which, all I receive from Caitlan is a raised perfectly sculptured brow.

"Besides, Suzanne really isn't a pole dancer. She's married with a daughter, but she's separated from her husband who is a top heart specialist. She lives in Buckinghamshire with her mother and daughter."

"Sure she does."

"You sound as if you don't believe me."

"You really should be a writer. You've been watching too many Vin Diesel films or whatever. I bet you don't even own a gun and even if you did, you'd have to have a license and stuff. Anyway, it's life now for firearms possession. Why should you need a gun? Oh I forgot," she stifles another giggle, "in case drug dealers kidnap Ruairi."

"Okay, ask Ru, he'll tell you." This is incredible. I've been pouring out my heart, scared I'm going to lose her if I tell the truth but she doesn't believe me, thinks it's all a joke. That I'm a fantasist.

"You don't have to invent all this tough guy James Bond stuff to impress me. I know you can handle yourself. You proved that the night you took Shaun Blackwood on. Okay, you sound sincere enough to make me believe there is no other woman. Wait 'til I tell Mollie…"

"No!" I rasp. "No, don't tell Mollie." I entertain the feeling that Mollie will believe me and attempt to persuade Caitlan that it's true and if she does discover it's the truth, will she still laugh and consider me a fantasist? "I don't want her to ridicule me too."

"Och, I'm not ridiculing you, Aidan? So where were you really? And you really weren't with another woman were you?"

"No, sweetheart, I wasn't with another woman. Ru and me got a wee bit hammered, that's all. I'm sorry," I lie.

She allows me to pull her into my arms and crushing my lips to hers, I feel her respond. When I release her, the beautiful emerald eyes rake mine with so much love. Lifting her into my arms I'm about to lay her down onto the bed when there's a couple of strident raps on the door and Mollie calls from behind it, "you alright in there, Caitlan?" I hear Niall whisper, "leave them alone can't you?" in an embarrassed voice.

"I'm fine thanks," Caitlan calls, a giggle behind it. "How can I not be with James Bond?"

"I wonder what she'll make of that." I laugh.

*

She does, however, display surprise when she sees the Mercedes. Exclaiming, "you bought a Merc while I was away?"

"No, sweetheart, it isn't mine."

She regards me with an element of suspicion.

"I didn't steal it. Jesus."

"I didn't say you did. Maybe 'M' gave it to you."

"M?"

"Haven't you ever seen any 'James Bond' movies? Me and Mollie used to watch 'em all the time."

"Not really my thing."

"Well it wouldn't be, would it?"

I fire the ignition. The beautiful car purrs into instantaneous life. A far cry from my old Cabriolet. "Why wouldn't it be my kind of thing?"

"Well, not if you live it."

"Och stop it," I laugh, cuddling her affectionately. I swing the Mercedes into the street, carefully because it's not mine, and when she asks who I borrowed it from, I spare no pains to tell her that it is Treveleyan's motor.

Still she laughs. "See I told you, 'M', only this is some Treveleyan guy. You said he has this Agency. Och, I almost forgot." She is suddenly subdued. "Mollie told me about Shaun Blackwood."

At the mention of the man who had attacked me, almost blinded me and whom Mitchell shot dead, despite my carefulness, I almost collide the Merc into a lamppost as we exit the car park.

"What about him?" I hear the huskiness prevalent in my voice.

"'The Irish Times' is full of it apparently."

"'The Irish Times'?"

"Seems Shaun Blackwood's body was found floating face down in the Liffey. It didn't half scare the people on one of those river restaurants. Good riddance is all I can say. The Garda are still looking for his killer. Apparently he was shot. Something to do with drug dealers, they reckon."

"Really?" It's all I can say because of the constriction in my throat. How the hell could that have happened? A man shot dead in London ends up in the River Liffey in Dublin. A cold chill encapsulates the length of my spinal column. To have taken his body back to Dublin, someone must have flown it and it makes me wonder how far reaching are Treveleyan's tentacles? How strong his desire to help me is, enough to make the police believe that Blackwood, a native of Ireland, should have been killed there. What of Blackwood's two companions? Maybe they had been 'dealt with' as well.

We return to Brid's and I am pleased to discover that Patrick is there. Instantly he sees me he flings himself into my arms. "Daddy, where were you? I missed you."

Ruffling his dark curls, I tell him that I missed him too. He even manages to acknowledge Caitlan, for which I am pleased. Brid hugs me in relief that I'm okay and I enquire where Ru is.

"He's in Mark's room. Mark's staying with his Dad for a while." Her tone drops to a conspiratorial level. "I had his telly brought over, Ru's that is. I'm a wee bit concerned for him. He spends a lot of time in his room," she says, before turning her attention to Caitlan, "we thought we'd lost you."

Caitlan sports a frown, I conjecture it's the 'we' bit, not that 'Aidan thought he had lost you' as if Brid and I are of the same mind. Maybe sometimes we are.

"I love your present, Daddy," Patrick is saying. Jesus, I've been so mixed up in all this I had forgotten to buy my son a Christmas present, obviously someone else has.

"Present?" I echo.

The 'present' turns out to be a 'Mario vs Sonic at the Olympic games, 2012'. Well I guess that's something I wouldn't have dreamed of buying my son in a million years. No matter, he seems pleased with it and I'm swift to discover the culprit when I clock Caitlan smiling impishly. "For his 'Nintendo DS'," she explains. I mouth, "thank you," to her, and reason how thoughtful she is.

"You know what Dads are like," she tuts.

"So you met the redoubtable Mollie?" I ask Brid.

"Sure I did and Caitlan, you are so different from your sister in every way," Brid says.

"I like to think so," Caitlan agrees quietly.

"Can I talk to you, Aidan, when you have a minute?" Brid says.

"Sure Sis." I attempt to read her expression, but her features remain impassive. Patrick demands my attention and when we've talked for a while and he's demonstrated his game, I inform him that I should go and see Uncle Ru.

Ru is seated on the bed. His torso bare, he's only wearing his jeans. His hair falls long and unkempt and looks badly in need of a wash. He's watching 'The Simpsons' on TV.

I peer around the door and say his name, somewhat tentatively. I have no idea what his reaction will be.

"You can come in, Aid. 'The Simpsons'," he gestures to the television. "They're safe."

"So how are you, Ru? You okay?" It's odd but I'm beginning to feel a little awkward with my brother. I believe it stems from the fact he pulled a gun on me.

"I'm fine. Why does everyone have to make such a fuss?" he shrugs. "Brid keeps coming in with this concerned look on her face."

"We're just that, concerned."

"Well you don't have to be."

"What did you mean 'The Simpsons' are safe?" I recollect Ru and I watching this when we were kids.

Ru shrugs once more. "I dunno. I used to like all those action movies and stuff. I can't watch 'em now. That's what I meant. I'll be okay."

"I'm sorry I put you through all the stuff I did." He allows me to slip an arm around his shoulders.

"I don't know how you sleep at night, Aid. I mean after what you and that Mitchell guy did."

"I've never slept too well at night, Ru."

"You tell Caitlan?"

"Sure. Or at least I tried to tell her."

"Jesus and she's still with you. You manage to bring her back?" I nod affirmatively. "You really do have some charm, mate, where the birds are concerned."

I relate what happened when I attempted to confide in Caitlan all that had transpired. "She said I was a fantasist," I conclude.

"A fantasist. Then she didn't believe you?"

"Not a word, apparently, and don't you back me up. It's best she believes I'm a fantasist. I don't think she can handle the truth."

"But it's over, right?"

To which question I mentally keep my fingers crossed. "Sure it's over. Anyway, I've got a wedding to plan."

"A wedding! You!" Ru regards me in much the same vein as Caitlan has done when I'd related I'd shot and killed the drug dealers.

"So when you planning to get wed then, man?"

"14th February," I reply and wonder where that came from.

"Really? St Valentine's Day. I never figured you for an old romantic."

"I haven't mentioned the date to Caitlan yet."

"It'll be cold. February. Most people get married in June. You could get married on your birthday. I mean, next year you'll be 30."

I make a face. "Don't remind me. I'd like to get married before then."

"Before you draw your pension you mean?"

"Fuck off," I grin. "Our baby will be born in August. Anyway, I want you to be my best man. We'll go to Italy for our honeymoon. I'd like you to come too."

"On your honeymoon? I know we're all pretty close…"

"You know what I meant. We all need a holiday, Bruv."

"So where you planning to get wed? In London?"

"No, not here. In Dublin. After all, it's Caitlan's home. Let's put all this behind us, hey. It's almost New Year, 2012. And that club. I don't want any more to do with it."

"You could always sell it."

I am considering it, when Sammy and Patrick, followed by Caitlan, enter the room. The latter is apologetic because she is unable to prevent the children from coming in but Patrick is missing his Daddy and Sammy "wants cuddles from Uncle Aidan." She's glad I look less like a pirate now without the eye patch.

My sister calls through the door that tea is ready. This is the life I want. Sisters making tea. Getting married. My family. In the New Year, after we get wed, maybe I'll put a mortgage down on a house. After all, this flat is too small when the baby comes.

However, I lapse soberly once more, my enthusiasm evaporating. To achieve all that, I'd have to either work for Treveleyan or sell the club, as Ru suggests. The latter sounds far more appealing.

I reluctantly ease myself from Caitlan's arms and whisper that Brid needs a word. When I remind my sister of that fact, she ushers me into her bedroom and closes the door.

"I have some news. I haven't said anything yet but I've decided to get married in Dublin and go on holiday to Italy."

"That's grand, Aidan, but there's other stuff you need to sort first."

"What other stuff? What is it, Sis?"

"That thing in the drawer," she gestures to her bedside table. "In case you've forgotten, the g-u-n. If the children were to find it they might think it's a toy."

"Most toy guns are made of plastic."

"Kids don't always realise that, Aidan. I don't want it in my house. You meant well I know, but just get rid of it, okay?"

"Sure, anything for you."

"Good. Anyway, how did you manage to get Caitlan to come back with you?"

"We knew how much we love each other."

"And you told her about all the stuff that's been happening?"

I confided in her Caitlan's reaction at my confession of the things we've been experiencing of late. "She thought I was a fantasist. She reckoned it all sounded far too James Bond to be true."

"I suppose it does. Except I know you, Aidan, and I know the kind of people you've mixed with. That Dennis Mitchell for instance."

"What about him?"

Brid clears her throat predominantly, her face crimsoning. Because she has not responded to my question, I repeat it.

"Is… is he seeing anyone?" issues the more than surprising enquiry.

"What? Dennis?" I stifle a rising tide of laughter. "You're not suggesting what I think you are?"

"I know he fancies me."

"Jesus, Sis. Don't even think it. Mitchell's bad news. You know that. What about Father Mulligan? I thought you and him…"

"He's a priest."

"I know, that's why he's called Father Mulligan. That's never stopped you before."

"There never really was a me and him," she shakes her head sadly. "I cared about him, maybe more than a parishioner should care about her priest. I think it was reciprocated but in the end, it was either me or the church according to his Bishop. The church won I'm afraid."

"I'm sorry." I hug her against me. "But don't set your sights on Dennis Mitchell. You can do better than that."

"He used to smile at me when I came to visit you in Maidstone."

"You know what he was inside for?"

"GBH and armed robbery."

"Bad news like I said. So forget him, okay."

Besides, he knows far too much about me. A few drinks inside him and God knows what he'll tell her.

When Brid opens the bedroom door, the kitten, which my sister informs me Caitlan has called Mew Mew, sidles against my leg. Lifting the small animal into my arms, I stroke its back and follow Bridget into the lounge.

Caitlan sees me and smiles, the way she does, and I wrap my arm around her and kiss her on the lips in the knowledge that a loving family, and this woman, is all that I ever want.

CHAPTER THIRTY-NINE

–

AN EX'S EXPOSE

Caitlan and I are married in Dublin, with ould Flanagan to give her away and our reception is held in the 'Liffey Bar'. She wanted us to travel down the river on one of those boat restaurants but I failed to envisage dwelling on the fact that Shaun Blackwood was discovered floating face down in the river.

The date of our wedding is St Valentine's Day. It is cold but the snow has dissipated. Although the air is frosty, the sun is out. When she and I walk down the aisle, I am in my best morning suit, Caitlan in yards of organdie and lace. The dress is loose at the waist, enough to conceal the evidence of the new life inside her. She is now almost three months pregnant.

Ruairi is best man of course. Bridget, matron of honour. Mollie and Sammy are bridesmaids. I feel that Caitlan's sister remains disapproving of our marriage but Niall seems to have miraculously calmed her down. She does look lovely, I have to admit, and much less shrewish in an orange, lace, looped skirt and cream, silk bodice. Patrick is a pageboy, a proper little Lord Fauntleroy, although he admits that a black, velvet suit and white ruffle shirt is hardly 'his thing'.

Mollie and Bridget have helped out, both financially and practically, with our wedding. When Brid first saw me in my grey suit and cream silk tie, she burst into tears and cried on my shoulder, although I reminded her that she's supposed to save her tears for the bride rather than the groom. She says she's crying because I look so handsome and I'm her brother and she loves me so much and that she'll miss me while I'm away. I placate her that I'll only be gone for a while. It's then she confesses that now I'm out of prison, she hates to allow me out of her sight. I jokingly tell her that it's as if she and I were getting married to which I receive the oddest expression from my sister and one that remains with me all day, no matter how much I dismiss it.

Harry has arrived from Milan, minus Sue, Antonio and Gina. Gina is attending college out there and he is back to doing landscape gardening.

Dad is there. He had been reluctant to return to Dublin at first but couldn't possibly miss his son's wedding, he said. Even though, whenever he spotted a member of the Gardai or a police car, he'd deliberately conceal himself behind one of us, usually me, being the tallest. Luckily, we have heard nothing more from across the water concerning the Docherty business.

Aunt Clodagh and Uncle Sheamie are in attendance of course. I feel saddened to see the latter in a wheelchair. Aunt Clodagh informs us that he has prostate cancer and is undergoing chemotherapy and radiotherapy at St Patrick's. She whispered to Brid and I that he didn't have long. My sister is concerned that she'll be on her own and why doesn't she come and live with Dermot in London? "Live with Dermot!" she exclaims in disbelief. Not only does she have her friends in Dublin but if she ever lived with that man again, he'd either drive her to drink or she'd drive him to it, probably the latter. If it hadn't been for us kids she would never have survived the last time, she says, even if he is her brother. She also confessed that she was closer to Marie than she ever was to Dermot. It is odd but aunty also related how, if it weren't for her faith, Marie might have left 'that man' a long time before her death.

Brid has booked a few days off from work, so she and Dad decide to remain in Dublin with her aunt and uncle for a while, but promise to return to London before we arrive back from our Italian honeymoon and that she'll pick us up at the airport.

Harry, Ru and myself decided to have my stag night at The Liffey Bar. Where else? I elected to remain marginally sober, having imbibed but a couple of Guinness's and making them last, although according to Flanagan, "you may as well enjoy it, boy, 'cos the women, they keep their eye on your spending and your drinking." A sadness appears in his eyes. I guess he remembers his late wife and misses her.

While I am in the bar. I long to resurrect the memory of Shaun Blackwood to Flanagan. Because Ru and Harry are present, I decline, although I would have appreciated the canny barman's opinion. Flanagan did, however, refer to missing Caitlan and her music and that the place isn't the same without her.

*

From Dublin, Caitlan, Ru and I, with Patrick (Judy actually allowed him to come with us), fly out to Milan for our honeymoon. Ru and I might be close, but even he is excluded from our honeymoon hotel and he and Patrick stay with Harry and Sue. Tony is there but I learn that Gina resides near the college. She's dating an Italian boy named Carlo, Sue duly informs me.

Everything seems so perfect now, away from London. Caitlan and I are happy. No more psychotic episodes. She's brought an ample supply of her medication.

We love Milan and we journey to Rome also, to view the art galleries. We marvel at the sights, particularly the Coliseum. Ruairi is in his element too. Here the world of his beloved art is opening up to him, as it is to me. I'm actually beginning to feel assured that nothing can possibly go wrong now.

Harry suggests, for the umpteenth time, why didn't we settle here? I'll admit it is tempting. Judging by his sun bronzed complexion, his relaxed demeanour, it's obvious that he's unlikely to return to England for a while. Away from London, I find myself more relaxed, and I am not drinking so much. Yet, I know it all has to come to an end, that we'll have to return and we'd arranged a flight from Milan to Heathrow.

As Ru has a gap year from Uni, Harry attempted to persuade him to stay. He insists it would be nice to have at least one of his brothers there, but Ru tells him that he'd miss me too much. Quite naturally, particularly after what I've put him through, I can't help but be touched by this. Somehow, despite all those earlier recriminations, in Italy, Ru and I draw close again.

The flight back to England. Predictably, I guess to match my mood, the day dawns grey and gloomy and leaves me in a bad temper for the first time in three weeks, since we'd been away. I snap at Caitlan for some stupid thing about her not being able to locate my passport when I asked her to look after it. I had afforded her the responsibility of looking after mine and Patrick's. Concerned that someone might have taken it, I was growing edgy again and we hadn't yet landed on English soil.

Caitlan snaps back at me something about looking after the passports myself, if I can't trust her. Before I can open my mouth to apologise, Patrick retorts how she "has to stop nagging at my dad. That if he gave her the passports, then she should be responsible for them." So I have to retaliate about him not upsetting my wife. When Caitlan manages to locate the passports, she discovers they were in her bag all the time, that she must have overlooked them. I counsel her not to worry, as long as we have them, while Patrick mutters, "women," under his breath as if he's 10 years older. Then Ru wanted to bring back a painting, only to discover that it was far too large to pack into his case. Harry promised to look after it for him but Ru continues to be fractious.

∗

Arriving at Heathrow, we have our luggage checked and wait for Brid after I've text her for the umpteenth time, while Caitlan is in the toilet, also for the umpteenth time. Patrick occupies the edge of my suitcase, a bored expression on his face. Ru paces, reminiscent of a soldier on sentry duty, muttering, "where the fuck is she?"

I'm about to light a smoke, when I receive a text that I expect to be from my sister and I mutter, "about fucking time," except the text isn't from Brid. It's one that causes a shiver to permeate my spinal column because the text is from Sir George Treveleyan. "Aidan. Hi. Now you're back in the country, I've a job for you. Call me. Treveleyan." I mutter, "fuck you," about to press the delete button when Ru wants to know who it's from. "Is it Brid?" So I lie that it is.

So how the fuck did he know I was back in England? I've only just arrived, for Christ's sake. 'I've a job for you,' Jesus, already and what kind of job?

Brid duly arrives some half hour late and bemoaning about the traffic getting through London, and that Judy has rung requesting we drop Patrick off. She'd been without her son, and is missing him so much.

So we drive down to Esher first. I suggest taking Patrick in while the others opt to wait in the car. Ru reckons he'll never darken her doorstep and fashions the sign of the cross with his fingers, which I find amusing but stifle an element of laughter as I walk up the path to her house.

But it appears that Judy is 'all sweetness and light'. She hands me a small, beautifully wrapped wedding present. The card reads 'Love to Aidan and Caitlan, from Judy and Ralph'. "It's nothing special," she says, "a selection of scented candles. I hope you'll both be happy. I'll see you again when you take Patrick out and next time bring Caitlan in, I won't bite."

Even when I tell her that Caitlan is expecting my baby she informs me that she already knew, that Brid had told her. "Don't look so worried, darlin'," she oozes, with a smile, "I'm pleased for you, Aidan, I really am."

I vacate her house with a lighter step than when I entered. I had no idea what to expect from my ex-wife. A tantrum, a slap across the face, sulks. Sexual come-ons.

I return to the car with the present. Predictably, it's Brid who asks, "What's that, Aidan? Not a present from Judy."

"Scented candles, apparently." I pass the silver wrapped parcel to my wife.

"That's nice," she responds and reads the card.

"Scented candles, blimey," from Ru in the front seat.

I ask him what's wrong with scented candles. "I know they're a wee bit girly."

"I think it's a nice gesture," Caitlan says, unwrapping the parcel to reveal the three large boxed candles inside. The smell of them is quite strong. I detect vanilla, strawberry and a sort of mint.

"I wouldn't light them if I were you, Caitlan," Ru warns.

"Why not?" she asks.

"They might blow up in your face. This is Judy, Aid's ex we're talking about," Ru says.

"She's not jealous is she?" Caitlan asks anxiously.

"No, sweetheart," I slip an arm around her. "In fact, Judy couldn't have been nicer and wished us well."

"Well, my dear brother." I catch Brid's green eyes in the rear view mirror regarding me speculatively. "You'd better read this."

"Read what, Sis?" I ask, puzzled, when she tosses a newspaper onto my lap, which I observe, is 'The Sun'.

"Read it," she urges before concentrating on her driving.

"'Terrified man dies of fright in locked hotel room'" Caitlan reads, "or is it the stuff about the X-factor?"

"Not that," Brid says. "I think it's on page 4. Your previous nice ex-wife has only been talking to the newspapers and that's not all."

I quickly turn to page 4, note it's also on pages 5 and 6 as well, with pictures. But it's the headline.

'CURSED NIGHTCLUB BURNS TO THE GROUND'

My senses reeling, I hear Caitlan's anxious gasp.

"What the fuck!" I hiss and read on, my heart beating much too erratically. The devil made me do it, says DJ Arsonist.

"Who the fuck is DJ Arsonist?" Ru asks. "What is it, Aid?"

"My fuckin' club burns down and you didn't think to tell me?" I'm practically yelling at Brid, anger surfacing.

"I'm sorry, Aidan, I… I didn't want to worry you," Brid says, suitably humble.

"You didn't want to worry me. Jesus. What's all this…?" My throat is suddenly constricted and there is an infinite ache in the pit of my stomach because I see a picture of HER, my Leanne. In the rather grainy newspaper offering, she wears a skimpy striped bikini. She stands next to Frankie Lamond, his arm around her waist. He's wearing these ridiculously coloured baggy shorts, no top. Even in the photo, his flaccid belly, hanging over them, is plainly discernible and I recollect thinking at the time, how can she stand this 'fat pig' draped over her? I knew the picture well, probably because I was the one to take it with Frankie's expensive Nikon. The shot was taken in Marbella.

"The infamous 'Black Garter club', even renaming it 'The Athenry' could not dispel its nefarious reputation, was burned to the ground in the early hours of Sunday morning. The person believed to be responsible for the arson attack is Paul Lucas, 25, a one-time DJ at the club. Mr Lucas had vowed to 'get even' with the temporary owner, Dublin born Aidan McRaney, 28, whom Mr Lucas called a 'racist f----- Paddy'."

"Well, sure now, they've dropped a year off my age," I mutter grimly and feel the sensation of Caitlan tremble next to me while I reluctantly read on.

"The Black Garter's original owner, Raymond Lamond, 53, was found dead in his cell at HMP Lexford five days ago from a perforated stomach ulcer after he was attacked."

"What the fuck!" I hear the animation in my voice as I read on. "Lamond's dead!" I look at Ru, he stares at me non-plussed.

"Jesus, Aid. Then it really is over. That's good news, for you I mean?" he says quietly.

"Sure it is," Brid interjects.

"But why didn't you tell me?" I accuse.

"Because I didn't want to spoil your holiday. I could tell from your postcards you were all so happy. Besides, it's not your affair. That evil man's dead, that's all that matters. I'm sorry about the club."

"No you're not," I retort.

"No, maybe I'm not, Aidan. That place was cursed and you know it."

"Cursed…" Ru fashions the sign of the cross and makes spooky noises in accompaniment.

"Shut the fuck up, Ru," I mutter.

"Yeah, shut the fuck up, Ru," he admonishes himself.

"And not so much swearing you guys," Brid says. "I apologise for my brothers, Caitlan, although I guess you're used to them by now."

"Sure I am." She agrees and the smile she directs me radiates her beautiful face, despite the fact I'm still coming to terms with the knowledge the club has burned down, and Lamond's dead. Both brothers now. It really is the end of an era.

Still, there is more news.

"Paul Lucas, known as 'Pauly' to his friends, had been a DJ at the club for almost a year when Mr McRaney took over. He'd had no complaints, he said. McRaney reckoned he didn't like the kind of music he played. Lucas suggested it was because he intended to install his younger brother Rory 21, as DJ at the club."

"I bet they've spelled my name wrong," Ru puts in.

"Yeah, Rory," I tell him. "At least they got your age right."

"Read on," prompts Brid. "There's more."

"Mr McRaney was unavailable for comment as he is on his honeymoon. He married his club singer, Irish country star, Caitlan McKenna, 19. We spoke to McRaney's sister Bridget Collier, 36."

Ru and I exchange raised browed grins at Brid's expense. "36, Sis," Ru jokes. "You been holding out on us?"

"No, I'm 34 for God's sake," she hisses tersely.

"But Mrs Collier refused to comment, except to say 'that her brother's business should remain private'."

"Unlike Mrs Collier, however, McRaney's ex-wife, Judith, 30…"

"She's fuckin' 31," I mutter. "I bet she made them say that."

"Was more forthcoming. She spoke quite freely about 'The Black Garter club' when her husband worked there as minder to the previous owner, Frances Lamond in 2002/2003. How her husband, then 21, left her alone most nights with their baby son. She revealed how he had shot and killed, in his capacity as minder, Lamond's potential assassin, a Brian Fitzwalter. The incident occurred in 'The Copper Kettle' restaurant, now a taxi rank, in Wardour Street, Soho. The woman who was killed was 23 years old Leanne Harlow, who at the time, according to the ex-Mrs McRaney, was 'having it off' with her husband in the upstairs room at the club. Frances Lamond, the intended victim, was shot in the spine and confined to a wheelchair in an Eastbourne nursing home until his death this year."

The 'Sun' describes Leanne as a beautiful ex-model, who could have been something, if Frances Lamond hadn't 'taken her away from all that'. Apparently, Leanne had run away from home after arguments with her father. Leanne Harlow had once graced the centrefold of 'Penthouse' magazine.

"Tall, leggy, (I'm certain he injected that description himself), slenderly built with long, copious, strawberry blonde hair, at 5' 10" tall," Ru relates when I angrily toss the paper at him. I'd heard enough but Ru, being the tenacious wee bastard that he is, savours the article as if it's a three-course meal. As it is, I hardly dare to look at my bride because guilt assails me at every word he delights to read. When I dare flick a glance to her face, I see it's white and she tugs her lips with agitation.

"What the fuck is it with you and leggy blondes, Bruv?" Ru quips, only to be admonished by Brid again for swearing. I cuddle Caitlan, kiss the top of her head, feel her stiffen against me.

"According to the ex-Mrs McRaney, it was common knowledge at the time, when Leanne Harlow was killed, that her husband emptied his gun into the assassin claiming that 'he did it for her', at his arrest and trial. In 2003, McRaney was sentenced for eight years for manslaughter. It seemed that a drugs deal had turned sour between Lamond and the Fitzwater's. Brian, also known as Bram, left a pregnant wife, Joanna. A ex-model turned photographer, Joanna Fitzwalter has since disappeared and was reported missing by her brother Jeffrey."

Now I face the window without glancing at anyone because I know exactly where Joanna Fitzwalter, aka Sheldon, really is.

"There's a picture of you, Aid," Ru jolts me from my reverie. After what I've been thinking, it leaves my heart pounding.

"A picture of me?" I attempt to keep the anxiety from my voice. "Where did they get that from?"

"Not me, Bruv," Brid is quick to respond. "I'm no party to any of that stuff. I gave them short shrift, that's probably why they upped my age by two years." Her mouth is tight as she concentrates on getting us through the conglomeration of traffic.

"I guess Judy gave them the picture. No wonder she was being so bloody nice. She really dished up the dirt on you, big time."

"I'm sorry you had to hear all that," I attempt to placate Caitlan. She has not so far spoken. Her complexion remains chalk white. Even after I apologise, she merely offers me a perfunctory nod. Finally, clearing her throat, she says, "I'm not tall or leggy or blonde," so quietly, her words are scarcely audible.

"And I'm glad, darlin', that's why I love you," I say. "And I think we've heard enough, Ru."

"There's just a bit more, Aid. Listen to this." Animation heightens his voice. "Some people suggest, the girls who danced in the club mainly, that they call her 'La Harlow' as if she's some kind of diva… was she a diva, Aid?"

"I don't fuckin' know," I mutter under my breath curtly. Oh sure, maybe she was a diva. All I know is she was the loveliest woman I had ever seen. That sex with her was incredible. "What else do they slander her name with now?"

"Only that she allegedly haunted that upstairs room, searching for the Irishman."

"That's a load of crap, Ru, and it could have been any Irishman. That place was never haunted."

"They'll write anything to sell papers won't they? They liken 'The Black Garter' to 'Borley Rectory'," Ru says.

"Well you can see the resemblance," I mutter sarcastically.

"What, that place in, where was it, Essex? The one that was supposed to be burned down by spirits or something?" Brid says.

"Yeah, they reckon that Leanne burned it down," Ru adds.

"Sure she did. She came from the spirit world with a box of Swan Vestas," I quip.

"There's more on Pauly Lucas," Ru continues regardlessly. "Mr Lucas gave himself up to the police who described him as being in some sort of a hypnotic trance or a daze."

A trance or a daze, I muse. A Manchurian Candidate perhaps? Someone wanted that club destroyed, using Lucas as a scapegoat. After all, he had a motive didn't he? He had accused me of being a racist Paddy who hadn't approved of his music.

"What's this!" Ru is obviously intent on reading more and much against my better judgement, I find myself listening to what he relates.

"Leanne was the daughter of John and Bettina Harlow. Apparently, John, or Johnny, as he was commonly known, was a small time crook in the seventies and eighties. According to the London underworld, Johnny had trodden on some important toes in the criminal fraternity and was found shot dead in his car in January 2004, murdered by person or persons unknown. Harlow left three children, Leanne, Lorna and Luke.'"

"Jesus, man, I didn't make no connection at first." Ru snaps his fingers suddenly, startling me from my uneasy retrospection. "Luke Harlow. I know him. If it's that Luke Harlow of course. We're in the same drama and set design class at Uni. He lives out Camden way. He's also my best friend."

THE END